Praise for *New York Times* bestselling author Lori Foster

"Emotionally spellbinding and wicked hot."
—Lora Leigh, *New York Times* bestselling author, on *No Limits*

"[*No Holding Back* has] compassion, interesting family dynamics, troubled pasts, killer fight scenes, and of course, swoon-worthy romance. Highly recommended."
—*Harlequin Junkie*

"No one writes alpha heroes and sexy, swoon-worthy romance like Lori Foster."
—Jill Shalvis, *New York Times* bestselling author

"Hang on for this completely unexpected hard-hitting ride!"
—*Fresh Fiction* on *No Holding Back*

"Hot enough to start a fire!… A delicious and dangerous tale that proves why Foster is one of the best in the genre."
—*RT Book Reviews* on *Fast Burn*

"Count on Lori Foster for sexy, edgy romance."
—Jayne Ann Krentz, *New York Times* bestselling author

"Foster knows how to turn up the heat, delivering numerous steamy passages that crackle with chemistry and build essential connections between the characters."
—*Entertainment Weekly* on *Cooper's Charm*

"Teasing and humorous dialogue, sizzling sex scenes, tender moments, and overriding tension show Foster's skill as a balanced storyteller."
—*Publishers Weekly* on *Under Pressure* (starred review)

"Foster is a master at writing a simmering romance."
—*USATODAY.com*'s *Happy Ever After* blog on *Fast Burn*

Also available from Lori Foster and Canary Street Press

Osborn Brothers

The Dangerous One
The Fearless One

The Little Flower Shop
The Honeymoon Cottage
The Summer of No Attachments
The Somerset Girls
Sisters of Summer's End
Cooper's Charm

The McKenzies of Ridge Trail

No Holding Back
Stronger Than You Know
Watching Over You

Road to Love

Driven to Distraction
Slow Ride
All Fired Up

Body Armor

Under Pressure
Hard Justice
Close Contact
Fast Burn

The Guthrie Brothers

Don't Tempt Me
Worth the Wait

For additional books by Lori Foster, visit her website, lorifoster.com.

LORI FOSTER

THE FEARLESS ONE

CANARY STREET PRESS

ISBN-13: 978-1-335-51713-5

The Fearless One

For questions and comments about the quality of this book, please contact us at CustomerService@Harlequin.com.

Canary Street Press
22 Adelaide St. West, 41st Floor
Toronto, Ontario M5H 4E3, Canada
CanaryStPress.com

Printed in U.S.A.

Big thanks to Jeffra Page, a super-helpful reader who visits my Facebook page. Jeffra answered my posted request for inspiration when I was writing the dog character in the book. I often ask readers for names, pets' personalities, jobs and more. Jeffra's dog, Tuff, makes quite the charming character! I hope everyone enjoys him and, of course, the whole story.

Lori Foster

CHAPTER ONE

For early April, the Colorado weather was unseasonably warm. Probably in the low sixties with enough sunshine to make it feel warmer. Jedidiah Stephens, who went by Diah for short, loosely held Tuff's leash in the only available finger she had. Loaded down with supplies, she made her way along the rutted, occasionally muddy road leading to the budget campground.

Hard to call the miserable path an entry, though. Surely the guy who'd bought the place planned to fix it up a little before he opened in mid-May. If not, she'd see what she could do about it. At the very least, the potholes needed to be filled and everything regraveled. Otherwise, anyone pulling a camper was in for a really bumpy ride, possible damage to the undercarriage of their travel trailer, and there was a good chance they'd get stuck.

Checking the time on her phone, she saw that she was thirty minutes early. Hey, it wasn't easy to be timely when she relied on others for her transportation. Good thing she'd found a nice woman who'd let her, her number-one guy, Tuff, and her luggage hitch a ride in the back of her pickup. Talk about getting jostled, and now she was more windblown than ever.

Not that she cared. This was the chance she needed

to solve the mystery, rid herself of nagging questions and finally get on with a new, better life. *Free.*

Oh, how she wanted to be free.

She couldn't change the past or stop the occasional nightmare; she understood that. But by God, she could put an end to running, and in the process forge a new future.

If she let it, excitement and even a little nervousness would take over. Ruthlessly, she tamped down those two disagreeable emotions. The owner's brother had sent her here, so her early arrival shouldn't be a big deal. Supposedly, she was a shoo-in for the job.

"Can't be too much farther," she said to Tuff, who looked up at her with a frown of concern. For real, her dog was a world-class worrier, but this time Diah had to agree with him. It was starting to feel creepy. The long road in, lined by tall aspens and pines, was plenty isolated. Other than the sounds of critters in the trees, the area was dead silent.

Don't be such a chickenshit... You gotta toughen up... Jesus, you're a scaredy-cat.

She'd heard those comments too many times to count. Worse than hearing them?

Knowing they were true.

To the right of her, something rustled in the underbrush—and effectively stalled her breathing. Tuff went alert, staring in that direction, then dismissed it. Almost immediately to her left, a flock of birds took flight, stripping a year off her life. Tuff sidled closer.

Automatically, she sought to reassure him, and in the process reassure herself as well because Tuff's nervousness always became her own, and vice versa.

Putting a hand on his neck, appreciating the contact with another living creature, she gently rubbed. "Yeah, maybe I should have asked that lady to drive us right up to the campground, huh? I hadn't figured on it being such a hike, though. His street sign should give a damn clue, right?"

Tuff looked forward and perked his ears.

"Squirrel?" she asked, because she could handle a critter. "Rabbit?" But no. She heard it now, too. *Singing.* And there up ahead, finally, the winding road opened to a clearing, with a small parking lot on the right and a wooden shed that served as a gatehouse and check-in station on the left. Right now the shed was empty, but it had been recently painted and looked big enough to accommodate a few people. Nearest the road was a drive-through window, so visitors wouldn't have to get out to check in for their stay.

Thank God they'd finally reached the campgrounds. With a duffel bag hanging from one shoulder, her packed tent slung over the other, and a suitcase in her hand, her shoulders were killing her. The soft suitcase was a roller, but not on this pitted, bumpy path.

Seriously, she wished she were stronger. Wished she were braver, too.

Sometimes she wished she were someone else entirely.

As Tuff strained against the leash, he almost got away from her. Quickly readjusting her free hand, not just a few fingers, Diah said, "Quiet," in her low command voice, and although Tuff's furry lips rippled, he didn't make a sound. Such a smart boy. So many times over the past two grueling years, she'd given thanks that Tuff had come into her life. He was her best friend, her protector and pretty much the only reason she ever smiled. "We'll sort of sneak in, okay?"

A muffled, *"Fft,"* was Tuff's reply. And yup, she grinned.

When she got to the check-in, Diah unloaded her belongings beside it. Looking around, she took in several small cabins that appeared newly repaired. Some trees had been trimmed, RV and tent lots were mostly cleared, but overall the grounds were a work in progress.

Straight ahead, not too far from the entry, a larger cabin—which by no means made it large—appeared to be the source of the singing. She heard, *"Love me, love me, saaaay that you love me,"* in a high falsetto and couldn't help but laugh.

"Oh, man, Tuff, do you hear that?"

"Lovefool" by The Cardigans. If she hadn't heard it in a bar during karaoke night, she'd have no idea. The drunken chick who'd sung it then hadn't done as good of a job as this guy. He really belted it out with gusto.

Snickering, she said to Tuff, "No time like the present," and led him along to the cabin, around to the side and there… *Ho boy.*

Naked.

Using an outside shower.

Forget the warmth of the sunshine. It was freaking *April* in Colorado.

Thank God a concrete block half wall kept her from seeing him in all his glory, but holy moly, what he showed was enough to keep her gawking. Dude had seriously hot, muscular shoulders and flat abs… Heck, she could see the tops of his hip bones, too. It was a mighty fine display, one she hadn't been prepared for.

Tuff sat down, maybe mesmerized. Diah's legs were suddenly shaky enough that she wouldn't mind sitting, too.

Lounge back and watch the show? Would've been nice.

Unfortunately, she was a human adult, not a dog, so she had to announce herself. She tried loudly clearing her throat, followed by a sharp "Ahem."

Nothing.

Face turned up, he sang out another verse while rinsing shampoo from dark brown hair a few inches too long. When was the last time she'd seen anyone built like him, all firm, ropy muscles on a tall frame?

Yeah, that'd be never.

Not once in her twenty-four years had she ever encountered any guy, anywhere, who looked like this one.

Shameful to admit, but she eyeballed him a little longer before saying again, louder this time, *"Ahem."*

Pausing in midverse, he cocked open one dark blue eye, framed by spiked lashes. He spotted her and at his leisure, without a hint of haste—or modesty—pushed back his wet hair and got both eyes open.

Intently watching her now, no longer singing, he… continued his shower.

What. The. Hell.

A big soapy hand went over his throat, the back of his neck, across his chest and beneath one arm.

He was so damn attractive, her heart ping-ponged around in her chest. Since he didn't speak, she assumed she'd have to. "Hi, I'm, um…" *Who was she?* Oh, yeah. "Jedidiah Stephens. Appointment at three."

Turning his back to the water, not at all put off by being caught in the buff outside, his gaze moved over her body, but quickly came back to her eyes. "I don't have any appointments."

She went blank for a moment before the obvious answer came to her. "Oh, hey, I'm sorry for disturbing you." Belatedly remembering that people were usually put off by her intent stare, she turned to give him privacy. But yeah, she wasn't comfortable with anyone at her back so she shifted again, facing to the side. If he tried to leave the shower to approach her she'd catch him in her peripheral vision, but at least her gaze wasn't directly on him. "I'm looking for Memphis Osborn."

"He's busy showering."

Confusion hit her. "You're both showering?" How… Why…? Thoughts of mud wrestling or some other sexy activity flashed through her mind. Two sweaty guys. Muscles straining…

Sucked that she'd missed it.

A gruff, short laugh came from him and he said, "You're not seeing the big picture. I'm Memphis, I'm showering and I don't have any appointments."

Chagrin brought her around so that she fully faced him again. Yup, still gloriously naked. How could she *not* stare? "You own this place?"

Beside her, Tuff stirred. The poor dog was as tired as she was and no doubt ready to bed down somewhere for a nap.

"Guilty. As you can see, I haven't opened yet."

"I *know* the place isn't open." She resisted adding "Duh." As if explaining to a little kid, she spoke slowly. "I have an appointment about a job."

His gaze dipped over her bare legs, making her wish she'd worn jeans instead of shorts. Yeah, if only she'd had a chance to do laundry, but it wasn't always possible on the road. His attention lingered for a mere heartbeat before returning to her face…and roaming over her every feature as if figuring out who—or what—she was. Rude!

Because she'd ogled him, too, she couldn't really get huffy about it… *The hell she couldn't!* She was fully dressed, not prancing around outside bare-assed. "Take a picture, why doncha?"

"You wouldn't mind?" He reached for the cell phone he'd left on the top of the half wall near a folded towel. As he lifted the phone, the music that came from it abruptly died.

The sudden quiet was jarring.

He pretended to take aim.

Belatedly, she found her voice, which erupted with irritation. "Look, I was told to be here and that you'd hire me."

"Sight unseen?" Shaking his head to deny that, he set the phone aside, turned off the water and reached for the towel—which he only slung around his neck. "I don't think so."

Swear to God, she could see steam rising off those impressive shoulders. Her palms tingled at the idea of touching him, maybe coasting her fingers over the swells of muscle. "Aren't you freezing?"

"Little bit."

Yet, he didn't dry off. "Is there a reason you're showering out here instead of inside somewhere?"

"Yeah."

She waited, but he didn't elaborate. Fine, she could play this game. "Wanna share?"

Amusement tugged at one corner of his *very* sexy mouth. "Might as well, since you're still here." He made a halfhearted effort at drying himself. "I've been living in this cabin, which is the biggest on the grounds, but still not big enough for me."

"Seriously?" It looked great to her.

"The shower was especially small," he explained, "so I'm extending the back end with a larger bedroom and bathroom. It's not quite done and until it is, I have more room out here." He eyed her again. "Used to have plenty of privacy, too, until some girl and her dog just showed up out of the blue."

Odd that the words were disgruntled, but the tone not so much. If anything, he seemed amused. Maybe she was going about this all wrong. After adjusting her tinted glasses, she tried on a congenial smile. "This is Tuff."

"What is?"

"My dog. His name is Tuff."

Glancing down, he gave a short laugh at the dog's sleepy expression. "Hey, boy. Are you really that tough?"

"T-u-f-f," she explained. "He came with the name when I adopted him. He's fast, smart and super protective." She tacked on the last just in case he wasn't as easygoing as he seemed and had any thoughts of hassling her.

Disinterested in all the human chitchat, Tuff yawned.

"He's also tired." Memphis searched the area. "Where's your car? I didn't hear you drive in."

"I walked."

Skeptical, he asked, "From where?"

Right. Nowhere was near so the question made sense. "We hitched a ride in the back of a woman's truck. She dropped us off by the camp sign."

"The camp sign that's a little over a mile away?"

That far? Hmm. Maybe she could garner some sympathy and that'd soften him up. "Only a mile?" To add an edge of drama, she put a hand to her back. "Felt longer with me carrying all my gear and leading the dog. I think it took me a good forty minutes."

Lacking even an ounce of pity, he grinned. "Great exercise, right?" He turned a finger in the air. "I'm stepping out now, so unless you want your feelings hurt, you might want to turn around."

"Why would it hurt my feelings?"

He hitched one of those big shoulders. "No idea, but you're acting all affronted that I'm out here naked, on my own property where you shouldn't be, showering in a place that's none of your business, so I assumed you'd object." After spewing that mix of nonsense and censure, he waited.

Left with no choice, she gave him the truth. "Eh, since you're a stranger and everything, I'd prefer to keep an eye on you."

"What a weak excuse. Admit you want to see me."

Of all the… She folded her arms and tried to glance away. Couldn't quite do it, though. "I won't stare." *She wouldn't.* Her stare had gotten her into trouble too many times.

Had gotten her hurt as well. *A long time ago*, she reminded herself, and yet it was a lesson she'd never forget.

"Suit yourself." The towel wasn't nearly big enough to adequately wrap around his lean hips, but he came out from behind the block wall anyway.

And strolled away.

"Hey." Diah hustled after him. "Where are we going?"

"I'm going for clothes, and you aren't invited." He glanced back. "Much as you'd apparently love to watch."

Damn it. She had to do better about staring—and usually she did. Given how good he looked, she'd cut herself a little slack for the lapse.

Ignoring his jibe, she aimed for a marginally reasonable comment. "I'll wait out here."

Keeping his back to her, he said, "No reason. I'm not hiring you."

Unacceptable, so she stalled with a question. "You don't have a shower room here for guests?"

Idly, he pointed in the direction of a concrete building farther out. "Right there, but it's still loaded with spiders."

Even as she shuddered, she prodded him by asking, "Squeamish about bugs?"

"Not particularly, but I'd as soon not shower with them." He went up a few wooden steps to his front door.

Rather than keep chasing him, Diah acted like everything was on track. "Go ahead and get dressed, then I'll explain."

At that, he dropped his head forward and laughed.

She waited to see what he'd say, but with another shrug, he opened his door and went inside.

Damn. Now what?

Pacing away, her every step kicking up debris in the gravel walkway, Diah tried to plan. She came up blank. He *had* to hire her, period. In fact, thanks to Memphis's brother and his wife, she'd already considered herself hired. They'd offered her assurances.

Could she use that to her advantage?

Twenty minutes later, he still hadn't returned. People didn't take that long to get dressed. It was a nice day. Underwear, shorts, a shirt…presto. He'd be done in under a minute.

So he was dodging her. Did he think she'd give up and leave? Fat chance.

She considered knocking on his door, but that wasn't a great way to make a good impression on a job interview.

If she could turn this into an interview.

If she hadn't just been completely dismissed.

Crap, what if he was calling the police or something?

Tuff whined, and that helped strengthen her resolve. She hadn't come this far just to give up. True, she wasn't the bravest person. So what? She had perseverance and initiative. "Come on, buddy. We both need a rest and Mr. Naked can just do whatever the hell he's in there doing. I'm not budging unless I'm dragged away."

Having done it many times now, in many different places, she methodically moved her gear to a cleared site, dug out Tuff's bowl and filled it with water from Mr. Naked's outdoor shower. While the dog drank she got set up.

Naturally, she'd chosen the spot closest to his cabin.

He'd figure out that she wasn't leaving. She couldn't.

One way or another, this was where she had to be.

WHILE MEMPHIS HASTILY pulled on boxers and loose cargo shorts, he watched the woman through one of the specialty one-way mirrored windows installed on his cabin as she literally—and expertly—pitched her tent.

On *his* property.

As if she had every intention of staying, despite anything he'd said. It nettled him big time, and yet it also had his blood pumping. Exhilarating. He hadn't been this enthralled since moving here and buying the campgrounds.

Sure, he went into town every so often, and he'd visited with his brother and sister-in-law a few times. At least once a week he conferred with Madison, who was not only hardcore at tech but also claimed to be his BFF. Most best-friends-forever would visit in person more often. So far, he'd only met Madison in person a handful of times. Not a biggie since her husband and brothers were scary dudes who excelled at intimidation.

They didn't intimidate *him* only because he understood them. They were big-time enforcers of justice, and on a smaller scale, he could help do the same from this campground.

To make the idea a reality, he'd been mostly working alone, setting up security cameras, motion sensors and reliable public WiFi for the guests—which he could easily monitor when necessary.

Eventually, he'd finish some of the necessary things, like cleaning out the showers and fixing the entry road, but any contractors he had around would be clueless to the real reason he had this place.

In fact, the only people so far who knew were his brother, sister-in-law and Madison.

After thumbing his brother's number on his cell, he waited, and as soon as Hunter answered, Memphis said, "What the hell is this?"

"Memphis?" Hunter asked with feigned innocence.

"Yes, it's your brother. I thought you loved me."

"Do," Hunter said, then asked, "So what's the problem?"

"You sent someone here for a job."

"I told you about that."

"You told me about a *guy*—Jedidiah—not a pushy girl." A girl with super-long, *gorgeous* legs, silky-looking brown hair with blondish ends, and an arresting set of eyes partially hidden behind rose-tinted glasses.

Eyes that instantly captivated.

She also had a totally funky fashion sense.

Not that he didn't appreciate her cute coverall shorts worn with a faded pink long-sleeve top.

Hunter stated, "Jedidiah is a woman."

"No shit."

"You called her a girl."

"You *know* what I meant."

"She's qualified. Has an amazing background as a handyman—"

"Woman," Memphis said, throwing the correction back at his brother. "Handywoman."

"—and she can fix, or oversee the fixing of, all the things you still need repaired. Plus, Jodi liked her."

Memphis hated to admit it, but an endorsement from his sister-in-law counted for a lot, because Jodi didn't trust many people. "Background check?"

"We figured you'd do more, but overall she's clear."

Overall clear and yet she'd watched him shower without a single qualm. That definitely felt shady…or at least ballsy. Worse, though, she'd heard him singing. Being fickle, he grinned and said, "I don't like it."

"You mean you don't like her? Will it help if I tell you she's a lot like Jodi?"

"Good Lord." No, that definitely wouldn't help. If that was true, he shouldn't have left her unattended.

Good thing he could see her walking around the grounds, inspecting one thing, frowning at another, testing the sturdiness of something else.

"I'll share your reaction with Jodi."

"Don't you dare." He adored Jodi and though she didn't need it, he felt very protective of her.

"So what's the problem? You were all about me marrying Jodi."

His stomach dropped. "What the hell does any of this have to do with *marriage*?"

"I just assumed if you had any type of issue with Jodi, you wouldn't have sacrificed me."

Sacrifice? Ha! He'd have liked to see anyone try to separate his brother from Jodi. Satan himself couldn't have accomplished it. "Jodi, with all her special talents, is perfect for *you*—but you and I are very different people and you know it."

"Jodi swears that in the most elemental ways, we're the same and she wants you to hire Jedidiah."

Damn. Memphis watched as the woman sat cross-legged on the ground, then dug around in her duffel bag and found an apple. *When had she last eaten?*

"Memphis?"

"I told her to leave," he murmured aloud, as much to himself as his brother.

"Did she?"

"No." Bemused, he watched her fill a bowl with dry food and set it before Tuff. First a water dish, and now this. What else did she have in that pack?

He kind of liked that she'd taken care of her pet first.

"Memphis?"

"She seems to be settling in," he grumbled. "Now I'm going to have to oust her."

"Hang on."

Alarm drew his attention off Jedidiah. "Hunter, don't you dare put me on with—"

"Hey, Memphis."

Damn it. "Hey, Jodi," he said in his nicest happy-to-hear-from-you voice. "How's my favorite sister-in-law?"

"I'm your only sister-in-law."

"Even if there were a dozen, you'd be my favorite." He saw Jedidiah yawn with an elaborate stretch, her arms reaching high, back arching, before she relaxed again.

Fascinating.

Showing visible impatience, she pulled the band from her ponytail, finger-combed her hair and deftly began braiding it over her shoulder.

Mesmerizing.

"You're piling it on a bit thick, aren't you?"

Jodi's droll tone again gained his attention. "Not at all. You're special. You know I've always said so."

"Well, as someone special, I want you to keep her."

Memphis rubbed the back of his neck where droplets from his still-wet hair trickled down his spine. He really needed to finish dressing so he could confront his unwanted guest. "Putting an attractive woman here with me isn't wise." He snatched up the towel and roughly ran it over his head.

"You think she's attractive?"

Memphis rolled his eyes. "You're not blind, honey. You know she is."

"I guess, but hey, I'm assuming you can control yourself."

"Can I?" He'd never had to before. Given how Jedidiah had stared at him, the interest would be returned. If she became an employee, he couldn't very well react to basic urges. Or could he? He'd never been a boss before.

Then again, if he didn't hire her, she'd leave. Hmm.

"I know you can," Jodi said. "And, Memphis, she really needs the job. Give her a shot. See how it goes. You have a little time before you open, and I guarantee she'll help you get the last few things in order."

That casual *last few things* should have alarmed him, because seriously, he didn't want others knowing why he'd bought the campground and how he planned to use it.

Hung up on a different part of what Jodi said, he harked back to, "What do you mean, she needs the job?"

Jodi huffed out a breath. "You met her, Memphis. Does she look like someone with a lot of resources?"

She'd hitchhiked in. She'd pitched her tent. Worse, she looked exhausted, so… "No." Did she carry all her personal belongings with her? If so, she didn't have much. "Spell it out for me."

"Look, it's her business, okay? All I'll say is that if you send her packing, she'll be sleeping in the woods somewhere."

Sleeping in the woods? "What the hell are you getting me into?"

Hunter rejoined the conversation, saying, "Madison recommends her, too."

Of all the… They'd already discussed this with Madison? "Listen up, brother. Women do not run my life."

Jodi's laugh came through loud and clear. "Keep her, Memphis."

"She's not a stray dog, you know."

"Definitely not." With more humor than the situation warranted, Jodi said, "You'll like having her around. Trust me. I'll check back with you in a few days."

"Jodi—"

"Later, gator."

Well, hell.

Hunter asked, "So that's settled?"

Had he given Memphis a choice? He hated to disappoint Jodi, and now if Jedidiah left, he'd worry about her. No woman should be alone and unprotected in this area, much less alone in the woods.

And it wasn't just the wildlife and weather that concerned him.

Memphis watched her stretch again, then pet the dog. "How did you and Jodi meet her anyway?"

"She was asking around town about you."

His brows went up. "How so?"

"Curious about the campgrounds at first. When she found out you owned it now, she wanted to know your plans for the place. When you'd bought in, how long you'd been out there, stuff like that. Jodi got wind of it."

"Of course she did." Most likely, Madison had clued in Jodi. For a guy raised with only one brother, Memphis now had two awesome women in his life—a sister-in-law and a tech wizard bestie. He enjoyed them both; Jodi because she *was* special, both cunning and kind, and she made his brother very happy, and Madison because she was brilliant, connected, and it was nice to talk shop with someone who understood.

"Once we located Jedidiah, Jodi spoke with her."

"Bet that was an interesting conversation."

"Actually, Jedidiah seemed skittish at first, and you know Jodi. That made her extra curious, too, but also sympathetic. Jodi claims Jedidiah is here for a reason."

That was the only conclusion that made sense. Why else would an attractive, healthy woman choose to hitchhike through Colorado and then apply for a handyman job at a remote, rundown campground? "She could be dangerous."

"You can handle yourself. Plus, Jodi said she wasn't armed."

He hadn't even thought about her having a weapon. "Jodi would know." His sister-in-law was more astute than most, and deeply aware of everything and everyone. Sad, how and why she'd learned to be that way—but it had made her perfect for Hunter, and vice versa, and that was what mattered most, not any tragedies in the past.

Did Jedidiah have a tragic past?

Seemed possible. After all, Jodi had a nose for recognizing kindred spirits.

"Memphis?"

That particular tone from his brother put him on guard. "What?"

"Give her a try, okay? If it doesn't work out, if you have legit reason for wanting her off your property, Jodi and I will help you make it happen."

"Why is it you two think you know everything I need?" He didn't wait for an answer. "Fine. She can stay the night and we'll see how it goes." He'd make no promises beyond that. "I should check on her now. She's been out there stewing while we talked."

"Ass," Hunter said in exasperation. "Go take care of her, and let me know if you need anything."

"Thanks." He stuck the phone in his pocket, finished toweling his hair, grabbed a T-shirt from the drawer and stepped into old sneakers.

A singular sense of anticipation, something he hadn't felt in forever, took him back out to the grounds and right up to where Jedidiah Stephens sat with her dog.

No way did she miss his approach, especially now that his shadow encompassed her, yet she continued to pet Tuff without acknowledging him. The dog, however, sat up and let his tongue loll out—cautious, ready, but not yet aggressive.

Memphis waited, but Jedidiah said nothing, which meant he had to. "So do you have a reference?"

Squinting against the sun, aqua-colored eyes peered up at him. "Your brother and sister-in-law aren't good enough?"

"Afraid not." Was it the pink-tinted glasses that made her eyes that unique shade, a cross between blue and green? Or perhaps it was compliments of colored contacts. For certain, he'd never seen eyes like hers.

She quickly glanced away, but as if she couldn't help herself, her gaze returned to him. "Then no, I don't have a reference."

When she didn't stand, he crouched down in front of her, noting her touch of wariness. Long lashes lifted, brown eyebrows went up…and then drew down.

"What?" she asked, her tone defensive.

"I'll keep you on a trial period."

Miraculously, her expression changed to one of relief mingled with joy. "For real?"

Happiness made her even more appealing. "A week."

"Awesome." A big smile put dimples in her cheeks. "That's time enough to convince you that I'm good to have around."

Bothered by her nearness, Memphis stood again. "Would you like the use of a cabin?"

"A cabin?" Finally, she came to her feet, too, and though she fought it, her attention flickered to his place. "Where?"

So much suspicion. Had someone mistreated her? It didn't really feel like a specific concern as much as general caution. A good idea since she was a woman alone, in an isolated area with a large man she didn't know. If Jodi was right, she didn't even have a weapon to protect herself.

Standing in front of her, he guessed her to be around five feet seven inches—which put her a good five inches shorter than him.

The braid she'd refashioned was crooked but cute, and his fingers curled with the urge to see if her hair was as silky as it looked. Traces of dust clung to her arms and cheeks. Wisps of hair around her face had darkened with sweat.

None of that should have stirred him, and yet it did.

"What?" she asked again, this time in annoyance. She straightened those silly colored glasses, flipped her braid over her shoulder. "Something wrong?"

Unfortunately, everything seemed right. "No." Gesturing to the cabin across from his own, he asked, "Will that do? It's small, only a loft bedroom, kitchenette, love seat with a TV, and a tiny bathroom." He needed her to be close by so he could keep an eye on her.

"Sure. Or I can stay in my tent."

"And then shower with the spiders?"

Her lips scrunched to the side. "Yeah, okay. Cabin it is. Er… I mean. How much?"

Benevolent, Memphis held out his arms. "It comes with the job."

Her eyes narrowed. "Is there a catch?"

So much distrust. "Yes. If I'm not satisfied with the job you do, you lose the cabin."

"That's it? For real? I'll do a great job, you'll see."

He believed her. "Would you like to know how much you'll get paid?"

"I suppose I should."

Meaning she'd take the job regardless? Things got more interesting by the minute. He named the amount—slightly more than he'd intended to pay—but why not? She looked like she needed it. When her eyes widened, he felt good about upping the pay. "Will that suffice?"

"That'd be terrific, yeah."

One issue down, now on to the rest. "Have you eaten?"

"You watched me eat an apple."

He blinked.

"Dude, you have reflective windows. I know what they are. You look out, no one can look in." She smirked. "Besides, I could feel you staring."

His fascination grew. "I was on the phone with my brother."

"Did he sing my praises?"

"Why would you think that?"

"He seemed all gung ho on you hiring me. His wife did, too. They smiled about it a lot."

Yeah, Memphis just bet they did. The lie came easily. "Actually, they cautioned me."

Her brows dropped. "About what?"

He started her toward his cabin with a wave of his hand. "You asked about me around town."

Nothing. Not a word as she followed along.

Prodding her, he asked, "How did you hear about the campground?"

More silence. He glanced at her and caught her concentrated frown. Ah, so she and this campground had a history? He'd have to look into that.

"The thing is…"

Understanding about secrets, he said, "Never mind, we'll get back to that later. Would you like to come in while I get the keys to unlock your cabin?"

She peered around him, gave it some thought and looked at Tuff. "I can't leave him out here alone. He'd go bonkers."

"Should I assume you'll only be able to work when the dog can be beside you?" That'd certainly limit what she could do.

"This is our first day here. First hour, even. He'll relax once he gets used to the place. Usually, I can leash him nearby and he's fine." She shifted, then asked with dread, "Is that going to be a problem?"

Memphis shook his head. Instincts were a very real thing and his were telling him to accommodate her. "Tuff is welcome inside as well."

For only a second, she showed her surprise. "Oh, okay, then sure. I can check out your bathroom, too, if you want." Verbally backpedaling, she said, "I mean, to see what else has to be done."

He let that go without a joke. "You have plumbing skills?"

"Give me the right tools and a little more muscle and I could pretty much build a house from the ground up."

"No kidding?" He opened his door and stepped aside for her to enter. "A formidable skill for a… How old are you?"

After the slightest beat of hesitation, she said, "Mid-twenties."

"And so exact." He came in behind her, which had her quickly turning to face him. Right, her aversion to having people at her back. Without making an issue of it, Memphis strode around her toward the kitchen. "Had some experience in contracting?"

"It's mostly what I've done." Leaning against a wall, she watched as Tuff sniffed everything—each piece of furniture, cabinet and along the floor. "I tried other jobs, but then I realized I have a knack for handyman work and pick up on stuff easily, so I've stuck with it."

Unlocking a large cabinet on the wall, Memphis surveyed the labeled keys on tiny hooks, each with multiple duplicates, and withdrew the one he'd need. "Was your father in construction?"

With deep interest, she continued to stare at the cabinet.

It took Memphis a second to figure out why, and once he did, compassion overshadowed everything else. Whatever was going on with Jedidiah, she'd learned to be extra cautious. "I need duplicates in case one gets lost." Her gaze shot to his and held. Such remarkable eyes. She didn't just look at a person, she fixed on them as if nothing else existed.

The only time Memphis could recall a woman gazing at him like that was during sex, and even then, the attention hadn't felt so intense.

Should he tell her that the tinted lenses did nothing to lessen the impact of her stare? Probably not—at least not yet. Not when she looked so mistrustful.

"Each cabin has a dead bolt on the inside of the entry door so when you're inside, you're safe. I have extra keys just in case someone locks themselves out, or loses the key."

She needlessly adjusted her glasses and glanced away. "Right." The uneasy smile she flicked his way didn't include her endearing dimples. Giving her attention to the rest of the kitchen, she said, "I know how it works. No worries."

"Oh?" Happy to give her the change in topic, he asked, "Have some experiences with campgrounds, too?"

"We visited them often when I was a kid."

Something in how she said that made him wonder: Had she been to *this* campground? Trying to be subtle about it, he asked, "When was the last time you and your family visited—"

She interrupted to ask, "Mind if I take a look at your addition now?"

Huh. Apparently, discussions of her family were off the table. His curiosity grew, but again, he let it go.

Knowing her preferences, he stepped around her to lead the way to his bedroom. "It's back here." As they walked down the hall, he asked, "So other than an apple, have you eaten?"

"This morning."

"Got a meal hidden in your gear? Because I don't have the camp store open yet and even when I do it'll be for basics without a lot of meal choices. The cupboards in your cabin aren't stocked, either."

Her hand went to her stomach, but instead of answering his question, she said, "I heard you're making this a budget place, right?" Studiously ignoring his bed, she moved along to the extension.

In between his special projects for the campgrounds, he'd gotten the bigger bedroom and bathroom semifinished. The doors and all the windows were in, so the room was secure. The drywall was up, the seams mudded, but they needed to be sanded.

"It'll be an affordable stay, not at all fancy. Only the

basics offered." Which meant that less reputable people would find it appealing. The grounds wouldn't be on anyone's radar. Low-key, unobtrusive—quick in and quick out. However, while guests were here, Memphis could do all the digging he wanted on their extracurricular and often illegal activities.

Jedidiah moved on, inspecting everything. "Electrical, plumbing and HVAC are all roughed in?"

"Yes." He glanced around at the incomplete work. Once the room was closed up, he'd put finishing it on hold to focus on other projects that he considered key to the campground. "The shower only needs to be caulked."

"So rather than caulk it, you choose to shower outside in April?"

"The weather has been mild and I find it invigorating." Only a partial lie. There'd been times when he'd thought he'd freeze his balls off, completing his shower in under two minutes and racing back into the warmth of his cabin. "I sing to scare off the bears."

"There aren't any bears around."

"Guess my singing is working."

She snickered. "Want me to caulk it for you?"

"Why?" She sounded so earnest, he lifted his brows and teased her. "Just because you're here, you don't want me showering outside anymore?"

The humor slipped and her expression went blank. "I mean, no, sure…" Confusion brought her brows together. "Did you still plan to?"

Fighting a grin, he gestured at the bedroom. "At least until the rest of this is done." When it was finished, his bed would get moved in here and he'd have the old, crowded bedroom to use as office space. "A little sanding, trim, paint… Won't be much longer anyway."

Determined, she faced him. "I can do all that."

Never before had he met anyone so eager to take on work. "No kidding?"

Again moving past his question, she explained, "You've had your final inspections, right? I can do the hookups for the electrical, plumbing, HVAC—all that. Plus, I'm really good at trim work and I've done drywall plenty of times. Painting isn't a problem, either." Squaring her shoulders, she said, "I'll even clear out the spiders in the public showers."

Damn. Did she think she needed to work sunup to sundown? "Jedidiah…"

"Call me Diah. It's not such a mouthful."

"Diah." Pretty name and it suited her. "All right."

This time her smile showed only resolve. "I promise I'll be a good worker."

"I never doubted it." He realized Tuff wasn't with them and turned to see the dog snuffling into his closet. Quickly striding to him, Memphis said, "Hey there, Tuff, how'd you get that door open?"

Before he could reach the dog, Diah darted past him and pulled Tuff away. "Sorry." Stiff and unsure, she stood protectively in front of the dog. "He gets nosy."

Her moods bounced around too fast for Memphis to keep track, but always, to one degree or another, the uncertainty was there. Now, when it came to her dog, she did her best to shield him.

What did she think he'd do? Wondering about that, Memphis gentled his tone. "First, there's nothing awful in my closet so I wasn't worried." To reassure her, he reached out and opened the closet door the rest of the way. She could see the clothes in front, but not really the shelving in the back. Not that he was hiding anything but he didn't think she wanted him to give her an accounting of his belongings. "Even if I was hiding something top secret, I would never mistreat an animal. You don't have to worry about me with Tuff. I just didn't want him eating my shoes."

"Tuff would never!"

Her affront on behalf of her dog was endearing. "If you say so. My brother has this goofy basset mix who seems to like the laces in my shoes."

The mention of Turbo eased some of the defensiveness from her posture. "I met Turbo. He makes funny noises."

"That he does. His barker is broken or something. He came that way when Hunter rescued him so we're not sure how it happened, and now it's just a very Turbo-like thing to hear a dog quacking."

The dimples reappeared in her cheeks. "He's bottom heavy, too, and bounces when he's excited."

"I imagine he was excited to meet Tuff."

"Very." Putting her hand on Tuff's head, she said, "We didn't know what to think, did we, bud?"

Tuff said, *"Fft."*

"That's his quiet bark, his way of keeping things understated. When he's mad he sounds demonic." Realizing what she'd said, she quickly backtracked. "Oh, but he doesn't get mad often, only when something is really wrong or..." Her voice trailed off.

"Or he thinks you're being threatened?"

CHAPTER TWO

"DIAH?" HER LONG silence bothered him.

Predictably, up went her chin. "Tuff is a friendly guy."

"I believe you." Memphis stroked a hand over the dog's neck. His fur was sleek and soft, proving she kept him well-groomed and cared for. It bothered him how she seemed so cocky, even irreverent one moment, then very unsure the next.

By the minute, Memphis's interest grew. Not just because she was pretty in a very natural way, and not because she had gorgeous legs, a quirky smile and eyes that mesmerized.

He liked her protectiveness of Tuff, that she was anxious to get to work, and that she truly seemed knowledgeable about her skill set. It was nice to hear her openly state her talents without unnecessary modesty.

"Here's what we're going to do—and please remember that I'm the employer, you the employee, so I'd appreciate it if you wouldn't argue."

Her eyes narrowed and her mouth flattened, but she didn't say anything.

He waited a second more, but she contained herself, making him smile. "I'll unlock your cabin and help you get your stuff inside. When that's done, I'll take you on a quick tour of the place in the golf cart. The campground is tiny compared to most." Which made it perfect for him since he planned to keep a close eye on everyone and everything. “Fifty-seven campsites in all, thirty for RVs with full hookups, seventeen rustic sites for tents and ten cabins, besides mine—nine since you’ll be using one.”

“I don’t mean to deduct from your revenue. I don’t mind using my tent.”

Was there anything she wouldn’t tackle? Didn’t seem likely. “Employer,” he stressed, pointing at himself, and then to her, “employee.”

Those soft lips compressed again and she grudgingly nodded.

At least she knew when to stand down—or her reasons for being here were too important for her to haggle over small stuff. “You’ll use a cabin for multiple reasons, one being that it’s safer.”

“Safer?”

“More protected?” Fearing that he might have spooked her, he elaborated. “From wild animals.”

“You could just sing around the clock,” she suggested with a quick grin.

Her dimples were extremely cute and preferable to her frowns. He hoped to see more of them.

“Sorry, but my voice doesn’t affect the weather or falling trees.”

Boggled, she asked, “Falling trees?”

“I made that up.” But now that he’d said it, it became a concern. He’d have to check the grounds to see if any dead trees should be removed. “Anyway, when we finish the tour you can refresh yourself and join me for dinner.”

Skepticism narrowed her eyes. “Dinner where?”

Here inside his cabin without the bright sunlight, he

could see that her eyes were mostly blue but had green striations that gave them the aqua hue. Her thick lashes and brows were a few shades darker than her hair, all set against fair, peachy skin.

He was naturally darker than her, plus all his work outside had added color to his skin.

Rather than push his luck by staring at her any longer, Memphis said, "There's a drive-through place near here. They have fried chicken, hamburgers and hot dogs, soup of the day, onion rings and fries, simple stuff like that. So that Tuff can go along, we'll eat at one of the picnic tables they have around the place. How's that sound? My treat on the meals until you get your first paycheck."

Pride had her saying, "I'm not destitute, you know."

No, he didn't know, but he said honestly, "Glad to hear it."

"I don't have a car, though, so…" She gave in with a wince. "Will we pass a store where I can get some stuff?"

"What kind of stuff?"

"More dog food for one thing. I was starting to run low so that's a top worry."

Because he couldn't hug her, he continued to pet Tuff. "Can't have that, can we? What else do you need?"

"Snacks for Tuff and me both. I assume there's a refrigerator in the cabin so I could put some drinks in there." She considered it, then added, "Maybe milk for cereal—that is, if you have a bowl and spoon?"

Right. She literally had nothing. "You have a small fridge, and I'm sure we can scrounge up some dishes and cutlery." He should have suggested eating before the tour. Too late to backtrack now, though. She'd catch on and no doubt be prickly about it. "After we eat, we'll hit up the little grocery. You have a stationary grill outside the cabin, too, if you enjoy grilling." He stared down at her, noting the added color in her cheeks and how soft her mouth appeared when she wasn't pinching it in disapproval or worry. As businesslike as he could manage, he stated, "Since it'll only be the two of us for a while yet, it might be easier to grill together but that's up to you." Forestalling any argument she might make, he got her moving again.

Tuff stayed right at her side as they exited his cabin and crossed over to the one she'd be using. Leaves and twigs cluttered the short deck, and a cobweb hung from the porch light.

Once inside, he found it even smaller than he'd remembered. Not that she seemed to mind. As he opened a few windows to air it out, she looked around with barely banked excitement.

"Wow, this is great."

Not really, but he knew families sometimes used the cabins so he supposed it'd work for one woman and her midsize pet. The loft bedroom might be a problem for Tuff—but as he thought it, the dog bounded up the narrow steps with ease.

His brother's dog, Turbo, with his heavy butt and short legs, wouldn't have made it, but the younger, longer-legged Lab had no problem at all.

Memphis frowned as he glanced around. "I don't know if there are sheets up there or if I need to collect some from the storage. Same with dishes and stuff."

"For tonight I'll use my sleeping bag. Do you mind if I leave the tent up?"

"It's not a problem." He did wonder why, though. Not for a second did he think it'd take her long to pack it up.

When they stepped outside, she locked the door, put the key in a back pocket, then patted it while wearing a huge smile. "Seriously, thank you. It really is terrific."

Damn it, it bothered him to see her happy about a tiny cabin with barely enough room to turn around. "Tomorrow we can go through the storage building to see if there's anything else you can use. Lawn chairs, outdoor string lights, stuff like that."

"Sounds fun." She rubbed her hands together. "Almost like Christmas shopping, right?"

Not really—at least not to him. Her enthusiasm bothered him, not because he was wealthy, far from it, but he'd always been comfortable. If there was something he wanted, he generally bought it. No big deal.

Even campgrounds.

Things like a roof over his head were taken for granted. Snacks? He'd never given them a thought because he always had them. Diah, though, had been living out of a tent.

Chased by an absurd sense of guilt, he led the way to the golf cart. He didn't know her background, but he assumed it hadn't been great, certainly not as easy as his own. Growing up, he'd had amazing parents who showered him with love, always backed him up, provided for him, protected him and guided him.

He had a kick-ass, slightly older brother who, despite going through a bit of hell, had remained one of the finest men Memphis knew. Never, not a single day in his life, had he ever felt alone.

Even while living on the campgrounds, he'd known he had family who'd be there for him in a heartbeat if he needed them. He spoke with Hunter and Jodi often, his mom and dad weekly, and Madison a few times a month.

He'd always been *safe*... But Diah'd clearly had a very different experience.

When they reached the golf cart, she whistled. "Fancy."

Hopefully, his grin hid his unease. At thirty, he'd saved plenty of money and with his tech skills, making more hadn't been a hardship. "It's a little out of place in the run-down campgrounds." Especially since he intended to leave them run-down—at least as far as appearances went. "An older one came with the property, and I enjoyed it, so I started shopping around..."

"And decided to buy yourself something top-of-the-line?" She ran her fingertips gently along the seat. "Nothing wrong with enjoying your life."

A refreshing attitude, so why did he feel like a jackass? "Guess it is pretty slick, isn't it?" He frowned at the metallic black four-seater. "Will Tuff be okay riding in it?"

"Tuff doesn't complain about much, plus he's tired. He'll probably just nap, won't you, boy?"

For an answer, the dog hopped into the back, spread out over both rear seats and released a lusty sigh.

Memphis lifted his brows. "Guess that means you're riding up front with me." He offered her a hand, which she ignored as she climbed in, so he got behind the wheel. "The other golf cart still runs so I'll make it available to you and Tuff."

"I don't mind walking."

Would she resist every offer he made? Seemed so. "Employer to employee—I prefer you have it."

"You're wearing out that line, you know."

He liked it when she was snarky. "Yes, I'm enjoying my position of power. Somehow I think you might be the only employee who ever grumbled about benefits." Steering out of his parking spot over the rough ground jostled her so that she grabbed on to the side rail instead of arguing. Maybe he could use that to his advantage, too. Anytime she disagreed, he'd go over a rut.

The sun remained bright, but typical to Colorado weather, the temps were dropping fast. He should have suggested that she get a jacket.

Did she *have* a jacket?

Holding on tight, Diah said, "These lanes need to be smoothed out."

Very true. "Why don't you start tomorrow by making a list for me? Write down whatever you see that needs work, then we can go over it and decide on the order of priorities."

"No problem." Still with one small hand wrapped tight around the sidebar, she took in her surroundings.

"Even though we don't have a lot of units, it's still spread out and covers a lot of ground, especially once you get near the lake. Oh, and a river cuts through the property, too. Shallow in some places, but it continues into the woods and it can get dicey out there." He frowned with that thought, then added, "I don't want you in the woods unaccompanied."

Her gaze slanted his way, but she kept quiet.

Not for a second did he take that for agreement. He'd need to keep an eye on her, for sure.

Over the next half hour, he pointed out the dump station, public restrooms and showers, laundry, tent camping sites, small store that'd sell necessities, and finally the storage building. They were just about to head back when he decided to show her the lake.

Big mistake.

The second they got near it, Tuff jerked awake from his nap and with an excited bark, he leaped off the golf cart.

Unfortunately, Jedidiah leaped off after him.

"TUFF, NO!" When the dog took off, the leash slipped from her loose hold. Instinctively, she grabbed for it, lost her balance...and landed *hard* facedown on the ground. *Oof!* She just barely managed to get her fingers around the end of the leather leash, jerking Tuff to a halt.

Immediately, the golf cart slammed to a stop.

"What the hell!" Running around and crouching beside her, Memphis asked, "What happened? Are you okay?"

Oh, Lord. A nervous, embarrassed snicker tried to crawl up her throat, but since she'd knocked the wind out of herself, all she managed was a pathetic wheeze. Dry weeds stuck her in the face, and she was pretty sure she'd just skinned both knees, bruised a forearm and convinced her new boss that she lacked any common sense.

"Jedidiah?" Cautiously, his big hands took her shoulders as he attempted to lever her onto her back. "Answer me."

"Can't." She wheezed again and thrust the leash at him.

He took it, and then she had to suffer through Tuff snuffling around her face in apology.

With a heartfelt groan, she struggled up to her elbows. "Don't. Let him. Go."

"No, I won't." Memphis patted the ground beside him. "Come here, boy. Sit."

Tuff obeyed, not that Memphis had seemed to expect anything different.

Looping the leash around his wrist freed up his hands, and he easily assisted her into a sitting position, then lifted her arms high. "Breathe. Slow and easy. That's it."

Oh, wow. His "help" put them up close and personal. Like kissing close.

Not that she should be noticing that right now, but hey, her thoughts were all over it. In fact, her gaze focused on his mouth. A really nice mouth, framed by what could be the start of a mustache.

Had he skipped shaving for a few days? *Why do I care?*

She managed a broken breath that sounded really pathetic.

"That's it. Easy."

If he didn't stop crooning to her, she might just faint.

A light breeze played through his hair. Man, it was thick. And his hands on her elbows were hot and firm, but in no way restraining.

"Are you dazed? You look dazed." He released one arm to cup her face, and in the process almost stopped her heart. "Can you focus?"

Unable to look away from his penetrating stare, Diah nodded.

He looked away—and scowled at the sight of her banged-up body. "A few more breaths."

Right. Her greedy lungs agreed that breathing was necessary. Luckily, it got easier by the second. "The water." She dragged in another breath. "He'd have… gone in… Soaked."

"Ah, I see. So you dove headfirst to the ground to keep the dog from getting wet?"

Said like that, it sounded beyond asinine so she frowned at him.

Rough-tipped fingers gently brushed dirt from her face. "No, really. Makes perfect sense."

Soon as she had enough air, she'd tell him to stuff his sarcasm—but he could keep touching her if he really wanted to. It was nice. Stirring. A bonus experience, now that she was finally at the campgrounds with her end goals in sight.

Flustered, she reached to adjust her glasses—and realized she'd lost them in her fall. Her gaze shot back to his, and she found him staring into her eyes. Whoa.

"Huh," he murmured with a small smile. "I thought maybe those pink lenses somehow enhanced your interesting eye color, but I guess that's not it."

He said nothing about her stare, and it didn't seem to bother him, but still… Blinking fast, she looked away. "Sorry."

"For diving off my golf cart?"

Yeah, sure. "I was…staring?" She needed another breath, then clarified, "At you, I mean." The last thing she wanted to do was spook him, but if she gawked at him too long, he'd probably be like the others and want her gone as soon as possible.

Gently, he said, "I didn't mind that part." Now *he* stared. "The mix of blue and green makes your eyes look aqua, but I noticed there's a little gold in there, too." Finally dragging his gaze away, he picked up her glasses and cleaned them with the hem of his T-shirt. "Here." He handed them to her.

Thankfully, they weren't broken. Placing them on her face returned her false sense of concealment. Plus, the glasses gave her something to fidget with when she remembered she shouldn't stare.

Focusing on Tuff, she realized he had his head on his paws and his ears down as he fretted.

"Ah, buddy." She still sounded strained, but at least she could speak. "It's okay."

Memphis continued to watch her. "Better?"

"Yes."

"You know how to make an entrance, Jedidiah Stephens, I'll give you that."

If he wanted to converse, she'd need a little more time. She concentrated on getting her lungs to function properly.

"First you sneak in and watch me shower—"

"Didn't sneak." She couldn't deny the watching part. Immediately, she got another visual of him standing there tall and strong, his skin slick with water and soap, and she felt her face go warm.

"—and then you do a belly flop off a moving golf cart. You could have broken your neck."

"I tried to grab the leash." And lost her balance.

"I see your words are returning." He smiled at her.

That smile, especially with him so close and being so nice, nearly made her breathless again. Finding it necessary to get it together, she deeply inhaled once more. "I'm okay now."

"Not sure Tuff believes you yet."

Tuff could muster the guiltiest expression she'd ever seen on human or animal. It never failed to have her apologizing to him, regardless of what he'd done. "No swimming right now, buddy. I need dinner." She rubbed his soft ears. "Food is better without wet dog fur."

"Incredible." Wearing an expression of mock surprise, Memphis said, "You got out three whole sentences."

His teasing, probably meant to put her at ease, had the opposite effect. How would she ever get through her time here if she turned to mush every time he grinned? It'd help if he were older. If he wasn't such a specimen of gorgeousness.

If he wasn't so blasted considerate.

Concentrating on the dog, she leaned down to kiss the top of his head. "I'm not hurt."

Tail thumping and ears remaining back in apology, Tuff sat up.

"He's sensitive," she explained.

"I'm equally sensitive."

Before she thought better of it, Diah quipped, "Want me to rub your ears, too?"

"Mmm...maybe?"

The grin tugged at her lips, making it difficult to fight. How was it she'd just met him, already liked him and *almost* trusted him? Not good.

More seriously, he asked, "You're sure you're all right?"

"Yes." Other than feeling foolish. "It wasn't the smartest thing to do."

"Gut reaction. I understand."

She appreciated that he'd let her off the hook, especially since he'd seemed genuinely concerned. Even now, he patiently sat there on the rugged ground with her as if it was no big deal.

Trying not to look at the dusting of dark hair on his muscular calves, she took in a few more breaths without issue. "I should have had a better hold on his leash. If I'd realized the lake was so close..."

"I should have told you." Casually, he draped one forearm over a knee. "Tuff was all set to dive in."

"He has a serious love of the water and can never resist it, but his thick fur takes forever to dry."

"Plus, that water is like ice, and I bet the temps have dropped ten degrees in the last half hour." He studied her arms. "You have goose bumps mixed with bruises."

Yeah, it was getting chilly.

"Ready to get back to your cabin? You'll need to clean those scratches before we head out. For tonight, I'll give you a few towels and some soap, and tomorrow we'll go through supplies and put together whatever else you need."

Before she knew his intent, he stood, hooked his hands under her arms and lifted her to her feet as if she weighed nothing at all. Never, not in a decade, had anyone touched her as much as Memphis had in the last few minutes. Out of sheer surprise, she stiffened, but he casually released her and took Tuff back to the cart. "Up you go, bud." Tuff looked at her, waiting.

Right, she needed to get a move on. Annoyed with herself, doing her best not to react to the sting on her knees and forearms, Diah slapped dirt and dried leaves off her clothes and returned to the passenger seat, then encouraged Tuff in, too.

She was so hungry, she'd have preferred to go straight for food. Without Memphis's offer to show her around, she'd already be munching on crackers. The idea of fried chicken was too good to ruin by snacking now, though, so she talked over the growling of her stomach on the blessedly short ride back to their respective cabins.

"Thanks." She gestured lamely. "For everything, I mean."

"No problem. So far it's been…interesting." After he parked, he said, "Give me just a second," and bolted inside, returning a minute later with folded towels, washcloths, a package of soap and a first aid kit. "I'll carry this in for you."

"I can take it."

Memphis walked past her. "You can hold on to Tuff so he doesn't decide to find the lake after all."

One look at the dog and she accepted the possibility. Hurrying ahead of Memphis, she got her door open. "Just set everything on the couch. I'll be ready in ten minutes."

"Perfect." Smiling at her—another really devastating smile—he turned to go. "I'll be waiting."

The second he stepped out, Diah closed and locked the door, grabbed what she'd need and raced into the bathroom. A glance in the mirror assured her she looked even worse than she'd realized. Oh, well. Who cared?

Not her.

Unwilling to take up too much time, she soaped up the cloth and cleaned her face, her neck and her limbs. Her abraded knees stung, as did one arm, but her biggest current complaint was her empty belly.

She dabbed a little ointment on the worst of the scrapes and covered them with plain adhesive bandages. With food on her mind, she hastily removed her messy braid, tipped her head forward to finger-comb her hair and then twisted it into a topknot. Done and done. Tuff had sat there watching her, his head tilted in curiosity, waiting to see what they were doing.

She found a thick sweatshirt and grabbed it. Memphis was right. It'd be downright cold in the next hour or so. "We'll unpack everything else and get set up when we get back. For now, let's go."

He gave an agreeable *"woof,"* jiggled a little and happily followed her out the door.

Memphis sat on his step, staring off in the distance, literally waiting.

Elbows braced behind him, long legs stretched out, knees casually open.

Such a guy pose.

The curled ends of his dark brown hair rested behind his ears and along his nape. A comb hadn't come anywhere near that thick hair, so his part was messy, off-center in front. His expression looked intense. And sexy.

She might have a different lifestyle, one devoid of normal social interactions, but she wasn't oblivious. She knew sexy when she saw it, and Memphis Osborn defined the idea.

When she closed her door, he sat forward. "Ready?"

He wore the same casual clothes of shorts and T-shirt, which reassured her since she hadn't changed, either. Like her, he brought along a zip-up sweatshirt. "You don't mind the dog in your car?"

"Truck, and no. It's fine."

To give him his due, she said, "You've been incredibly accommodating."

He rolled a shoulder. "You wouldn't leave, remember? What choice did I have?"

The complaint stalled her. Was he serious? True,

she'd been pushy and if he belatedly got pissed, well, she couldn't really blame him.

"Come on, then," he said, his expression enigmatic.

Fine. She'd prove to him what a good hire she was. Give her a week and he'd be thanking his lucky stars that she'd come along.

Unlike his fancy golf cart, his truck wasn't as new, but it was still super nice. Clearly, he took care of his stuff. Other than a little dust on the black exterior, it was clean.

He opened the door for Tuff to get in the backseat, then surprised her by opening her door, too. Since he seemed to think nothing of it, she tried to be blasé. Not easy. She couldn't remember the last time a man had opened a door for her. The courtesy after the complaints would have quickly made her suspicious except that she'd met his brother and sister-in-law, and others in town who knew him. Memphis was respected and liked.

"Having second thoughts?"

She glanced up and realized he'd been standing there, one hand on the top of the open door as if waiting for her verdict. "No." She climbed in and got settled. "Why would you think that?"

His expression was far too intense. "No reason." He took a step back, said, "Buckle up," and closed the door to circle the hood.

Diah felt the sudden pounding of her heart, and it wasn't from nervousness.

It was all because Memphis Osborn impacted her in very unfamiliar ways.

Just getting through dinner seemed like a tall order—and here she'd be working for him for the foreseeable future.

FOUR HOURS LATER, fresh from a shower, her wet hair wrapped in a towel, and now wearing flannel pants, socks and a big, loose sweatshirt, Diah looked around the cabin with immense satisfaction. She had a soft bed to sleep on, food in the fridge and a full belly.

Idly, she walked around the minuscule space, admiring the conveniences. *I have a coffeemaker.*

Waking to a hot cup of coffee would be heaven.

True, she'd barely had enough room to store her supplies, but who cared? She was under a roof, the cabin was toasty and best of all she was safe. Simple things she would never take for granted.

Sprawled out on a cozy rug in front of the love seat, Tuff dozed. He'd had a busy day, too. The trip to the restaurant had been an adventure filled with stories from Memphis. He told her all about the area, the people he'd met, other employees he planned to hire; all in all he'd put her at ease—and he hadn't pried into her life.

How nice was that?

Usually, if she spoke more than two sentences with anyone, they started to grill her. Not Memphis. He'd asked if she wanted more chicken, what dessert she'd like and if she was warm enough.

That was it. Nothing nosy. Just good, old-fashioned civility.

From a mega-hot guy.

She enjoyed the novelty of it.

At the small grocery, he'd explained to the pretty owner that Tuff needed to come in with them. Although the woman hadn't liked it, it was clear she admired Memphis—*seriously, who wouldn't?*—and she wanted to stay on his good side.

While Diah pushed around a rickety basket with a

squeaky wheel, Memphis had stood at the counter letting MaryJo Durham flirt with him. Even while grabbing what she needed, Diah heard Memphis's low voice and MaryJo's giggle, and at one point she'd locked her teeth together.

Actually, it was a good thing that she'd gotten fed up with their inane chitchat, otherwise she'd have continued shopping when she didn't have enough space for it all.

Food now filled the cabinets and fridge. Snacks galore, cans of soup, lunch meat, cheese, condiments, bread, peanut butter and jelly, cold cereal and milk—so many wonderful things she hadn't enjoyed lately because they weren't easily packed and prepared for someone living in a tent.

Since she didn't have much, only a few changes of clothes and what she needed for Tuff, she'd stored her other gear, too. Except her tent. As they'd agreed, it remained in the yard. A long lead was fastened to the railing on her small deck so that when Tuff wanted out, she could hook him up. Tomorrow she'd put another near the tent. That way, when she was working, he could get out of the sun if he wanted.

The dog was always happiest when he could see her.

Thinking of the days ahead, she paced to a window and parted the blinds to peek out. Here in the campgrounds surrounded by tall pines, darkness had fallen early. Scattered security lamps were already on when they'd returned, and now only a faint purple tinge remained along the treetops in an otherwise black sky.

When she caught a spark of orange light, she froze in alarm…until she saw that it was Memphis making a campfire in a large stone fire pit near his home.

Once the blaze caught, his head came up and he looked directly at her cabin. Had he known she was watching him? Interesting.

Curiosity took her to the door and then out onto the small wooden deck where she could better see him.

In invitation, he lifted a lawn chair.

Don't do it, she told herself. *No reason to get that familiar.* She'd already had a heavy dose of Memphis's allure. Given the tingling in her stomach now, she wasn't immune. Far from it.

Sitting around a campfire at night had nothing to do with her reasons for being here, or with the job she'd been hired to do. She should keep things professional. Avoid him when possible. That was the only thing that made sense.

He waved at her, urging her to join him.

Don't do it, don't do it—her hand went up and she called, "Be right there." Damn. *No willpower at all.*

Turning, she almost tripped over Tuff. He, too, appeared excited by the prospect of joining Memphis.

Taking the towel from her hair, she hung it over the back of a chair at her tiny parlor table so it could dry. In the bathroom she grabbed her wide-tooth comb and as she stepped into sneakers, she told Tuff, "We'll only sit with him a little while. Maybe until my hair is dry. I couldn't go to bed with it wet anyway, right?" Lying to the dog wasn't really a habit, but for now it worked.

The truth, she knew, was that she felt drawn to join him. "The idea of having fun for the sake of fun is a mighty lure. Even when Memphis is being bossy, he's still fun."

Tuff had no reply.

She hooked the leash to his collar. "It's been a full

day for sure. Tonight we'll sleep inside on a real bed, so this will have to be a short visit. No arguments."

She turned to head out and there was Memphis, arms braced on the deck railing where he'd clearly heard her every word.

Well, hell. She'd have to remember how quietly he moved.

It was an interesting thing to watch Diah comb her damp hair in front of a crackling fire. Very pretty hair, even longer than he'd realized. As it dried, he noticed again that it was darker near her face and crown, but lighter toward the ends as if bleached by the sun. Not blond, more of a golden brown.

The glasses she still wore reflected the glow of the flames.

Between their chairs, Tuff sprawled out, sound asleep and occasionally twitching his paws as he chased dream rabbits or squirrels or something equally provoking.

So Diah considered this fun? The quiet crackle of the fire, the occasional night sounds that drifted over the cold air? The companionship? He hoped so.

"It's peaceful here at night," Memphis explained. "Hear that?"

Pausing, she tilted her head, then smiled. "What is that?"

"Frogs on the lake."

"They're so loud. Very cool."

"The sound carries." He listened a moment and caught a familiar squeaky screech. "And that's a nighthawk."

When her smile warmed even more, Memphis wondered why he was out here tormenting himself—but of course he knew. The thought of her going to bed all alone, owning nothing more than what she could carry, clashed with the pleasure he'd seen on her face as they'd brought in her groceries.

They hadn't even gone to a big grocer with a lot of variety. The peanut butter was a generic brand and she'd only had a few choices in cereal.

Hadn't mattered to her.

She'd taken extreme delight in shopping.

And it had almost leveled him.

It wasn't often he felt this torn. He didn't want her around, but now he felt compelled to make her as comfortable as possible. He didn't want to like her, but how could he resist someone who took such simple joy in basic things?

He sure as hell shouldn't be attracted to her, but yeah, he was a man with a healthy libido, so good luck on ignoring the chemistry. Not that he'd do anything about it. He was good and stuck and he knew it.

He needed to kick Hunter's ass for sending her here.

"Do you do this every night?" she asked, indicating the fire.

Thoughts interrupted, he looked at her again…and kept on looking. *What was it about her?* "I'm not a big fan of television, so when I don't feel like reading, I sit out here and listen to the sounds." Leaning forward, he used a poker to shift a log, sending a spray of sparks to dance upward. "It's important to only use the fire pits or stationary grills, and never leave the fire unattended."

That sent her gaze around the area. "I guess with so many trees a fire could be a real problem." She turned in the chair to face him. "What do you like to read?"

"A little of everything."

"Not *everything*," she teased.

Damn. Was she now comfortable enough to relax with him? Part of him hoped so while another part knew that would only add to his dilemma.

It seemed safer to focus on what she'd said rather than how she'd said it. "Words fascinate me, always have. Maybe because I'm a techie and spend so much time online—"

"You're into computers?" Arched brows lifted above her glasses. "I thought you were more the lumberjack type, out here reopening a campground."

"That'd be my brother, Hunter. He unwinds by chopping wood. I only pick up the ax when necessary." Yeah, he could tell by her expression that the words sounded more ominous than he'd meant them. "The wood doesn't magically fall into logs, you know. Some effort on my part is required."

"But you don't enjoy it?"

"Would you?"

She eyed the neat pile of wood. "I don't know. Next time you need some chopped let me know and I'll give it a try."

No, pretty sure he wouldn't do that. She'd already promised to take on enough without stealing his every chore.

"So," she said, getting his thoughts back on track. "You unwind by reading?"

Books were a topic he could dig into. "I like fiction of all kinds, but I read nonfiction, too."

"Like?"

"Sitting out here, I got curious about the trees and the birds, especially the night sounds, so I read books on Colorado to bone up on the wildlife and vegetation.

I can identify nearly every tree, wildflower and bird, and I know the habits for most of the visiting critters."

Thick lashes lifted, emphasizing her eyes as she grinned. "That's genius. You literally arm yourself with knowledge."

That was how he'd always looked at it, but interesting that she'd put it that way. "I've also read a lot of books on business, campground rules, any restrictions Colorado might have." *Crimes, criminals, most traveled routes they used...* But that wasn't something he needed to share. "Since I was alone here, I read some medical journals, too. How to treat most injuries, when something is more serious, stuff like that."

"Fascinating. I don't know why, but it doesn't surprise me."

"Maybe because you're intelligent enough to recognize right off that I'm an astute guy, equally intelligent?"

"Maybe. I mean, I did notice that you have emergency numbers on your refrigerator."

Memphis had the feeling that very little escaped her, which meant he'd have to be extra careful now that she was around. The numbers on his fridge were for locals. He'd programmed other, more important numbers, which had nothing to do with the community, into his phone. "I learned preparedness from my brother, who's like a freaking superhero." He said it, then shook his head. "No, scratch that. He *is* a freaking superhero." Hunter would deny it but it was still true.

Interested, Jedidiah set aside her comb, kicked off her sneakers, then pulled her legs up onto the chair and rested her chin on her knees. "How do you mean?"

The loose pajama pants now fell over her small feet.

In all her loose clothing, she looked like a very appealing pile of laundry…with gorgeous hair, intriguing eyes and those sweet dimples. "Hunter was a park ranger with an uncanny knack for seeing things others didn't. He'd look at a creep and know he was up to something. The thing with Hunter is that he has the follow-through, too."

"Follow-through?"

Taking in her expression, Memphis badly wished he could remove her glasses and look into her eyes. See them again without the barrier, as he had when she'd fallen from the golf cart.

There'd been a connection then—one he knew for certain she'd deny. Hell, he'd deny it as well.

He *was* denying it, right?

"Is your hair dry now? I don't want you getting sick." Her hair hung over one shoulder, thick, a little wavy, looking heavy and soft.

"I'm fine. Plenty warm enough."

No doubt. Her sweatshirt had to be three sizes too big. The cuffs nearly hid her small hands.

There were a hundred things he wanted to know about her, but she had willingly joined him, her posture was relaxed, her dog asleep, and he didn't want to disrupt any of that. For now, she needed to keep her secrets, so he tamped down the urge to question her and instead he indulged one of his favorite pastimes: bragging on his brother.

"Hunter sees trouble and he can deal with it—however necessary."

"So he's a park ranger here, but living in that little town… What was it called?"

"Triple Creek. Thirty minutes away, but we're in Knockoff."

She grinned. "For real?"

"Yeah, you didn't notice the name of the place when you rode in?"

"Guess I had other things on my mind. Plus, we were in the back of a truck, facing the wrong way, so I wouldn't have seen road signs until we passed them. I just told the driver where I was going and she said she'd go past it." Shoulders lifting in a shrug, Jedidiah said, "So here I am."

Here she was.

And here he was, completely drawn by her.

"Hunter isn't a ranger anymore. He dealt with some shitty stuff..." Routine, run-of-the-mill thugs, right up until things had gone off the deep end. Memphis shook his head. "He was used to awful things. Arsonists intent on starting fires, dealers selling drugs, even some truly awful suicides—he handled it all, no problem. My brother is a rock."

Sympathy brought her brows together. "But?"

"It's a long story that I'm going to make short because neither of us needs nightmares."

An alert wariness entered her gaze. "It's bad enough to give me nightmares?"

He rethought things in an instant. "Maybe I should save this for another night..."

"Don't you dare stop now." Preparing herself, she hugged her knees and burrowed down into the layers of fabric of her huge sweatshirt. "At this point I need to know the rest."

Wishing he hadn't gone down memory lane, Memphis stared at the fire. As always, it tortured him thinking what his brother had endured. Skating past details and going with the big picture seemed the way to go. "Some women were missing." Knowing how it had ended, he worked his jaw, then continued. "They'd searched everywhere and couldn't find them, but Hunter had a hunch that they weren't looking in the right place. Higher-ups didn't listen. They wanted to concentrate the search in the last known area."

"Where they'd last been seen?"

"That's usually the way to go. People lost on foot don't wander too far." People taken, however, weren't where they should be.

"Guess they were wrong?"

He gave one curt nod. "On his off day, my brother hiked into an area where no one ever went." Slumping back in his seat, his gaze unseeing, Memphis said, "He found one of the women, barely alive. Tortured."

"Oh, my God."

Drawn back to the here and now, Memphis frowned at her. She looked at him over her glasses, probably without realizing it. Her eyes were huge, worried.

"I shouldn't be telling you any of this."

"Oh, no, you don't." She leaned toward him. "Was he able to save her?"

"Yeah, he did." Such a reaction. Fear, but also anger. "He saved her and he killed the men responsible."

"The other women…?"

"It was too late for them."

"Damn," Diah whispered.

"Hunter got hurt and stranded in the mountain." His stomach clenched with the awful memory. "My brother, with a concussion and a badly distressed and wounded woman, still got them both out alive because that's who he is."

"You're right," Jedidiah said decisively. "He's a superhero."

"Told you so." Scrubbing a hand over his face, Memphis decided to wrap it up. "You know how the news media likes to sensationalize a story? Well, they painted my brother as complicit in it all."

"What? No way!"

Memphis appreciated her attitude. "Fucked up, right? The thing is, how he fought those men..." Badly wanting Diah to understand, he said, "Hunter was forced to use necessary violence."

"He stopped them from torturing her!"

Exactly. "That's how any sane person would see it, right? She was innocent, they were not. Unfortunately, until the survivor recovered enough to clear him, Hunter was labeled a monster. He'd seen things no man should ever have to see, and still the fucking reporters hounded him and my family. Once Hunter got his name cleared, he moved here and lived in isolation."

For several moments, she was quiet. "What do you mean, *in isolation*?"

They'd lost him. "He checked in every now and then, but my badass, outgoing, take-charge brother was MIA." A new memory intruded, giving Memphis a small, relieved smile. "Then he met Jodi."

"His wife, right?"

After all that, Diah was really into the story. Did she in some way relate? Living on her own as she did, it seemed possible that she'd faced threats, even violence. He'd like to know more about her, but he sensed she wasn't in a sharing mood.

A listening mood, though? Yeah, Diah was all ears right now.

"Jodi turned his world upside down. I don't think Hunter knew what to make of her at first, but right off the bat they fell hard for each other and somewhere along the way I got my brother back."

"You make her sound like a miracle worker."

"Maybe another superhero." Just in a different way. Where Hunter's dangerous ability was quiet, almost understated, Jodi's was in-your-face and full of challenge. Apparently, it was exactly what his brother had needed. "Overall, it was love that really did the trick." He watched Diah, waiting for her reaction. "Love can make all the difference, you know."

Relaxed posture vanishing, she asked, "To *what*?"

"Anything? Everything?" He shrugged to lighten the mood, and nodded at Tuff. "You love him, right? Look how secure and happy he is."

They both stared at the dog, now with his furry lips quivering from a deep snore.

Softening, she said, "We love each other." As soon as the words left her mouth, she stiffened again. "So are you and your brother alike?"

"In what way?" They shared a similar appearance, though he was a little looser than Hunter, not nearly as intense.

Those intriguing eyes stared into his. "Do you also have hero tendencies?"

For a second there, with her watching him, he got lost.

She blinked fast and looked away. "Sorry."

"For...?"

"Staring again."

She did seem to worry about that. Choosing to play it off, he lifted his brows. "Were you?"

"It's a bad habit." She glanced at him, then away. "I've been told I stare too much and it makes people uneasy."

Was that all there was to it? "Didn't make me uneasy." No, it had just sharpened his awareness of her.

"Really?"

Memphis tugged at his ear. "We'll be working together. When I'm explaining something, I'd prefer to have your undivided attention, so stare away."

"You *want* me to stare?"

How the hell had they gone down this verbal road? "I'd prefer that you be yourself, without giving it another thought."

Showing how that idea appealed to her, she smiled. "You mean that?"

Memphis held out his arms. "We're the only two people here. I plan on being myself, so I expect the same of you."

She watched him a second more, and the smile turned into a small laugh. "All right, sure. But if it ever does bother you, just let me know."

So apparently, she planned to do a lot of staring?

"Now, about those heroic traits...do you have them, too?"

For her, he wished he did. "Sadly, no." It was a terrible admission, but he owned his shortcomings. The world was an ugly, unpredictable place without enough heroes. Hunter had made a difference plenty of times, and now Memphis wanted to do his part, too.

But *behind* the scenes, not dodging bullets or duking it out with psychopaths. When compared to Hunter he definitely came up short. "Not even close, sorry."

Wearing a quizzical frown, she asked, "Why are you sorry? We can't all be heroes. I'm definitely not. Besides, I wasn't asking out of personal reasons."

So then why did all of this feel so personal? Making light of it, he said, "Didn't want to disillusion you, that's all."

Her gaze went over him, then her smile turned cynical. She pushed her feet into her sneakers and stood. "Believe me, I have very few illusions."

Now, what was that about? He stood, too. "Good. I'm just a tech geek." Lifting a hand to indicate their surroundings, he tried to be convincing. "Turned campground owner, of course. There's not a single heroic bone in my body."

Picking up her comb, she hesitated, stared at the fire and then around the area. "Oh, I don't know, Memphis. I think there's more to you than you let on."

Wow. Felt like she'd just thrown down a gauntlet. "Maybe," he admitted. "Just a little."

That must have been the right answer because she nodded. "Thanks for this. It was the perfect way to wrap up a perfect day, but I think Tuff and I need to call it a night."

The second she said his name, the dog came awake with a start. Head lifted, expression alert, Tuff waited.

Memphis didn't move. She looked like she might break into a run if he did. *What secrets are you hiding, Jedidiah Stephens?* Before he turned in, he'd do a little research and find out what he could. "I enjoyed it. If you need anything—"

"I won't." She patted her thigh and the dog got to his feet to join her. "Good night."

"Night."

He watched her fast-walk to the cabin, saw her hesitate before the deck so Tuff could sprinkle a few weeds, then without looking back, they both went in.

Memphis knew she immediately secured the door.

Not just for safety…but to lock him out.

She didn't yet trust him. Given the briefness of their association, he understood that.

Yet, her wariness still bothered him.

He waited outside until a few minutes later, when he saw all her inside lights go out. Only then did he store his chairs and tamp down the fire.

Too bad he couldn't tamp down his growing interest, too.

The more he spoke with her, the more questions he had.

Now to find some answers.

CHAPTER THREE

DOING RESEARCH WAS tricky for Memphis. He could find almost anything he wanted, but sometimes in doing so he also piqued Madison's interest. Once she had decided they were besties—something that still amused him—she kept tabs on him.

Especially when she thought he might be ferreting out trouble.

Did Diah count? Since he didn't yet know anything about her past, he couldn't say how much trouble might be brewing around her. *Plenty*, his instincts insisted.

Using advanced techniques, he'd uncovered quite a bit about her, including the fact that she'd changed her last name a few times. To hide, or for some other reason? Far as he could tell, and he was good, she didn't have a criminal background. Over the past two years she'd moved from job to job. She'd often changed her hair, too—darker, lighter, shorter, longer… He liked it long as it was now, and given the color of her brows and lashes, he assumed it was natural. Some might have had trouble recognizing her in her various disguises.

For Memphis, there was no mistaking those eyes. Not just the color but the almond shape, how they dominated her face, and the intensity of her gaze.

He could ask Madison to do a more thorough search,

since she had access to technology not yet available to the general public, but he didn't want to. For reasons he'd rather not analyze, he felt protective of Jedidiah. Instinct told him that exposing her could also endanger her, and that he wouldn't do.

Many considered him a tech guru, but Madison was an outright genius. Hopefully, given the time of evening, she was away from her PC and with her husband, enjoying something more physical than online research. He could only hope.

If she was online, which was often the case, Madison noticed whenever he accessed the special research and facial recognition programs she allowed him to use. He knew Madison tried not to be intrusive, but her ability was such that very little ever got by her. She had a tendency to note every tiny detail.

Two hours later, with his eyes feeling gritty, Memphis sat back and frowned. Jedidiah Stephens was previously known as Jedidiah Stelly…from age fourteen. Prior to that, he couldn't locate her.

She'd lived with an older man, Glover Stephens, and even though he was listed as her father, Memphis knew better. He hadn't gotten too deep into his research on that yet. All he knew was that the two had started appearing together when Diah was fourteen.

Awful possibilities burned his brain, putting thoughts there that he didn't want to ponder.

Like why a girl so young would be with a sixty-year-old man. With what he'd uncovered, the relationship looked more like a guardian and dependent, but Memphis never accepted first impressions. There was always more beneath the surface.

A private message popped up on his screen. What are you doing?

Damn it. Knowing Madison wouldn't be ignored, he typed back: Why aren't you with your husband?

:) He's right here, grousing because ur up to something & now I'm distracted.

Great. Madison's husband had a scowl that could send murderers running. If he took more than five seconds to consider his reply, Madison would only dig in more. Being curious and finding answers was what she did, and she was extremely good at it. New employee. Just doing a thorough background check.

I call BS on that. Try again. Or should I just call?

No. He did not want to be on the phone with her right now. I'm sure Jodi mentioned Jedidiah, right? Well, ur not the only one curious.

She's hot. Giving u ideas?

Where the hell is your husband?

Lol. Okay, fine. Keep ur secrets.

Um… Not trusting her, Memphis typed: Thanks?

FYI, Glover Stephens was Glover Holt. Crook. Swindler. Sometimes muscle for a crime boss. Jedidiah's family all died in what appeared to b house fire. She disappeared—til we just found her.

Memphis sat back in amazement. *In what appeared to be a house fire.* Meaning there was more to it than that.

Of course Madison couldn't let it go. God, how he'd love to have her superior skill. He supposed having access to her skill was the next best thing.

Ur welcome.

Belatedly, he wrote: Thank u. His fingers hovered over the keys, but no, he would not have her breach Diah's privacy more than she already had. I'll talk to her, see what else I can find out. Could u—

Find out even more? Sure.

Respect her privacy! *And give me a chance to think.* Pls.

Seconds ticked by where Memphis imagined Madison already digging, uncovering every awful thing in Diah's past, secrets that she wouldn't want to share with anyone, especially someone of Madison's ilk, but by digging, he'd opened her up to this—

Ok. For now. Anything happens tho u tell me.

Agree. To butter her up, he added, Ur the best.

I know. Luv ya, bestie.

His mouth quirked into a grin. Back atcha. He waited, but Madison appeared to have moved on. Honest to God, it was a wonder her husband hadn't come after Memphis yet. Most men wouldn't be so comfortable with a wife constantly chatting with another man, especially when each exchange ended with proclamations of love.

Then again, Madison was a distinctive personality, so it figured her husband was as well.

Putting Madison from his mind, Memphis decided he'd try talking to Diah over the next few days, to subtly find out more about her, her life, her family, the god-awful fire...and this Glover person who'd apparently taken her in. With any luck, she'd share.

And if not, *then* he could resort to deeper research.

TWO WEEKS WENT by without a single issue. Amazed, Diah took in all she'd accomplished and gave herself a mental pat on the back.

Some of the jobs were bigger than others. The showers were not only spider-free now, they were also pristine, but yeah, that had been an undertaking.

Memphis's addition was ready to be painted, with everything else done. He claimed they'd work on that soon.

It amused her that he always called a halt to work before she did. Heck, she'd continue on through the night if he asked it of her. After all, he'd given her a home nicer than anything she'd known in years. Or maybe ever.

"That was before your time," she said to Tuff, who currently lolled on his back. "Some of the places I've lived..." She let the words trail off, unwilling to remind herself in detail of how horrid it had occasionally been.

Tuff said, *"Fft,"* as if he understood.

"You like sleeping in a comfortable bed as much

as I do, huh?" It had taken her a month to get used to camping in her tent, but only hours to feel at home and cozy in the cabin. "If I can find what I need here, we'll never have to sleep in another tent."

Tuff eyed her.

"I know. We enjoy the evening campfires, don't we?" Sometimes they even roasted marshmallows. It was relaxing. It could also be romantic, except that she fought that idea. There were times she had to chant "employee" in her head to keep from losing sight of her goals.

There were also times when Memphis watched her a little too closely, but oddly enough it didn't alarm her. If anything, it ratcheted up her awareness of him, of his dark blue eyes and the way his mouth lifted when he smiled…

So odd.

She hadn't looked at men as anything other than total bores or possible threats in so long, at first she hadn't recognized the interest for what it was: normal, sexual and probably not unexpected for most women.

For *her*? Unthinkable.

The more she got to know Memphis, the more she liked him. Even his longer hair and often-scruffy beard shadow was sexy. Add in his easygoing manner and it was no wonder she enjoyed Memphis Osborn so much.

Tuff rolled to his feet, shook the dust from his fur and gave her another, *"Fft."*

Using a hoe, she uprooted a weed. "Sorry about last night, bud. I have to resist sometimes, you know?" Tempting as it was, she occasionally opted out of sharing a meal, forcing herself to suffer a little alone time so being with Memphis didn't become a habit. He never complained.

Tuff did, though.

Her dog had quickly taken to Memphis and when they didn't join him, Tuff would sit on the love seat and stare morosely out the window, watching for any sign of him.

Funny that her dog would make her feel guilty even when Memphis didn't.

The biggest problem she had with their arrangement was that she couldn't explore in the evening. She really wanted to search the area, but repeatedly, Memphis warned her about walking too far. He detailed all the dangers to be found in the Colorado wilderness.

As if she didn't know.

It wasn't the black bears, mountain lions, or even the deadly snakes and spiders that worried her the most. Long ago, she'd learned that worse things could lurk in the dark.

It was her motive for being here, and the number-one reason she was grateful to Memphis.

Though he didn't realize it, he'd given her the access she needed to solve a decade-old puzzle. Here in this campground was a clue to solve the most tragic event of her life. Evidence that she needed so she could move on, so she could understand.

So she could exact revenge.

But first, she needed him to trust her enough to let her out of his sight. So far, that hadn't happened. She'd had to resort to sneaking around in the dead of night, with Tuff behind in the cabin. For a chicken like her, it was nerve-racking. Each sound seemed alarming when you were alone with woods all around. Her imagination conjured every nightmare she'd ever seen in a horror movie—and the actual nightmare that she'd lived through.

If only she could explore the area in the light of day without the darkness closing in on her.

Maybe she needed to be a little more open with Memphis. Should she try flirting? Did she even know how? Not really.

She could try smiling at him more. Maybe do something with her hair… No. She was so far out of fashion, she couldn't even spell it at this point. She was female, though, right? And he was most definitely male. Very, *very* male, so maybe she could—

"Hey," he said from right behind her.

Wielding the hoe like a baseball bat, she swung around to face him—and the makeshift weapon was snatched from her hands. So easily, too.

His brows shot up. "Whoa. Didn't mean to startle you." Yet, he'd taken the hoe from her with ridiculous ease. For such a laid-back, casual guy who claimed to only be a techie, he had amazingly fast reflexes.

She glared at Tuff. "Thanks for nothing."

Belatedly, the dog gave a happy bark of greeting, the traitor.

By way of apology, Memphis offered back the hoe. "I didn't realize you were lost in thought."

Oh, God, had he listened to her talking to the dog? A scorching blush climbed her neck and bloomed over her face, which was dumb because no way could he know her thoughts, and yet, something in his deep blue eyes seemed intimate.

Focus, damn it, focus. She accepted the yard tool and mumbled a breathless, "Sorry."

Hands in his pockets, no doubt trying to appear nonthreatening since she'd reacted so fiercely, he smiled.

What a smile it was. It left her mouth dry and made her heart race.

Why did he have to be so attractive? It was grossly unfair. Her memories of campgrounds, vague as they might be, did not include walking, talking temptation. A breath sort of strangled in her lungs, sounding broken as she tried to exhale.

He continued to return her stare and she couldn't seem to draw her gaze away.

"Why are you staring at me?" she whispered.

His smile warmed. "Because you're staring at me."

Oh. She should really look away, but it was like they'd just become connected or something. Physically. Emotionally.

At least until Tuff leaned against her, pushing her off balance. Stumbling, she finally found her voice. "Sorry again."

"I told you, Diah, I don't mind."

No, he didn't. He was probably used to women gawking at him.

She frowned at his thermal shirt—a shirt that fit snug to his shoulders, chest and pecs, but draped more loosely over his trim midsection. With the cooler weather, he wore jeans instead of shorts. If she hadn't been laboring on the grounds, she might've needed a jacket.

"You're doing it again."

Damn it. She blinked. "If you weren't so…"

"So…?" he prompted.

Sexy. Appealing. Another broken breath. "Never mind." She indicated the pile of uprooted weeds. "I got a lot done today."

Memphis shifted, and three more heartbeats later he got his gaze off her. "It all looks great."

"Thanks." Above them, against a darkening sky, lightning flickered. "Storms are moving in."

He gave little attention to the sky before asking, "Do storms bother you?"

For some reason, his assumption annoyed her. "No. It just looks cool, don't you think?" Vivid purple hues backlit the mountains, pierced by splinters of white lightning. "How far away do you think it is?"

"Time-wise? Another thirty minutes or so, if it's even coming this way. Out here, the weather can be deceptive. If you're hoping to shower, you might want to get to it."

"Will we lose electricity?"

"Depends on how bad it gets. It happens occasionally."

Looked to her like it might get bad. One minute the skies had still shown daylight, but it was darkening quickly. For much of the day she'd been lost in working on the grounds, digging in the dirt and removing troublesome weeds. Every inch of her was sticky with sweat. "Guess I should get to it, then." She eyed the remaining weeds she'd planned to remove.

"They'll wait." Memphis nodded at Tuff. "Do storms bother him?"

"If the lightning gets too close he doesn't like it. I guess he can feel the static in the air or something. Otherwise, he doesn't seem to mind."

Appearing troubled, he asked, "Have you ever camped out in a storm?"

Not really something she wanted to go into, so she merely lifted a shoulder.

As usual, Memphis didn't press her. "Taking him out to do his business might be your biggest issue tonight. You'll both get soaked since you don't have much of an overhang."

Wind suddenly gusted through the trees, playing havoc with his hair. It always seemed pleasingly messy, as if he didn't care enough to do more than finger-comb it after his shower. She loved how the ends curled against his nape.

Right now, thanks to the weather, his hair was again parted more in the middle than the side. "I have a rain slicker," she said absently. A cheap plastic thing, but it had kept her mostly dry before. "I'll put it by the door."

He raked a hand through his hair, moving it out of his face. "I appreciate that you always walk Tuff out. Some people just stick their dogs on a chain and check back an hour later."

"I'd never do that to Tuff." Hearing his name, the dog looked up at her adoringly. In so many ways he'd become her entire world. "Sometimes I hear coyotes around here, especially in the middle of the night." It was another reason she hadn't ventured too far yet in her nightly explorations, and why she left Tuff in the cabin. Or at least, it made a good excuse whenever she gave up and turned back. "You ever hear them?"

"All the time. When they get together, the yipping is almost deafening. Coyotes are smart and known for playing with dogs long enough to lure them away from safety."

Hearing him voice one of her worries made her frown at her own shortcomings. If only she was as brave as his brother and sister-in-law. She wasn't. Overall, she was a person who'd taken the easy way out far too many times in her life.

Another blast of wind stirred up dust around them.

Memphis turned his attention to the sky. "We could use the rain."

She had nothing to say to that. Rain would only hinder her tonight. She needed to extend her searches. Until she found what she needed, she'd have to keep sneaking out.

"Here's the thing." Aggrieved, Memphis came forward a step. "I'm just me, okay? A man with plenty of flaws. Remember, I told you I'm going to be myself. Well, I can't change who I am at this point, and I won't deliberately crowd you or anything like that. It's just..."

Well, hell. Was *he* afraid of the storm? That was sort of endearing, bringing her a little nearer, too. "The storms worry you?"

Incomprehension flared in his dark blue eyes. "What?"

She touched his forearm. "It's okay, you know. Everyone fears something." Would it make him feel better if she admitted that she feared almost everything?

Humor glittered in his eyes. He chuckled, and then outright laughed.

Offended without knowing why, she withdrew. *"What?"*

"I'm tempted to let you believe that. Seriously." Leaning toward her, he teased, "Would you sympathize with me, Diah?"

Annoyed, she said, "No," and turned away to get Tuff's leash.

He dogged her heels. "Would you hang out with me? Hold my hand when the thunder got too loud?"

"Screw you."

"Is that an offer?"

She whipped around again, already breathless, flushed…

He held up a hand. "No, don't answer that. Damn, I'm sorry. That was over the line."

Did he have to keep confounding her? He'd said it, so he could at least own up to it. Unless of course… Maybe the idea was so repugnant he'd wanted it clear up front that he'd only been joking. "I don't know what you're blathering about."

"I swore to myself that I wouldn't do that."

Ready to put him on the spot, she asked, "Do what?"

His mouth opened, then closed again. He frowned. "I wouldn't treat you as a…"

"What? A *woman*?"

He said nothing.

"Well?"

"I'll treat you *only* as an employee." Appearing satisfied with that explanation, he let out a breath and smiled. "You're my employee. So again, my apologies."

Crossing her arms and cocking out a hip, Diah said, "You could have given me a chance to answer."

The second the words left her mouth, they both froze. She couldn't believe she, Jedidiah Stephens, had said such a bold thing. It wasn't like she welcomed a come-on. Right? *Right?*

Well, maybe she would.

For his part, Memphis considered her…then pretended the exchange hadn't happened. "Storms don't bother me at all. Actually, I like them."

One insult after another, never mind that she stood there in utter confusion. *He* certainly wasn't confused.

No, just very disinterested.

Well, she could be disinterested also—and maybe confuse him a little in the bargain. "Me, too." As if in confidence, she leaned in to share, "I've always found storms to be sexy."

His gaze locked on hers. She heard his slow inhale.

Huh, maybe she knew how to flirt after all. It must be like a natural phenomenon when around someone appealing. Human nature, an ingrained response and all that.

Memphis looked ready to speak, but he stalled, then tried again. "It's you I worry about. Do you even have a phone? You're out here all alone, and if we lose power it gets blacker than you can imagine."

Irked that he'd still blown past her comment, that he seemed hell-bent on ignoring her attempts to…tempt him, she said, "Oh, I can imagine a lot."

That he jumped on. "Want to talk about it?"

He had to be kidding. "Nope."

More hesitation, and he actually shifted before asking, "Okay, then do you have a flashlight?" He leveled a serious look on her. "Would you even tell me if it bothered you, or are your secrets so deep that you'd just suffer it?"

What the hell did he know of suffering? Or of her secrets! *Nada*, that was what, and she'd keep it that way. "I have a cell phone but I don't use it often." Actually, as rarely as possible. "A laptop, too. It's pretty old, but it still works. Since I've lived on my own, sometimes pitching my tent in the middle of nowhere, of course I have a flashlight, as well as a solar-powered charger."

"You've been here a while now. How about you stow away the tent? I'm sure you have it anchored, but with a storm blowing in…?"

"Right. I'll take care of that now." The way he watched her only irked her more. She paused and turned. "Anything else, boss?"

"Diah," he said.

"Employee," she replied, pointing to herself, and then at him, "employer. Don't worry. I haven't forgotten."

Regret sounded in his gentled voice. "Will you let me know if you need anything?" Before she could reply, he continued. "What if you fell out of the loft and got hurt? If you see a rattler, or a bear? Even if you take on a job that's a bit too much for you, *anything*, would you let me know if I could help?" Again, before she could answer, he added, "That's what I meant about me being me. I'm helpful, or at least I try to be. And my mother raised me to be considerate. If you were another guy alone, an elderly woman, hell, a small family—anyone out here trying to make it work—I'd want to lend a hand when I could."

He'd said a lot, and yeah, he had a few points about accidents and whatnot. She was already acquainted with his helpful nature. Memphis Osborn might deny heroic tendencies, but she knew there were all kinds of heroes.

She was only here now, alive and well, due to a most unlikely hero. "Do you see rattlers this time of year?"

"This is when they're the most active and aggressive." Accepting her question like an olive branch, he moved closer again. "I haven't seen any around the campgrounds, but that doesn't mean we won't. If you ever do, I'd want to know right away. Under no circumstances would I want you to deal with it on your own. Understand?"

"It's your place, boss. So sure, I'd let you know."

His mouth firmed over being called *boss* again.

Too bad for him. "Have you ever fallen out of a loft?"

"Damn near. I was going through all the cabins, looking them over, and tripped on a loose floorboard. I lost my footing and if it wasn't for the handrail I'd have gone down. I've since finished inspecting them all and made any needed repairs."

That made her think. "How old are the cabins?" From the looks of it, her cabin and a few others nearby could be newer than the rest.

If he considered the question odd with an impending storm moving in, he didn't say so. "The four up here, including mine and yours, are only eight years old. The six that are farthest back on the property are older."

"How old, though?" She tried to see them clearly, but night settled around them. Along with the scent of rain, a turbulent wind was building. Without the sun and activity that had kept her warm all afternoon, she felt chilled.

Noticing her shiver, he said, "We can talk about the cabins tomorrow if you want."

"But—"

"Stay here a minute. I'll be right back." He jogged off, bounding up his steps and leaving the door open behind him. Less than half a minute later he returned with a large utility light. "Here." He handed her a business card with his name and number on it. "That's the landline for the campground, but I wrote my cell on the back." He offered her the light. "I have more flashlights, so I'd appreciate it if you took this just in case."

"Sure, thanks." She stuck his card in her back pocket and held the handle on the light.

Still, Memphis hesitated. "Promise you'll let me know if you need anything."

It was such a novel thing to have anyone sincerely concerned for her. "All right, I promise."

Bending his knees so he could look directly into her eyes, he asked, "Is that a sincere promise, Diah, or a way to shut me up?"

She couldn't help but grin. "Little of both?" When he stayed like that, admonishing her with a frown, she laughed. "I promise. Cross my heart and all that."

"Want me to get your tent taken down for you?"

She snorted. "I can do it in no time. Somehow I don't think you've had a lot of practice at it like I have."

"Very true." Straightening again, he briefly stroked Tuff, then nodded. "Get your tent, and then get your shower. Tomorrow let's talk over coffee. I have a few new chores to discuss."

"Yes, boss," she replied, but this time with a grin, which earned her a laugh in return. Ready to wrap it up and hoping she could figure out when those original cabins were built, she started backing away. "See you tomorrow."

"Sleep well, Jedidiah."

After everything they'd just shared, sleep might be hard to come by.

She wanted in those cabins.

At this moment, though, she wanted Memphis more.

Too bad he'd rejected her efforts at flirting. Had she been terrible at it? Was that why he hadn't reciprocated? Or did she just not appeal to him? It was entirely possible that she'd misread the signs. Odds were, Memphis teased with all women, gifting each and every one of them with his sexy smiles.

Going forward, she'd pay better attention and then she'd have to decide how far to take it. Yes, she wanted the evidence that she knew must be hidden somewhere on these campgrounds.

But…yeah. She might want Memphis Osborn, too. At least for a little while.

Long enough to see what she'd been missing all these years, and then she'd get on with her life.

THE STORM RAGED ON—outside, and within Memphis. *She was alone.*

Never mind that she had Tuff with her, or that she'd laughed over the idea of thunder and lightning bothering her.

He still didn't like it, but he did like her.

Stacking his hands behind his head, he stared up at the ceiling while another flash, followed by a rumbling boom, shook his cabin. They could have kept each other company—except, yeah, he knew he wouldn't be able to keep his hands off her. Not with the static in the air, the darkness all around them…and the crackling chemistry between them.

He shifted in the bed, knowing if he didn't divert his thoughts, he'd never get any sleep. But then, thinking about her was more fun than sleeping, anyway.

Was she curled up in the loft bed, Tuff near her feet? Was she already asleep, or was she, like him, thinking other things?

The possibility caused his shallow breathing to quicken. *What is it about her?* Images flashed through his mind like answers. Gorgeous hair, bold attitude tempered by glimpses of vulnerability. Stunning eyes. Her obvious love of Tuff. The visible appreciation she felt for a bed, groceries and kindness.

The look on her face whenever she stared at him.

Remembering that look was enough to push him over the edge. He gave up on sleep, threw off the covers and stalked through the darkness until he reached the window that gave him a view of her cabin. Other than the light outside her front door, he couldn't see much through the rain, not until lightning temporarily brightened the area. There were no interior lights showing against her windows. Her front door remained secure. Everything was quiet.

And yet, still, he sensed that she was also wide-awake, thinking, imagining, wanting. Knowing he couldn't do anything about it, he stifled a groan and went back to bed. He wouldn't sleep, not yet, but he could give himself relief, and hopefully in the morning he'd have a clearer head.

AMAZING HOW MUCH Memphis anticipated coffee the next morning, all because Jedidiah would join him. Last night he'd convinced himself that feeling this way was dangerous, yet the second he saw her striding in her long-legged way, Tuff at her side, he made a split-second decision.

Yesterday she had openly flirted. With any other woman—a woman who didn't work for him, who didn't possibly have a troubled past—he'd know exactly how to react.

Given their obvious attraction, he'd have already invited her to his bed.

With her, though, there were too many unanswered questions and he didn't quite trust his instincts.

This morning she wore her long hair in twin braids that draped over her shoulders, bouncing against her breasts with each long stride she took. The chilly morning air fogged her breath and turned her cheeks rosy enough to match her glasses. Well-worn jeans hugged her hips, and paired with scuffed, laced-up boots, a long-sleeved gray shirt and an unbuttoned flannel shirt, she somehow became the most appealing woman he'd ever seen.

Must be the isolation, Memphis reasoned. That was why thoughts of her had kept him from getting enough sleep, had, in fact, almost tortured him with what-ifs. Sure, he found most women attractive in one way or another. He wasn't choosy; high-maintenance or low-key, petite or voluptuous, long hair or short, curvy or understated… He'd yet to focus on a "type," except that he didn't like mean-spirited people of any kind.

And yet, *this* woman, who changed moods often, flirting one minute and shutting him out the next, skulking around his campground in the dark and so appreciative of bonfires, totally did it for him.

If he started thinking about her *doing him* again, he'd end up making the wrong move even before he followed through on his new plan.

Leaving the window, he met her at the door before her raised fist had a chance to knock. She smiled up at him, an innocent smile of greeting, and he wanted to kiss that mouth so badly that he backed up.

Tuff saved him by charging in and bringing Diah with him.

"Hey," she said, eyeing Memphis curiously. "Everything okay?"

"Yup." Except that continued arousal simmered just below the surface.

"You invited me over for coffee, remember?" With a frown, she added, "I hope you haven't changed your mind because I didn't make any and now that I've been thinking about it, I'm almost salivating."

"This way." She still liked to keep him where she could see him, so he preceded her into the kitchen where a fresh pot of coffee scented the air. Tuff hurried in next, found a sunny spot in front of a window and sprawled out with a contented huff.

He needed to pick up some dog treats and toys so that when they visited, Tuff had something to do. "I played homemaker and even put some sugar cookies in the oven."

Pausing, eyes closed, she inhaled deeply. "Wow, that smells good."

Memphis averted his gaze. Until that moment, he hadn't realized that braids and expressions of bliss went well together. "They're just refrigerated cookie dough that you bake, but still good when they're hot." Now, if only *he* wasn't so hot. "Grab a seat and I'll pour your coffee. Cream and sugar are already on the table."

Diah pulled out a chair, dropped into it, then tipped her head to study him. "You're being weird."

Weirdly turned on. Yesterday, after accidentally spooking her, he'd been overflowing with protective instincts. He'd wanted to promise her…what? About a dozen things, really. Then when she'd tried her hand at flirting, those feelings had morphed into a sleepless night, caused by his heated and sexual thoughts.

Forcing a smile, he set the steaming mug in front of her. "Cookies coming up." Donning an oven mitt, he removed the tray from the oven and set it on the stovetop. Expertly—because yeah, he liked hot cookies—he sprinkled sugar onto them, then moved them to a plate.

Unable to dodge her any longer, he and the cookies joined the party.

"So," she said.

"Two?" he asked. "Three? I'm taking three."

"They smell great."

All he detected was her and the clean, crisp scent of the fresh outdoors clinging to her skin and hair—sunshine and pine and something infinitely sweeter, a fragrance unique only to Diah. *Talk about salivating.* He put three cookies on a napkin and handed them to her.

Diah bit one in half, made a "Mmm," sound, and sipped her coffee. "So you and your morning weirdness. What's up?"

"I'm going into town today. Do you need anything?"

She looked at him in near alarm. "You're leaving?"

"Not permanently or anything. I'll be back." It'd help if she'd trust him just a little, but she'd been here two weeks now and other than her flirting last night, she remained guarded. Friendly, yes. Teasing sometimes, sure. But if he got too close, if he asked a question? She shut down really fast.

Staring at him, the cookie in her hand forgotten, she said, "I know you'll be back. It's just..."

No doubt she wondered why he hadn't invited her to come along. Fortunately, he'd thought of the perfect solution to that. First, he repeated, "Do you need anything?"

She looked away, then gave her attention to her coffee. "No."

Damn it, she appeared hurt and it bothered him. "I figured you could go through the cabins today."

At that, she perked up again. "The cabins?"

"You wanted to talk about them, right? I assume we

should go through them again, see what each one needs, like bedding, dishes and stuff like that, before we open. You could make a list."

"Okay, sure." New excitement showed in her eyes. She practically vibrated in her seat. "How long will you be gone?"

"A couple of hours." Long enough for her to snoop around. "I want you to be extra careful, understand? Keep your cell phone on you and if you run into any problems, give me a call. You still have my number, right?"

"Yeah, sure, I have it."

"Where?"

"What do you mean, where?"

"Is it stored in your phone?"

"Um…no. I left your card on the counter."

Which wouldn't do her a bit of good if she fell or ran into a snake. Rethinking the idea to leave her, even for a short time, Memphis frowned.

"Hey, seriously, ease up, why don't you? I'll go to the cabin and store the number in my phone first thing." Trying to look casual and failing utterly, she sipped her coffee. "No worries, boss. You can take your time today. I'll be fine."

Biting into another cookie, Memphis knew she wanted him gone as soon as possible. For whatever reason had brought her here, she wanted in those cabins. "You asked about them last night."

"What's that?" She licked sugar off her thumb. "About what?"

The gesture sent his temp a few degrees higher, but he didn't buy in to the innocent act. "The cabins. You seemed awfully interested in how old they are. Want to tell me why?"

"Idle curiosity." She smiled. "You said they're older than the cabins we're using."

"Nearly twice as old. I checked the information given to me when I bought the place."

She looked over her glasses at him. "And?"

Idle curiosity, my ass. "Fifteen years old or thereabout."

"Still in good shape, though?"

Leaning forward and folding his arms on the table, Memphis said softly, "You know, if you told me what you're looking for, I could help."

She went still, then forced a laugh. "I'm looking for another cookie." Reaching toward the plate, she asked, "Do you mind?"

"Eat as many as you'd like." Accepting that she wouldn't confide in him yet, he downed the last of his coffee and stood. When he opened the key cabinet, Tuff came alert, watchful as always. After gathering the keys she'd need, Memphis went to a drawer and pulled out a notepad and pen. "I'll stop at the store to get him some treats. Write down whatever he likes and anything else you might want while I'm in town."

"The little grocer where we went?"

"Actually, I'm heading to Triple Creek to see my brother, so I'll shop there." He had his own purchase to make, just in case.

No, he told himself. *You don't need condoms because you aren't going to touch her.* He glanced at her, and knew it'd still be a good idea to have them around.

Deftly, he hooked the numbered keys on a single ring to make it easier for her. "Triple Creek is small, but they still have a better selection."

Calculating, she tapped the pen against the table. "I

can't think of anything right now, but maybe you could give me a call before you head back, just in case something comes to me."

More likely, she wanted advance warning on when he'd return so she'd have a chance to cover her tracks. "Or you can call me." Giving her a tepid smile, he put four more cookies in a container and handed it to her with the key ring. He picked up her note with a brand of dog bones listed. "I can tell you're anxious to get started. After you finish your coffee, I'll get going. You can take a few cookies with you."

"Gee, thanks." Ready to see him on his way, she tipped the mug to her mouth and quickly downed the rest. He was about to take the empty from her, but she went around him to the sink, rinsed it and put it in the dishwasher. "Fancy." Giving him a cheeky smile, she said, "Too bad all the cabins don't come with added appliances."

"Have a lot of dishes to do?"

Her smile widened even more. "No, and even if I did I wouldn't mind. It's sort of fun being domestic. Making my bed, doing dishes, sweeping my deck… I've been wandering for so long, it feels good to have a routine."

There she went, stealing another piece of his heart. "Your chores for the campground have been different nearly every day."

"True. But the rest… You know—" her hand flagged back and forth between them "—seeing you in the morning for my to-do list and sleeping in the same comfy bed each night. It's nice."

No longer in a hurry to go, Memphis leaned against the counter. "Visiting around a fire? Chatting?" he prompted. “Come on. You can give me a small compliment and I swear I won’t let it go to my head.”

She snorted. “Small? Are you serious? I have *huge* compliments for you because you’ve been awesome, way more generous than I expected.”

He’d paid her a salary, period. Okay, maybe a little more than he would have offered someone else, but still, it wasn’t like he threw money or gifts at her. They shared a few meals. She got use of a cabin. Big deal.

Oddly displeased with her answer, he insisted, “Plus, you like my company.”

Her mouth twitched. “When you’re not being contrary, sure. I enjoy your company.”

“Well, that was like pulling hens’ teeth.” Very frustrating, except that now she laughed and he did like seeing her dimples.

Unwilling to be the first to leave, Memphis waited—and Diah caught herself.

“Oh, sorry. You’re ready to go and I’m lingering.” Tossing him another smile, she patted her thigh for Tuff, hooked his leash to his collar, then said, “I’ll have a report on the cabins by the end of the day.”

“No rush.” He walked with her and Tuff to the door. “Remember, be careful and call me if you need me.”

Giving him another snort, she and the dog headed out. As soon as she entered her cabin, Memphis locked up and went to his truck.

Diah had relaxed with him because he kept things light and didn’t pester her about personal stuff. How pissed would she be when she found out he’d been researching her all along?

If things got too boring, maybe he’d tell her and see what happened.

DIAH STOOD IN her open doorway, waiting until she saw his truck leave the campgrounds. It was a funny feeling, excitement at being able to explore, mixed with an eerie dread at being completely alone here.

Odd how quickly the sound of his tires on the muddy rutted road faded, only to allow silence to descend. Her heart pounded erratically.

Having another human around, even when she didn't see him, made such a difference. With Memphis gone, the campgrounds now felt like the middle of nowhere.

You'd think by now she'd have gotten used to isolation.

Tuff sat before her, waiting patiently as he always did, so she worked up a reassuring smile for him. Her nervousness always became his and she didn't want that. It was bad enough that she often scared herself; she didn't need to scare her dog, too.

Holding Tuff's leash, she stepped out to her small deck and listened. A light wind rustled through the spruce and pine trees. Birds soared overhead. Insects chirped.

Funny, but on her way to see Memphis just a little while ago, she hadn't noticed any of that. Her entire being had been focused on her visit with him. A sizzling sort of anticipation had kept her smiling from the time she woke up.

What was it about him that grounded her, chasing away her fear and letting her be a more normal person? His quiet confidence, maybe. It was such a counter to her fitful worries and constant uncertainty.

She wanted this. She *needed* this in order to move forward. Finding out the truth once and for all, and exposing those responsible, would hopefully give her some much-needed clarity. She was tired of looking over her shoulder, tired of wondering *why.* She had so many unanswered questions that she often felt like half a person. Someone stuck in the past, held there by a fear of the unknown. Once she'd accomplished her goal, she could get on with a real life.

Settle down. Think about a relationship. A future.

Resolute after her pep talk, she stepped off the deck and led the dog down the winding lane. One day soon the campgrounds would be filled with people and activity. She had vague memories of being here as a kid. There'd been laughter and constant movement as families set up picnic tables and campfires, as they'd rolled out awnings and played music. Even when she'd been kept inside their small camper, she'd heard it all and imagined many happy family scenarios.

For now, the area just felt deserted. And creepy. "I'm glad I have you for company, Tuff. We'll start at the older cabins farthest back. We don't mind stretching our legs, do we?" Sure, Memphis had given her use of a golf cart, but she preferred to walk. God knew she'd done enough walking in the past two years that she should be sick of it. The thing was, on foot she could run. Hide if necessary. Duck behind a tree and be as silent as she needed to be.

She drew a deep breath of the chilly morning air and kept going. Honestly, she was afraid if she stopped at all, she'd turn back and run. *This is too important.*

She kept going, and finally ahead of her she saw the first of the six older cabins. They were all dark and empty, a dewy mist lingering near the ground.

Damn, there went her heart again. *Thump, thump, thump.*

The key ring jangled in her hand until she closed her fist tight around it.

The cabins lined up, three on the left of the lane, three on the right, each nestled in between towering white birch trees. The early-morning sun played peekaboo with the foliage, leaving everything in heavy shadows.

"This can't be worse than the spiders in the showers, right?"

Tuff gave a reassuring, *"Fft."* Truly, he showed no concern at all.

If there was a problem, he'd let her know. "My good boy. We're braver together, aren't we?"

He glanced up at her, and as if he understood her hesitation, he stepped up to the first deck and waited at the door.

She released a tense breath. "I wish I knew exactly what I was looking for. That'd sure make it easier." She unlocked the door, winced at the loud screech of the squeaky hinges and stepped inside.

Thankfully, no spiders.

In fact, other than a musty smell, it wasn't too bad at all. Set up much like her cabin, only tighter, meant she already knew her way around.

The cabins were each identical from the outside, so she could assume they were all the same on the inside. Maybe this wouldn't be so bad after all.

Holding the door open a moment to allow in fresh air, she looked up the narrow steps to the loft, where it was darker with a low ceiling and lack of windows. No, she'd check the main floor first. It was small enough that it wouldn't take her long.

"You may as well get comfortable," she told Tuff.

She patted the small love seat under a window and said, "Feel free to take a nap, okay?"

Instead, Tuff sat and looked at her.

"Suit yourself." She had to remember that this was a chore assigned by Memphis, so while she searched she also had to make notes on what the cabin might need. After closing the door and unleashing Tuff, she pulled the small pad and pen from her back pocket—and realized she hadn't brought her phone. Well, shoot.

He'd only just left, so there'd be no reason for him to call yet. She could at least get through a few cabins before she walked back to get it. After all, what one cabin needed, they'd probably all need, so it should be fairly routine.

Now, where would an evil cretin hide evidence?

CHAPTER FOUR

IT SEEMED IRONIC that Hunter was in his backyard chopping wood when Memphis arrived. He heard the steady *thwack* of the ax splitting logs. Bypassing a knock to the front door, he went around the side of the house and there was his brother.

Seemed every time he saw Hunter, he was more shredded. Had to admit, the outdoor activity agreed with him.

Jodi was pretty damn good for him, too.

"Hey," Memphis called out.

Pausing in the act of placing another hefty log on the block, Hunter looked up, spotted him and used his forearm to wipe sweat from his brow. "Memphis." He glanced at the still-closed back door. "I didn't hear you come out."

"I never went in." Hands in his pockets, Memphis moseyed closer. "Is it my imagination or are you getting bigger?"

Donning a half smile, Hunter moved to the pile of logs and swiped up his shirt, using it to mop his face and chest. "Jodi says I'm more muscular."

"Bet she doesn't complain."

"No," Hunter confirmed, still looking pleased, "she doesn't." Then with more gravity, he asked, "What's up?"

Usually, Memphis called ahead to announce his visits. Knowing he'd gone off half-cocked, he looked out at the thick woods behind his brother's house. "I should kick your ass, that's what."

Behind him, a more feminine voice said, "You could try."

Rolling his eyes, Memphis turned to face Jodi, with Turbo the dog standing silently beside her. "You say that as if I wouldn't have a chance."

"Wouldn't. I'd probably shoot you first."

This time he rolled his eyes at Hunter. "You let her run around making threats—" Before Jodi could blast him, he lifted his hands. "Figure of speech, hon. I know he doesn't *allow* or disallow."

"Damn right, he doesn't."

Memphis frowned at Turbo. "Traitor. I used to brush you. We had sleepovers together."

Turbo wagged his hefty butt. As a basset-beagle mix, he was a pretty funny dog, heavy on the bottom with a droopy face, long, floppy ears and a truly bizarre bark.

Giving Memphis a light swat, Jodi said, "Don't take it out on Turbo."

"I suppose you're the one who's taught him to sneak up on people?"

"He emulates her," Hunter said, pulling his wife to his side.

"Damn." Feigning alarm, Memphis nodded at the Glock beneath Jodi's loose shirt. "Does that mean he'll be packing heat next time I visit? Will his barks turn sarcastic?"

Jodi grinned. "It's a good thing I know you love me, otherwise I'd take offense."

Yeah, he did love her—for the unique, awesome person she was, as well as the incredible effect she'd had on his brother. "I really do." Pulling her away from Hunter, he gave her an exuberant hug. "I don't even mind when you threaten me."

"Yeah, well..." She huffed out a breath. "That was mostly bluster, anyway."

"Mostly?" Amused, Memphis let her go and appreciated how she immediately snuggled back to Hunter's side.

"He does get the say-so on a few things, just as I do." Hunter kissed the top of her head. "Because what each of us wants or doesn't want matters."

"You're both nauseating, you know that, right? Seeing all this perfect harmony makes my eyes burn."

Jodi made a big deal of looking around him. "Where's Jedidiah?"

"She prefers Diah, and I left her at the campgrounds doing *her job*." He remembered she was an employee, even if these two didn't. Looking at Hunter, he said, "I wanted to talk to you alone a minute." When Jodi didn't budge, he grinned and amended, "The two of you, away from everyone else."

"Meaning," Hunter said, "that you want to talk about Jedidiah. What is it? Something in your research set off alarm bells?"

"Not really." Not yet. To Jodi, he asked, "You?"

She shrugged. "I imagine you know as much as I do."

Doubtful. Jodi was friends with Madison, and despite Madison's halfhearted promise to leave the research to Memphis, he knew her curiosity would get the better of her.

Rather than debate it, he shared his info. "Her last name was actually Stelly. She changed it when she took off on her own."

"How old was she?" Hunter asked.

"Twenty-two. Before that, she lived with an older guy. Like a father figure, I think, but he wasn't her actual father. When he died, she hit the road."

Jodi said, "Hmm."

"What?" Focused on her, Memphis stepped closer. "Tell me what you're thinking."

"I'm thinking that you know so much, I'm not sure what you want from us."

Hunter spoke before Memphis could explain. "She's looking for something at the campgrounds." Casually, he pulled on his shirt, ran a hand through his hair and then gave Memphis the familiar "big brother" frown. Crossing his arms, brows together, he stated, "You need to know what she's after before anything gets out of control."

Interesting that Hunter had come to that conclusion so easily. "Whatever it is, I'll eventually figure it out."

"It could be dangerous."

Possibly, but that wasn't Memphis's biggest concern.

Catching on to her husband's worry, Jodi said, "Madison might know more."

"Has she said anything to you?" He watched Jodi closely, but when she shook her head, he believed her. Jodi was always up front. He trusted her completely. "I'd prefer that Madison not get too involved."

"Good luck with that," Hunter said.

Exactly. Memphis had a feeling Diah's past might lead down a very dark road. If Madison started digging, God only knew where that would lead. "That's not why I'm here, anyway."

"Should we go in and get comfortable?" Jodi asked. "I know how to play hostess every now and then."

Memphis shook his head. "I can't stay long." Discussions around the kitchen table tended to drag out because everyone settled in. "Here's the thing. Diah is jumpy one minute, then she sort of..." He eyed his brother, saw his keen interest and decided *screw it*. He focused on Jodi. "Sometimes she flirts, too."

Jodi lifted her brows. "So?"

"So she's sending mixed signals. I don't want her to feel pressured—"

"And she works for you," Hunter pointed out, always the practical one.

"There's that, yeah, but it's not conventional employment, right?"

Frown darkening, Hunter asked, "How so?"

"We're there alone." Completely, totally isolated. "We've shared dinner more often than not, which makes sense, right?"

His brother and sister-in-law stared at him.

Shit. "That got started because she arrived with nothing," he pointed out. "You know that. She doesn't have a car to go out for fast food, and it's not like I have a diner open on the property."

The continued silence felt condemning.

Memphis stiffened. "We also sit around the fire pit nearly every night. She likes it. She's been alone too long."

"Definitely not a typical employer/employee relationship," Hunter agreed.

Jodi shrugged. "Probably too late to change that now, at least not without hurting her."

"Right? That's what I think, too." He didn't want to change it. He'd instigated the closeness after all. "The thing is, she made a few teasing comments, and I..."

Memphis faltered on how to explain his lack of reaction, or rather, how he'd deliberately skated past her interest.

"What'd you do?" Jodi asked, not really with accusation, but still she frowned.

"I'm pretty sure she was outright flirting, but again, she's an employee, so..."

Jodi said, "And?"

"I didn't play along." There, that sounded reasonable.

"Even though you're interested, too?"

He definitely was, but still... "I couldn't reciprocate."

Appalled, Jodi whispered, "You *ignored* her?"

Did she have to make it sound like the worst of insults? "Basically, I just pretended it hadn't happened."

Jodi glared at Hunter. "Are you certain he's your brother?"

Hunter half smiled. "Cut him some slack, honey. Women are complicated."

"Always," Memphis agreed. "And this situation is more so than usual."

Still full of attitude, Jodi crossed her arms. "So what happened?"

He wished he knew. "She seemed pissed."

"Well, duh." Dropping her arms, Jodi took a step closer. "I'd have been pissed, too. Like you said, Jedidiah's been alone and odds are she doesn't get the chance to hook up often. You must've been throwing it out there to make her think it'd be okay with you."

"The hell I was! I only tried to be considerate." He didn't know what Diah might've gone through, how she might really feel about intimacy. The woman had more secrets than he could count.

"He's always considerate," Hunter remarked, playing peacemaker. "And it is a tough situation."

"Men," Jodi complained…as she leaned against *her* man. "Guess Hunter's more intuitive than you. He knew right off what I wanted."

Hunter choked. "Not exactly true. I knew what *I* wanted, but I wasn't your employer."

"We were neighbors, though."

"Not the same thing, honey. Plus, you were pretty up front about things—what you'd accept and what you wouldn't. That made it easier. Sounds like Memphis is dealing with an entirely different situation."

"Different from anything I've known." Memphis appreciated his brother's support. "That's why I'm here. The last thing I want to do is make Diah uncomfortable, but at this point I don't know what's worse. Ignore the flirting, or take her up on it."

"Memphis," Hunter warned.

"No offense, but you're not a woman so I'd rather hear Jodi's take on it."

Jodi chewed her lip. "I know what I'd prefer, but I don't know Diah well."

"Let's say you have some things in common."

Her mouth curled with cynicism. "So she's damaged goods, too?"

Both men immediately protested that, Hunter by drawing his wife protectively closer.

Memphis by stating the truth. "You were never that. Defensive, sure, with good reason." She still carried a weapon or two on her at all times. "As far as I'm concerned, you're absolutely perfect."

"Perfect for me," Hunter agreed.

"You two are such sweethearts." Jodi's grin widened. "Be like that with Jedidiah, okay?"

Another example of women being confusing. “Like…how?”

“Just be you, Memphis. All sweet and understanding. Funny. Smart.”

Grinning at the compliments, Memphis theatrically preened.

“See, that’s cute, too.”

He nudged Hunter. “Your wife thinks I’m *cute*.”

“You’re a dumbass, but whatever. I guess you have your moments.”

Jodi spoke over them both. “If Jedidiah is anything at all like me, she’ll make it clear if she wants you. If not, I figure she’ll shut you down.”

If only it were that easy. “Would it be the right thing to do, though?”

“Look at it this way,” Jodi said. “If she’s feeling frisky, do you really want her looking somewhere else?”

God, no. Definitely a giant fucking *no*.

Hunter clasped his shoulder. “Before you get into any of that, I suggest you head back and tell her outright that you need to know why she’s there and what she’s planning.”

“Maybe, but I don’t want to spook her.”

“Does she spook that easily?” he asked.

Lately, no. But if he started pushing things? “Hard to say.”

“Huh. Then I’m surprised you left her alone at the campground knowing Remmy will be there.”

Everything inside Memphis went cold. “Remmy…?”

Jodi frowned. “He didn’t tell you?”

Son of a… “When did he tell you?” Memphis was already headed to his truck.

“Not long before you got here.” She, Hunter and

Turbo all trotted after him as his angry stride carried him around front in a rush. He could hear the laughter in Jodi's voice. "He probably figured you'd be there, right?"

"He damn well should have called me first."

"Like you always do?" Hunter asked.

Rounding on him, Memphis said, "One time! Can't a brother drop in unannounced?"

"Whenever you want," Jodi assured him. "Seriously, Memphis, Remmy is mega gorgeous—"

Hunter growled.

"—but so are you. And she knows you already. I'm assuming she likes you since you two have been hanging out. Trust me, it'll be fine."

It wasn't Remmy Gardner's appearance that bothered him…much. True, the guy was tall, muscular, blond and brown-eyed. Memphis had seen women give him second and third looks.

Remmy definitely got around. So what? Remmy wasn't married or even involved in anything steady. He was allowed to enjoy himself. Before buying the campground, Memphis had, too, so he'd be a hypocrite to condemn Remmy for hooking up.

And although Remmy had once been a thug, he'd intervened when others had planned to hurt Jodi.

She considered him a friend now, Hunter tolerated him, and Madison worked with him. Remmy was a trustworthy guy.

But Diah didn't know that. She thought she'd be alone. She thought she'd have plenty of time for snooping.

And now she was about to get a massive surprise.

With a quick pat for Turbo, a hug to Jodi and a slap on Hunter's back, he got in his truck and drove off. As soon as he was out of the driveway, he tried calling Diah but she didn't answer and that amplified his worry.

Fortunately, most of the roads had very little traffic, allowing him to drive faster. Normally, he enjoyed the views, but not today. Twice he tried calling her again.

Still no answer.

Good thing he'd done his shopping before visiting Hunter, because he wasn't about to stop now. Not until he reached Diah. Until he knew for sure she wasn't afraid.

Until he made it clear to Remmy Gardner that Diah Stephens was off-limits.

Now and for the foreseeable future.

SHE'D MADE IT through three cabins without finding a thing of interest. She had her list, so Memphis couldn't accuse her of slacking. Not that he would. He really had been terrific. Almost too good to be true.

Did guys like him actually exist in the real world?

And *why* was she thinking of him again?

Over and over, her thoughts had returned to him. His smile, the intensity in his dark blue eyes, the casual strength in those super-fine shoulders and brawny biceps. The way he spoke to Tuff.

How he spoke with *her*.

The man was an enigma, enticing, sometimes flippant, usually open and caring but occasionally distant. Always generous. And understanding.

Too much so, maybe. Enough that he wore her down without any visible effort.

Determined to make the most of the time given her today, she walked with Tuff back to the maintenance shed and retrieved a few tools she'd need. It made sense to search each cabin thoroughly before moving on to the next. That way, if another opportunity presented itself, she'd know where to pick back up.

Returning to the first cabin, she paced the floor. She'd already searched the very tops of the cabinets, behind every nook and cranny and under the few furnishings. Trying to see the cabin with new eyes, she stepped forward…and heard the squeak of a floorboard.

Interesting. Going to her knees, she knocked on the floor in an attempt to determine where the squeak originated. A hollow sound led her to the love seat where Tuff reclined.

"Sorry, boy. I don't mean to disturb you." Since she'd already looked under the seat, she sat back on her heels and sighed. Tuff continued to watch her, so she sent him a wan smile. "Everything is fine. I'm just disappointed."

Hopping down, Tuff snuffled against her face. While he was up, she wrestled with the love seat again, overturning it and knocking on the floorboards once more.

Clearly, one of the long slats of wood had been repaired. Or had it? Her heart started to race. She could see that no one had cleaned under the love seat in a very long time. Dead bugs and a lot of cobwebs took up space.

She made a mental note to do a thorough cleaning beneath the furniture in all the cabins before Memphis opened for business.

Disgusted, Diah used her hammer to clear it all away, and then examined the board again.

She still had time, right? Shoring up her courage, she went about prying loose the board, using utmost care not to break it. Tuff watched her nervously.

Right. If Memphis caught her, what could she say?

That she'd decided to clean *under* the floor? She snorted at herself—and the wood came loose. Beneath it she found…nothing interesting.

The cabins had pier foundations, making it easier to access the electricity and plumbing. Not that she planned to crawl under there. Even thinking it gave her the shivers.

Damn it, she needed a flashlight but like her phone, she hadn't thought to bring one of those, either.

She was the worst sleuth ever. No way in hell was she going to stick her hand in there. What if there were snakes? Massive spiders? Heck, even a loose, rusty nail could do damage—

She yelped when Tuff suddenly went rigid, his ears perked. In a whisper, she asked, "What is it?"

He gave a low, threatening growl.

Oh, shit. Nervousness radiated out to encompass her entire body. Tensed, she glanced around and… Dear Lord, a man was staring in the window!

A shrill scream strangled in her throat.

For a second there, her vision narrowed and she feared she might pass out.

Coward.

Trying to remember all her lessons, she struggled for control, drew a long deep breath and gradually the gray fog receded.

Frowning, the man hurriedly moved away from the window. It struck Diah that he was probably going to the door.

A door she hadn't locked.

When she lurched to her feet, the movement seemed to galvanize Tuff. He began viciously barking. She reached the door at the same time the man did. Panicked, she fumbled with the bolt, got it turned just as he tried the doorknob, then she stumbled back.

Through the small door window, he gazed at her, glanced down at the dog and heaved an impatient breath. “You’re okay now?”

Terrified, but otherwise... She nodded.

“Will the dog bite?” he asked loudly over the racket Tuff made.

“Yes!” She let Tuff continue his deranged dog impersonation. “He would mangle you.”

“You could restrain him.”

She shook her head. “No.” Hell no.

Downright annoyed now, the guy asked, “Who are you and what’re you doing on this property?” Before she could come up with an explanation, he threatened her by saying, “I’m calling the owner.”

Mouth dry and heart trying to thunder out of her chest, Diah asked, “You’re not the owner?” just to test him.

“No.”

“Then who is?”

“Since you’re locked in there, I assume you’ll meet him soon. Doesn’t matter how cute you are, honey, he won’t appreciate you destroying one of his cabins.”

How cute...? Indignation stiffened her backbone and she returned to the door. On tiptoes, she glared at him in challenge. “If you know the owner, then give me a name!”

“Memphis Osborn.”

Oh. She dropped back to her heels. Well, okay, so he knew Memphis. That relieved her marginally. “What are you doing here?”

“He has a job for me.”

Memphis had hired someone without telling her? That stung. Sure, she was only an employee herself, but still, they talked daily and she'd started to feel like… more.

Her, Jedidiah Stephens, the girl without a background, always on the run. She knew better than to make connections.

One day, she promised herself. But not today. Not until she found what she needed to put the past to rest.

"Hey, did you fall asleep in there?"

Diah scowled at him. Over the last few weeks, it seemed like Memphis could have taken the time to clue her in on other employees. Not because they'd grown closer—apparently, they hadn't—but out of common courtesy he could have told her that she might not be alone today.

"What job are you supposed to be doing?" Given that Memphis was always so considerate, skepticism lingered. Taking a page from the interloper's book, she didn't give him a chance to reply before saying, "You look like a thug."

Slowly, a grin crept over his strikingly handsome face. "No kidding? So I've still got it, huh?"

Her insult had flattered him? Not her intent.

"And here I figured I blended in real well now."

"No," she assured him. No blending. The calculating way his dark eyes took in everything, how he studied her, it was as if he saw her fear, recognized it and understood it.

Damn it, she didn't like being dissected.

Giving her a magnanimous smile, he held up his hands. "Tell you what, honey. If this is a simple robbery, I'll just let you go. Memphis doesn't need to know."

She would most definitely tell Memphis all about this. "He'll know because I plan to tell him."

"Aw, so you do know him? Great." The guy nodded at her. "Go ahead and give him a call."

Right. She'd have already done that if she hadn't forgotten her phone. Making her smile as mean as she could, she suggested, "If you know him so well, why don't you do the honors?"

Studying her anew, he rubbed a hand over his sensual mouth. "All right, fine. Give me a sec." Stepping away from the door, he pulled his cell from a back pocket of his jeans, swiped a thumb over the screen and touched a number…

Then turned his back on her!

Diah moved closer to the door. With the guy now a short distance away, she could see that he was tall, likely as tall as Memphis, with hard shoulders and lean hips. He had a strong build, and damn him, he was exceptionally good-looking. Not that she gave a flip what he looked like. He could be the most gorgeous man alive—which would be tough since Memphis was still breathing—and she'd want to skewer him anyway for scaring her half to death.

At this point, she wasn't sure what would be worse: if he was simply there as an employee who'd caught her tearing up the floor, or if he *was* a crook who still might try to get to her by breaking a window.

If he went that route… She snatched up her hammer to use as a weapon, shushed Tuff and strained to hear the guy's conversation.

He glanced back at her. "Memphis wants to know why you're not answering your phone."

The groan bubbled up but she repressed it. "I forgot it in my cabin."

"Which cabin?"

Her mouth firmed. No way would she tell him where to find her belongings.

With a grunt of frustration, he turned away again and did more muffled talking. She heard him when he raised his voice to say, "I can't give her my phone because she's locked me out. No, I didn't try to break in! I thought *she* was breaking in… Ha! Wait until you see the cabin. It was a logical conclusion." Aggrieved, he said to her, "Memphis wants you to know he's on his way."

"Great. When?" Couldn't be soon enough for her.

"He said a few more minutes."

Her eyes narrowed. *If* Memphis was on his way, and *if* it'd only be minutes, the guy could still do a lot of harm.

"Sorry, Memphis." As he spoke into the phone, the stranger gave her a charming grin. "Not sure she believes me."

Diah blew out a breath. She did—sort of. But she'd long ago learned not to take chances. No one was to be trusted. She could never take a risk.

She had to toughen up.

"Right, sure," the stranger said. "I'll wait for you there."

What? He'd wait *where*? She preferred to keep him where she could see him, but off he went, his rangy stride taking him out of sight.

New fear intruded, and Diah raced around the cabin, ensuring the few windows were locked tight and then wedging a chair under the door. With that done she sat down to wait.

Almost laughable. She'd learned to survive on her own, eventually she'd learn how to snoop. Not today, though. For now, she was good and stuck.

"YOU TOLD HER I'm on my way?"

"Shouted it through the barricaded door, yeah."

Memphis checked the time on his dash. "Thanks. Just leave her be until I get there."

"Fine, I can do that, not that she'd have let me bother her, anyway. When she first saw me, I thought she was going to keel over. Went white as a corpse. Luckily, she managed to regroup."

"Damn."

"You didn't know she was the anxious type?"

Not like that. Guarded, sure. Sometimes flippant. Usually cautious. But panicky?

She hadn't been panicky with him.

He thought to ask, "Was she wearing glasses?"

"Some big-framed pink things. Girl has a deadly stare, doesn't she?"

As he'd told Diah, he liked the way she stared.

When he didn't reply, Remmy forged on. "Just so you know, a crew will be showing up here shortly. Four men. You'll want to keep your little hedgehog away from them."

Memphis bit back his frustration at the shitty timing. "It's what I asked for, then?"

"You bet. Shady fucks, all of them. I might have reconsidered them if I'd known you'd have a complication."

"If you mean Diah—"

"Well, I don't mean her dog, though he was losing his shit, too, snarling and growling and ready to eat me alive."

"Really? I haven't seen that side of him." Good to know the dog would be so protective. Diah had said he would, but he liked having it confirmed. "If they get there before me—"

"Right. I'll keep them occupied by putting them to work."

Fortunately, when Memphis pulled in, no one else had arrived yet. As with everything that had to do with the campground, he'd already read up on what was required to fix the entry drive. He knew once they got started, getting in and out would be tough. They'd have to use ripper teeth to tear up the old gravel and level the ground, and with trees lining the drive there wouldn't be much room to maneuver.

With Diah there, he'd have managed one way or another, even if it meant parking by the street and jogging in.

He saw Remmy right away and drove up alongside him. "Before they start work, I'll need a sign at the entrance so no one else pulls in."

"Get a lot of company, do you?"

"Not really, no, but I've spoken with a few other people about jobs." Impatient, he asked, "Which cabin is she in?"

"On the right, third cabin back." He didn't step away. "Seriously, Memphis. She's a looker."

His jaw set. "Meaning?"

"Meaning it wouldn't be great for them to know she's here, in an isolated area, unprotected."

"She's protected. By me." He wasn't without weapons, strength or common sense. Whatever it took, he'd see that no one bothered her.

"Twenty-four seven?" Remmy pressed. "Do you have her glued to your side at night?"

No, but he had cameras everywhere. Before the day was through, he'd install a few more so he'd know if anyone got near Diah's cabin.

Put out and not bothering to hide it, Remmy said, "It's risky enough that you're here alone. You know it makes you an easy target."

Which was part of what Memphis had planned.

"But a woman? That puts a whole new spin on things."

Yeah, it did. "Give me a few minutes to collect her and I'll get her inside my cabin until they're gone."

Remmy lifted a brow. "Not her own cabin?"

He lifted a hand. "She's staying right there, and there's no way they wouldn't hear her or the dog inside. I agree it'll be better if they have no idea that anyone else is here." Anxious now to be on his way, he said, "Head back to the entrance. Stop anyone from pulling in until I get back."

"Sure." Then Remmy said with a grin, "Later, I'll expect a proper introduction."

Actually, Memphis wouldn't mind hiring Remmy to stick around longer term. Could he finagle that? Given Remmy's concern for Diah, maybe.

As long as he understood the parameters.

Instead of parking his truck and taking a golf cart, Memphis drove right up to the cabin. Even before he'd completely left the truck, the door opened and Diah strode out to him, Tuff leashed beside her.

He started to explain, but she grabbed him in a tight hug and his mind went completely blank at the same time his body came alive. Gently, he put his arms around her in a protective embrace that felt incredibly right. "Hey." She smelled good, felt soft and warm, and he let his lips brush her hair.

"Jerk." She shoved him back. "You hired him?"

From grateful to furious in a nanosecond. It was almost amusing. "Remmy Gardner, yes, I did. Recall that you insisted the entry drive needed repairs."

"Of course it does, but you could have told me! He about gave me a heart attack."

"So he said." Memphis stooped to greet Tuff. "I hear you were ferocious security, my man." He used both hands to rub Tuff's neck, earning a doggy smile and a wagging tail.

"He was scared, too."

"Not how Remmy described it. Seriously, I'm glad Tuff feels so protective." His gaze lifted to look into the cabin, and he gave a low whistle. She had the love seat turned onto its back and part of the floor pulled up, scattered tools around it. How would she explain it? "You've been…busy."

Reciting a well-rehearsed excuse, she said, "There was a squeaky floorboard so I decided to fix it."

Standing again, Memphis looked down at her. "I see."

Her chin lifted as if daring him to doubt her. "It would all be done if you hadn't forgotten to tell me that we'd have company."

"Remmy isn't company. I didn't know he'd be here today and I wasn't aware I had to check in with you when hiring other workers."

She made a rude sound. "Common courtesy, that's all."

Damn, he liked the way she got miffed. "Why did it scare you so badly?"

"Who says I was scared?"

"Remmy?" He added, "Or maybe I just assumed after that tight hug you gave me."

"Relief," she explained, shrugging off her extreme reaction, then dished it right back at him. "I didn't know another worker would be here, and you're the one who is forever cautioning me about how dangerous it can be here."

"Snakes, bears, spiders," he reminded her.

"For all I know, this Remmy person could have been a serial killer." Glancing around, likely to ensure Remmy wasn't anywhere near, she whispered, "He looks dangerous, don't you think?"

Astute. He liked that about her. "He can be, when necessary." Walking up to the cabin, he closed and locked the door.

"I can put everything back—"

"Later." Clearly, whatever she was searching for, she thought it might be well hidden. To accommodate her, he said, "For the next few days, take whatever time you need to look over the cabins and do any necessary repairs."

She jumped on the edict with alacrity. "Absolutely. No problem."

Damn it, she'd have to come clean with him soon. When he had time tonight, he'd look at the security feeds from the cameras placed around the grounds and see if he could pick up any special interests from her activity. "For now, I need your cooperation."

Her brows came together. "What does that mean?"

"A small crew of men will be here any minute." He urged her and Tuff to his truck, then he got behind the wheel. "I need you to stay in my cabin, out of sight, until they've finished the entry drive and gone."

"Your cabin?" she asked while fastening her seat belt. "Why not my own?"

Making sure Remmy hadn't returned with anyone, he drove up to his cabin. "I don't want them to overhear you or Tuff. I'll make sure they don't venture beyond the entry drive, and you'll make sure you stay out of sight. Understand?"

She chewed that over, and then asked, "Who are they?"

"I told you. They're a crew."

"Okay… Then why should I hide from them?"

He couldn't explain, so he chose to be autocratic. "Because I am the employer and you are the employee and that's what I'm telling you to do."

The seconds passed in strained silence. He put the truck in Park and turned to scowl at her. "Jedidiah?"

"Fine."

"Good." He stepped out and strode around to her door, hurrying now since he could hear some commotion. "Let's get inside. Soon as I can, I'll bring Remmy to introduce you two."

"That one I'll gladly avoid."

"Ah, sorry, no can do." If things worked out as he'd prefer, Remmy would be around more often, so she'd have to get accustomed to him, and vice versa. He got her and Tuff inside, said, "Stay put," and jogged to her cabin to get Tuff's lead from the front deck. He also got the dog's food and water dishes in the kitchen, and he located Diah's cell phone on the counter.

For a woman set on a sketchy course, she wasn't very prepared.

He could hear the trucks coming down the drive when he locked her cabin door and ran back to his, pausing only long enough to get his purchases from his truck.

Diah was at one of his specialty windows in the kitchen, peering out in curiosity. “It wouldn’t kill you to tell me who they are.”

He set the food and water dish on the floor, and the new treats for Tuff on the counter. “Let’s just say it’s in your best interest to stay completely off their radar.”

“So…criminals?” She turned to face him. “Small-time or something worse?”

Memphis almost laughed. Here with him, she didn’t seem at all concerned, merely intrigued and insistent. He hoped that meant she trusted him to keep her safe. “I’ll put Tuff’s lead out the back door in case he has to go. No one can see him from there, but are you able to keep him quiet?” If the dog started barking, they’d notice for sure.

“Usually. He understands caution.”

“Great. Let’s hope you do, too.” He strode to his bedroom to put away other things he’d bought, then went out back to hook the lead, shortening it so Tuff couldn’t get around to the side of the house. It’d be temporary, and for now, necessary.

When he got back inside once more, Diah was again at the window. Her brows were drawn in curiosity, but because he’d irked her, she tried to ignore him.

On impulse, Memphis pulled her into another hug. It surprised her enough that he was able to press a brief kiss to the top of her head before she even thought to react. “Be good, Diah. Stay inside. I mean it.”

Bemused, she stared up at him with wide eyes and slightly parted lips.

He straightened her glasses for her, brushed a fingertip over her cheek and said, "Make yourself at home. I'll be back in a few minutes."

ED HURLEY NEVER missed a thing. It was why Otto relied on him to gather even the tiniest details. So far, what he'd noticed most was the complete and total lack of security. That didn't make any sense—which meant he couldn't trust it.

Sure, the campground was the same as he remembered. Rough around the edges with plenty of woods for concealing activity, enough space that the lots weren't crammed too close together and a "who gives a fuck" atmosphere.

Without the usual amenities of pool and playground, no respectable family would stay here long, which meant the disreputable businessmen, like Otto Woodall, could freely carry on without interference.

"The place looks deserted," he said to Remmy. "You sure it's opening soon?"

"Few weeks." Remmy eyed the other men, then as usual he tried to take over. "Listen up. The owner doesn't want anyone wandering around, so no one goes beyond this point. Understood?"

"What if I have to take a piss?" Charlie asked, making his brothers Vic and Syd both laugh.

"Commune with Mother Nature for all I care, as long as you don't go into the park."

"That's bullshit." Ed didn't like Remmy, but then he never liked the pretty boys. Couldn't trust them. They always thought they were better than him. "There's no reason they can't use the public—"

"I gave you a reason." Gaze dark and hard, Remmy

crowded closer. "I don't plan to repeat myself so make up your mind if you want the job or not."

Self-righteous prick. "And if we walk?"

"You think I can't find four more just like you?" He showed his teeth in a mean grin. "Wouldn't take me an hour."

One solid punch to that smug mug and Remmy wouldn't be so cocksure of himself. Of course, Remmy tended to punch back—hard and fast. From everything he knew, the man didn't take shit of any kind, which meant it'd be better to avoid a physical conflict.

Remmy Gardner was the type of man you blindsided, not one you went at face-to-face. Besides, Otto had been clear. He wanted info on the layout of the place, the level of security and the players involved. That meant Ed had to hang around.

"Gentlemen." Another man, just as pretty but a lot more jovial, stepped up to Remmy's side. "Thank you for being here. I hope you can finish the job today because I have other work being done soon. I need the entry passable."

So this was the owner. Interesting. Ed reached forward in greeting. "Mr. Osborn."

A big hand, solid and strong, clasped his. "And you are?"

"Ed Hurley. These are my men, Vic, Charlie and Syd. We can do the job today, no problem. It's just—"

"I heard, and I do apologize for any inconvenience. It's an insurance thing, you understand." He flashed a congenial yet steely smile. "Until the last inspection, I can't have anyone on the property without running the risk of an injury, for which I'd be liable." As if in confidence, he added, "I'm doing the bare minimum for it to open and be operational. Getting sued would defeat the purpose of cost cutting, now, wouldn't it?"

Bare minimum, huh? Otto would enjoy that detail. "You're opening when?"

"Well, now, that depends in part on you, Mr. Hurley. Can you finish today without overstepping or will I need Remmy to hire a new crew? That would push us back, but hey, I'm flexible."

One glance showed Remmy's satisfaction. He'd probably like to send them all packing. If he did, there'd be hell to pay with Otto. "We can start right now. We weren't scheduled until tomorrow, but we got the backhoe and box blade early." It helped that they had influence with all the local companies. You didn't tell Otto no, for any reason. "We'll get the bad areas prepped in time for the delivery of the crushed limestone."

"Already arranged the limestone, too, huh? Very efficient, Ed."

"I know people," he said, issuing his own challenging grin, but no one asked him for specifics.

Remmy said, "With all the equipment here, it's just a matter of leveling it out. We'll—"

Memphis held up a hand. "Fascinating, but spare me the details. If I find the time I'll walk out to watch, otherwise I'll leave the supervision to you and the execution to Mr. Hurley and his crew."

Remmy half laughed. "I forgot your aversion to labor."

"It's not an aversion," Memphis denied, still with good humor. "More a lack of capability." He shared another smile.

One that Ed didn't buy, but whatever, they needed to be here so he couldn't quit. "Leave the dirty work to us. We've got it covered." He gave a nod and walked off to get started.

He heard Memphis say, "Remmy, if you can spare a minute, I'd like to discuss something with you before you get too involved."

"Sure."

"We can talk inside my cabin."

Remmy glanced at the men. "I'll be right back."

"We don't need you," Ed said. "Take your time." As long as they were both out of sight, he could survey the property all he wanted without making anyone suspicious. Could use his cell phone to take a few pics, too.

For now, that'd have to be enough—but he was willing to bet Otto would want him to return, maybe in the dark of night.

When Memphis Osborn would be all alone.

CHAPTER FIVE

It didn't surprise Memphis to see that Diah had pulled the kitchen chair around to sit and was still watching the crew through the window. Without a word, he joined her, putting his hands on her shoulders as a reminder to her that she wasn't alone.

Plus, the connection helped him to tamp down his anger.

For reasons he couldn't yet pinpoint, he'd badly wanted to smash his fist into Ed Hurley's face. Playing the amicable stooge didn't always come easily for him, not when facing cruel people.

What kind of criminal was Ed? A run-of-the-mill goon, or someone truly evil? A man who traded in drugs, guns…or lives?

He'd find out from Remmy, but first he'd make introductions. "Diah, I'd like you to meet Remmy Gardner."

Startled, she stood so fast that her braids swung out. She glared at Remmy in accusation. Tuff sat up to do the same while staying at her side.

Next, her hot gaze shifted to Memphis. "You brought him in here?"

"It's my cabin," he reminded her.

Her smile wasn't nice. "That's right, boss. I haven't forgotten."

Remmy huffed on a laugh, then coughed to cover it.

Whether Diah liked it or not, he wouldn't allow her to be at risk. That'd be asking too much of him. If she wanted to get cross, then so be it. "Remmy will be around off and on." More *on* if Memphis could arrange it. "He's a reliable friend, so I asked him to arrange employees for a few other projects."

"I could handle all your projects." Her attention landed on Remmy like a laser beam. "You don't need him."

Stubborn as a mule. "Nonetheless, he's been hired."

Remmy stayed silent, his expression understanding. Did he, like Memphis, sense Diah's uncertainty? It seemed likely. One of the things he liked most about Remmy was his keen perception of people and situations.

"Remmy," Memphis said, trying to lighten the mood, "this is Jedidiah Stephens, who prefers Diah. A competent jack-of-all-trades and a certifiable workhorse."

Straightening from his slouched position against the wall, Remmy extended his hand. "Ms. Stephens."

Warily, she accepted the polite offering.

When she would have pulled back, Remmy held on. "I'm sorry about earlier." Gently, he pressed her hand between both of his. "I didn't mean to take you by surprise, and of course I understand your caution. I hope, going forward, if you need anything—"

"I won't." Retreating, she stood closer to Memphis's side, close enough that he could feel the tension going through her, and breathe in her scent. It was as if she carried the fresh outdoors with her.

A really nice fragrance—and one that affected him.

To everyone's surprise, Tuff yawned, stretched and then went to Remmy for a few pets.

"Hey, boy. All is forgiven? I'm glad. You're a fierce one when triggered." Remmy grinned at Diah. "Bet you learned that from her, huh?"

Flirting? Memphis would shut that down really quick.

Unamused, Diah finally dragged her keen attention off Remmy and onto Memphis. "I need to talk to you."

"All right." He needed to talk to her as well. "Just let me discuss something with Remmy first—"

"It can't wait." Her small hand curled around his wrist, her fingers chilled as she tugged him toward the hall. "Tuff, stay."

Obediently, Tuff sat and stared at Remmy.

"Sure." Remmy crossed his arms and leaned on the wall again. "I don't mind waiting."

The irony in his words couldn't be missed.

Diah didn't attempt to drag him far. She urged him down the hall and just outside his bedroom. Casting a suspicious glance back toward the kitchen, she lowered her voice and said, "Those men are crooked."

The fact that she still held his wrist threw Memphis off, and it took him a second to ask, "The workers?"

"Yeah. They're not men you want to have around. Trust me on this."

Fascinating. "How do you know?"

"I can just tell." Realizing that she still held him, she jerked her hand away and tucked it into a pocket. "You can't?"

Unwilling to give himself away, Memphis shrugged. "They're sketchy, sure. It makes them cheaper. That doesn't mean they won't get the job done."

"I don't believe you." She appeared ridiculously disappointed in him. "Memphis, they're scoping out the place. Seriously, you didn't see it? You don't *sense* it?"

Yes, he did. Hoping to get some insight into her experiences, he said, "Tell me what it was about them that alarmed you."

She threw up her hands. "Their eyes for one thing."

"They aren't close enough for you to see their eyes."

"I don't have to get close. Those men have very mean eyes. It's there in how they look at you, how they look at Remmy when his back is turned and how they're checking out the campgrounds."

A mixture of pity and protectiveness brought Memphis closer. "You know something about men with mean eyes?"

Her frustration visibly mounted. "*Duh.* I've lived on my own for a while so naturally I've come across all kinds. That particular look isn't exclusive to men, though, so keep that in mind." While schooling him, she flexed her hands, her gaze on her feet as she thought things through. "It's also the way they carry themselves. Alert—sort of like Remmy, actually—and with their heads tilted a certain way, almost like they want to provoke someone."

"They didn't provoke me," he reminded her.

"Because you're dense or something." She glanced at him. "No insult intended."

"No, of course not," he said, deadpan. "How could I take offense at being called dense?"

"This isn't a joke! They're dangerous and Remmy shouldn't have brought them here. If you want the entry drive done, I can—"

"They'll do it, and no, it's your turn to listen, Diah."

Stiffening at his authoritative tone, her mouth flattened and her shoulders squared, but she kept silent.

For now, he'd call that a win. "Everything you saw

with those men, I saw as well. I hate to disillusion you, but I'm not dense, not even close to it." Forestalling anything she might have said, he added, "I can't explain right now, but there's a reason for the things I do."

"Don't you dare tell me that you're shady, too." Her hands tightened into fists. "That'd make *me* dense, because I figured on you being a good guy."

"Diah." Reaching out, he took her hands in his, carefully loosening her fingers until they relaxed in his hold. It was a familiar touch, one of concern and friendship, but it felt like more. She was so much smaller than him, so often wary and defensive. She'd recently had a fright with Remmy…while searching one of his cabins.

Eventually, he'd have to figure that out, but right now he had bigger priorities.

"I know it's too soon to ask you to trust me, but I'm requesting a little time."

"Time for what?"

Gently, he lifted one of her hands to his lips and brushed a kiss over her knuckles. Seeing her eyes widen, he said softly, "When I can, I'll explain the reasons for what I'm doing and why, just not right now. Until then, I need you to know that I *am* a good guy. More importantly, you need to know that I would never hurt you, and I won't let anyone else hurt you, either."

Slowly, she inhaled. "You swear you're not up to anything…criminal?"

Memphis winced. What was and wasn't criminal could sometimes be up for debate depending on who you asked. "I swear that I want only to protect innocent people. Is that good enough?"

After scrutinizing him for far too long, one corner of her mouth twitched, then lifted the tiniest bit. "This is getting interesting. Okay, sure. For some reason, I believe you."

"Maybe because you know I'm not a liar?"

Leaning in, she lowered her voice even more. "But does that mean you're playing vigilante?"

Unbelievable. It took Memphis a second to order his thoughts, especially since what he really wanted to do was kiss her taunting mouth. How dare she look so tempting right now? Diah was always attractive to him, but with that playful glint in her unusual eyes?

Irresistible.

Sidestepping the question seemed the best way to go. "It means that, on occasion, there will be shady characters around."

She eyed him, no longer with irritation and distrust, but with something a bit warmer. "Okay, then. Am I going to be expected to hide in your cabin every time these *shady characters* show up? If so, I don't know how I'll be expected to get any work done."

Good point. While he considered the complications, he said, "On occasion, it will be necessary."

"Uh-huh. Can I at least get prior notice next time so some creep doesn't take me by surprise?"

Damn, now that she said it, his brain locked on the possible ramifications of others—those not as upstanding as Remmy—finding her in an isolated spot on the campgrounds. He couldn't be everywhere at once, and she was right, she needed to be able to do her job.

"Solving world problems, Memphis? Because I have to tell you, if you pull the boss/employee move again, I'm going to get irked."

He smiled. "Can't have that now, can we? And no, it's not a world problem, but certainly, it's important to me."

"What is?"

"Your safety. For that reason, until I sort out a few things, it occurs to me that the easiest way to handle having other employees around is to..."

Her brows went up. "What? Spit it out."

Watching her, curious to see her reaction, he said, "We could pretend we're a couple."

That wiped away her improved mood really quick. "A couple?" she croaked, not quite sounding appalled, but definitely stunned. "You and me?"

"I didn't mean me and Tuff."

"You want me to pretend to...be your girlfriend?"

Her incredulity almost made him laugh. "Unbelievable, I know, but I'm hoping you can bear up under the pretense, at least long enough for me to get some things in line."

Calculating, she narrowed her eyes and studied him from head to toes and back again. "How long?"

Oh, honey, you have no idea what that visual stroke just did to me. He shifted closer still. "Would it be too much to request two weeks?"

"All right."

Astounded at her quick agreement, he asked, "Is that a yes?"

"Sure, why not? I've never really been anyone's girlfriend."

Never? "That can't be true."

"Eh, when you explain, I will, too. Until then, I have a question."

Assuming she'd want some clarification, he said, "Let's hear it."

"Do I get the girlfriend benefits as well?"

Blank astonishment leveled him. Certain that he misunderstood, he said, “Excuse me?”

“Benefits.” She hip-bumped him, saying playfully, “You know, closeness, consideration…sex?”

His mouth worked, but it took him two tries to finally repeat, “Sex?”

“I have no idea why you’re strangling.”

Lust, that’s why. A sudden, powerful surge of lust that gripped him hard.

Rolling her eyes, she said, “Don’t expire over it. It’s not a deal-breaker or anything.”

He’d offended her when that wasn’t his intent. He tried again, saying with more heartfelt optimism, “Sex!”

Her dimples appeared. “That’s better, and yes. I mean, kissing first would be good. We’d have to work up to the actual sex stuff, but two weeks leaves plenty of time, right?”

He drew a slow, deep breath. “Yes.” *Was he really agreeing to this?* Scorching heat rushed through his blood. With any encouragement at all, he’d be hard. He gave a horribly clichéd clearing of his throat, and managed to sound mostly rational when he said, “If that’s what you want, consider me on board.”

“Excellent.” She patted his chest, let her hand linger a moment, then withdrew with a sigh. “I guess we should check on Remmy.”

He’d rather get clarification on those benefits, but he knew she was right. “You can trust Remmy.”

“I don’t yet trust you, so don’t go pushing other men on me.” She stepped around him. “Besides, I can’t quite get a bead on Remmy. It’s like he’s a tough guy, but with good intentions.”

“Actually, that nails Remmy perfectly.” It hit Memphis that Diah was ahead of him, meaning he was behind her...when up until that point she hadn't wanted him at her back. Progress? He chose to think so.

Sex with her would be no problem at all. Count him in. Hell yeah. But damn, her motives were murky at best.

Then again, so were his own.

As they reentered the kitchen, Remmy watched them warily. "All good?"

Diah smirked. "I'm surprised that word can even leave your mouth."

"Yeah, it surprises me sometimes, too." He gave a final pat to Tuff, ignoring the sharp glance Diah sent his way, and said to Memphis, "Guess it's my turn."

To Diah, Memphis said, "Make yourself at home, but don't leave my cabin."

"Yes, sir." Giving him a smart salute, she took up her position by the window again. "In the meantime, I'll keep an eye on your goons."

He and Remmy shared a look. With a shrug, Memphis gestured for him to head down the hall.

REMMY WAS FIRMLY caught between enjoyment and caution. When he'd first agreed to help Memphis with his plans for the campground, he hadn't imagined anyone like Jedidiah being involved. In some ways she reminded him of Jodi—bossy but guarded, sexy without effort, capable but also fragile.

Unlike Jodi, Jedidiah was painfully wary. Jodi had a tendency to meet a supposed threat head-on, whereas Jedidiah had damn near hyperventilated.

Obviously, she was already attracted to Memphis,

which was all well and good since he'd sworn off nice girls.

At least for now.

Until he got his life in order.

Getting used to the straight and narrow took some adjustment. No reason to muddy his transition with that type of complication.

Gaining dubious privacy at the end of the hall, Memphis asked, "How would you feel about moving into one of the cabins?"

Taken aback, Remmy stared at him. "You want me here around the clock?"

"Initially, I didn't," Memphis admitted. "When I first asked for your input, it was only to get the ball rolling."

Right. Because he knew scumbags—having been one himself. "Now there's Jedidiah to consider."

Rubbing the back of his neck, Memphis said, "It changes everything."

Already knowing how it'd go over, he suggested, "You could fire her."

"No, I couldn't."

That gruff admission brought a quick smile to his mouth. "I didn't think so." Guess Memphis was as interested in her as she was in him. He folded his arms over his chest and studied Memphis. "I'd like to know how you and your brother find such interesting women."

Memphis gave it a little thought, then said, "Maybe it's not a matter of finding them, but recognizing them."

Huh. Could be. When was the last time he paid attention to a woman other than for a few hours of pleasure? Well, of course he knew: Jodi—who was now Hunter's wife, Memphis's sister-in-law...and Remmy's friend.

He wouldn't change that for the world. He owed Jodi

a lot, since she was the first to trust him, to see him as more than a brute thug.

"So," he said. "You and Diah?"

"I'm sorting that out, and in the meantime, don't get any ideas."

Remmy grinned. Memphis gave off a more laid-back vibe than Hunter, but he wasn't fooled. The brothers were different in many ways, but they both had a core of strength, intelligence and determination.

"Do you have to think about it?" Memphis asked.

Remmy shook his head. "Just weighing the pros and cons."

That had Memphis straightening. "I just told you—"

"I mean about staying on longer term. Relax. I wouldn't overstep." He glanced around Memphis's home, but knew the other rentals didn't compare. "The cabins have indoor plumbing?"

Appeased, Memphis nodded. "All the comforts of home, but with minuscule showers. You might prefer to use the bathhouse, but then that could mean showering with someone using the stall right next to you. The cabins are small, basically a loft bedroom with a low ceiling, a tiny kitchen, narrow couch and a shit TV with lousy reception."

"I mean, how could I resist all that?"

They both laughed. "I'll provide decent WiFi, and since I'm offering the cabin free you'd save on rent."

Remmy ran a hand over his mouth. "I'd have to clear it with the McKenzies." With Jodi's urging and Madison's backing, they'd hired him on, saying they saw his potential. They were strict but fair, and always supplied enough action to keep him engaged. Who knew it could be so much fun helping people? Sure beat the hell out of aligning with criminals. "Since Madison worries about you—" he flashed Memphis a fake smile "—I don't think she'd mind."

Memphis rolled his eyes. "Madison enjoys keeping an eye on my every move."

"Not just you, dude. She does that to everyone. I wouldn't be surprised if she knew we were talking right now." That seemed to strike Remmy, and he glanced around. "She can't have this place bugged, right?"

"No, but could she tap into my phone or PC and somehow listen in? Probably. She has skills I can't even imagine."

"All the McKenzies," Remmy said, then he fell quiet. "No lie, they blow me away."

"You enjoy working for them?"

"I do, and I owe that to Jodi." He gave that quick thought, then added, "And your brother, too. He has enough sway now that he could have nixed the deal for me."

"Hunter probably likes to know you're keeping busy. Less time for you to cozy up with his wife."

"Don't even joke."

Memphis cracked a half grin. "Yeah, I imagine Hunter doesn't take it well, does he?"

"He's a possessive junkyard dog."

"Accurate," Memphis said with a laugh. "At least when it comes to Jodi."

This was why Remmy liked Memphis. He didn't get insulted easily, and usually handled every situation with good humor.

"You know the whole story with the McKenzies, right? I mean, now that your brother has married into the family." Jodi wasn't blood related to any of them, but they considered her family all the same, and that made Hunter family as well. Hell, he was pretty sure the McKenzies now counted Memphis among them, too.

"Yeah, I do," Memphis said. "You?"

So neither of them would say it out loud? Worked for Remmy. He supposed with the way the elite group operated—under the radar and often dodging legal channels—it made sense to keep it quiet. As far as he was concerned, their methods of rescuing victims from human trafficking and forced labor were to be applauded. "I know enough to see that you're starting to take part."

Denying that, Memphis shook his head. "What I want to do can't begin to compare, but I hope it'll make a difference."

"I assume you'll be able to keep an eye on anyone coming or going?"

"True, except for in private cabins, tents or RVs. Even then, I'll control the WiFi so there are always ways to monitor things. Understand, Remmy. I have no interest in eavesdropping on you, or other everyday people."

He already knew that. "This way, you'll get a heads-up when drug or arms deals are going down—"

"Or when innocent people are being targeted." As if relishing the idea of protecting others, Memphis rubbed his hands together. "I'll have an inside track on corruption."

It was plain to see how he anticipated things going. They both knew there could be problems, though. "Jedidiah is going to be a distraction."

"She's agreed to lay low until the current crew finishes their job. I'll be interviewing new employees, too, but for the next two weeks, as far as anyone will be able to tell, we'll be a couple."

Skeptical, Remmy asked, "But you aren't really?"

"We just covered this."

Remmy held up his hands. "I wasn't asking out of personal interest. I know you two are already connecting."

Memphis eyed him a few seconds more, then nodded. "I don't know where things are going, or where I want them to go, but I do know Diah is searching the grounds for something and it worries me. I don't want her hurt in any way, not frightened, not threatened, and I'll break the arm of any man who dares to get grabby with her."

"Works for me. So am I to do the same? Break arms or heads or whatever if anyone gets out of line with her?"

"Absolutely. I can't be everywhere at once and she rarely leaves the campgrounds since she doesn't have a car. There will be times when I can't take her with me on errands and I prefer that she not be alone."

"Got it. No sweat." Possibilities ran through his head. Here, on a smaller scale, he'd have more input and influence than he did with the larger-than-life, alpha McKenzies. "Count me in."

"How soon can you make it happen?"

"I can ensure the guys wrap up today, then run home and grab enough stuff to last me a few days."

"I'd like you here for the entire season."

Now that he'd thought about it, he'd like it, too. Fresh surroundings for a fresh start. "Once I see the place and figure out what I need, I can move in the rest of my stuff. How's that sound?"

"Perfect." Memphis shook his hand. "I appreciate it."

Remmy didn't yet leave the hallway. "Which cabin is Jedidiah's?"

"The first one when you come in. Why?"

"Maybe it'd be a good idea to pretend that it's mine." Remmy didn't want to be a braggart or come off too cocky, but facts were facts. "Ed doesn't like me so he puts on a show of animosity, but I know his type and I've dealt with them for years. He doesn't actually want to challenge me. If he tried it, I'd take him apart before he could blink."

"Unless he shoots you in the back."

"Something he's capable of, for sure, but he knows he wouldn't be able to sneak in on me, so if they think I'm staying in Jedidiah's cabin, odds are they'll leave it alone."

"I like it. It's a solid plan. Thanks for thinking of it."

"No problem. Thanks for including me." A guy like Memphis wouldn't realize what it meant to be trusted, but to Remmy it was the best possible compliment.

"Can you give me a quick rundown on Ed?"

Knowing Memphis was anxious to get back to Jedidiah, he summed it up quickly. "Ed is like a school bully with delusions of being a mobster. He works for Otto Woodall, which is where he gets his clout."

"Otto Woodall?"

"By all accounts, a truly foul character," Remmy said. "Doesn't take a lot of research to know in the last few years, he's been accused of grand larceny, extortion and assault. Dig a little deeper and you'll find that he also got off on rape and kidnapping charges a few years ago."

Memphis locked his jaw. "Nothing sticks?"

Shrugging, Remmy said, "The women changed their stories." Or were forced to change them.

"How many women?"

"Two that I know of. One moved to the Midwest, the other vanished." For all they knew, the woman could be dead and it infuriated Remmy. He had a better understanding now of just how evil some people could be. He thought of Jodi—and then he thought of Diah.

It would be his extreme pleasure to help Memphis take down Otto Woodall and anyone working for him. "The important part of this is that Otto is still free, still a pig, but now he always has cover. I get the feeling that a lot of shit goes down in his hotel." Thugs shared more than most realized. It hadn't taken Remmy long to find out about Ed, and in the process he'd learned more about Otto, too. "Now he thinks of himself as an untouchable king, and unfortunately, with others to take the fall for him—"

"Or remove evidence?"

"—he might be right." Scowling, Remmy added, "He even changed the name of the hotel to *Castle Getaway.* His slogan is that you get treated like a king." It didn't escape Remmy's notice that the slogan in no way included women. It was directly targeted to men, and Otto got away with that because there were just enough bottom-feeders to keep things profitable. "So tell me, Memphis. What's the plan?"

CHAPTER SIX

VARIOUS EMOTIONS AND concerns bombarded Memphis. Hotels with their automatic check-ins/check-outs and the requisite guest privacy requirements would be ripe for abuse of the worst kind. Maybe he should have bought a hotel instead of a campground. Here, people were seen driving in. Even with an online registration, they couldn't be anonymous, not like at a hotel.

He'd have to give it some thought, possibly set up an "after hours" arrival and then lure the bastards away from hotels like Otto's so he could then turn them out to the right people and put an end to their vicious sport.

Thinking out loud, but also keeping Remmy up to speed, Memphis said, "I'll research him and his business tonight, and I'll put out a few more cameras so I'll know if anyone approaches the road in or tries to sneak through the woods. I want to know what Otto looks like, all his employees, and any weak spots he might have."

"Let me know how I can help."

"Thanks." He'd known that Remmy would be an asset, providing all the learned experiences missing from Memphis's squeaky-clean upbringing. "Let's go. I don't want to leave Diah on her own too long."

"Probably not a good idea."

Memphis shot him another look, but Remmy merely smiled as if sharing an inside joke. He wished he could find it funny, too. If it was happening to someone else, maybe, but it was happening to him and the confusion Diah caused him, how she stirred him without even trying, would take a lot of getting used to.

Around her, he felt like a stranger, like a man he didn't know and couldn't quite understand.

Determined to have her cooperation, Memphis returned to the kitchen and stated the plan to make it look like Remmy was using her cabin.

He was all geared up to insist, to argue with her if necessary.

Jedidiah listened, then nodded. "Sounds good."

The easy agreement left Memphis and Remmy both surprised enough that Diah shook her head at them.

"What? You expected me to refuse? I'm the one who pointed out that they're trouble. I definitely don't want to be on their radar. If you say that big, bad Remmy scares them, then hey, that works for me."

Remmy hitched his chin. "I don't *scare* them, exactly."

"Yeah, yeah. You fight back and they're pretty sure I wouldn't. Or couldn't." Rolling a shoulder, she turned back to the window and her voice dropped to a low grumble. "They'd probably be right. As you already know, I tend to freak out under pressure."

That just plain irked Memphis. "You don't give yourself enough credit."

"I know my limitations."

"You've got guts." Whether she believed it or not, he knew it was true. More than most, Diah understood the risks, yet she was still here, still up to *something*.

"You're deluded," she mumbled.

He didn't think so but debating it now, with Remmy's eagle-eyed attention involved, wouldn't change anything. “Regardless, you’ll have no reason to panic or to feel pressured,” Memphis assured her. “As long as you do as I tell you.”

She snorted, and he wasn’t sure if that was a sound of agreement or indictment of his delusion.

Before he could get clarification, his cell buzzed with an incoming call—no doubt from Madison—and he groaned. “Sorry, I need to take this.”

“Dude,” Diah grumbled, “you should put in a turnstile with all this coming and going from the kitchen.”

“I’ll only be a minute.” He started backing away, hesitant to leave them alone.

Diah eyed Remmy.

Tuff eyed him, too.

For some reason, Remmy found that funny. He said, “I don’t know what you’re getting me into, Memphis, but one way or another, it’ll keep me busy.”

“Both of you, play nice.”

This time there was no mistaking the disagreeable sound Diah made, and it worried him. He cautioned her with a look, then had no choice but to return to the hall for privacy, saying into the phone, “Sorry, Madison, but you’ve got to make it quick. I have my hands full at the moment.”

“I’ll get right to the point. Are you stealing my guy?”

“*Your* guy?” Memphis laughed, recognizing her teasing tone.

“You know what I mean. I had plans for him.”

“I hope your husband knows that.”

“Ha! Crosby has no worries in that regard.”

Of course not. Memphis let it go. “Let’s just say I’m borrowing him.”

Amusement infused her impatience. “For how long, Memphis?”

“The camping season, if all goes well.” His eyes narrowed with suspicion. “How did you know Remmy was here, anyway?”

“He works for the McKenzies now, remember? I knew he had a job with you today and that he’d brought along that pack of cretins he corralled.”

“That doesn’t explain how you knew I’d asked him to work for me.”

She blew out a breath. “Relax, Memphis. It was an educated guess, that’s all. I know Remmy, I know you, and I’d already thought about suggesting a similar scenario.”

“With Remmy as an employee to the campground?”

“Among other things. But to put you at ease…”

“Yes?”

In a softer tone, she said, “You’re my bestie, remember? I wouldn’t wiretap your home, and I wouldn’t pry into anything private. You have my word.”

He wanted to believe her, but Madison could probably monitor the president and the pope if she wanted to. “Describe *pry*.” He thought to add, “Describe *private*.”

“Your home is your sanctuary. I wouldn’t intrude—well, unless I saw thugs forcing you inside at gunpoint or something. Then I absolutely would monitor things while I sent backup. Other than extreme situations like that, I respect you too much to overstep.”

Her idea of overstepping baffled him, since she usually knew every move he made. “I appreciate it. Now tell me that it’s okay for me to borrow Remmy.”

“He’ll be a great help to you. Take him with my blessing.”

"Appreciate it."

"If you need anything else, we McKenzies have great resources."

Didn't he know it? "You don't have to run everything, Madison. Some of us want to do our part, too."

"Ah, got it. Okay, then." Still, she hesitated.

Ripe with impatience, Memphis asked, "Something else on your mind?"

"You really are my best friend, you know that, right? I'm super close with my family, and I'm madly in love with my sexy husband."

Memphis bit back a laugh. "Noted."

"With you, though…you get me and what I do. We can talk shop together. You're a true friend, Memphis. Thank you."

Suffering a moment of guilt for being short with her, Memphis dropped his head. Madison was brilliant and because of that she was sometimes too forward and occasionally awkward. He had to remember that, because one thing was true: "I value you as well." He'd learned a lot from her, he greatly admired her and she was special in many ways. "Thank you for putting up with me, even though I'm not on your par."

Immediately, she shook off the unfamiliar reserve and reverted to her normal confidence. "Few are, but you come closer than most. Just remember, if you ever need me, I'm there."

"Back atcha. Now, go relax and quit worrying about me."

She laughed and finally disconnected.

Ready to return to Diah, Memphis started that way, but paused at what sounded like a serious conversation.

"You may as well tell me," Diah insisted. "I already know something is going on. Don't bother denying it."

"I'll let Memphis do the honors," Remmy countered.

"Will he, though?"

"You think he'd keep anything important from you?"

"He reminds me often enough that I'm a lowly employee and he's the boss." Sounding more than a little disgruntled, Diah said, "I'm guessing our ideas of important probably differ."

"Huh," Remmy replied with a note of bogus humor. "That doesn't sound like Memphis."

"Well, he doesn't use those exact words, but it's what he means."

"I doubt it."

Memphis appreciated Remmy's loyalty. Again, he moved to join them, but paused at Diah's next remark.

"Okay, fine. I'll have to figure it out myself, then."

"Or," Remmy suggested, "you could be patient until Memphis finishes his call and then he can—"

"What? Clue me in on what little bit he wants me to know? I'm not big on being kept in the dark."

"You'd rather plow forward on assumptions?"

"Hey, assumptions have worked for me so far, but I'll admit when I'm wrong."

Remmy gave a theatrical gasp. "You've been wrong about something? Hard to imagine."

Rather than be insulted, Diah laughed. "Sure I have. Let's take you for instance."

"Uh, no, let's don't."

Of course that didn't stop Diah. "You seem so good-natured now, I have to rethink my earlier assumptions on you."

With obvious discomfort, Remmy asked, "How's that?"

"I think you're not as bad as you first appeared. I mean, I was alone in the cabin, I didn't know anyone else was showing up and you definitely have that edgy vibe, so naturally I was spooked."

Zeroing in on only one part of that, Remmy repeated, "Edgy vibe?"

"Yeah. Like a guy who's seen some shit and knows how to handle it."

"Ah…"

"I don't think much spooks you anymore."

"You're wrong. The more I've seen, the more aware I am of how fast a situation can go sideways."

Apparently finding common ground, Diah said, "Now, there's an undeniable truth."

"What do you know of it?"

"Only that people can be pretty sick and twisted." As if they shared a philosophy on life, she added, "Sometimes ignorance really is bliss."

Those softly spoken words clenched around Memphis's heart. What had she seen? The thought of Diah being exposed to cruel, ruthless people made him even more determined to shield her from now on.

"Jedidiah," Remmy began.

"Friends call me Diah."

There was a long pause before Remmy continued. "You were right about me. I'm not the kind of man you want as a friend."

"Yeah?" Sounding unaffected by his confession, Diah asked with a touch of mockery, "Because you're a *bad* guy?"

"I hope I'm not anymore, but yeah, I did things in my past that I'd rather forget."

"Who's good and bad is sometimes an obscure thing, right? It comes down to perspective."

"How do you figure?"

It was Diah's turn to pause. Finally, her tone gentler and her words reluctant, she whispered, "I knew a bad man who did a very good thing."

Memphis frowned in concern.

Remmy must have felt the same, given his reply. "That didn't make him a good man, though."

"People are complicated." In a brisker tone, she said, "If he hadn't been a bad man, he wouldn't have known anything about the situation and wouldn't have had the skills to keep me safe."

"He helped you?"

"He's probably the only one who could. I'm grateful to him for what he was and who he later became. Not many would have understood the situation, but he did. He knew what to do for himself, and for me."

Could she be speaking of Glover Stephens, the man she'd lived with? If so, what trouble had she been in that she'd needed him to save her?

Remmy murmured, "Interesting that you'd share all this now, with me."

"Right? The thing is it's a perspective some might not have if they've lived a normal life."

After a beat of silence, Remmy said, "I haven't."

"Same." She let out a breath. "I'm testing my theory on you before I share with Memphis—because he's had a different life, thank God. I'm glad about that. But given you're here now, and those shady dicks are hanging around outside, I figure Memphis has *something* going on, right?"

"I imagine there's a lot about Memphis you don't yet know," Remmy said.

He heard the grin in her tone when she said, "I'm working on it."

"Glad to hear it."

Memphis sensed a moment of camaraderie, and damn it, he envied them that. His own life had been nothing short of blessed, Diah was right about that, so whatever hardships they'd endured, he couldn't share in that. Done skulking around like a spy, he stepped into the kitchen.

Diah glanced at him, and then didn't look away even as she spoke to Remmy.

"So you and I have some things in common. I won't judge you if you don't judge me."

Naturally, Remmy agreed. "Sounds like a plan."

Moving to Memphis's side, she remarked, "If you're done running up and down the hallway, will you tell me what's going on?" Prodding him, she said, "Remmy assured me you would."

With a grin, Remmy said to Memphis, "I'll head out and keep the others in line. Join us whenever you're ready." Appearing relieved to be let off the hook, he strode away.

They both heard the door close behind him, but neither of them moved.

Expression curious, a smile teasing her lips, Diah stared up at him thoughtfully. "Got an earful, didn't you?"

So she'd known he was there all along? He didn't care. Making sure he didn't move too quickly, Memphis rested his hands on her shoulders. For such a workhorse, she had a delicate bone structure. He searched her face but didn't see indignation. "I'm curious why you'd have a heart-to-heart with Remmy."

"Are you going to pull the boss card again and tell me employees aren't allowed to socialize?"

"Since I've been *socializing* with you all along, no, I won't say that."

Her humor increased. "Then...are you maybe jealous?"

She felt very soft beneath his hands. "Little bit."

Her grin broke free. "Good. Serves you right for hiding around corners and listening in."

"Diah." He drifted his hands up her shoulders, along the silky skin of her throat, and carefully wrapped his fingers around her braids. "I hope you're not getting ideas about Remmy."

"Like what? Pretend boyfriend ideas?" Her gaze landed on his mouth and stayed there. "No. I'm not dumb. I wouldn't play games with a guy like him."

"But you don't mind playing games with me?"

She smiled. "With a guy like *you*, I think it's going to be fun."

Fun? Here he was, tortured by thoughts of having her, and she dared to smile up at him with humor. Recalling Jodi's advice, he asked outright, "Are you making moves on me?"

"I think I am." The second the words left her, she went on tiptoe and pressed her mouth to his.

Not about to waste the moment, Memphis cradled her closer to maintain the contact, prolonging the kiss while his thoughts spun out of control and his body warmed. What he wanted to do? Easy.

He wanted to open his mouth over hers, taste her, stroke his hands over her body, even bend her over the table and—

"Wow," she whispered, breaking the contact by half an inch. "Again."

He brought her in for full-body contact, deepening the kiss until they both breathed harder. Her glasses were in the way, going askew until he thought they might fall off her face.

With her hands on his chest, she curled her fingers in reaction to the kiss before sliding them up and around his neck.

Damn. All day, it had seemed his timing was off. Now was no exception.

"Diah." It took a lot of effort on his part, which was strange since Memphis couldn't remember getting so carried away so quickly. He enjoyed women, everything about them, but never before had a kiss seemed so…intimate. Like it was more than just a kiss. He brushed his thumbs over her cheeks. "I hate to do this, I really do."

"Explain *this*," she breathed. "Because if you mean kissing, I enjoyed it an awful lot."

Hell, he enjoyed it too much. "This, as in calling a halt." *For now.* He smoothed a hand down one of her braids, then straightened her glasses until they sat perfectly on her narrow nose. "Don't forget that I have goons working outside, plus I have a detailed plan to enact with Remmy, and several things that I need to explain to you."

"Right." Urgently, she kissed him once more, this time using her tongue to devastating effect and scorching him with her enthusiasm. Then, completely on her own—because he wasn't much help—she stepped back. "I needed that."

Memphis had no idea what to say. He was too busy fighting elemental urges to come up with a reply.

Gathering herself, Diah heaved a deep breath, let it out slowly and turned businesslike. "Okay, first things first."

Anticipating all the questions she'd ask about the

notorious plan he'd mentioned, as well as what he had to explain, he tried to clear his head.

She surprised him by asking, "We'll be doing more kissing, right?"

Fearless, that's what she was. Oh sure, she'd been taken off guard by Remmy showing up. And from day one her wariness had been easy to see. Yet, she stayed in the campgrounds despite any worries, and that impressed him. *She* impressed him.

And now, with complete candor and honesty, she admitted to wanting personal involvement. "I vote yes." To punctuate that, he put another quick kiss to her mouth, straightened her glasses once more and gave her a smile.

"Great." Wearing a look of satisfaction, she pulled out a chair and dropped into it. "Then feel free to put explanations to me last on the list. I mean, who knows what those creeps are plotting, and Remmy probably thinks he's invincible so you'll need to keep an eye on him, too, plus I'm stuck in here, anyway. Since it's your cabin and you have to come back, I'll get all my answers soon enough."

Remarkable. "You don't mind? You swear you'll stay right here?"

"I won't budge. Tuff and I will kick back, relax, but hey, don't leave me hanging too long."

While she was so agreeable, he said, "Thank you for going along with the pretense of Remmy staying in your cabin. I agree with Remmy, since I witnessed their caution with him already."

"It's a good idea, so I don't mind." She dug her key from her pocket and tossed it to him. "I didn't leave anything private laying around, but don't even think about touching my laptop or going through my things."

"I wouldn't."

"Memphis?"

"Hmm?"

"Thanks." She played with the end of one braid, her gaze steady. "I know you're trying to watch out for me, even though I haven't given you much reason to care, and I appreciate it."

That made two times today that he'd gotten gratitude from remarkable women. Maybe he should buy a lottery ticket.

But first, he had a few things to get in order.

DIAH WAITED UNTIL he was gone, then she gave up her careless attitude and bolted to the window to watch. Once Memphis and Remmy were engaged in talking to the crew, she bolstered her courage. "Do it now," she told herself. "You'll have at least a few minutes before he returns."

Full of skepticism, Tuff tilted his head.

"It's fine," she argued. "I have to do this."

The dog didn't look convinced.

"Damn it." Turning away, she trotted down the hall and peeked into Memphis's office space, which had once been his bedroom. Going through that, she entered his bedroom. Thanks to her, it had turned out beautifully and he now had a lot more room.

The connected bathroom was especially nice with a roomy shower and masculine touches that she felt sure Memphis enjoyed. Of course, a woman could easily pretty it up—and what did that matter? The only woman around was her and she didn't plan to use his shower.

Would be nice, though. Did girlfriends, even the pretend kind, get to shower with their boyfriends? Memphis wet and soapy...she had the visual from the day they'd met still seared into her memory. It'd be nice to reenact it, with full participation involved.

Maybe she should make that another stipulation of her cooperation with whatever scheme he had brewing. She wasn't unfamiliar with schemes. Over the years, Glover had executed numerous schemes to elude danger and keep her safe.

She ran her own scheme now, to search the campgrounds until she found the clue she needed. Whatever it might be. Wherever it might be hidden.

Lord, it did feel like an impossible task, but what choice did she have? Give up? Continue hiding? No. She was twenty-four now and ready to start living a real life, one without bogeymen from her past.

Trying to be methodical, she peeked into his bedroom closet, this time pushing his clothes out of the way to see the shelving behind them. So. Many. Books.

He hadn't lied about reading.

On impulse, she pulled out a hardcover and saw it was by Stephen King. No, thank you. Judging by the creepy cat head on the cover, she'd have nightmares if she read it. She pulled out a paperback with a badass-looking dude on the cover. Curious, she read the back and discovered it was a romance featuring a special agent written by April Hunt. Interesting.

Grinning, she slipped it back into place.

Next, she found a sci-fi, and then a comedy, something on trees, a few on wildlife, financial investments… He literally read everything!

Realizing how much time she'd just wasted, she rifled quickly through his clothes, the shelf at the very top of his closet, and a box that held an album of old photos, a few small mementos and a batting glove. Talk about eclectic. The closet scored a great big zero. Not a single clue to tell her who Memphis really was, and why he'd decided to buy the campground.

Under his king-size bed she found a rifle. Drawing back in surprise, she clunked her head on the frame. While she rubbed the spot, she stared at the weapon. Instinctively, she knew the thing was loaded, even though her knowledge of rifles was pitiful.

Worried about getting caught—and anxious to get away from the deadly weapon—she hurried back to the kitchen window. She was just in time to see Remmy unlock the door of her cabin and stride in as if he owned the place. Memphis, damn him, stayed behind talking to the crew. She assumed he did that to ensure no one followed Remmy.

But damn it, Memphis was the one she trusted, not Remmy. He should have gone along to ensure her privacy. For all she knew, Remmy was going through her things…the same way she was going through Memphis's. That realization caused her only the slightest twinge of guilt.

Fortunately for her peace of mind, Remmy quickly returned with a bottle of water, as if he'd only gone in for that reason. She had to admit, it was good cover and a casual way to indicate that the cabin was his.

One of the men immediately questioned him, and Remmy gestured at the cabin with a smile. Memphis did his part, nodding now and then and laughing at something Remmy said. The other man did not look amused, but he did seem appeased.

They had no idea that she, a woman, had actually moved in there.

Since they were all still occupied, she rushed back

to her search but still didn't find anything of interest. She even went through his dresser drawers, and in one nightstand she found a Glock. The man had too many weapons, in her opinion.

She was grumbling about that when she spotted a bag, peeked inside and found an unopened box of condoms. Okay, that was…interesting.

A receipt fell out. Curious, she read the date.

He'd bought them *today.*

Sitting back, she stared at the condoms and wondered just why he had them. Precautions, just in case? Or did he figure she was easy?

Blowing out a breath, Diah accepted the truth: she'd jump his bones right now if he wanted, so maybe having protection around—at least that type—was a good thing.

Struggling to keep her thoughts on track, she reentered Memphis's old bedroom space, which was now his office. He hadn't yet furnished this room and was using a folding table for a desk. Atop it were a few pens, scattered papers and power cords from where he'd unplugged his laptop. A cabinet was arranged against one wall but the drawers wouldn't open.

To Tuff, she said, "If only I'd learned how to pick a lock."

He looked away, somehow appearing judgmental.

Frustrated, she paced back to the main room. Lo and behold, there on the coffee table in front of his couch was his laptop.

Disbelieving, she inched closer.

She could almost picture Memphis sitting on the soft, tan leather sofa, his feet propped on the dark, heavy table, maybe the TV on a sports program and a drink nearby, while he worked online.

It was a cozy image.

A long time ago, she would have imagined herself snuggled up on the couch beside him, a throw blanket over her legs, her head resting against his shoulder.

Sadly, she'd given up on fairy tales when she was fourteen years old.

Tuff had trailed her as she'd pried through Memphis's things, but now he pushed past her, jumped up to the cushions, snuffled around and made himself comfortable for another nap.

"You slug. You've slept the day away."

"Fft." He barely left enough room for her, making her smile.

"Mooch." Squeezing in next to him, she continued to stare at the laptop.

Did she dare?

Memphis had said he was techie, right? Who knew what awesome things he might have on there? Things that would give her a few clues about his real reasons for owning a campground.

Not for a second did she think he'd bought the place as his livelihood. Not a guy like Memphis. Not a scorching-hot, super-smart, talented, funny and capable guy with protective instincts and kindness galore. It didn't fit.

No, he was up to something. She'd really like to know what.

Giving in, she reached for the laptop, opened it and stared as the screen flickered to life.

THE SECOND THE alert sounded on his phone, Memphis knew his mistake: he'd not only left his laptop accessible to Diah, he hadn't locked it, either. In his defense, when he'd left that morning, he hadn't guessed that Remmy would be over, that she'd get spooked, that he'd end up stashing Diah and her dog at his place, or that she'd kiss him, making him forget his usual precautions.

Yeah, that kiss had pretty much blown most rational thought.

Now all his thoughts were on sex with Diah. He seriously had to get it together.

Naturally, she'd take advantage. He'd expect nothing less considering her behavior since arriving. Just that morning she'd been taking apart the floor in one of the rentals to look for something.

Enough. It was past time he got some answers from her.

It took all his concentration not to take off immediately for his cabin. Instead, he moved away from the tree where he'd casually studied the men, watching their habits, memorizing how they moved while pretending to be a mere spectator. He had a knack for recognizing small things, like a certain type of gait, how a man shifted his arms or turned his head.

Now, after watching them, he could pick them out of a crowd even if they were disguised.

He'd also listened in on idle conversation. It didn't take a specific talent to figure out that Ed was in charge with Vic, Charlie and Syd following his lead. Presumably, then, they all worked for Otto, with Ed having seniority as the oldest.

Glancing at his phone and opening a mirrored screen to his laptop, he saw exactly what Diah was doing. Damn. She'd gotten right to the heart of things.

Concerned that she'd come stomping out of his cabin at any minute, he called out to Remmy, "I have some paperwork to do so I'm heading in. If you need anything let me know."

Ed said, "What if I need something?"

Miserable prick. "I assumed you and your men would bring everything you'd need with you." He smiled. "Isn't that how it's usually done?"

"Oh, I see. Somehow Remmy is better than us?"

Remmy snorted. "Was there ever any question of that?"

"He lives here now," Memphis said. "You gentlemen do not."

"We weren't invited."

Pushy bastard. Memphis showed his teeth in a not-so-congenial smile. "Once we open, you can register the same as anyone else." He hoped that'd be the end of it.

Apparently not.

He heard Ed ask, "You still got your place in town, Remmy?"

Silence seemed to descend on the area. Memphis looked back to see Remmy stalking toward Ed, his posture aggressive. *Well, shit.*

"Why," Remmy asked in a near growl, "do you give a fuck where I live?"

"Screw you. It was just a question."

Of course Remmy didn't relent. He went right up to Ed and invaded his space. Immediately, the other men clustered closer as backup.

Not that Remmy appeared to care. He kept his attention strictly on Ed as if the others didn't matter.

Given what he knew of Remmy, maybe they didn't.

The situation was literally saved by the arrival of the limestone.

Grumbling that they weren't yet ready, Ed broke eye

contact and retreated. The other men followed him. Remmy stood there, all but heaving in his agitation—until he glanced at Memphis. Then he grinned and left to greet the truck.

So it was all an act?

Clearly, there were facets to Remmy's personality that he had yet to discover. Right now, though, it was Diah who concerned him.

Without obvious haste, he went to his front door and—at the last second—chose to sneak in.

Silently, he turned the knob and swung the door open. "Hey."

Diah nearly bounded off the couch, badly startling Tuff. In one agile leap the dog came to her defense, legs stiff, scruff up, lips pulled back, then he realized it was Memphis and went all goosey in relief, rushing forward with his tail going wild.

With Diah standing there, the laptop still open before her, Memphis stepped in and clicked the lock into place behind him.

While she shifted in apparent uncertainty, he knelt to give Tuff a few pats to put him at ease. "Good boy. Always ready, aren't you? You were up in a flash and I swear, Tuff, that vicious look scared me." The dog jiggled all over. "Yes, it did," Memphis said in a goofy voice. "Such a vicious dog. So scary."

Tuff loved it.

Diah huffed.

Keeping his voice high, Memphis added, "If I'd been up to no good, you'd have changed my mind. Such a mean doggy. Yes, you are." The praise seemed to work, because when Memphis finally stood again, Tuff happily returned to the couch to continue his nap.

The silliness with the dog had given Diah time to regroup.

She stood there glaring at him over her glasses. "You're snooping into my life."

So she'd go on the attack? Nice ploy.

Reasonably, and with a touch of irony, he pointed out, "You're snooping through my things."

A flush colored her skin, and with the rosy glasses perched on her nose she looked decidedly pink. And really, he shouldn't be thinking about pink, not when he was imagining her naked. Damn it, now he felt his own skin flushing but for a whole different reason.

"What else did you go through?" He glanced down the hallway and at the door he'd left open to his office and bedroom, and somehow he already knew. "I hope you didn't disrupt anything."

"Like a rifle? A gun?" She folded her arms defensively. "Box of condoms?"

Mimicking her pose, minus the attitude, he leaned back on the door, yet he couldn't help grinning. "I'm a decent shot but could use more practice. You?"

"I despise guns."

"I see." But he didn't. Instead of getting answers, more questions cropped up. He had to believe that eventually she'd give him answers. "I bought the condoms today when I went out for Tuff's treats."

"They sell those with pet supplies?"

"No, smart-ass." She did keep him amused. "You should see yourself. Hair in braids, round glasses in place, guilt all over your face, but you want to brazen your way through things with accusations."

Brows coming together, she dropped her arms and

jabbed a finger toward his laptop. “You’re all up in my business!”

Going on a hunch, he said, “Your laptop has similar info on me.”

Her mouth dropped open before she caught herself and offered a swift denial. “It doesn’t!”

“Only because you aren’t as good at it as I am.” He held her gaze. “Admit it. You tried.”

Looking mulish for only a moment, she huffed. “Fine. I tried to figure out what my *boss* is really up to, because I’m certain you aren’t just the owner of a campground.”

“You sneer well,” he said, enjoying her and oddly turned on. She was sharp, brave and far too daring. If he’d been a different man, someone more like Ed or, God forbid, Otto, she could be in big trouble right now. “I haven’t seen your laptop, by the way. I just assumed you’d done your own checking.”

She gasped again. “You *lied* to me.”

“Let’s call it a bluff.”

“Let’s call it a lie!”

“Considering what you’re doing, all this outrage is a little ludicrous, don’t you think?” He nodded at his open laptop. “As to my research, I wanted to know who my star employee is, because you’re here for a reason and it has nothing to do with a job.”

“Had nothing to do with condoms, either.”

Oh, she was quick. He liked it. He especially liked that with him, she had little to no reserve. “Not at first. But now? I’m thinking it might.”

Indecision held her for far too long, then humor made her lips quirk as she looked away.

“Are you going to smile?” Drawn to her, Memphis

pushed away from the wall, then bent down to see her averted face. "You are."

"It's ridiculous." She fought to keep her lips stiff. "We're yelling at each other and we're both terrible."

"You did all the yelling. I've been the epitome of a reasonable adult."

"*Too* reasonable—and it makes my Spidey senses tingle. It's not natural." As he reached her, she softened, her beautiful eyes filling with confusion. "My business is private."

Cupping her face, a face that showed him a dozen different emotions, he said, "I haven't shared with anyone. So you know, I think it's admirable that Glover turned his life around for you." At least he hoped that was true. After hearing her with Remmy, he thought it was.

Not quite believing him, she asked, "What are we doing?"

He wished he could remove her glasses.

He wouldn't mind removing her clothes, too—and he could just imagine how she'd react to that thought. "I'm about to reassure you."

"Sounds interesting." Relaxing against him, she said, "Go for it."

"I don't think you're terrible. I think you have a goal, one that I don't yet understand, but it's obviously important to you. Also, I'm not terrible..." He hesitated, but fair was fair. "And I have a goal as well."

She dropped her forehead to his chest. "Fine," she said. Her arms came around his waist, her thumbs hooking in his waistband at the small of his back.

It amazed him that she could be so antagonistic one moment, and then familiar the next. So far with Diah, he rarely got the expected. It was refreshing.

"So tell me, Memphis. Who's going to go first?"

Damn. It would probably have to be him. He was considering the pros and cons when he heard a commotion outside. Scowling, he went to the window, well aware of Diah following him. One of the workers, Vic or Syd, was cursing a blue streak and holding a bloody hand. "Damn it."

"Go on," Diah told him. "Tuff and I can entertain ourselves."

"Stay off my laptop."

"Spoilsport."

He wanted to trust her, but didn't, so he snatched it up and carried it with him as he went out the door. He could hear Diah's quiet laughter behind him, and though this was all serious business, he couldn't quite stop smiling.

CHAPTER SEVEN

SEVERAL DAYS HAD passed and nothing much had come of her girlfriend status. Sure, on that momentous day a week ago, Memphis had gotten sidetracked with the goofy worker who'd cut his hand. Since one of the other workers drove the accident-prone guy to the hospital for stitches, Memphis had pitched in to help finish the work.

It was an eye-opening experience watching him labor. He could pretend to be no more than a desk jockey interested in his computer, but his stellar bod told a whole different story.

Typing and using a mouse did not give a man biceps or pecs like that. It did not turn his shoulders into boulders or his abs into a washboard.

Remmy had taken Memphis's active role in stride, but the roughest-looking of the three men had seemed very nonplussed by it. Their conversation didn't reach her, but it appeared they'd expected Memphis to play chauffeur—not strip off his shirt, run heavy machinery, rake and shovel.

The dummies had underestimated him. She could have told them he wouldn't leave the campground with only Remmy to watch over it.

Since that afternoon, they'd each been avoiding the other. She assumed Memphis was as reluctant to share his secrets as she was, because he hadn't mentioned Glover and she certainly hadn't brought it up.

If he would go first, and tell her everything...but then, he probably felt the same about her. Someone would have to show trust first. Diah wanted it to be him.

After completing her search of the first cabin, she'd finished repairing the floor so it was as good as she'd found it, and then she'd gone through all the other cabins as well.

She hadn't found a thing, but the cabins were now all spick-and-span and ready to be rented.

Memphis had kept busy interviewing potential employees for a few other positions, and in the process he'd started assigning job titles. He deemed Diah as the official maintenance technician, and Remmy as the custodian.

Sable Feigley, a stocky, fifty-something woman with a bum leg that gave her an unsteady gait, was now the official camp store manager. Sable had a disagreeable personality and distrusted everyone, but she also had experience for the job. She would officially get underway when they opened, and until then she'd help Memphis figure out what the store should carry, how much stock to order and what to charge.

Diah would have grumbled about that, except she didn't know diddly about the camp store. In her few visits to the campground ages ago, she'd never, not once, gone into the store. Wasn't like her family would have let her spend money when they barely let her out of the camper.

Brooding, Diah realized that Memphis had been busy with Sable for three afternoons in a row.

So much for their sharing—and pretending to be together. Secrets she understood, but now she was starting to feel insulted. When she'd kissed him, he'd seemed interested enough in the mock-relationship stuff.

Or maybe it was her own overblown reaction to him that made her think so. What if she'd put him on the spot, and he'd agreed under duress just to sidetrack her? A humbling conclusion that completely soured her mood, but what else could it be?

The sun was setting and he was still in the store doing God knew what. How long did it take to figure out supplies for such a small building? Good thing Sable was old and mean, otherwise Diah might be jealous.

"You look like a thundercloud."

Gasping, she whipped around to face Remmy, one hand over her heart. She'd been so busy staring at the stupid camp store, she hadn't heard him approach. "Don't sneak up on me!"

He merely gave her a look. "Jumpy as you are, you should learn some situational awareness."

Glover had told her that many times over. It had been his biggest complaint; her fear and lack of instincts had always worried him.

Flippant, she asked, "How does someone learn that?"

Taking the question seriously, Remmy sipped his Coke, then gestured for her to join him on the steps to his cabin.

Unsure how he planned to instruct her, she waited for him to sit first, then took the step above him and braced her elbows on her knees. It was cooler today so she'd worn her hair loose, letting it cover her neck. Her extra-large sweatshirt hung to midthigh over her skinny jeans.

Tuff squeezed up around Remmy and accepted the

affection he offered. "You could start by focusing a little less on Memphis. Whenever you're outside—hell, even when you're in your cabin—pay attention to everything."

He had actual advice? Well, she wasn't a fool. She'd be glad to learn from him. "What else?"

"Never listen so closely to one thing that you tune out everything else." He glanced back, shook his head with a laugh and said, "Like that. You're so absorbed in what I'm saying, someone else could sneak up on you and you wouldn't know it."

She flushed, realizing that she'd been staring. It was a damned curse. "Sorry."

"Hey, it's not a problem except that when you're so focused on hearing me, you miss other things."

"So… I shouldn't listen to you?"

"Listen, but stay aware of other things. Like Tuff does. Look at him." Remmy scratched around the dog's ears. "He looks like he's in heaven, right? But if a twig snaps, he hears it and tunes in long enough to figure out what it is." Remmy gave it some thought, then said, "We could practice if you want."

Every day now she'd chatted with Remmy. She was starting to like him, yet he still made her nervous. He was just that type of guy, the type she'd been taught to recognize and avoid. "How?"

"You sit here and I'll go behind the cabin. I'll sneak around one side or the other and you have to figure out—"

Shaking her head, aware of her heart already tripping, Diah said, "No sneaking up on me." Just the thought of it made her anxious. "I get way too jumpy."

"Diah." Sympathy made his brown eyes appear even

darker. "Whatever you're up to, you know you should be better prepared."

"I'm not up to anything," she lied.

"Baloney. I see it and so does Memphis."

She winced. "No, really, I..." Yeah, better to just let that go since she clearly couldn't lie well enough to convince him. "I don't like being startled."

"No one does, so stop blushing. Besides, I'm not going to jump out and scream *'boo,'* I promise. And you have Tuff here with you. Odds are, he'll let you know which side of the cabin I'm on. It'll just be practice, that's all."

So many times she'd disappointed Glover. Remmy wasn't anyone special to her, but still, she didn't want to disappoint him, too. "If you deliberately scare me," she warned, "I'm going to be pissed."

Grinning, he put his Coke aside. "Promise I won't."

Anxious, Diah stared at him. "What do I do?"

"Sit right there if you want."

"Nope." She immediately shot to her feet and went down the steps.

Remmy ran a hand over his face. "How the hell do you..."

"How do I what?"

"Nothing." He started walking away.

"No, you don't." Diah took a few quick steps after him. "How do I *what*?"

Put upon and not bothering to hide it, he asked, "Live on your own? Snoop around the campgrounds?"

Feeling defensive and not sure what to say, she tried to wipe all expression off her face.

"Right. That's what I figured." He reached out and

gave a light tug to a long hank of her hair. "Listen for my cues." Again, he walked off.

Idly, Diah smoothed her hair. The playful way he'd touched her left her confused. Sliding her fingers over the lock, then flipping it over her shoulder, she stared down at Tuff. "Are you ready?"

Unconcerned, the dog rested his snout on his paws.

"Where is he, Tuff? Do you hear him?" She stepped out to better see both sides of the cabin he was staying in, wondering from where he'd emerge. Her gaze bounced left to right, waiting.

Nothing happened.

"Remmy?" she called. No reply. Again, she looked at Tuff. He lifted his head and listened. Something rustled to the right and she shouted, "Aha!" as she stared in that direction, but then from behind her she heard a different sound.

She turned, but didn't see anyone. Her hands trembled. What if something had happened? What if he was playing this game and there were actual dangerous people around?

Another sound, like the snapping of a twig, had Tuff sitting up to listen. Even though the dog didn't appear concerned, it left Diah frazzled.

Damn him, he toyed with her. "Remmy," she demanded, moving to the left to see that side of the cabin. *"Answer me."*

"I'm here," he said from the right.

Didn't matter that he spoke calmly or that he stood a good ten feet away. Her hands clenched and she shouted at him, "Swear to God, my heart almost stopped."

Unlike Glover, he didn't show disapproval. "You knew it was me. All you had to do was listen."

He sounded so calm that it calmed her, too. "I tried, but you were making noise everywhere."

"That's how it happens, hon. No one sneaking up on you would announce it. They'll try to confuse you." He went for his drink, took a long swig and then said, "Let's try it again." He walked off once more.

Diah wasn't at all sure that she wanted to keep up this game, but she definitely wanted to get past her anxiety, so she made herself play along.

Now that she understood how Remmy would do this, she drew a few deep breaths and tried to calm her rioting heart. She'd never understood how kids could play hide-and-seek.

She waited, but didn't hear anything. A minute passed, then another. Tuff yawned, stretched out on the step and closed his eyes. *Don't focus on the dog*, she told herself. *Keep listening. To everything.*

A slight rustling of leaves came from the left, then a bird emerged, pecking at the ground. Realizing she was staring, she quickly looked away. Funny, but she could hear herself breathing.

A few seconds later, a small rock landed to her right and she knew Remmy had thrown it. Maybe to get her investigating that area and then he'd come from the left. Or...did he expect her to assume that and go left, then he *would* come from the right?

Just listen. Biting her lip, her gaze constantly moving, she heard a sound behind her, quickly turned—and found Remmy several feet away, smiling at her. This time she only jumped a little.

"Good job." He stepped up and patted her shoulder. "I circled behind two other cabins to get around you. Remember, you have to listen everywhere, to everything."

Blushing again, this time over his praise, she asked, "Is that even possible?"

"It is. We'll keep practicing and soon it'll be natural for you." Suddenly, he went still and stared toward the campground entrance. In that same calm tone, which now held a note of gravity, he said, "Grab Tuff and go get Memphis. Don't talk in front of Sable, but let him know we have company."

Her jaw worked but nothing came out. Remmy gave off an unconcerned vibe but she still felt his urgency. Finally, she squeaked, "Company?"

"It's fine," he told her without looking away from the entrance. "Now go." He headed back behind the cabin, this time in total stealth mode.

Well, hell. Rushing, she grabbed up Tuff's leash and hustled with him toward the small block building that would serve as the camp store. She kept looking back but she could no longer see Remmy. The damn sun had faded behind the mountains, and heavy shadows stretched out everywhere.

With a quick tap at the store door, she opened it and stepped in. Overhead fluorescent lighting showed Sable hunched on a stool behind the counter, browsing through a computer with papers stacked beside her and a pen in her hand.

Memphis walked up and down the shelves, adding sticky notes here and there. "Canned goods will go here, bottom only to help stabilize things." He added another sticky note, finally looked up, and seeing Diah, he said in an even, amicable tone to Sable, "Finish getting those prices for me. I'll be back in a minute."

Sable narrowed mean eyes on Diah, made a rude

sound and stretched. "I've got two left to mark, then I'm out of here. It's getting late."

"Of course. Leave the notes there on the counter. Lock up when you leave." He reached Diah, took the leash from her hand and stole a quick kiss from her lips. "Come on."

MEMPHIS HAD GOTTEN to know Diah better than she realized. The second he saw her, despite her forced smile, he knew something was wrong. They'd barely cleared the door when he asked, "Where's Remmy?"

Keeping her voice low, Diah said, "He told me to tell you we have company."

Anticipation ran through him, hastening his steps. "He's near the entry?"

"I don't know," she said in a rush, hustling to keep up with his long strides. "He told me to get you and then he disappeared into the woods behind my cabin."

"I see." Impatient to join Remmy, he dug out his key and handed it to her. "Go into my cabin and—"

"Enough with the orders. We were supposed to talk and instead you've been avoiding me."

"Just as you've been avoiding me."

"No, I—"

"Diah." They really didn't have time for this now. "You know where I am every minute of every day. All you had to do was bring it up."

She glared at him.

"Right." He knew exactly why she hadn't mentioned it. "You didn't, because then you'd have to explain a few things, too."

"I have more to lose than you do."

"And more to hide?" Her flush said it all. Patience,

he was finding, wasn't always a damned virtue, especially after those kisses they'd shared. She'd apparently backed off that idea, though, and he wasn't about to pressure her. "We've both been busy," he said, giving her a reprieve—for now.

She nodded fast. "And we've accomplished a lot."

He'd spent time installing more surveillance near the entrance. Hidden trail cams and microphones so he could pick up nearly anything. Each night for a few hours he watched the feeds, seeing the occasional car go past, a few animals hunting. In the morning he checked them again on fast-forward, finishing before Diah was up and about.

And he'd researched her more, as well as Otto's operation. Hotel, his ass. Otto Woodall did a sight more than rent out rooms, he'd bet his life on it. How much more, that's what Memphis needed to find out. If his visitors were Ed and his cronies, as he assumed, now might be his chance.

Diah stopped and propped her hands on her hips. "If you'd only tell me what was going on, maybe I could help."

He took her arm and continued her on toward his cabin. "Right. Because you're all about sharing."

"Unfair! You said we'd talk but haven't."

"And once I tell you everything, you plan to do the same?"

"Well, no. Probably not *everything*." She dared to look regretful, then offered as an olive branch, "But maybe some."

Some was better than none, he supposed. "Deal. You share a few tidbits and I'll share a few."

Her scowl darkened.

Yeah, no one liked to be strung along with half-truths. Going for expedience, he said, "So how about you *please* wait in my cabin with Tuff so I can see what's happening, then we'll have dinner and discuss things?"

"Dinner," she repeated with skepticism. "I suppose you'll ask Remmy to join us again so there's no chance of discussing anything important?"

Is that what she thought he'd been doing? God, no. Including Remmy had been his insurance against coming on to her. He wanted Diah to make a move, as she had before, so there'd be no question of what she wanted.

And because... Hell, he didn't have another good reason except that things were moving too fast and it worried him. For her, but for himself as well. He wanted to trust Diah. He *needed* her to trust him.

He supposed they had to start somewhere.

"Tonight will just be us." Saying it made his muscles twitch. Without spelling it out—to her or himself—his body reacted to the idea of being alone with her, in the evening, in his home.

Anything and everything could happen. Somehow he'd have to keep it in check.

She sized him up with a look. "So we'll finally play the whole boyfriend/girlfriend thing?"

Keeping it in check just got very dicey. "End the inquisition and go into my cabin right now, and I'm pretty sure you can convince me to play."

With a roll of her eyes, she grumbled, "Fine," and took the leash from him. "You better not keep me waiting too long, though."

"My laptop is no longer accessible to you. I trust you won't break anything trying to hack it?"

With a snarky smile, she said, "Scout's honor."

Not the least bit reassured, he said, "Lock the door behind you." He watched her go inside, and after he heard her click the lock into place, he broke into a stealthy jog while taking his phone from his pocket. Melding into the trees, sticking to the shadows, he put his phone on dark mode and then texted Remmy. Who's visiting?

Ed + 1

Hmm. Easing from tree to tree as silently as possible, Memphis texted, Where r u?

Remmy appeared with a finger to his lips, indicating that Memphis should be silent.

Damn, he was good.

Pointing toward the entry road, Remmy drew his attention to two shadowy figures creeping along. Memphis blended into the outstretched branches of a Douglas fir, but kept his eyes on the men. Though they'd dressed in dark clothes with hoods up on their sweatshirts, he recognized Ed and Charlie by their physiques and how they moved.

He wanted to see what the men were up to, how far they'd intrude and what they'd do once there.

However, he wasn't willing to let them get anywhere near Diah.

He was deciding how to proceed when they all heard the closing of a truck door, then an engine starting.

Startled, the two men ducked for cover—coming in Memphis's direction.

Well, shit.

Going perfectly still, grateful for the darkness of the woods, he waited. Luckily, Ed and Charlie didn't go far from the road, choosing to hunker down behind scrub bushes and rocks. Seconds later, the headlights of Sable's truck danced across the winding road.

Ed said, "What the fuck. That's not Osborn or Remmy, so who is it?"

"No idea," Charlie answered, then growled, "But I can find out."

"Otto wants to know everyone coming and going from this place."

"Maybe we should follow her?"

"Not a bad idea." As soon as it was clear, they both stood and headed back toward the entrance. To follow Sable. To then…what?

Question her? Intimidate her?

Not happening. Hunkered low so they wouldn't see him, Memphis used his phone to activate an alarm on one of the cameras. It sent a red beam of light across the road ahead of them and started loudly chirping and flashing.

"What the fuck?" Ed grabbed Charlie back. "Are we fucking being recorded?"

"I'll smash it," Charlie said, hefting up a thick broken branch from the ground.

"Don't be an idiot." Ed jerked the branch from his hands and tossed it. "Hide your face, for God's sake!"

Obeying, Charlie pulled his hood farther down to better conceal himself. "If we don't hurry, we won't be able to follow the—"

"Forget it. I don't want some fancy security thing taking my picture. We'll figure it out later. Probably just a new employee or a repairman or something. Come on, we'll take the long way around through the woods."

Cutting entirely too close to where Remmy stood, the two men lumbered through the woods with a lot of noise.

Memphis didn't take chances, so he watched through other camera feeds on his phone until they reached the main road, trotting along like two very out of shape dupes to where they'd left their truck.

"Coast clear?" Remmy asked.

"Yeah, they're driving off." He clapped Remmy on the shoulder. "Thanks for being here." Without his help, Memphis wouldn't have dared taken his attention from the men to watch the video feeds.

Remmy knew about the cameras because he'd helped to keep an eye on Diah while Memphis installed them. He'd worried, even then, that Diah would sneak out on her own while he was occupied, and he'd wanted Remmy available to dissuade her until Memphis finished.

"Neat trick, making it go off like that." Remmy moved closer to see the camera that would now have to be moved.

"You can get damn near anything these days." Memphis deftly removed the small camera, scowling as he tried to figure out where to put it now.

Rubbing the back of his head, Remmy looked around, too. "You have others up, right? Let's look at it again in the morning when there's more light. In fact, it might not be a bad idea to get better lighting out here."

"This place is turning into a money pit." Grumbling wouldn't help, though. He was elbow deep in his plans and no way could he pull back at this point. Memphis blew out a breath.

"Shouldn't be too complicated. The poles are in so we could probably just change out the single lights on top for doubles and that'll help."

Anything involving electricity concerned him. "I'll need an electrician for that."

"Nah. Diah and I can handle it. It's not that complicated."

They walked on while Memphis considered that. He wanted Diah to befriend Remmy because he'd be a good ally for her. Backup when Memphis wasn't around. Someone who understood her…

"It's not like that, you know."

Memphis said, "Hmm?"

"I like her, but I'm worried for her. Whatever she's up to, she's out of her element. She might be a workhorse as you said, but she's not cut out for danger."

"I agree, yet she's pressing on, no matter what."

"True. I don't get it. I don't trust it."

Hearing what he didn't say, Memphis asked, "But you trust her?"

"For the most part, yeah. I don't think she'd do anything to screw you over, and I'm more certain that she wouldn't hurt anyone. Those are the top concerns, right?"

Top for Memphis was her safety. He'd rather she, as Remmy put it, *screw him over* than get hurt in whatever scheme she had going right now.

Remmy suddenly grinned. "She was jealous of you spending so much time with Sable."

"Ha! She should pity me. That woman is depressing and disagreeable, but she has experience running a camp store and I don't, so it seemed logical to hire her."

"You don't worry that her personality will chase people away?"

"I spoke to her about that. I nicely explained my expectations on customer service. She frowned even more and told me she damn well knew how to treat people and I shouldn't worry about it."

Remmy laughed. "I assume you researched her?"

"Yes." How was he supposed to carry through on his plans if he constantly got distracted with other people's problems? Especially since it seemed everyone had a sad story. "She's lonely. Her husband died two years ago." Of course, that had bothered him. "They had a store together and for twenty-five years they'd worked side by side. This will be her first foray back into the workplace. Overall, I think she'll do an adequate job and it'll be good for her. Get her out and about instead of sitting at home, lonely."

Remmy gave him a funny look. "Diah will win her over."

"Or she'll throw her out." Memphis grinned. "Sometimes I think she considers herself the one running this place."

"She's a little bossy," he agreed with a smile, but it didn't sound like an insult. "Probably comes from being on her own."

Memphis thought it also indicated Diah's role in her relationship with Glover. He could almost picture her as a teenager playing as host, housekeeper, shopper and organizer. From what he'd read about Glover, the man hadn't been domestic, yet he'd managed to settle into a routine with Diah.

For Diah.

As they neared his cabin, Remmy paused. "It's late."

"Well past dinnertime." Now to explain.

"Diah's waiting for you. She's probably at the window watching us right now."

"I'm sure she is." He could actually feel her attention on him. "About dinner—"

"Not tonight. I want to grab a sandwich and kick back with a movie. You two should enjoy an evening alone."

Memphis still wasn't certain that'd be a good idea. "You're not going out for food?"

"Not unless you need me to. Now that we know Ed was poking around, I'd rather stick close. He's likely gone for the night but why take chances?" Remmy looked at him a minute, then said, "It might not be a bad idea to get Diah to stay with you, at least until you can put a few more security lights outside her place."

Which would definitely cause her to ask questions. "Motion-activated would be good. A lot of elk and deer are around right now, but still..."

"A bit of unsolicited advice—level with her. I assume you'll have involvement with Otto, so she needs to know the risks."

"Probably." With Diah's penchant for sneaking around, he should probably go ahead and make the first move on sharing.

With a slow grin, Remmy said, "Pretty sure you can handle things with Diah, but if you need any help let me know."

Someone else might have been offended, but Memphis laughed. He felt confident in most things but this particular woman definitely kept him on edge. "I might tell her you said that." Remmy's eyes flared, causing

Memphis to laugh again. He walked off, leaving the other man to wonder how serious he might be.

Proving she'd been watching for him, Diah opened the door right before he reached it. She started to speak and Tuff pushed past her so he could greet Memphis first. He caught the dog's collar so he didn't get past the door, then gave him a few rubs.

It was a nice welcome, even with Diah frowning and Tuff slobbering. A woman and a dog. He could get used to this. "Do you think he needs to go out?"

Tuff answered with a single bark.

Giving up, Diah huffed and went back for his leash. Once she'd fastened it to Tuff's collar, they walked off the deck together with Memphis urging her toward the back of the house.

For now, Ed and Charlie were gone. If they'd circled back, an alert would have sounded on his phone. Still, it'd be a better habit to use the back, away from prying eyes...just in case.

They stood together in the near-total darkness. Memphis realized he needed more light here as well. By design, he'd left many of the areas dark both to economize and offer privacy to the campers. During busier times, campers would light the area with bonfires, torches and the silly lights some liked to put on their awnings.

Most who'd choose to come here would appreciate the shadows.

They heard a noise and Tuff, who'd been in the middle of doing his business, lifted his head. A curious red fox paused under a stray beam of moonlight, its little nose lifted to the air, its long, fluffy tail trailing behind.

Tuff gave his patented quiet, *"Fft,"* and the startled fox darted away.

Memphis had already tightened his hold on the leash just in case Tuff took offense to a visitor, but the dog didn't give chase. He finished his business, kicked at the ground a little and came forward to sit, staring in the direction where the fox had gone.

"You," Memphis said, stroking along Tuff's neck, "are a remarkably kind and well-mannered dog."

"He's had to be." Restless and not bothering to hide it, Diah moved around the area, not going far but looking at the next nearest cabin, a massive rock, up at a tall tree and then at the sky, where stars began to show.

In that moment, Memphis wanted her so much he wasn't sure what to say.

"Sometimes when we were camping, Tuff and I would be so silent that animals would get really close. Luckily, none of them were aggressive."

For him, that visual was almost intolerable. "Dangerous."

She put her foot against that large rock and pushed, but of course it didn't budge. "I have bear spray."

Bear spray. So basically, she had no protection at all.

"Never saw any bears, though." Adjusting her glasses, she stared off at nothing. "It's so silent tonight."

"Sometimes." No sooner did he say it than an eerie screeching started, like the sound of a frantic baby or a wet cat.

"Good God." Diah jumped closer to him.

"The fox." Because he couldn't resist, he put his arm around her.

That diverted her really fast and she stared up at him in question.

What a stare she had. The glasses didn't blunt the

impact of her gaze one iota, but if it made her less self-conscious about staring, he didn't mind them.

He just wished she didn't feel the need to wear them with him.

"Boyfriend move," he explained. "All the boyfriends do it."

"Okay." She eased closer still. "You're sure the fox isn't hurt?"

He didn't have a guarantee, but what he said was, "I studied up on it. First time I heard it, the hair on the back of my neck stood on end. Sounded to me like a banshee wailing or demons coming through the woods."

Her eyes widened. "Gee, thanks for sharing that."

And…then he couldn't resist brushing a kiss to her forehead. "I'll protect you," Memphis whispered. "It's what a boyfriend would do."

This time she laughed, shouldering into him playfully. "Since Tuff appears to be done, maybe we could enjoy the boyfriend moves inside?"

"You don't think it's romantic out here?"

"With wailing banshees? After you and Remmy dealt with…something? No, I don't think it's particularly romantic." She frowned in thought. "I like it when you have a bonfire, though."

"Maybe tomorrow." After he ensured Ed and his bud wouldn't sneak back in. He glanced to where Tuff had done his business, but whatever. It was too dark to see clearly right now.

Knowing his thoughts, Diah said, "I'll get it, but if you wouldn't mind, I'll wait until sunrise tomorrow."

"I need a light out here." The three of them headed back to his door.

"Agree. Even though my cabin doesn't have a door

to the back, I've been thinking of adding more light, too. Would you mind?"

She'd just made that way too easy. "I insist, and I'll cover the expense. Remmy and I think the lights along the entry should be brighter. He suggested double light heads might do the trick."

"Good idea." As Memphis got the door open, she stared toward Remmy's cabin. "Whatever's going on, he'll be okay there by himself?"

"Yes." Of that much, at least, Memphis felt certain. "Remmy can take care of himself."

They stepped inside, he closed and locked the door, and Diah asked quietly, "Will *I* be okay?"

SHE KNEW IT was a stupid question. Never, not once in her entire life, had her safety been guaranteed, and that wasn't likely to change. If she could accomplish a few things here, her odds might get better, but as she'd told Remmy, she now knew the dangers in the world. It wasn't something she'd ever forget.

After the game with Remmy, and then whatever company they'd had, she was extra jittery, more so than usual. It seemed so dark tonight, as if the stars weren't quite as bright and all the shadows were somehow closing in. Plus, the awful sound that fox had made… She shivered.

For sure there'd be no sneaking out from her cabin. Once she got inside, she planned to lock the door and stay put.

"Come on." Memphis took her hand and led her toward the kitchen, where he automatically pulled out a chair at the table for her, refilled Tuff's water dish, gave him a treat and then washed his hands.

It struck her that she'd grown used to the seamless way he did things. He rarely faltered or hesitated. He saw things to do and he did them, including taking care of her.

That was the dangerous part, far more dangerous than critters in the night.

She hadn't traveled this far, risked so much and taken so many chances just to lose her autonomy. Didn't matter how nice it was to have a guy be a gentleman or to show affection to her dog.

She had to stand on her own two feet. She had to get things done. It was time for her to get back on track.

"Hungry?" he asked.

Sniffing the air, she realized that he had something simmering in a large slow cooker. "I am now."

"First," Memphis said, "you will absolutely be all right. I want you to know that your safety is a top concern of mine."

See? It made no sense. Somehow she was losing her grip on independence. She already knew that Memphis was a natural protector, plus he was her employer, and the fact that he was the owner of the campground meant he could be liable for anything that happened.

Yet, the way he watched out for her went far beyond all that so she asked another question: "Why?"

"I care about you."

Wow. He said that like it wasn't profound. Since it wasn't at all what she'd been expecting, her astonished gaze shot up to his. She tried really hard not to stare at people, but Memphis so often took her by surprise, it just happened. Plus, once she looked at him, she could never seem to look away. "You do?"

"Pretty sure you already knew that and you're just in denial." He continued with, "I care about you and I want us to come to an understanding."

An understanding. What exactly did that mean? Still watching him, she waited.

He gave her a small smile and asked, "I have stew ready, made the way my mother taught me with beef, potatoes, carrots and onions."

Without a single blink, she said, "Sounds delicious."

"Mom used to bake fresh bread to have with it, but all I have is regular sliced bread. It's still good with plenty of butter."

Rising from her chair, she forced herself to look away from him. "How can I help?"

"Pour us some drinks?"

"Sure." So many nights now they'd shared dinner. She liked it. It was a routine sort of like what she'd had with Glover, except Glover treated her like a niece and he hadn't had Memphis's ease in a kitchen. In fact, she'd done the majority of their cooking. The majority of housework, too.

She'd wanted a home, and Glover had done his best, but it wasn't an easy fit for a man used to a bachelor life.

After washing her hands, Diah got down a glass. Knowing Memphis's preference, she poured him iced tea but chose a bottle of water for herself. He put two steaming bowls of stew on the table, along with the bread, butter and a knife.

After they'd each gotten their food ready, and she'd

taken two bites, she said, “This is great. I guess your mom is a good cook, huh?”

“Really good, but then I might be biased since I love her and I grew up on her home cooking.”

“I bet that was nice.” She could almost see Memphis as a boy coming in all grubby from playing outside, forever hungry the way growing kids were, always anxious to eat.

“It was exceptionally nice. My family ate together in the kitchen nearly every day. Mom and Dad, Hunter and me. If we had company we used the dining room, but it wasn’t often.”

“Did you have a big kitchen?”

“Big enough, I guess. Middle-class size.”

That sounded perfect to her. She didn’t think her makeshift family of mother, stepfather and stepbrother had ever sat together for an actual meal. Actually, regular meals were rarely provided. They’d lived in a more “fend for yourself” mode, meaning she’d often heated up canned soup or made a sandwich.

Memphis smiled at her again. “During dinner we’d talk about everything and nothing. Sometimes Dad would grumble about work and Mom would tell him if she needed anything to be repaired or replaced.” He paused, thinking about something that made a smile flicker over his mouth. “I always knew I could tell them anything.”

“Like what?” After adding a little more salt, she spooned up another big bite.

“Problems, questions.” He waited until she had her mouth full to say, “I remember when we had a discussion on condoms and sex and responsibility.”

Diah nearly choked. She couldn't imagine discussing something like that with family! Not only had her family not been interested in what she had to say, she'd also been too young to bring up anything personal like sex with them. Then with Glover... Well, good grief. No, they'd never discussed anything sexual.

Memphis laughed at her. "For real. Mom was big on us being responsible. No topic was taboo if she thought we could learn from it. I think Hunter was in sixth grade when he asked her about condoms. It was based on something he'd heard in school, and me being younger, I was fascinated."

"I bet." It almost made her face hot just to think about it.

"It got discussed right then and there, over a pork roast and sweet potatoes." He leaned slightly forward to share, "Dad looked uncomfortable, but Mom handled it the same way she did everything."

After a big drink and a slow breath to ensure she wouldn't choke again, Diah asked, "And that is?"

"Straightforward. Plainspoken." He settled back and his smile softened. "Honest."

She couldn't imagine such a thing, or people like that. A *family* like that. "Was your brother embarrassed?"

"No. Later that night, though, we cracked up, mostly about how Dad had acted. Poor guy barely got through the peach cobbler Mom served. Later, Hunter told me from then on when he had questions, he knew to wait until after dessert."

She started snickering and couldn't stop. For most of her life, she'd had no one to talk to. For her, it sounded like a fairy tale. Talking with Memphis was always enjoyable, regardless of the topic.

Until he asked, "What about your parents?"

There went all her humor, right out the door. It took her only a second to find a way to deflect. "Before we get into anything with me, you need to tell me about your visitors, and why it was such a problem."

CHAPTER EIGHT

To Memphis's credit, he didn't try to dodge the question. It was almost as if he'd just been waiting for her to ask again.

Did that mean he had a rehearsed explanation?

"Ed and Charlie returned, unannounced of course. I already didn't trust them, but tonight I know they were up to something."

"How?"

"Well, let's see. They parked on the road and were walking in. Why not just drive up?"

Why indeed.

"And I know it's cooler tonight, but they were dressed in dark sweatshirts with the hoods up."

That didn't really convict them of anything except being weather conscious.

"When Sable drove off, they jumped into the weeds and hid."

That bit certainly got her attention. Walking a mile in, dark hoodies and then hiding—things were really adding up. "What do you mean, they hid?"

"What I said. They ducked down at the side of the road and cowered to make sure she wouldn't see them."

Interest had her leaning forward, the delicious food forgotten. "What did they want?"

"They didn't exactly say, but I overheard them planning to follow Sable so I set off an alert and it distracted them enough that they couldn't catch up with her. After that, their plans changed and they took off."

Memphis was far too nonchalant about the whole thing to suit her. "If they were planning something, they'll be back."

"I assume so."

Flattening both hands on the table, she stood and said, "I *told* you they were shady!"

"You did, but it wasn't news to me." He waved a hand at her food. "Let's finish eating, then we'll talk."

She looked at her nearly empty bowl…and decided she was still hungry. She was also too warm. After stripping off her enormous sweatshirt and hanging it on the back of the chair—all under Memphis's fascinated observation—she asked, "Mind if I have seconds?"

"Sure." Pulling his gaze off her, he started to rise.

Diah waved him back. "I've got it." Trying to be as casual about things as he was, she refilled her bowl, then when she noticed he'd eaten most of his, she refilled his as well.

"Thanks."

"Thank *you*. You've really gotten me spoiled." Knowing her questions might lead to *his* questions, she tried to ease into things. "While on the road, sometimes all I had was a protein bar or something equally blah. Hot food like this still feels like a treat." And damn it, dinner with him was special. So far, everything with Memphis had been wonderful and unique and she enjoyed it far too much.

He watched her while saying, "I like sharing my dinners with you."

"Me *and* Remmy, usually. It's better than eating alone?"

"I didn't mind, but now that you're here I prefer your company."

A thoughtful answer. "I know how to cook, so maybe one of these days I can return the favor." The idea of playing house with Memphis… Man, how it tempted her. Not that her cabin wasn't awesome, but he'd really set his up as a home. It was organized and just messy enough to know he lived in it and wasn't too fussy. Everything felt warm and friendly, especially the man himself.

It hadn't taken her long at all to get completely used to sharing meals with him, as well as thoughts, laughter, plans for the campgrounds…

"What's your specialty?" he asked, drawing her back around.

"I don't really have one. I learned enough to get by so we…I mean *I* wouldn't starve." She didn't want to talk about Glover, or how funny it was that he mostly cooked eggs. Scrambled eggs, boiled eggs, egg salad. She'd taken over cooking just to have some variety.

Without really thinking it through, she said, "I do best with breakfast."

"Yeah?"

Grinning, she boasted, "I make a mean pancake."

"Now I'm intrigued."

How he said that, all low and sexy, caused her heart to skip a beat. "Um, so dinner—let's see. I probably baked pork chops the most. Did a beef roast or two. Baked potatoes were easiest for me." Her mashed potatoes tended to be lumpy. No reason to admit that now, though. "I can do spaghetti or chili." What else? "I got pretty good at making chicken and rice."

"You're a multitalented woman."

His continued admiration left her flustered. "I get by, and I like to think I'm self-sufficient." Unlike him, she'd had to learn by trial and error. She didn't have a mom willing to teach her, or a family interested in helping her learn new things.

Reaching across the table, Memphis gently folded his fingers over her own. He had such strong hands, his fingertips rough and warm. "I meant what I said, Diah. I like you and I like spending time with you."

Looking into his direct, heated stare, she started wanting things she couldn't have. Not now. Maybe not ever.

It was unfair of him to tempt her like this. *Protect yourself,* Glover had instructed. *Always.*

Managing a half smile, she gingerly eased from his hold. "Back atcha. You know, there's something sexy about a man who cooks." Something sexy about a man who listened, who wore a shirt that fit his stellar shoulders so perfectly, who didn't care when his hair got a little long but did care about a newly hired grouchy employee…

That brought her right back to her main concerns. "You said those men wanted to follow Sable?"

He returned to his food. "They didn't know it was Sable driving but they're interested in the campgrounds and wanted to know who's coming and going. If they'd caught up with her, they'd have figured an older woman was an easy mark so they probably would have tried to use her to get info on me."

Because he was the owner and this place wasn't exactly known for being on the up-and-up. Were they planning to use it for illicit deals? And if so, in what way?

More importantly, did all this put Memphis at risk? "If they research you—"

He shook his head. "They won't find anything other than what I want them to know, which is all superficial stuff. Remember, I'm good with technology." He bobbed his eyebrows. "I know how to hide things."

Huh. "Well, there's normal techie and then there's spy-grade know-how, right? You make it sound like you're into some real heavy-duty stuff."

Suddenly, Memphis looked around. "Where's Tuff?"

Oh, good grief, had she lost her dog? Jumping up, Diah sent her frantic gaze around the kitchen and then walked briskly into the living room—where she found Tuff stretched out on Memphis's couch, snoring away.

Something about the sight sent emotion spiraling through her. She wasn't the only one comfortable visiting here now.

Her dog had not only let down his guard, he'd also made himself at home.

Stepping up close behind her and settling his hands on her shoulders, Memphis whispered, "Let him sleep while you finish eating. I'll clean up, then we can get to the heart of our talk."

Right. The all-important talk that she both anticipated and dreaded, and that probably wouldn't amount to much, anyway. She had her secrets and he had his and that, more than any other reason, was why she shouldn't be leaning back against him, shouldn't thrill at the feel of his breath on her temple.

His mouth grazed her jaw and she heard the smile in his tone when he said, "You worry too much."

Being a realist wasn't worrying, but whatever. Diah allowed him to steer her back to the kitchen. As she sat, she marveled aloud, "I didn't even notice when Tuff left because he never leaves my side."

"He feels safe here."

True. Here with Memphis she also felt safe, even though she knew it was wrong. With him, she lost sight of other things—her goals and the ever-present danger that shadowed her existence.

In a daze of conflicted emotions, she finished her food. She badly wanted to play with that whole boyfriend/girlfriend scenario. She also wanted to understand what was going on with the campgrounds and what real purpose Memphis might have for owning it.

But sharing her life with him? Did she dare?

It wasn't something she'd ever done before. Only she and Glover knew about her past, and now Glover was gone. If something happened to her, the truth would never come out. It'd be like she'd never experienced it all, like she hadn't lived through a horrific nightmare.

Maybe if Memphis actually shared, if he told her anything substantial, she could throw caution to the wind and share just a little bit, too.

By the time they finished eating and tidying the kitchen, mostly in silence now, she still hadn't decided what to do.

"Diah." He took the dish towel from her and draped it over the front of the sink. "You've gotten so quiet."

"Thinking."

He tipped up her chin.

Oh, how she loved the way he did that. Somehow it seemed gently dominant, like he demanded her undivided attention and wouldn't be satisfied with anything less.

Whereas others hadn't wanted her eyes focused on

them—had actually been unnerved by her direct gaze—Memphis wanted it.

She knew if she chose to walk out right now she could, but there was a push-pull playfulness between them that she'd never experienced before.

Prior to Memphis, if a guy got close, she put up her guard and immediately distanced herself. Now… She stepped up against him.

His hand slid from her chin to cup her face. "What were you thinking about?"

"So many things." Her gaze dropped to his mouth.

"We're going to talk, remember?"

She traced his lips with a fingertip.

"Diah," he warned. "Behave."

"You're not my…" The words trailed off and she suppressed a grin.

"Boss? Oh, but I am."

He looked so devilish, she *really* wanted a kiss. "This is me," she said, all prim and silly, "behaving."

"I doubt it'll last, so let's get to it."

Getting to it sounded good to her.

He took her hand. "We should sit. Our talk might take a while."

They turned for the living room—and both drew up short. "Sit where? Tuff is taking up most of your couch and your chair isn't big enough for us both." She slanted him a look and tried for a little guilt. "Poor guy is all tuckered out after the excitement of your visitors."

Proving he was listening, Tuff's tail did a couple of hard thwacks against the leather, but he didn't open his eyes. "You big faker," Memphis said to the dog. "You just like to nap, don't you?"

Another tail thwack, this time accompanied by a lazy, *"Fft."*

"Basically," Diah said, "he just told you to leave him alone. I don't think he trusts you to be honest any more than I do."

MEMPHIS LIKED THIS TEASING, affectionate side of Diah, but then he liked it when she was quiet and introspective, or annoyed and bossy, too. Overall, he just liked her, everything about her. Too much.

"Clever dog." And clever woman. To get the ball rolling, Memphis pressed another kiss to her temple and stepped away. Squeezing onto the couch, he encouraged the dog into his lap—an invitation that was eagerly accepted—and got Tuff settled, half on him, half off, then he scooted over to make room for Diah. "Problem solved." He patted the empty space beside him.

"Tuff likes you." She plopped down on his free side. "That goes a long way since he's a great judge of character."

"Is that why you've decided to like Remmy?"

"*Like* him? Not sure I know him well enough for that, but I figured if you like him, and Tuff doesn't want to bite him anymore, he must be okay."

"He's very okay, and I hope you learn to like him." Memphis took her small hand in his. It was a simple touch that packed a punch.

Because everything about Diah impacted him on a deeper level. He recognized it as special whether she did or not.

Talking with her, touching her, even arguing with her, felt like the start of something important.

He wanted that, and yet there was still so much he

didn't know about her. He liked to think of himself as a calm, easygoing, pragmatic person, which meant he shouldn't be feeling so strongly about her without knowing her motives first.

"How long will you be here, Diah?" At her questioning look, he asked, "If you find what you're looking for tomorrow, will you bolt?" A worse thought occurred to him, making him frown. "Am I going to wake up one day and you'll be gone?" He didn't like that idea at all.

She took a second to consider her words. "Okay, truthfully—" As if the words struck her, she narrowed her gaze on him. "We're both going to be truthful here, right?"

"As long as it's mutual."

She agreed with a nod. "A few days ago, I would have just lied and told you a long story."

That's what he figured, damn it. "And now?"

"I kind of like the idea of having a coconspirator. At least enough to promise that if I do decide to leave, I won't sneak off. I'll let you know and give you a few days to find someone else."

Knowing Diah, how could he want anyone else? "You promised to be a girlfriend for two weeks."

She shot back, "And for damn near a week you've done nothing!"

True, and it had about killed him. He had a strong will, but she was mighty tempting. "You know I've been slammed."

"Baloney. You had time for *something*."

Did she want him as much as he wanted her? He could almost believe it. "Here's the thing, honey. I don't want to get used."

She drew back as if insulted. "Used?"

He stroked back her hair. "I keep telling you I like you, and you keep clamming up when I do."

Her jaw loosened. "So you think what? That I'll somehow take advantage of you?"

Meeting her gaze and baring himself, he said, "I think that I'm getting far more involved than you are and then if you take off, I'll be left feeling like a fool."

Her eyes flared wide behind her glasses. After a second she blinked and, abashed, glanced away. "I never thought of it like that."

With a touch to her chin, he brought her gaze back to his—and received her cheekiest grin. "What?"

"I like when you do that, when you touch me like that, I mean. It's sexy."

He gave a small laugh.

"Plus, I like it that you don't mind me staring at you. Like you said, around you I can be myself."

"Before me, you couldn't?"

She started to look away again, caught herself and admitted softly, "Everything here with you is different."

Not a direct answer, but he'd take it. "Tell me you'll stay and we'll do a lot more touching."

With a firm nod, she said, "I already committed to two weeks."

Pushing, Memphis asked, "How about two months?" Laying out valid reasons, he added, "The season will be underway, so the campground will be more settled." *And by then, hopefully you won't want to leave.*

A lot of trepidation crept over her expression. "It's been a long time since I've hung around one place for a month, much less two."

"We'll get to your reasons for that in a minute, but

look at it this way. We're rolling up on a month already and it hasn't been bad, right?"

Her mouth quirked to the side. "It's been so amazing, it almost scares me." She glanced around at his cabin, at him beside her and her dog sprawled over him. "I… I'm already too comfortable, that's the problem."

"You think it's dangerous for you to stay in one place?"

Her expression grew remote and she closed down on him.

"Diah." He turned her face up to his and pressed a warm, firm kiss to her stubborn mouth. "Before I share any of my plans, promise me a two-month guarantee." One more kiss…which led to another. "It'll help."

"Help with what?"

"Confiding in you." *Dealing with how fast I'm falling.* No again. He wouldn't do this alone. If Diah was shady, if she was only using him to get something on the property, he'd find out and deal with it.

Somehow.

Sighing, she confessed, "I'd like to trust you, too." Her gaze searched his. "I don't want to spook you or anything, but a few years ago I lost the only person I'd ever really been close with, and until you, I didn't want to chance going through that again. No one else has even tempted me."

That was more sharing than he'd dared to hope for. "You've been completely alone?"

Her shoulder hitched. "Except for Tuff but he's not big on conversation." She smiled at the dog. "He's a good listener, though."

He assumed she was talking about Glover's death.

She'd have been only twenty-two, far too young to be cut off from other people. No family, no friends.

Now she could have him, if he could convince her. "So why don't we give it a chance? I promise I'll be a good listener, too."

"I already know that." She closed her eyes, her expression pained. "This is going to sound so freaking needy, but I'm tired of being alone. I'm tired of being scared, too. I'm tired of…" Her mouth turned down. "Guarding myself against everything and everyone."

Nothing in the world could have stopped Memphis from putting his arms around her and holding her closer—not even her dog on his lap. "Then don't be alone anymore. Trust me. Stay with me."

That got her eyes open in surprise.

Right. What he'd just said sounded almost like a long-term proposition. Even a proposal. He seriously needed to retrench and fast. "Two months," he reminded her. "That's not asking a lot."

"It's asking for eight and a half weeks. Sixty some days. Too many hours for me to add up in my head."

Grinning, Memphis said, "Let's just leave it at two months for the sake of simplicity." She fit to him perfectly, resting the side of her face to his chest, her hand now on Tuff's neck, which made the dog snuffle in contentment.

In so many different ways, Memphis wanted her. To hold her like this. In bed and out. "Two months," he cajoled.

Tilting her head to smile at him, she said, "Sure. Two months it is."

His eyes narrowed. "You agreed so suddenly, I'm not sure I believe you."

"Then don't." The smile morphed into a grin. "But I meant it."

"What convinced you?"

"I don't know. I guess it's that this is all new, so I figured why not? I like having a bed at night, a door to lock and food at hand. Plus, a real shower has been pretty sweet." She wrinkled her nose. "Using sinks in gas stations or paying to shower at truck stop stalls isn't nearly as appealing."

"So hot water won you over? I should have known."

"Wash in the rain or a cold stream a few times and believe me, hot water will become a serious incentive." She lightly nudged him. "But hey, the conversation has been nice, too. The area is beautiful. I've enjoyed working and it's nice watching the campgrounds come together." She fell silent a moment. "The real clincher is that for the most part, I feel safe here."

Knowing it was private territory, he ventured carefully. "I take it you don't usually feel safe?"

"Not for a long time. But here, with the trees all around us, it feels really serene. Even at night when it's quiet and creepy, it's not too bad."

Damn. Once she knew that he planned to deliberately court trouble, he'd probably have a hard time getting her to stay. One thing was certain: he couldn't keep it from her. "That might be a problem."

"That I feel safe here?" She started to move away from him. "What? You're freaking me out looking all guilty like that."

Memphis held on to her and spoke fast. "I don't want you alarmed, but I know you've snuck around at night. It's why I gave you access to the cabins."

Her mouth dropped open, followed by the beetling of her brows. *"You..."*

"Going out alone is dangerous, so I chose to make it easier for you without intruding." He gave her compressed lips a firm kiss. "So sue me for worrying, for trying to find the least intrusive way I could to let you go about your business without risking yourself."

Scowling, she asked, "So why tell me now?"

"Because we're coming clean with each other, right? I need you to know that the purpose of the campground, my entire setup, is to find trouble before it escalates."

She straight-armed away from him, her eyes now curious, but not quite as angry, behind her frames. "The one-way windows?"

"They allow me to observe things without people knowing they're being watched."

"*I* knew."

At least she'd stopped pulling away. "Can we agree that you're a little more suspicious than most?"

"Ha! This kind of thing is exactly why I'm suspicious."

Good point.

"I'm also more astute because I've had to be." Appearing impressed, she said, "I think I get it. You want to watch people, see when they have little private convos that look shady, or if they're scheming something. You'll see when they're sizing up a mark."

A mark meaning a victim. "That's about it, or part of it, anyway." He figured it'd be best to share the rest and let her deal with it. "I have security cameras hidden everywhere—well, not *everywhere*. Not in the showers..." Although he might consider a microphone that he could activate if he felt anyone was using that building to plot. "Around the campgrounds, out on some of the trails, near the RV hookups and tent sites, and even by the lake."

"That's how you know I've gone out?"

He gave one short nod.

"Damn." Her frown was back. "You saw how nervous I was!"

"You *should* be nervous! It was a reckless thing to do." Wasn't easy, but he dredged up his usual calm demeanor. "Understand, I have no intention of spying on anyone who's going about their business, you included, but this place has a history of lawless activity."

Her eyes narrowed. "I assume drug deals and gambling. That sort of thing?"

"That, and illegal gun sales, fights, drunkenness, prostitution." And worse. "There was so much trouble here, the owner shut it down. It was already in bad shape, needing a lot of renovations." His thumb moved over her knuckles in an effort to help her relax. "I liked what you said to Remmy about good and bad guys being subjective."

"Come off it, Memphis. I can't see you as one of those in-between people."

He was, but that wasn't his point. "It reminded me of what my brother went through. He most definitely falls into the good-guy category."

"Right. Sounds to me like he's a hero through and through."

"But if he hadn't been ruthless enough to take down two men, if he hadn't been able to do what *had* to be done, another woman would have died."

Diah stirred, tipping her head to meet his gaze. "And since then?"

He brushed two fingers over her cheek, then along

the frame of her glasses. Eventually, she'd be comfortable enough with him to leave them off. And then he'd be able to see her beautiful eyes without the filter. "Let's just say the world is fortunate that he's the man he is."

"I think you're a man like that, too."

He hoped so. He despised injustice and the slow seep of apathy and cruelty overtaking society. "Hunter told me once that no one really knows who or what they are until they're put to the test. Sometimes disaster strikes, leaving behind victims and revealing survivors. We figure out the alphas, the twisted ones who take advantage and the strong ones who step up and help everyone else."

"You're a helper," she said with conviction. "You've been helping me since I got here."

"I've tried," he agreed. "You don't make it easy, though. You're so independent and hardworking, so damned fearless, you haven't let me do much."

"Fearless?" She reared back with an incredulous laugh. "Me? Not even."

Some very real hurt sounded in the denial. "You don't think so? So who is it who's been on her own, traveling from God knows where with just a tent and a dog?"

"From Phoenix, but I used to live in Colorado so that wasn't—"

Good God, she'd traveled from Phoenix—without a car? "Who marched into my campground demanding a job from a naked man?"

"I didn't *march*," she said, then added with a laugh, "or demand, and I didn't know you were naked until I spotted you."

"Singing." He could almost be embarrassed about that. "Even after you saw me, knowing we were the only two here, you didn't take off."

Her mouth twisted to the side, either in chagrin or an effort not to laugh.

Maybe a little of both.

She lightly shoved his shoulder. "You know I didn't have anywhere else to go."

A truth that broke his heart. "Since you've gotten the job, you've nearly worked yourself into the ground."

"You are such a storyteller! A little hard work never hurt anyone. I told you, I've enjoyed it."

"You don't get enough sleep."

Her brows lifted. "I sleep just fine."

"Maybe you would if you weren't out snooping around all the time."

Guilt stole her smile.

"No more, okay? I mean it." When she didn't reply quickly enough, he made it easier for her by stating, "As your boss, I'm telling you. No more sneaking around the grounds at night."

She huffed. Loudly.

Tuff gave her a look and apparently, like Memphis, he decided it was all bluster. "Your dog doesn't let much disturb him, does he?"

"If he can sleep through your audacity, then I guess not."

Was he audacious? Maybe a little. Yet, he knew prowling the grounds at night wasn't something she wanted to do, she just felt she had to. If he could help her to figure it all out, he would. "Even during the storm, you went out. That's dangerous. Admit it."

"Sure it is. But I've also done my job."

"Above and beyond." Every day, all day, she worked around the camp and it now looked very different. More welcoming than he'd ever intended. He wondered if she deliberately expended energy to block out unpleasant memories. "But from now on, I won't interfere and you won't risk yourself."

"Deal." She huffed again. "Actually, I'm relieved. I may as well admit that I'm afraid of everything."

She was always so hard on herself. "You weren't afraid of the spiders in the shower rooms."

"Yes, I was, but it needed to be done."

That made him frown. "You're not afraid of me."

She mumbled, "I probably should be."

That was as good as an admission, prompting Memphis to initiate another kiss. He started slow, his lips moving over hers until she parted them, allowing his tongue to tease. Tilting his head, he fit their mouths together, deepening the kiss, tasting her, determined to devastate her senses.

Given how she slowly curled against him, the way her hands slid into his hair and the soft moan she gave, he was successful.

Tuff protested, grumbling at them both and lumbering off the couch without much concern for who he bumped or where. When his back paw landed firmly on Memphis's crotch, he quickly shifted with a wince.

Breathing hard, Diah stared at him. "What?"

"Your dog just tried to maim me."

"Tuff would never. Look at him. He's just finding a more comfortable spot to continue his nap."

"He stepped on my nuts."

"Oh." She tried and failed to repress a grin. "Sorry?"

"I don't think you are." Stretching out his legs now

that he had a little more room, Memphis scooped up Diah and drew her onto his thighs. "You can take the dog's place."

"I'm not sure I like how you put that." Rather than seeming offended, though, she got comfortably situated. "Now what?"

"Let's talk."

"We were talking until you decided to kiss me instead."

Looping both arms around her, he said, "About Glover Stephens."

She sprawled back as if collapsing. "Guess it's my turn?"

Memphis thought she looked incredibly cute. "That's how this should work. I share, and then you share."

"All right, I'll try to be fair." She sat up and settled against him, her cheek to his shoulder, her face against his neck.

Memphis wondered if it would be easier for her without looking at him. If so, he was okay with that. "Glover is the man who helped you, right?"

"Yes."

She said nothing else, so he asked, "How did you meet him?"

Idly, she smoothed her hand over his chest. "Glover and my stepfather worked together so he was around a lot. I never paid much attention to him because they didn't want me hanging around when they were doing business. Usually, my stepfather would send me to my room." She lapsed into another short silence, then finally said, "I spent most of my time in my room, so I didn't mind, but I saw Glover enough to know he didn't like my stepbrother."

Stepfather, stepbrother… He'd get to her family dynamics later. "Why didn't Glover like him?"

With a negligent shrug, she said, "Rusty was not a nice guy."

Something in her tone put him on alert. "Was he close to your age?"

"Twelve years older, and he hated me. Whenever he could, he made sure I knew it."

Memphis trailed his fingers over her hair. "How?"

"Mostly he'd just say nasty things."

Mostly. His jaw clenched. "Glover heard him?"

"A few times, and he never liked it. He called Rusty a coward." Her fingers curled into his shirt. "Rusty argued with him, but Glover wasn't the type of guy you provoked, you know? I hadn't seen my stepfather nervous very often, but he told Rusty to knock it off before Glover lost his temper."

So all along, Glover had felt protective of her. "Did Rusty listen?"

She was quiet for a while. "Actually, later that day Rusty took it out on me."

Memphis's arms tightened. "Will you tell me what happened?"

"He came into my room…" She tucked closer to him. "I was twelve and chubby, with messy hair and acne, and I was so damned backward."

Sounded to him like she'd been neglected. It was hard for a kid to blossom when her own family ostracized and ridiculed her.

"Rusty started slinging insults at me again and… I don't know, he was so vicious about it. I was trying to pretend it didn't matter, but then he said no one wanted me around, that my stepdad barely tolerated me, and my mom would be better off if I killed myself."

Jesus. Memphis's heart thumped hard in both rage and sympathy. "What a bastard."

She lifted one shoulder. "I knew it was probably true so like a pathetic dope, I started crying. Bad move, because Rusty hated that even more than he hated me. He smacked me for it, then smacked me a few more times, like it wound him up or something. Pretty soon he was throwing me around the room, knocking over a lamp and a chair, and I was totally hysterical."

"He was a grown-ass man, hitting a child." Memphis crushed her closer, rocking her a little. "I'm so damned sorry."

"Luckily, my mom got home and she had a conniption. Rusty slapped her, too, even harder than he'd hit me. She landed flat on the floor and at first I thought she was dead."

He couldn't begin to imagine how awful all of it was for her. "She should have shot him."

Diah shook her head. "It took her a second, but even though she was dazed, Mom got back to her feet and stepped in front of me. I was just…numb. Scared to breathe, you know? A complete coward. But Mom stood up to him."

Enraged on her behalf, Memphis growled, "You were a young girl who'd been brutalized by a man. *Not* a coward, so don't say that."

She tilted back to see him. "Hey, you okay?"

"I'm fucking furious. If Rusty was here right now, I'd rip out his heart."

Her fascinated gaze searched his and he knew the

second her expression softened that she believed him. "Yeah, well. He gave up and stormed out. Mom's mouth was bleeding, her lip split, and I could see her cheek was already bruising. She told me to stay away from Rusty, but it wasn't like I'd been bugging him or anything. I always steered clear of him."

"Your stepfather should have handled things."

"I don't disagree, but unfortunately he almost always let Rusty have his way. The next day, I was sitting on the front stoop, staying out of the way like Mom said, when Glover came over. He saw the marks on my face and exploded. It was like he went on a rampage or something, shoving into the house and shouting Rusty's name. My stepfather chased him, warning him not to start anything, but Glover went from room to room until he found Rusty. I heard a lot of crashing and cursing and then Glover dragged Rusty out to the yard."

Thank God she'd had a champion. "I hope he beat some sense into him."

She shot him a look. "Wasn't like Rusty just went along. He tried not to, but Glover was determined. At the time, I didn't know what to think, but like everyone else in the neighborhood, I watched. My stepfather tried to jump in again. I still remember what Glover said."

"Tell me."

"He said Rusty was due a lesson about bullies and he was going to deliver it. He sounded so ominous, I didn't know if he was going to kill Rusty or not. He seemed old to me, you know? Rusty was big and fit, but for the first time that I could remember he looked scared. Really scared. Glover told my stepfather that if he wanted the same lesson, he'd get it."

Satisfaction burned into him. "And did he?"

"No. He lifted up his hands and stepped back, telling Rusty that he'd warned him."

"It's like pulling hens' teeth with you," Memphis complained. "What the hell happened?"

Diah laughed. "Usually, when this particular memory catches up with me, it leaves me feeling hollow."

Shit. "I'm sorry." He put his forehead to hers. "Forget I asked. I'm an insensitive prick."

Another laugh, followed by a kiss, and she said, "Here with you and your impatience, I'm finding it kind of funny."

Memphis wondered if she understood the significance of that. "So...you don't mind telling me what happened?"

"An old-fashioned ass whooping, that's what. All over the front yard with the entire neighborhood watching. No one called the cops—no one ever did in our neighborhood—so it lasted as long as Glover wanted it to. Rusty got in a few hits, but they didn't seem to faze Glover. He manhandled Rusty like he was a little kid. By the time he stopped, Rusty had way more bruises than I did, a broken nose and a couple of loose teeth. My mom didn't say a word, just stood there with her arms crossed, watching and looking smug. Then, with everyone listening, Glover told me if anyone ever bothered me again, I should let him know. He glared at my stepdad, like he was including him."

"He probably knew the bastards would come after you, since they couldn't match up with him."

A sad smile flickered over her lips, there and gone.

"I always tried to stay out of everyone's way, and after that they all avoided me, too."

He didn't like how she said that. It put an image in his mind of a lonely little girl, ignored by those who should have loved and protected her. "Your mother…"

"Eh, not to sound pitiful or anything, but she'd work all night at a club and then sleep most of the day. What free time she had, she spent with my stepfather, and Rusty was usually with them, so…" Diah rested against him again. "Mom didn't have time to dote on me, and I was okay with that. But then about a year and a half later, when I'd just turned fourteen, Rusty started acting different with me."

Memphis wasn't sure how much more he could take—and yet she'd lived through it. "He came on to you?"

"Hardly that." Brows pinched in a frown, she said, "Coming on to someone implies flirting or honest interest, right? Rusty would just make snarky comments on my boobs or butt, or he'd ask what bra size I was wearing, how far I'd gone with boys, what turned me on. He'd be as crude as he could, but he didn't touch me. I had a horrible feeling those questions were leading up to something, though. I'd look at him, and I could almost see what he was thinking."

That probing stare of hers. "So at that point he was… what? Twenty-six?"

"Yep. A man while I still felt like a kid."

"You *were* a kid. Fourteen is far from being an adult."

"Rusty said I looked like a woman." Her mouth twisted. "Seemed like my extra weight converted to boobs and butt."

Memphis growled, "At fourteen, he had no damned business noticing."

"I agree. I felt so awkward around him. He was always watching me, so I ended up watching him."

"Guarding yourself."

"He didn't like it. He'd curse at me and say I had witchy eyes. My stepfather agreed with him. They'd both swear that I stared on purpose."

Like a scared kid would provoke two grown men? Assholes.

She started to say something else, stopped herself and blew out a breath. "I never meant to stare, but sometimes it would just sort of happen."

"You were worried about them bothering you, so you kept an eye on them. Nothing wrong with that."

She gave him a crooked smile. "Except that Rusty said I creeped him out. He warned me not to look at him anymore, and if I even glanced his way, he'd blow up. He swore I was evil, that he could see it in my eyes."

"You have incredible eyes, you know that, right?"

Uncomfortable with the question, she looked away. "I know people have always told me that my eyes are different. Some have said eerie. I try not to look at people too long since it unsettles them."

Memphis snorted. "Anyone unsettled is a jackass."

"My eyes look a lot like my mother's did, but on her they were beautiful."

Her mother...who hadn't done enough to protect her, and then had died in a fire. Tangling his fingers in her hair, Memphis muttered with heartfelt sincerity, "I hope you told Glover that Rusty was hassling you again."

"I might have." She lowered her voice. "But then the house caught on fire and they all died."

For Memphis, something felt very off. Sure, that was the story—but in his gut he knew that wasn't what had really happened. Measuring his words, he asked, "You weren't there?"

He heard her heavy swallow, then felt it when her hand clenched in his shirt. "I was sleeping."

In the house that had burned to the ground? That didn't make any sense, but he chose not to question her. Instead, he waited.

"I'd gone to bed before everyone else. I'm not sure what happened, but I woke up with a hand over my mouth and someone holding me so tight I couldn't scream."

Everything in Memphis went hot, and then ice-cold. He tried not to react, not to barrage her with questions.

In a low whisper, she said, "I got pulled off the bed and across the floor." He felt her quickened breathing against his throat. "The window was open, and he dragged me out, scraping my shoulder and my spine. My shin and my heel. I thought it was Rusty and that he was going to kill me, so I panicked."

"I'm so sorry," Memphis whispered against her temple, unable to bear the pain he heard in her voice.

"It was Glover," she explained, almost like she thought she should have known it.

But how could she have? "Torn from your bed like that, of course you panicked. Anyone would."

Without acknowledging that, she said, "I guess I fainted. Next thing I knew, I heard, *'Jesus, Jesus, did I smother you?'* I looked up and there was Glover hanging over me. He kept patting my face, shaking me a little." She frowned. "We were in a truck."

His heart felt trampled. Poor Diah—and poor Glover, too. He could almost imagine the fright the man had suffered while trying to save her—and he knew, without a doubt, that was what Glover had done. It couldn't have been easy to get a girl away from a house without anyone knowing.

Whoever had set that fire had obviously wanted Diah to die, too. Unbearable. He wanted to crush her close, but he also wanted—*needed*—to hear it all so that hopefully he could understand. And maybe, whatever she needed now, she'd let him help her.

"I probably wasn't out long, because..." Eyes squeezed shut, she whispered, "I could hear the fire and smell the smoke. People were screaming, neighbors, I think, but I'm not sure." She stared up at Memphis. "I didn't know what was happening but Glover kept one hand clamped around my wrist while he drove away. He kept saying he was keeping me safe and he wouldn't let anyone hurt me. I couldn't stop crying and shaking, but then I saw him wipe his eyes, too. He looked furious, but also scared, and swear to God, that scared me even more."

"Diah." Gently, Memphis cradled her cheek. "Why do you think Glover would steal you out of the house right before everyone else burned up in a fire?"

"Because he didn't want me to die."

Screw the details. Memphis no longer cared. His only concern was Diah here and now, with him. *Safe.*

Holding her, he pressed his mouth to her ear, her cheekbone, her jaw. "I'm so damned glad he saved you."

She drew a shaky breath and nodded. “I’m glad, too. But Memphis?”

“Yeah, honey?”

“I was never supposed to tell that. Not to anyone. Not ever.”

CHAPTER NINE

MINUTES TICKED BY in an oddly peaceful silence. She'd shared her greatest secret, yet no one appeared out of the shadows. The past didn't loom up like a great destructive demon. Nothing happened at all.

Well, not entirely accurate. Memphis had happened. Big, comforting, funny and secure Memphis.

God, but he'd demolished her self-control just by being himself.

Diah didn't know what had possessed her, but once she'd started she couldn't seem to stop herself. The words had kept coming, like each one was linked to the other and there was no way to break them apart.

What had she done? All her life she'd been told that she could never tell anyone, and here she'd just spilled her guts to a man she'd only known a few weeks. The problem was that in many ways, it felt like she'd known Memphis forever.

In other ways, she discovered something new about him every day.

Drinking in the scent of his skin helped obliterate the memory of smoke.

Feeling the strength in his hold eased her shivers.

His soft voice drove out the screams forever trapped in her brain.

"My opinion?" he finally murmured, his hands moving up and down her back. "You needed to talk about it. Keeping it bottled up inside couldn't have been good for you."

Probably not. "But it was safer." That's what she'd always been told.

"Maybe. I don't know it all yet, but I do know you can tell me anything." He rubbed his fingers over her scalp, lulling her. "You can trust me, Diah. Always. With anything."

God help her, she did.

Exhausted from dredging up so many emotions, she asked wearily, "Why you? Why now?"

Even though the questions didn't make sense, he understood. "Because we click. We have chemistry. Sometimes that happens."

Affronted, she shoved back. "It's happened to you before?"

"No." He took her mouth in an oh-so-gentle, lingering kiss that felt more about comfort than sexual need. His lips played lightly over hers, brushing, pressing, teasing, from her upper lip, to the bottom, and then the corner of her mouth. "I've enjoyed women, but none ever got under my skin the way you have. I could ask you the same—what is it about you? Out of all the women I've known—"

She gave him a halfhearted slug to the shoulder for talking about *all* the women, the braggart.

"—none ever took over my brain like you do. I think about you way too often. I've made reckless exceptions for you."

"Hey!" Clearly, none of this was about seduction for him or he wouldn't keep insulting her.

He pressed his forehead to hers. "I had goals, and

I came up with sound plans and a path to reach them. Then you showed up, ogling me and pushing your way in, and I haven't been the same since."

Half laughing, she protested, "Well, I like that! You sound pretty annoyed about it."

"I'm…completely undone." He stroked his fingers through her hair. "*Undone.* Do I like it? No. Do I like you?" Against her grumbling protests, he kissed her again, not quite as sweetly this time. She felt the glide of his damp tongue over her bottom lip before he straightened. "Yes, I do. More than makes sense." He scowled at her. "Why do you think I've been finagling to keep you around?"

Like she had a clue about the workings of the male mind? Not even. "I thought it was some latent hero tendency or something."

"Latent hero tendency," he repeated, trying to make light of it. "Not me, no. Where did you go to school while Glover was removing you from trouble?"

He slipped in that question, maybe to distract her from talking about him. It wouldn't work. He *was* a hero—she knew it, even if he didn't because in so many ways, he'd already saved her.

"For the first few years I was homeschooled with neighborhood tutors. He gave me a new name and he was worried about me forgetting it, so he said I had to live with it for a while before I was around other people." Her mouth twisted. "Poor Glover. He tried to give me what he considered a well-rounded education. He wanted me to know how to defend myself, how to shoot." As always, these particular memories left her both sad and grateful. "He had a way of complaining that would make me laugh. Not at all like Rusty. He wasn't mean, but he had these high expectations that I never met."

"Maybe I don't like him so much after all."

She grinned at that heartfelt comment. Amazing that she *could* grin when minutes ago she'd been reliving the worst event of her life. Sharing with Memphis had lifted a heavy burden from her, as if she'd just shaken off forty pounds of angst.

"Glover took really good care of me. It's just that I'm no good at hurting anyone. I can't fight and although I know how to use a gun, anytime I'm afraid or feeling threatened my aim is iffy."

"He wanted you to be safe, even when he wasn't around for you."

"I knew to avoid any and all suspect situations. When I finally went to school, I didn't talk to people much outside of class. Glover didn't trust any boys. He said he knew exactly what they all wanted."

"He was probably right about that, but it doesn't mean the boys wouldn't have been respectful."

"He let me date." If that's what you could call it. "I always knew he was nearby, though. Once, even at a drive-in, when this guy and I were walking back from the concession with snacks, I spotted Glover in the row behind us." Remembering made her laugh. "I was mortified because I'd been making out and I knew Glover never missed a thing."

Smiling with her, Memphis said, "Embarrassing."

"He never said anything, though. Days later, when he sort of mentioned it, it was just to say that he wanted me to have as much of a normal life as I could, as long as I remembered that it *wasn't* normal, that if anyone knew who I really was I'd be in danger." That heavy reminder stole her smile. "I was supposed to die but didn't."

Memphis frowned. "Am I really the first person you've told?"

"The first. The only." Lightly, she traced his mouth with her fingertips. Oh, how she'd wanted that mouth, pretty much from the first day she saw him showering outside. "I have no idea if the fire was a random act of violence against my family and now they're satisfied. If not, if they specifically wanted us all dead, then someone could be after me. That is, if they even knew I got away."

"That's a lot of unanswered questions."

"Tell me about it. So many times I asked Glover, but he wasn't big on sharing details."

"He probably figured the less you knew, the better."

She nodded. "Too often, kids talk. Glover was worried I might say the wrong thing to the wrong person. Reminding me that my life depended on me staying quiet became a nightly ritual. Before bed, we'd check the window in my room, making sure it was still locked." Glad that Memphis held her, she confessed, "After getting pulled through a window, I never wanted it opened. Most of the time I couldn't stand to go near it."

"That's understandable."

"It was a weakness. To a man like Glover, everything was a weakness. He said I had to be able to go out the window if I needed to. I had to think fast enough to know if he was grabbing me or a stranger."

"Jesus."

Yeah, she'd lived with so much fear for so long, it all became a part of her. Seeing the renewed ire on Memphis's face, she moved on. "He was fanatical about the security code, changing it often and then making me memorize it. He had a plan so that if anything happened, if he didn't show up when he should, I was to do certain things, go to certain places..."

"You realize that's no way for a kid to live."

Actually, it was the only way she *could* have lived. Without Glover and his plans, she wouldn't be here now. Like her mother, like her stepfather and Rusty, she'd have burned up in that fire. "Over and over he'd tell me that saving me was the only good thing he'd ever done, that he deserved hell ten times over." *But you don't, Diah, and I want to keep it that way.*

Hearing Glover's words in her head made her heart heavy, but this time it was different.

This time she was with Memphis.

"I miss him so much," she whispered. "It's been two long years, and I still think of him every day."

"I wish I could have met him."

She smirked at that. "You wouldn't have liked him."

"You'd be surprised." Then he asked, "Would he have liked me?"

"Sure. Everyone likes you, right?" This time she stole a kiss, murmuring against his soft, hot mouth, "You're a very likable guy."

"I suppose I have my moments."

It was more than a moment. It was a lifestyle. A personality. The makeup of a born protector. If she said all that to Memphis, he'd probably think she was falling in love with him.

But that wasn't something she could do. No, definitely not.

"Glover said that if others found him, they'd make bad assumptions about me, too. He made me rehearse how I'd explain, so that I'd never forget." She curled in against Memphis, prompting him to tighten his hold again. "He said I'd have to detail just what a bastard he was so no one would convict me by association. Swear, though, I'm not sure I could have done that. Glover wasn't perfect, but he was perfect for what I needed."

Absently, Memphis stroked a broad hand along her back. "Because he knew how to hide you, how to get you a new name. A whole new identity."

"How to steal a car," she said in fond memory, then with more gravity, "how to dodge creeps who may or may not have been looking for us." How to fight, defend…and how to kill if necessary. She wouldn't share that reality, though.

Memphis hesitated, then asked, "Has anyone come after you?"

"Not that I'm aware of. There were times when Glover would suddenly move us again, from one cheap motel to another. He'd go out for a while, come back in a rush, and we'd be on the road within a half hour."

"You must not have owned much if you were able to pack up that fast."

Fear was a great motivator for speed. "For a while, we lived out of suitcases." Nostalgia settled into her bones, roughening her voice. "He bought me this pretty case with purple and pink flowers on it." She sighed. "And then he bought me clothes to go in it." Glancing at him, she explained, "At first, all I had was what I was wearing—a T-shirt and panties. I didn't even have shoes."

Memphis looked devastated, and she realized it sounded worse than it had actually been. "Those first few days were wild, but after that it wasn't so bad. He rented a room and snuck me in, then made me swear over and over that I wouldn't make a sound or open the door to anyone while he was away."

"How long was he gone?"

"Just a few hours. He came back with nicer clothes than I'd ever had. The poor guy had done a rush job trying to get everything I might need." A silly smirk took her by surprise. "Can you imagine his reaction when I started my period a few days later? *That* he hadn't anticipated. Poor Glover had to go out again and I swear buying tampons unsettled him way more than fleeing the state. He wouldn't make eye contact with me for the entire day."

Not as amused as she'd hoped, Memphis said, "What I keep picturing is how hard that had to be for you."

"It embarrassed me, too," she admitted. "But his reaction was so over-the-top that I ended up amused. I think we had our first good laugh together that day. Glover's laughter had always sounded scratchy, like he wasn't sure how to do it right. He cursed like a seasoned pro, though."

Groaning, Memphis said, "You're making light of it, but it all sounds grim."

At times it had been, but she only shrugged. "When we finally got an apartment, Glover was so proud." A specific memory made her smile. "I think that's when it really struck me that he'd turned his own life upside down for *me*. He'd given up everything—his job, home, acquaintances… I don't know if he had family or not, but when I asked he said none of that mattered and I shouldn't worry about it. He risked everything for me. How amazing is that?"

"Sounds like he did what needed to be done, no matter the cost to himself."

That summed it up perfectly. "The idea of a home was foreign to him, but for me, he made the effort. After we settled in the apartment, he got us our own legit ride, and he looked out for me, better than anyone else ever had. And unlike Rusty, he didn't hate me when I made mistakes." The emotion Glover had evoked was far more life-altering than hate. "Instead…he loved me."

Trailing his hand down to her hip, Memphis said, "I bet you were very easy to love."

Had she been? It seemed doubtful since no one had loved her before Glover. "It was such an adjustment for me. I went from being mostly ignored, to having a guy worry about me eating breakfast. If I sneezed, he wanted to know if I had a cold. He cared if my clothes fit and if they were clean. He even noticed when I was moody or down about something."

"You know what that sounds like to me? Family."

Nice that Memphis really got it. "Yes, he was my family." Her…everything. And now he was gone and she had to know what they'd been running from. *Had* to.

If people had been after them all those years, then they weren't likely to give up now. But without Glover, how could she defend herself? The only way she knew was to expose them.

"How did he die, honey? Do you mind me asking?"

"Actually, I've enjoyed talking about him." Not the tragic memories, the fear and the danger, but how Glover had cared for her. He deserved to be remembered fondly. "For a while we knew he was dying with lung cancer. At first, he was a terrible smoker, but that was something else he gave up for me. He used to say that I was good for his budget, that because of me he no longer blew so much money on drinking and smoking."

"I guess by the time he quit, it was too late?"

Diah nodded. "He started getting sick when I was eighteen. At first, he was diagnosed with pneumonia, or what we thought was pneumonia. The doctor would give him meds, he'd get better…until he didn't. After that went on for a year or more, he saw a specialist who did more tests, and we found out it was cancer."

"Chemo?" Memphis asked gently. "Radiation?"

Her heart seemed to tighten in her chest. "He didn't want to do much. He said the odds weren't in his favor anyway and he'd rather enjoy what time he had left with me, instead of fighting the inevitable." Her nose tickled and her throat felt thick, but she would not cry. She *wouldn't*. "Even then he was worried about me. He wanted to make sure I was ready, that I knew what to do, how to take care of myself and stay safe. We practiced everything and I thought I was prepared, but…"

His arms were snug around her, holding her close. "There's no way to prepare for a loss like that."

Amazing Memphis. "No, there isn't. In my head, I kept going over everything Glover had taught me. I knew what he wanted me to do, how important it was to him, so I tried to focus on that."

"He had a plan laid out?"

"Glover never left anything to chance, not when it came to me." No lie, it helped more than she could explain that she was here with Memphis, that he wasn't judging or demanding explanations. He was just with her, caring and supportive.

Feeling Tuff's attention, she glanced his way and found him watching her with concern. Usually, he'd have been on her the moment he knew she was upset, but here, with Memphis holding her, Tuff just gave a few reassuring wags of his tail.

"You're a good boy, Tuff," Memphis said, also noticing the dog's concern. "A really good boy, but I've got her if you want to sleep."

Taking that as his due, Tuff settled on his side again.

She liked seeing her dog so comfortable. "It's funny how much he trusts you."

Memphis shrugged. "Like you said, he's a great judge of character." The way his hand moved over her hip felt incredibly intimate.

Not that she minded. She actually liked the familiarity.

It seemed the most natural thing ever to be sitting on his lap like this, spilling her guts about things she'd never told to another living soul. "He died in his sleep. When I found him, he looked peaceful enough, still in his bed. The second I opened his door, I knew. The air felt…empty. There'd been plenty of times when I'd worried, when I'd opened his door thinking he might be gone, but then he'd smile at me and we'd talk quietly. I'd ask if he needed anything and he'd remind me to be brave."

"I imagine that felt like pressure at times."

"Only because I'm usually a coward—no, Memphis, don't shake your head at me. It's true. I wish I could've been half as brave as Glover."

"You can't compare yourself with a man who'd lived life on the rough side."

"Maybe not." But she still did. "He should've been in a hospital, but even at the end, after he'd gotten weaker and so thin, he wouldn't go. From the day he got the diagnosis, his every thought was for me." She rubbed her tired eyes, displacing her glasses then had to situate them again. "I knew that when he was gone, everything would be different."

"I hate that you went through that alone."

Sympathy was a luxury she'd rarely had. "Before I could even call anyone, I had to go through his hiding place just as we'd practiced. There was plenty of cash, probably stolen or earned doing illegal things before he took me. He'd left a note with the money saying it was safe and I could spend it without worry of being traced." That was a huge admission to make, something she'd never thought to share. "There was a new ID, too. Over the years I'd gone from Diah Wilson, to Jedidiah Stelly, then to Jedidiah Stephens."

Memphis frowned. "So you haven't used Diah since you were a kid? It's an unusual name. Is it safe for you to use it again?"

"I think so. I look way different now than I did back then."

"Except for your eyes."

She shrugged. "Like I said, I used to be chubby and stared too much."

"I bet you were an adorable kid."

Silly Memphis. "Believe me, I was completely forgettable. Even though my eyes were always an unusual color, my face is a lot different now, thinner and obviously more mature. Plus, the tinted lenses help to hide the color. I've only worn these with you, but I have them in other shades with different-shaped frames, and I have some colored contacts but they've always bothered my eyes."

"One day," he said seriously, "you won't wear them with me."

"Oh, you think so?" she teased.

He traced a finger around the frames. "Not when we're in bed," he assured her. Before she could get too heated over that sensual promise, he asked, "If Glover left you money, why don't you have a car? Why aren't you living somewhere safe and enjoying life?"

Knowing she owed Memphis at least that much, Diah sat up and faced him. "That's what Glover wanted. He left instructions for me to get on the road and keep going."

Frowning, he asked, "Until you got here?"

"Actually, this wasn't part of his plan." She almost winced with that admission. "Glover wanted me to make my way to New Mexico or Texas, then I was supposed to lay low for at least another year, preferably longer, to live off the money he'd left me before I attempted getting a job."

"But...you had jobs."

"Yes." She often felt guilty for not following Glover's instructions to the letter. "He died two years ago. I've traveled during that time, always on the move, and yes, I worked different jobs while trying to convince myself to follow his plan."

"Yet, here you are."

"Here I am," she repeated quietly. "Because I couldn't do it. I couldn't keep running. Always looking over my shoulder, always being afraid—that's no way to live." And she wanted to *live*. She wanted that so much.

His hand cupped her cheek. "I agree."

Relieved that he understood, she let out a breath.

"That doesn't explain why you don't have a car."

Sharing an uncomfortable truth, she said, "The idea of trying to steal a car, switch out tags, stay in seedy places again..." She shook her head. "What little courage I had died with Glover, but I didn't exactly feel safe traipsing onto a car lot to buy something, either." In so many ways, she'd remained a coward.

"You felt safer *hitchhiking*?"

Understanding his disbelief, she explained, "I didn't. Mostly I took buses and the occasional hired driver. I've gotten a lift a few times when Tuff and I could ride in the back of a truck, and only from older women. I sometimes stayed in motels when dogs were allowed. Not foolproof, I know, but it got me here."

Instead of giving her a hard time, Memphis asked, "So why stop here? Why not follow part of Glover's plan and make your way farther south?"

"How can I get on with my life when my whole family was murdered? They wanted *me* to die, too, but I don't know why, or who did it, or if they still see me as a loose end." Her lips felt dry, her palms damp. "I don't think I've ever said all of that out loud. It's always just been in my head, but I *need* to know everything." Like who did it.

And why Glover felt he had to rescue her—only her. Was he somehow involved?

Her thoughts churned. Talking about it made it feel so real. "It probably has something to do with a job Glover and my stepfather were involved in together. They answered to other people, bigger people, but I never knew much about it."

Memphis tipped up her chin so he could study her eyes. "What about Rusty?"

"He worked with them often. He wasn't a regular, but he wanted to be. He was always trying to prove himself, maybe especially to Glover."

"He was still afraid of Glover?"

She nodded. "Definitely. Maybe that's why it was so important to him to measure up."

Memphis relaxed his hold on her. "What does all this have to do with my campground?"

He was such a sharp guy, she should have known he'd catch on right away. "Hidden with the money, the ID, the instructions on what I should do and the prearranged plans he had for his burial, was info about this place. It was buried at the bottom of his belongings, maybe not meant for me. I think it might've been something he was researching. There has to be a reason he had it, though."

"Like what?"

"I don't know. That's the frustrating part. I just need time to look. Would you mind if I continued searching the grounds when I'm not working? I swear I won't break or steal anything."

"That's not my concern." Gently, Memphis kneaded her shoulders. "You can search wherever you want, as long as you don't endanger yourself. That means no prowling around at night." He added tentatively, "I'll even help you look if you—"

"No." She hated to deny him, but she had no idea what she might find, if she found anything at all. Something incriminating against Glover…? No, she wouldn't share that, not even with Memphis. She'd never want to tarnish the memory of how Glover had cared for her. "Promise me that you'll leave the searching to me."

"All right," he agreed, "but I want some assurances."

That didn't sound promising at all. Maybe it was her own uncertainty at play, but she heard herself say, "Like what? If you're looking for a big payday, forget it. I doubt there's any extra money to be found."

The press of his finger to her lips silenced her. "That's a shitty insult, one I don't deserve."

Though he spoke in his usual calm tone, his gaze was blazing, his midnight-blue eyes direct. Feeling the burn of shame, she caught his wrist and lowered his hand. "You're right, I'm sorry. I don't know why I said it."

Being the amazing man he was, Memphis kissed her forehead. "You've just detailed a lot of stressful stuff. Honestly, honey, I think you were traumatized by the whole thing, and talking about it again has you off-kilter."

"You're not offended?"

"No. I just want us on the same page."

His understanding in the face of her pettiness deflated her even more. "Most of the time I have no idea what motivates you."

"Then let me make it clear. I want assurances of your safety. I want assurances that whatever you find, you'll come to me with it so I can help you. I want you to promise that you won't make a single move without me."

The demands made her laugh uneasily. "Let me guess? You also want the moon?"

He didn't share her levity. "I want us working as a team. I want you to trust me. If that's as unattainable as the moon, I don't care."

Somehow, he always got her smiling. "But *why*?"

"There's something going on between us and I want to see where it goes." He lifted a hand. "Easy."

Yeah, she sort of wanted that, too, yet to her it wasn't easy at all. "Problem."

"Let's hear it."

May as well, she decided. If he wanted to do this, she needed to do it right. "For most of my life, I didn't have anyone. Family, yeah, but they didn't..." *Care.* Her mother had tried on rare occasions, but the day-to-day stuff? She'd barely spared Diah a glance. "We weren't at all close." Such an understatement. "After they were murdered, I got incredibly attached to Glover. When he died... I can't even tell you how lost I felt. Since then, I've avoided getting close to anyone else. So what happens if we do...this—" she gestured back and forth between them "—and I get really attached to you and then you flake out and I'm left brokenhearted?"

His eyes widened a little and he went silent. She couldn't even hear him breathing. Yeah, it was doubtful any other woman had ever hit him up with that in-your-face type of question.

Ironic that he'd been pressing her, and now he sat there stunned. "Don't choke," she grumbled. "It could happen." Wasn't likely, because she'd gotten pretty good at protecting her heart. "I don't relish the idea of me getting hooked, and then you decide I'm not good enough."

"Good enough for what? Are you asking if I plan to marry you?"

Now she choked.

Seeing her expression, he smiled. "Not that I'm opposed to the idea of marriage someday. I always assumed I'd settle down and have a few little Osborns, but it's a bit soon for that, don't you think?"

Smothering a laugh, Diah gave him a playful shove and started to leave his lap.

In return, he caught her close and tipped her back so that she draped over his arm with him leaning over her. "Where do you think you're going?"

Hmm. Memphis in seduction mode was pretty damned hot. "It's late," she said, unsure if that mattered much or not. "I should get back to my place."

"Or," he said, his gaze on her mouth, "you could stay with me."

Funny how her heartbeat quickened while her breath slowed. "Stay with you?"

"You and Tuff," he whispered, while nuzzling against her lips. "Here, with me."

"Um…till when?"

"Morning."

The way he played his mouth over hers was distracting. She badly wanted his kiss, firm and damp and hot. She tried to draw him closer but he resisted with a grin.

"Agree to stay."

"You're asking me to spend the whole night?"

"Preferably in bed with me."

That sounded like a lot more fun than worrying about the past. "I suppose that would be preferable. I mean, you bought the condoms already."

He gave her a rascal's smile. "There's that to consider—but also, I want you. Have wanted you since the first time I saw you."

Oh, nice. So that hadn't been all one-sided. "Same from me, but then I saw you naked and wet."

His lips touched hers and he whispered, "I'd like to see you naked and wet, too."

Heat bloomed all through her body. "You do have that big fancy shower…"

"Exactly. I'm happy to share it with you."

Enjoying the silly banter, she said, "I mean, it's definitely big enough for two."

For a second he didn't answer, then in a rush his mouth pressed to hers, hungrily nudging her lips to part so his tongue could explore. She clung to him, pressing tighter to his body, trying to shift to get more of him.

Reluctantly, he lifted away but his breathing was ragged. "God, what you do to me."

She wanted to hit him with another witty quip but nothing came to mind. Mostly she just wanted to kiss him like that again.

"What do you need from your cabin? Not pajamas," he clarified. "You won't need those. But anything else? Maybe for Tuff?"

The dog lifted his head to give them both a lazy look.

Diah could barely think. "My toothbrush, I guess." Did she need anything else? She needed Memphis. At the moment, that was the only thing registering.

"Come on. Let's do this now before I self-combust."

"Do…?"

"Walk over to your place. Grab whatever you and Tuff need, let him sniff the grass once more, then we'll lock ourselves in and I can finally have you."

As he pulled her to her feet, she said, "Maybe I'll have you instead."

He groaned, laughed, but for once Memphis had nothing to say.

Awkwardly and with a lot of haste, he stuffed her back into her sweatshirt. Tuff decided it was all fun and games and started dancing around them, making it more difficult for Memphis to get the leash hooked to his collar.

Being in a bit of a daze, Diah wasn't much help with

anything. Her thoughts had already bounded ahead to nakedness and showers, condoms and sex…

And Memphis touching her, kissing her everywhere, moving over her—which meant she could do the same to him.

It hadn't even been a conscious thing on her part, craving to touch him, to feel his skin, to stroke her fingers through his hair, to again see everything she'd seen on that first day, but close-up and accessible.

Now that it was a reality about to take place, she knew the need had been there all along, stirring just beneath the surface. "No wonder I've been feeling extra cautious and uncertain," she murmured. "This, with you, is completely new."

"For me, too." He took her hand, leading her in a rush to the door.

Outside, the brisk evening air chilled her and she huddled into Memphis's side while he power-walked her and the dog to her cabin. It was a beautiful night, still and quiet, dark and cold.

Funny that it had seemed ominous until she found out she'd be having sex with Memphis Osborn.

She fumbled with her keys enough to get the front door unlocked and opened. First thing she did was flip on the front light so Memphis could see while Tuff did his business.

After climbing to the loft she pulled her duffel bag from the minuscule closet and hastily stuffed in panties, socks and a long-sleeved T-shirt to wear tomorrow with the jeans and sweatshirt she'd worn today.

When it came to clothes, she didn't own much, didn't want much and didn't mind doing laundry often. She wasn't anyone's idea of fashionable, but then, who cared? Memphis wanted her so she must be doing something right.

"Aren't you done yet?" he called up to her.

Earlier, after baring her soul and all her darkest secrets, she'd felt raw, but now she laughed at his impatience. Truth, her own hands were trembling with the need to hurry. "Coming," she replied.

"Not yet, but soon."

Pausing with one foot on the top of the narrow stairs, Diah snickered nervously then quickly climbed down. Darting into the bathroom she grabbed her toothbrush and hairbrush, a hair tie and some lotion. On her way out, she snagged Tuff's favorite blanket, which had the dog perking up in interest again.

"It's like his security blanket," she explained to Memphis. "We move around so much that he—"

"Moved," he corrected, his hand curving around her cheek as he zeroed in to take her mouth in a warm, firm kiss. "You moved around, but now you're staying put."

He sounded so set on that, she floundered. "For a few months," she agreed.

"For at least a few months." He kissed her again with brusque insistence. "Do me a favor and don't lock on to any plans yet, okay?"

She was just rattled enough to say, "Okay." Did he expect to control her this way? She had to admit, it wasn't a bad strategy. And besides, by the end of two months they'd surely be ready to go their separate ways…right?

And if not? Unwilling to think too far ahead—good God, two months was far enough—she shoved dog food and Tuff's blanket at him, closed her door and locked it. "Let's go."

On their fast clip back to his cabin, she couldn't help glancing at Remmy's. Only one light had shown from inside, and as she looked, it, too, went off. Without knowing why, she was glad that Remmy wouldn't know about her changed relationship with Memphis.

No sooner did she think it than Memphis murmured, "It wouldn't matter to him, so quit worrying about it."

"I work for you."

"Doesn't matter. Remmy won't think anything of it. He even suggested it."

Diah stopped so suddenly, she nearly tripped herself. "He… What… *Why?*"

Catching her arm, Memphis got her moving again. "That company we had? Remmy doesn't trust them, either. Until I get a few alerts installed around your cabin, he thought I should convince you to stay with me."

She tried to stop again, but since Memphis kept going, she did as well. "So that's why you suggested—"

"I should have remembered, but then you were finally opening up to me, and you were on my lap, and I forgot all about the bastards."

Well, that was nice. Still… "You and Remmy shouldn't have discussed me." They waited while Tuff found another spot to sprinkle, thankfully making it brief. "It's embarrassing."

"Why?"

Men could be so obtuse. "It's private, plus I've never really done this sort of thing." Seeing his expression alter, Diah shook her head. "No, don't go all shocked. I'm not saying I'm a virgin."

He let out a tensed breath.

"It has been a while, though."

Unlocking his own door again, Memphis asked, "How long are we talking?"

"A few years." Thinking she may as well say it all, Diah dredged up a nonchalant tone, girded herself for his reaction and admitted, "Actually, it was only the one time."

CHAPTER TEN

MEMPHIS HAD NEVER thought of himself as an old-fashioned guy, and he refused to believe he was clueless when it came to women's sexuality. Of course he knew women enjoyed sex as much as men.

Pretty sure every woman he'd ever been with had enjoyed herself. He'd done his utmost to ensure it.

Yet, Diah's innocent bombshell unearthed a tidal wave of possessiveness he'd never before experienced. He didn't want to know about the guy she'd been with because he already resented him.

How freaking primitive was that?

Thankfully, once Tuff figured out they were staying, he dragged his blanket to the couch, circled twice, yawned and royally dismissed the humans.

Memphis would have liked to skip the shower, but Diah had already made her preferences clear. His brain churned as he grabbed towels from the linen closet.

An almost-virgin.

Had her one and only time been any good? What were her expectations?

While he ruminated on the best course to take considering her inexperience and the fact that his blood was already rushing hot, she flipped her hair forward and secured it with a band.

And...yeah. Seeing her bent at the waist like that

tested his resolve big time. Diah didn't play it up, but she had a killer body and loads of sensuality. The natural way she presented herself only added to her sexiness.

She moved, spoke, showed a little attitude and everyone, male and female alike, paid attention.

Determined to make this, her *second time*, as memorable as possible, he clamped down on the lust and instead concentrated on prepping their shower. Deliberately keeping his attention off her, he opened the shower door and adjusted the temperature of the water, making sure it was hot enough. To expedite things, he set their toothbrushes and toothpaste inside, along with a washcloth. A five minute shower, he could handle that.

Utilizing a modicum of control, he straightened, turned—and found Diah naked from the waist up, in the process of stripping off her jeans.

Swear to God, his eyes almost dropped from his head. His cock, already twitchy, came to full alert.

Off went the jeans, which she neatly folded and set on the sink, along with a white bra. Her panties and the shirt she'd worn were bundled together, presumably for the laundry.

Adjusting her glasses, and now with her face bright pink, she stared at him defiantly. "You planning to shower fully clothed?"

"No." It took a lot of effort just to get that word out. His gaze drifted over her again and again, from one mouthwatering area to another. Her thighs were long and lean, lightly muscled. There was only the slightest curve to her smooth, pale stomach. For a double-beat of time, his gaze caught and held to the neat triangle of pubic hair before he forced his attention up to a narrow waist, her rounded breasts and rosy nipples already tight.

Breathing took concentration, but then who needed oxygen with Jedidiah Stephens standing there in the buff? Not him.

Her straight shoulders, now rigid in embarrassment, tensed even more. "Say something, damn it." Feet together, chin lifted, she waited.

"God, you're gorgeous."

Her mouth trembled, and she drew an uneven breath. "Mostly I just feel exposed, so could you..." She flapped a hand at him. "Take something off?"

Ignoring the request, Memphis stepped close and carefully slipped her glasses off her nose. "You don't need these now."

In a strained whisper, her gaze shifting away, she confessed, "Wearing them in the shower would be ridiculous, I guess. The thing is, I feel extra naked without them."

"Maybe because you are." Staying close to her, he reached back and snagged a handful of his shirt to strip it off over his head, then let it drop to the floor. Everything about her fascinated him, and since he could feel the warmth of her bare body, his thoughts just naturally turned into words as his attention tracked down her body again. "Your brows and lashes are dark, but I didn't expect—"

"Shush it," she said.

"It's just that your hair is lighter—"

"The sun bleaches it." She swallowed heavily. "Your body hair is darker, too."

Forcing his gaze away from her sex, Memphis reached for the snap to his jeans.

Diah moved in, brushing his hands aside and doing it for him.

"Careful," he warned, his breath held. He was hard enough to make the task tricky.

She must have been a natural-born tease given how slowly she dragged down the zipper…before lightly trailing her nails over his erection covered only by the taut cotton of his boxers.

His breath hissed. "Diah." Feeling like he'd waited years for her, he caught her shoulders and brought her naked breasts against his chest.

Her hot little palms coasted up his sides and around to his back. Her lips brushed his chest, then she gave him a soft love bite. "I've wanted to eat you up since that first day I saw you."

Struggling to hang on, Memphis promised, "You can do that all you want—but after." It wasn't easy with lust surging through his veins, but he smiled at her crestfallen expression. "If you really want a shower, we need to get to it because I'm a nanosecond away from having you."

Her eyes, staring into his, softened. "You mean that, don't you?"

"That I want you? Can you have a doubt?" Seeing a glitch in her determination, he offered roughly, "If you want to shower after, that's fine by me."

"Don't tempt me," she said. "I'm sweaty so it needs to be now."

To him she was perfect, her scent rich and warm, her skin soft and dewy, but what she wanted was his priority, so he reluctantly stepped back.

Wasting no more time, she hustled into the shower, leaving him to come in behind her.

Not a bad place to be, really. Wrapping his arms around her while she stood beneath the spray, Memphis enjoyed pressing his erection against that plump backside.

"This is decadent." She tipped her head back to his shoulder, her hands over his where they rested loosely at her waist. "You have so much room it's like a private spa."

Nuzzling the side of her throat, he suggested, "Stand still and I'll bathe you." Maybe if he spent a leisurely hour on that, he'd get her up to speed.

She slipped around to face him. "No way. I'd rather finish and get to bed."

"There's no rush."

"Ha! Speak for yourself."

Pretty sure that statement was for her and his dick. "Diah—"

Still going at Mach speed, she snagged the soap from the dish and began lathering up head to toe. Not in any seductive way, no, nothing like that from Diah.

It made him grin. Also made him ache because, yeah, her hands were sliding all over those incredible curves, breasts and rosy nipples, along her belly, thighs… Damn.

Diah might've kept a lot of secrets, and he imagined there were still things she hadn't told him, but she was always genuine. What she said and did was *real*, without pretense, and that really did it for him.

While her eyes were closed, her face covered in suds, Memphis stroked his hands over her wet body under the guise of helping her to rinse.

He moved his hands over her soapy breasts.

On a soft moan, she tried to turn away.

He caught her nipples between finger and thumb and lightly rolled.

Groaning, she shifted around to face him, eyes still closed and her body slippery, to kiss him hard… And wrap a small hand around his erection.

Dangerous. Trying to joke while going breathless, he said, "You're going to get soap in your eyes."

She laughed, then turned and splashed under the spray, getting some of her hair wet in the process. "If you don't hustle up, I'm going to think you're stalling."

"No," he lied, because he needed her to catch up. "Not stalling, but lingering long enough to enjoy you would be nice."

Edging around him so that he stood under the water, she grabbed up her toothbrush. "Sorry, but I'm anxious."

Memphis followed her lead and lathered up, but also asked, "Anxious as in nervous?" He didn't want that. Not that she acted nervous. Mostly she seemed bossy and in a mad rush, as if she thought the moment might pass and there'd never be another.

Fat chance. After this, he planned to have her again, preferably every day.

Twice a day if he could convince her.

"Anxious," she clarified, "as in I can barely wait. Remember, one of us has been on ice for a very long time. I have a lot of pent-up need." As if they'd been showering together forever, she vigorously brushed her teeth.

"Guarantee you I'm more anxious than you."

"Not likely," she countered while her gaze ate him up. "I'm just average me, but there's no way you don't know what a treat you are."

"Diah." He finished washing with more energy than

was needed. "There's not a single thing about you that's average."

"Maybe not my eyes," she agreed, leaning forward to rinse her brush and mouth. "And the awful way I stare."

"Your intensity is hot." Hell, he more than enjoyed it. When Diah looked at him, it was like she saw clean through to his soul. "I agree your eyes are incredible, but they're just a reflection of you."

"What a sweet thing to say." She set aside the brush and looked at him expectantly, reaching out a hand, lightly drawing her fingertips through his chest hair. "I can't believe I'm here in your shower with you naked talking about my eyes."

He was prepping his own toothbrush when her middle finger rasped over his left nipple, trailed down his abs and coasted along his dick.

A barely there touch, but lust punched hard, pushing him closer to the edge.

Doing his best, he stepped out of reach, cleaned his teeth, rinsed his mouth and proclaimed them, "Done." After shutting off the water, he opened the door and grabbed the towels, handing one to her.

"I've never brushed my teeth in the shower before. It's convenient. Saves time."

Right. Proof that he was going too fast. "Instead of rushing you, I should be pampering you. I should have washed you, maybe even got you off—"

With a heartfelt groan, she said, "Talk less and finish faster!" Barely dry, she stepped out, slipped on the floor but caught herself, tossed the towel on the vanity and headed toward his bedroom.

Damn it. "It's not a race," he called after her, almost laughing as he rushed into step behind her…where he enjoyed the show of her ass and the graceful line of her spine and the determined set of her proud shoulders.

She'd just reached the bed when he caught her. Very deliberately, Memphis tumbled her down to the mattress, his mouth finding hers, his hands catching her wrists so she couldn't incite him more.

Whether she understood it or not, she needed to catch up or their first time together wouldn't be satisfying enough to lure her back for more.

He most definitely wanted more.

This kiss was unlike any of the others, far hotter as his tongue explored, tasting her deeply. Damp skin sliding together. Body heat mingling.

He eased up, kissing her jaw, the side of her throat.

Pulling her hands free, she tunneled her fingers into his hair. "I really like your hair, Memphis. How it curls at the ends and is always a little messy."

Fitting himself closer to her, wanting all of him to touch all of her, he nudged his way between her thighs. "I like everything about you," he whispered against the warm skin of her throat while cuddling one breast.

They adjusted together, shifting, gently rocking.

Tipping her head, Diah gasped, "Get a condom."

"Not yet, babe." He opened his mouth on that sensitive spot where her neck met her shoulder, licking, sucking lightly, but careful not to mark her.

"Who knew?" she breathed.

Someone, Memphis decided, hadn't taken enough time with her. He would be different, even if it killed him. "Let's try here," he said, moving his thumb over her puckered nipple.

She inhaled a fast breath, held in heated anticipation.

After circling with his tongue, he drew her into the damp warmth of his mouth for a soft, leisurely suck.

Her body arched, and the way she wiggled against him, trying to get closer, told him how much she liked it. He switched to the other breast, treating that nipple to the same, then nipping carefully.

Making an inarticulate sound, Diah slid one thigh along his hip before she hooked a calf around him to give him a snug, whole-body hug.

Everything about this, about her, felt right on an elemental level. He wanted to take her now, and yet he wanted it to last forever.

An unsettling thought.

Savoring her, he nibbled his way down her body.

"Memphis?" Clenching her fingers in his hair, her breath coming faster, she tried to stall him.

"You smell so good." He tugged her hands away, kissed each palm and placed them on his shoulders. "I've been thinking about this forever."

"About…? Oh." She gave an audible swallow, then a soft gasp as he grazed his teeth along her hip bone, followed by a slow lick low on her stomach.

This time when her hands went into his hair, it was to stroke uncertainly.

Memphis looked up her body to her face. Her gaze was locked on him, those mesmerizing eyes heated and interested—no longer rushing him.

He took a soft love bite of her tender inner thigh and smiled. She smelled indescribably good, like the perfect aphrodisiac to fire his senses. Now that he could set the pace, he nuzzled against her.

Diah lay perfectly still except for a slight trembling.

Slowly, he spread her legs wider. She didn't resist, but she did hold her breath—until he licked over her.

Her sharp inhale was followed by a low, vibrating moan.

Nice. Lifting her now-limp legs over his shoulders, he settled in to enjoy himself, licking and teasing her swollen, sensitive flesh, lost in her heady fragrance, the taste of her excitement, the wetness and heat. With each pass of his tongue, her body shifted or twitched in growing readiness. Her breath caught, her fingers alternately gripped and stroked his hair.

She was getting closer, but not quite there yet.

Ready to push her a little more, he pressed one finger into her. She was tight but slick, her reaction a huge turn-on. While concentrating on her clit, lightly sucking, he worked in a second finger and felt her clench everywhere.

Her hips lifted against his mouth and she set the pace that worked for her. Each of her breaths came faster, deeper, building and building. He stayed with her, keeping the rhythm she liked until minutes later she bowed hard and let out a harsh groan, her body convulsing in pleasure.

So fucking hot. Memphis damn near came, too.

When her hips gradually eased back to the mattress, he sat up and fumbled for a condom. His own hands were shaking as he rolled it on, but then he'd never been this desperate for a woman.

Turning back to her, Memphis appreciated the sight of her, thighs and arms limp, eyes heavy with satisfaction, every inch of her skin flushed.

"Diah." He moved over her, kissing her hard and

finally, *finally*, pressing slowly into her. She was wet, ready… Christ, it was heaven.

Her body tensed and she squirmed to accommodate him as he went deeper, rocking a little to ease the way. He made himself pause.

"Memphis?"

He liked the huskiness of her voice after her climax. With a brief, soft kiss, he said, "I don't want to hurt you."

She wrapped her legs around him again. "Then don't stop."

His short laugh was more a groan than humor. "No, I won't. I'm just giving you time to—" Lifting into him, she took him deeper, and he knew he wouldn't last, but for now it didn't seem to matter.

She flattened her hands over the small of his back, then slid them down to his ass, trying to urge him closer to her.

Struggling to get it together, he thrust deeper, entering hcr, withdrawing, pressing in again. He whispered, "Okay?" She was so incredibly snug, he needed to hear it from her.

"Phenomenal." Her lips curled in a sexy, sated smile.

Would he ever get used to her unique blend of sass, candor and vulnerability? Doubtful.

And her eyes… He could almost understand someone saying they were witchy; he certainly felt bewitched. The difference was that he liked it, liked *her*.

Damn, but he was falling in love and there wasn't a single thing he could do about it.

He took her mouth again as he entered her, pressing deep, loving the feel of her holding him so tightly. Her reaction was swift and hot as he rocked against her, lost in the silky clasp of her body, the musk of her skin, the sounds of her pleasure and the all-consuming way she watched him.

With her legs around him, she spurred him on until he rode her harder, faster. "I knew," she gasped, countering his moves. "I *knew* it'd be like this."

So had he. They might have fought it, but from the very first moment it had been inevitable. She had to trust him completely. *Had to.* He needed that like he needed oxygen, food and family.

When she put her head back and cried out a second time, he let himself go, too, holding her tight—convinced he'd never want to let her go.

Gradually, his muscles relaxed and he sank against her, acutely aware of her smaller, softer body cushioning his. He felt cocooned in intimacy and satisfaction.

They eased into a comfortable embrace, arms and legs entwined with him slightly to her side so he didn't squash her. He touched his mouth to her temple. She returned an equally soft kiss to his shoulder.

He thought it'd be nice to hold her like that all night… Until he became aware of Tuff snuffling near the bed.

Oh, hell.

Raising his head, he looked at the curious dog and wanted to wince. This was a new one. "Hey, bud." Even saying that much took effort with the way his heart still galloped.

"Bud?" Eyes closed, her lashes resting on damp cheeks, Diah smiled. "Is that one of your usual after-nookie endearments? Seems like an off choice."

"Not for Tuff."

Her eyes snapped open. "Oh." She, too, lifted her head, saying again, *"Oh."* Then in Tuff's defense, she added, “He’s never…well, *heard* anything like that from me before.”

With a straight face, Memphis asked, “Like what?”

Fighting an embarrassed laugh, she said, “You know what I mean.”

“Groaning? Moaning?” Damn it, he was getting himself hot again. He cupped her breast and added, “Heavy breathing?”

Diah pushed him to his back and loomed over his chest. “Growling, gasping, *coming*?”

“You’re good at after-sex play.” He patted her satiny behind and asked, “Do you think he wants out?”

She turned to Tuff, who waited patiently. “Do you need out?”

“Fft.”

Softening, Diah smiled at the dog, reaching out a hand to scratch under his chin. “I’m okay, Tuff. Just a little excited, that’s all.”

As he listened to her, his furry little brows beetled, and his cars twitched forward. *“Fft.”*

“Everything is fine, I promise. You can go back to sleep.”

He looked at Memphis, back at Diah and must’ve decided all was well because he wheeled around and padded out of the room.

Staring after the dog, Memphis asked, “He won’t piddle on my floor?”

“Tuff would never! He makes it clear when he has to go.”

Memphis shook his head. “That dog is absolutely amazing.” Much like his owner.

“Yup.” She snuggled against his chest. “No idea how I got so lucky.”

Memphis put his arms around her and though she might not realize it, it was a possessive, protective embrace. Her life hadn't been lucky at all, far from it. Hopefully, now that she was here with him, that would change.

And he'd be the lucky one.

Otto Woodall—what a stupid alias—glanced in disgust at Ed. "It should have been easy to get in and out of the campground, but no. You had to fuck it up."

"I didn't know he'd thrown up security shit everywhere!" Ed protested from his position near the office entry door. "It was all new."

Or Ed wasn't as good at spotting it as he had claimed. Now he had to adjust his plans when he had little patience for delays. "Lay low for a while."

"But I'm sure I could find another way in."

If Ed hadn't been so loyal in the past, Otto would kill him now and be done with it. He leaned forward in his desk chair. "I don't want you anywhere near there until I tell you to go."

Disgruntled, Ed scowled, but of course he agreed. "Whatever you say, boss."

Exactly. Whatever he said was law and anyone in his employ obeyed—or else. "We'll leave it be for a while to avoid suspicion." Sitting back in his chair, Otto thought that what he needed from the campgrounds, what he had to fucking recover now that it would be operational again, well, it'd keep a little longer. "Once he opens for business, you can pitch a tent there and see what's what."

Expression comical, Ed repeated, "Pitch a tent? But Otto..."

For about the hundredth time, he regretted the name he'd chosen. It had been handy, stolen off a dead guy with few ties or family, but it didn't fit him at all.

The new identity did, though. He loved the power he'd acquired, the rewards he'd been given. No longer did he answer to others. He was the boss, the only one in charge, and that made everything, even the stupid name, worthwhile.

This life was better. His old life was gone for good... Or at least, it better be. He'd ensure it, once he recovered his property.

Eyeing Ed with distaste, he asked, "Do I need to hire someone else?"

"No, it's not that, it's just that I don't know shit about tents." Stepping closer, he said earnestly, "I could go there in a camper."

Fat chance. Swiveling his chair to face his office window, Otto looked out at nothing in particular. The hotel's parking lot. A few people checking in, some checking out. With a business like his, no one kept regular hours. "I'm not footing the bill on an expensive camper so you can avoid a sleeping bag for a weekend."

"You wouldn't have to buy it," Ed promised. "I know someone who has one. He'd let me use his."

Hmm. Maybe that was the way to go. A camper would give him a way to get into the park without being seen. Ed could drive while he relaxed in back. No one would know his business.

He made a decision. "Fine. Do that. But not until the campground opens."

With a note of relief, Ed said, "Yeah, sure. Whenever you want. I'll keep the guys clear of there until then."

It wouldn't be much longer, and then he'd find out

how Memphis Osborn planned to run things. In the past, the place had been used to conduct business safely away from nosy cops. These days, the hotel took up most of his time, but it'd suit him perfectly if he could step right back into that part of the operation, too. Making deals in the shadows, ironing out the details, bargaining—in person—so that he always came out ahead.

There, hidden in the trees and away from prying eyes, he could be himself again. *Not* that he missed his old life.

Not that he had any regrets over the choices he'd made.

He ran a rough hand over his face. He knew who to blame for how things had gone down, but she was long gone and out of his reach. *How* she'd gotten away, he didn't know, but every day he got better at convincing himself that he didn't care.

"Anything else, Otto?"

"Yeah." A budget campground, well off the radar, was the perfect place to deal with difficult people. You could hide anything there, even evidence of multiple murders. If Memphis Osborn became difficult, he just might have to go missing. "Get Lane up here."

"Sure thing. I'll call for her right now." Ed stepped to the other side of the room, his phone to his ear.

Out of all the girls at the hotel, Lane was the one he enjoyed the most, largely because she fought so hard to hide her fear. She looked young and ripe, and in some ways, she reminded him of another girl. *Damn it, I will stop thinking of her.*

Otto slowly filled his lungs, flexed his hands and rolled his shoulders, forcing himself to calm. Playing with Lane was one of his favorite pastimes, the perfect way to release tension. He knew eventually he'd tire of that game, and then he'd own her completely. Until then, he'd continue to have his fun.

"Uh, boss?"

Disliking that tentative note in Ed's voice, Otto turned, his hard gaze demanding an answer.

Ed shifted with uneasiness. "Apparently…" His gaze skittered away from Otto's. "I mean, the thing is…"

"Fucking spit it out."

"Lane is gone."

The words ignited his barely contained rage…and sent a queer sense of loss twisting through him. In a low rasp, he growled, "What the fuck do you mean, she's gone?"

"Her things are missing." Ed backed away. "No one has seen her all day."

Tension coiled, tighter and tighter until finally it exploded, leaving his voice no more than a tooth-grinding rasp. *"Find her."*

Jerking around with haste, Ed fled the room. Maybe hc wasn't so stupid after all.

THE NEXT THREE weeks were idyllic for Diah, the stuff of dreams, which made them sort of unbelievable. How could she trust in something that good? That peaceful and comforting?

For *her*?

No, it had never been that way. Even while living with Glover, there'd been endless worry and the drive to learn all that Glover wanted to teach her.

To make her braver. To better prepare her.

Yet, always, she'd fallen short.

With Memphis, it wasn't like that. No matter what she did, he enjoyed it. A walk around the park, count him in. A sleepless night having sex? He always aimed to please. When she wanted to try something new? Yeah, he was totally on board for that.

There were other things, too, though.

In the mood for fast food? He didn't mind at all. Her attempts at cooking? He ate whatever she served, and praised her even while giving her little tips. When she worked sunup to sundown, he was right there with her.

His friendship with Tuff…that really got to her. In her heart she knew he valued the dog as much as she did, and God, that mattered *so* much.

Whenever she asked Memphis endless questions, he always did his best to answer. When she wanted to talk about her own experiences, he was so interested that she felt truly valued.

It wasn't natural for her to be this happy, and that worried her. It was weird, like becoming a millionaire overnight or something equally bizarre. Somehow, in some way, things were bound to go wrong. She was just waiting for the other shoe to drop.

Today she'd been working with Remmy, a common occurrence, but Memphis was nearby. Always. That had to be deliberate, right? Keeping an eye on her, she knew, yet she wasn't certain why. She knew he wasn't concerned about her with Remmy. Heck, he'd encouraged her to befriend him.

He was probably just doing his own share of work since opening day for the campground quickly approached. She'd arrived here in early April, and it was nearly mid-May.

Time truly did fly when you were having fun.

His nearness now distracted her greatly. She looked at him and the ever-present lust overtook her every thought. Even after all their times together, she usually ended up rushing him and each time, Memphis found it amusing. He was fond of telling her that one day she'd learn to slow down and savor things.

One day…

But how many days did they get? Until the end of the busy camping season? And then what?

Would she pack up her gear and just walk away? The thought caused a hollow ache in her chest.

Overall, she had free rein of the campground now, which meant she and Tuff could wander before work and during her breaks, searching wherever she pleased. She knew, with Memphis's many security cams, that if she ran into any trouble or got hurt, he'd be there to help. She was no longer alone.

It was such an incredible concept.

"This one is ready," Remmy said, and she obligingly turned her mind back to work. Or tried to.

They were in the process of cleaning all the heavy picnic tables situated in and around campsites. Beneath them, cobwebs had filled with dried leaves and dead bugs. It was all pretty gross, but she didn't mind lending Remmy a hand.

Using a heavy scrub brush on a long handle, she was clearing them away—and thinking of Memphis again.

She hadn't officially moved in with him—he hadn't offered and she wouldn't have accepted if he had—but she spent every night with him. Waking with him wrapped around her was even better than the extraordinary sex.

"Want me to get this?" Remmy asked.

"What?" Diverted, she returned to her task. "No, sorry. I'll do it."

"Uh-huh." Skeptical, Remmy moved on.

Right. Since she'd started getting smokin'-hot sex from Memphis, she'd barely been able to concentrate on anything else.

There were times when she felt horrid for still holding back from him. Sadly, the need for secrets was so deeply ingrained, she couldn't quite trust herself to share everything. She wanted to, she'd even tried to, but the words wouldn't come.

Many things she'd already told him, but there were still parts—

"And," Remmy said, dragging out the word, "I've lost you again."

"Huh?" Being with Remmy throughout the day was another fun thing. She was used to working by herself, and even when she'd been on a crew, her attitude had caused most people to ignore her.

Remmy didn't. Memphis most definitely didn't.

How can I ever lose them?

"You're daydreaming." Remmy nodded toward Memphis. "Thinking about anything, or anyone, in particular?"

Grinning, she asked, "Can you blame me?" Since Memphis had removed his sweatshirt and wore only a snowy-white T-shirt that fit snugly to his oh-so-sexy bod, she forgave herself for getting sidetracked. "He is so delicious," Diah murmured.

Snorting, Remmy shook his head at her. "You have it bad."

Something she couldn't deny. She did have it bad, and she liked it. Wallowed in it.

And dreaded the day it would end.

Just then the chainsaw went silent and she glanced over to watch Memphis stacking more wood.

"It's okay, you know." Remmy mussed her hair like she was a kid, which made her frown. "Sex on the regular mellows everyone."

Sex on the... Forget her hair. Diah's mouth opened twice without a single syllable emerging. Should she deny it, ignore it or ask him how he knew?

He moved away, so the moment passed.

Determined not to let her new relationship affect her job, she turned back to the picnic table with a vengeance. Thank goodness Memphis had hired Remmy as the custodian. The table weighed a ton. Without Remmy, she would have had to crawl under it to clean it, but he'd effortlessly overturned it to make it easier. She'd concentrate on that, and not on what he'd said. In this instance, silence might be denial enough.

Forty minutes later, they'd finished every table in the area. While Remmy returned them to their upright positions, Diah used the pressure washer to clean the scarred tops. Beneath the built-up grime, she noticed different names carved into the wood. Every so often she felt compelled to trace a heart with her fingertip, or to laugh at a scratched-out, raunchy sentiment.

Obviously, some people had truly enjoyed their past stays at the campground. It wasn't fancy back then, and it wouldn't be now. A few existing porch swings, there from years ago, had been repaired, but nothing new had been added.

The April chill had faded away and the sunnier days of May were warmer. Over the past week or so, they'd put the finishing touches on everything. To Diah, it all looked pristine and she took a special sense of pride in helping to make it happen.

"Once we finish with these," Remmy said, making sure he stayed out of the spray of the power washer, "we only need to do the grills, clear out the rest of the dead brush and remove some fallen branches."

Then they'd be ready to open. With the last tabletop clean, she turned off the washer. "It all looks great, doesn't it?"

Remmy looked around. "Especially if you're into nature."

"I take it you're not?"

"I never was before, but it's peaceful here and I've enjoyed the work."

Not the best endorsement she'd ever heard. Probably a guy like Remmy would rather be in the middle of action. "I can't understand how anyone chooses to work in a stuffy office instead of being outside."

"It suits some people, but not everyone has a choice."

"I guess not, but some do." Choices. So many things came down to that.

Her stepfather and Rusty…and Glover for a while… hadn't chosen outside work or an office or any honest labor at all. Instead, they'd embraced a violent vocation of enforcement. They'd all been able-bodied men, intelligent enough, yet they'd taken the lazy and dishonorable path of brutality. With her stepfather and Rusty, it fit.

With Glover, she occasionally had a hard time reconciling the man who'd cared for her with the man who'd busted legs, maybe even killed people, just because his boss told him to.

Choices, she thought again. Life was full of them.

Remmy came closer to her. "We're not talking about accountants or secretaries, are we?"

Damn, he read her well. She brushed away a fly. "Just thinking back on some things."

"Ugly things, I imagine."

Very ugly, but she didn't want to dwell on that. "Let's just say *unpleasant*."

"All right." His gaze went over her face, then their eyes held for a few seconds.

Until Diah looked away. She liked Remmy enough that she needed to know, so she asked, "Do my eyes bother you?"

"Bother me? How do you mean?"

"You know, like do they seem creepy?"

Puzzled, he huffed a laugh. "Why the hell would you think that?"

Because she'd heard it numerous times. "So they don't?"

"Of course not. That's just silly."

That could have been an insult, and instead it lightened her worry. "So I'm silly, huh? Thanks a lot."

"That idea is, for sure. You have a direct gaze. You can pin a person in place with the way you stare."

Which was why she made people uncomfortable. She mumbled, "Sorry."

"Hey, that's a good thing. Usually, when people can't look you in the eye, it's because they're plotting something—or lying."

Hmm. Could that have been what bothered Rusty? Had he been, even back then, plotting against her?

"You're up front, Diah. I like it."

"Really?" Wow, she was two for two with these guys. "Good to know."

He crossed his arms. "I'm betting Memphis doesn't mind you looking at him."

A grin slipped into place. "No, he doesn't."

Remmy smiled, too. "Any guy who called you creepy is a dumbass."

"And that would exclude you and Memphis."

"Very true. Now back to working indoors or out—not that long ago I thought my options were limited. I won't give you the whole song and dance about the shitty childhood, but let's just say I hadn't been around many sterling role models. It was easy for me to see the appeal of the tough-guy act."

This time she didn't hesitate to look right at him. "Hate to break it to you, Remmy, but you *are* a tough guy."

"Tough enough, I guess, but I wasn't when I started. I was all bad attitude and hungry for what I considered easy cash. Sometimes it takes a good example and a little faith to make someone see the possibilities."

Interesting. "You've seen them?"

"I have—and I think you have as well."

Her eyes rounded. "We're not talking about me."

"Aren't we?" He chucked her chin—again, like she was a kid. "Pretty sure you're riding the fence, hon, and there's no reason." Arms open, he encompassed the area around them. "Possibilities are everywhere here, so I hope you take advantage and make the choices that are right for you."

She scowled…and wondered if he was right. Her efforts to uncover the truth about her family's deaths were now halfhearted at best. What had once been her top priority had quickly faded beneath carnal and emotional desire. When she had free time, she wanted to spend it with Memphis, not search for elusive clues to the past.

She'd wanted to be free, to finally feel safe.

Here, with Memphis, she did.

Giving her a second look, Remmy sighed. "You don't have to solve world peace, hon, but if you think you do, let Memphis help you."

"I can't—"

"You *can*," he stressed. "Trust me, he'd want to help, and not to come on too strong, but I'd be happy to lend a hand as well. Keep it in mind, okay?"

She was so touched by that, she had no idea how to thank him. She was still trying to find the right words when Memphis approached in his golf cart.

The wagon, now full of small limbs and debris, rattled behind him. Coming to a stop, Memphis studied each of them as if he knew he'd just cut through some tension.

Diah worked up a firmer smile to reassure him. "All done?"

"As much as I plan to do today. I'll unload all this, then get washed up for dinner. Say half an hour? I'm guessing you two are getting hungry."

Watching his mouth as he spoke, Diah wished she could kiss him. After what she and Remmy had just discussed, *not* kissing him took some effort.

Slanting her a look, Remmy grinned. "Sounds good. We're about finished here, too."

Tuff, who'd been watching them work from a nearby tree where he was tethered, barked at Memphis.

"Want to go with me, bud?"

Another bark.

Pulling herself together, Diah asked, "You wouldn't mind?"

"Course not. Tuff's good company in the kitchen."

In apparent agreement, Tuff said, *"Fft."* Because for real, they were good buddies. She loved that Tuff's circle of care had expanded.

Glad to have something to do other than blatantly moon over Memphis, she dumped the dog's water bowl, unleashed him and walked him over to the golf cart. Tuff jumped in with one agile leap, snuffled a happy "hello" against Memphis's neck and looked forward, anxious to be on the way.

Memphis took the leash and patted him. As Diah put the empty dish on the floor, he murmured low, "See you shortly."

Now, see? How was she supposed to keep bedroom activity off her brain when Memphis used his sexy voice? Face flushing in awareness, she nodded.

He'd barely driven away when Remmy gave her a light nudge.

Because she'd been oblivious to him, all her heated attention on Memphis, she stumbled. "Hey."

Laughing, he wrapped up the power washer. "It's okay, you know."

Unsure what he meant by that, Diah narrowed her eyes and stayed quiet.

"Such a hard case." He shook his head and began loading things into the golf cart they'd used. "I'm not dense, Diah. So you and Memphis have a thing for each other. So what?"

This time she couldn't ignore the insinuation. "Did he say something?"

"You know better. I'm guessing he's quiet about it to appease you." Straightening, he ran a hand through his hair, then leaned on the golf cart and studied her.

"You're human. Pretty sure you're enjoying the same things the rest of us do. No reason to hide it."

With Remmy more or less daring her, she couldn't keep pretending. "The same things…?"

"Sex on the regular."

Her jaw loosened.

Which Remmy found hilarious. Grinning at her, he said, "So you're a normal, healthy woman and you've found someone who does it for you. That's great." He quirked a brow. "No reason to hide it."

"I'm not exactly hiding it…"

"Bull. What I can't figure out is whether or not it's out of worry for what I'll think, which would be ridiculous, or because the idea of involvement scares you."

Involvement. What a weak word for everything she felt with Memphis, how encompassing it was, stealing her thoughts, redirecting her motivation and melting the layer of ice that had encompassed her heart for a decade.

Removing her utility gloves, Diah plopped down to sit on a stump. "I've never really had anyone to talk to about this stuff."

Remmy went on alert. "Uh…what stuff?"

"Sex stuff, and don't start backing off now. You're the one who brought it up."

"Your mom…?"

"Even when she was around, we didn't have that kind of relationship. Mom made sure I had a roof over my head and food to eat, but heart-to-heart conversations?" She snorted at the absurdity of it. "No close girlfriends, either." *No close friends at all.*

Uncomfortable but trying to man up, Remmy asked, "So what's the problem?"

"I don't know what I'm doing."

After a heavy pause, he lowered himself to a large rock near her. Wrists resting over his knees, he studied her. "You're not talking about sex, right? I mean, Memphis *does* know what he's doing, and he looks pretty happy to me, so I assume—" She swatted at him, but he leaned out of reach with a laugh.

The truth just sort of spilled out. "In comparison, sex is easy to the emotional relationship stuff." That wasn't entirely accurate, though. "With Memphis, it seems like it's more than just sex, only I don't know how much more. Or even how much more I'd want it to be." She ran out of steam and ended with, "See? No clue what I'm doing."

"I'd say you're probably falling in love."

Alarm shot her gaze to his. After she stopped strangling, she said, "I *can't*."

Sympathy softened his brown eyes. "Why not, hon?"

Oh, wow, that was a new tone for Remmy, gentle instead of teasing, familiar but in no way flirting. Maybe he'd make a decent confidant for the private emotional stuff—things she couldn't sort out with Memphis since it was all directed at him.

She rubbed at the corner of her eye, almost knocking off her glasses. See, this was why she shouldn't remove them around Memphis. Now there were times when she forgot she was wearing them! Quickly righting them, she stared at the picnic table. "For one thing, I can't stay here. Love means you stick around, right?"

"Can't say I'm an expert on love, but yeah, I assume you'd want to stay near Memphis. He's pretty invested in this place, and I don't mean only financially."

"He has plans, I know." Memphis spent an hour or so most evenings researching a hotel owner named Otto

Woodall, the guy Ed worked for. She didn't mind. It reassured her that she hadn't interrupted his life or his plans too much. On occasion, he'd talk with his friend Madison, too. He'd compiled an online file on the hotel, and told her he had suspicions about how Otto ran the place.

It was admirable, the amount of effort he put into caring about others.

The lowering sun turned the sky various shades of orange, from sharp tangerine to warm melon. God, how she'd come to adore the evenings here. Even the howling, screeching and yapping of various wildlife didn't alarm her as much. *Because you've given up on finding the truth.* Sad, how quickly her purpose had wavered. "The thing is, I had plans, too."

"Had?" His smile encouraged her. "Maybe your plans are changing just a little?"

With her jaw going tight, she shook her head, denying that even to herself. "They can't. *I* can't." Without the truth, how could she know when she was truly safe?

"Well." Remmy's smile faded. "You probably have a lot to think about, and even though it's none of my business—"

"Don't let that stop you."

He hesitated. "I pissed you off. Understandable. I shouldn't have butted in."

Given that she sometimes felt completely lost, she valued his input. Forcing herself to relax, she faced him. "I'm not pissed, I'm...confused. Do you mind discussing it with me?"

He hesitated again. "It's not that I mind, I'm just not sure I'm the right person for it."

"But there isn't anyone else." A sad truth.

"There's Memphis."

Her heart gave a heavy thump. *There's Memphis.* Damn, she wanted that to be true. "Don't you see, though? He and I are so different."

"And we aren't?"

Now he was just playing word games with her. "You know we aren't, not in the most important ways."

"Honey, I think we're as different as night and day. Knowing bad people and being a bad person isn't the same."

Remmy was not a bad person. She knew that even if he didn't. "Understanding the bad in people *is* the same," she insisted, but hey, she wouldn't force herself on him. "Never mind, though. I didn't mean to unload on you, especially at the end of a long day." She worked up an apologetic smile.

His sigh was hard and frustrated. "You're fine, so don't say that. I'm just…out of my depth."

"Still struggling with the whole good/bad thing, huh?"

The corner of his mouth kicked up. "Sometimes it's hard to see the difference. I envy people like Memphis, where it's all black-and-white."

"Me, too. I thought I knew what I was doing. It seemed important and…" How to explain it? "It gave me purpose, you know?" Find the truth, end the threat, finally live in peace.

"Yeah, I do. That's how I feel about being here, lending a hand and giving Memphis some backup." His smile widened. "The acts of a reformed thug. It feels good."

"Exactly." With her own humor restored, she said, "Not that I was ever a thug. A slug maybe."

"I'll never believe that."

No, she wasn't afraid of hard work, but in other ways she'd been a total slacker. "It doesn't matter. If you wouldn't mind sharing your thoughts, I'd like to hear them."

For several seconds his gaze probed hers. Funny, but Remmy and Memphis never shied away from staring into her eyes. Maybe they really weren't as witchy as Rusty and others had claimed—and as she'd always believed.

"All right," Remmy said, "so here it is. Memphis strikes me as an all-or-nothing type of guy. He doesn't play around the edges. It'd be hell for him, falling for a woman without knowing if she'd stick around."

The thought left her stricken. "You think I'm putting Memphis through hell?" Did she have that kind of power?

"I think he'd really appreciate knowing exactly where he stands. All this pretending to be only employer and employee. It's kind of absurd, don't you think?" He leaned in. "I know you two are banging."

"Banging," she repeated with a snicker. "Juvenile lingo."

"Should I have said *making love*?"

By the curl of his lip, she knew he didn't like that description much, either. "That sounds sort of dramatic and old-fashioned, doesn't it? You could just say we're having sex."

"Or you could stop trying to hide it so we have no reason to talk about it." Hands on his knees, he leaned in more. "You could just own it, then we'd all carry on, minding our own business and enjoying whatever pleasures we can."

She'd been trying to protect herself, but if Remmy was right, she'd hurt Memphis in the process. "So what do I do?" she whispered.

"That's for you to decide. Come clean with Memphis about how you feel, or keep playing games. Up to you." He stood. "I need a shower."

"And I need food." Plus, time to think. She pushed to her feet. "Thanks for the pep talk."

"You're welcome."

Smiling, she looked at everything they'd accomplished. "The picnic tables look great now." As the last word left her mouth, she saw it.

Her stomach dropped fast and heat flooded her face, making her light-headed. As she stared at the name, the edges of her vision closed in around her and she wavered on her feet.

"Diah?" Remmy was at her side in mere seconds, one hand taking her arm, the other at her waist, holding her securely. "What the hell? What's wrong?"

She blinked twice, and finally the fog began to lift, yet she still felt horribly unsteady. "I'm... I'm okay," she lied. She wasn't, not even close.

"You don't look okay." His secure hold didn't loosen. "You're white."

A deep inhale helped, at least with the dizziness. Nothing would help with the reality.

There, carved deep into the picnic table, was the name Rusty Wilson.

Her stepbrother.

She was close to finding the clue; she felt it in her bones. There'd be no giving up now, though, because she had to reconcile the fact of *when* Rusty had been here. Too many thoughts and suspicions converged at once, jumbled and yet, with a sick sort of logic.

Sensing things were about to get ugly, it would be best if she leveled with Memphis. She looked up at Remmy, gave him a wan smile and whispered, “Time for us to go.”

CHAPTER ELEVEN

MEMPHIS WAS RELIEVED when Diah and Remmy finally joined him. He hadn't yet washed up, hadn't unloaded and hadn't given a thought to finishing dinner prep. All his attention was on the young woman facing him, refusing to accept "no" for an answer.

Déjà vu, anyone? Another wannabe employee forcing her way into his campground and refusing to leave. The difference this time was the lack of snapping awareness on his part. Lane Robertson resembled a tall, ragtag, very stubborn teenager, though she claimed to be in her early twenties, same as Diah.

All he felt was sympathy, a touch of impatience and a complete lack of ability to deal with her.

"I can work with Sable. You know running the camp store 24/7 isn't a job a single person can do."

"It won't be open around the clock." He watched Diah and Remmy getting closer. The smile pinned on Diah's face wasn't quite as convincing as she might think. Something had happened. Nothing tragic, given that she held it together just fine. But *something*. He was so attuned to her in every way that he felt her moods like they were his own.

As if he hadn't spoken, Ms. Robertson continued. "Sable's a…friend, and she *wants* me to be her helper and backup."

"It's not Sable's decision. Besides, I wasn't planning two people for a single job."

"I'm cheap."

That blunt statement had Memphis reaching for rational arguments. It was obvious that for reasons of her own, Lane wanted to be here, yet he had no idea if her reasons would clash with his. "Look, it doesn't matter if you were free—"

"Sable will need breaks!" Her pointed finger came damned close to poking him in the chest. "What is she supposed to do if she needs to use the bathroom?"

Sensing her desperation, Memphis carefully moved her hand aside. Far more calmly than she'd managed, he replied, "Ms. Robertson, you seem to think you can *shout* me into hiring you."

Now that he'd reached them, Remmy asked, "Something going on here?"

"I," Ms. Robertson said, "am here for a job, and *he*," she stressed, staring daggers at Memphis, "is being unreasonable about it."

"Can't imagine why." After that insult, Remmy grinned.

Memphis noted that Diah's expression had turned keen with curiosity. Next, he took in the woman's sudden preoccupation with Remmy. An expedient conclusion occurred to him. "Remmy, handle this for me, okay? I need to talk with Diah."

Remmy's brows shot up. "How the hell should *I* handle it?"

Good question. Until this moment, Memphis hadn't delegated his authority, but when it came to Diah, he'd changed a lot of things so what was one more? "Use your best discretion. You understand the campground, the jobs that still need to be filled, the budget and the… purpose of things, so I'll stand by whatever you decide."

The woman immediately switched her laser focus and aggressive determination on Remmy.

Holding up a hand, Remmy told her, *"Wait,"* which left her standing there with her pert mouth open, no doubt ready to harangue him with all the excuses she'd used on Memphis.

Stomping away from her, Remmy muttered to Diah, "You okay to keep an eye on her? Just for a minute or two?"

Gaze bright with fascination, Diah smiled at the woman. "Absolutely."

This was exactly what Memphis hadn't wanted. "Damn it," he growled, then followed Remmy to the side of his cabin where they could talk privately, but he could keep his eye on the women. "Make it fast."

"Fine. Don't drop surprise shit on me."

"A woman is not surprise shit."

"She is when she's a potential employee."

With his attention glued to Diah, he saw her speak to the woman as if everything was fine, so maybe whatever had bothered her wasn't quite as bad as it had felt. Still, he wanted to wrap up this discussion so he could find out for himself. "It occurs to me that you're probably better at evaluating employees, anyway. She really wants, or possibly needs, to be here. Under those circumstances, she might be an asset or a liability. Could go either way, right? Try to sort it out."

"And if I hire her, you're okay with that?"

So much skepticism couldn't be ignored. "This might be a surprise to you," Memphis said with conviction, "but I trust your judgment. If I didn't, I wouldn't let you work with Diah."

It took a second or two, and then a slow smile cut across Remmy's face. "Appreciate it."

"If that's all." He started to head back to Diah, but Remmy stopped him.

"You'll need someone at the gatehouse," he mused.

"Easy enough job, right? Basically just checking the reservations online."

"When Sable needs breaks, she can call one of us."

"See, perfect." Again, Memphis started away.

Remmy spoke before he'd taken a full step. "She's floundering big time."

He pivoted back around. "Who?"

"Diah."

Which was precisely why he should be with her right now. "What happened?"

"Nothing to warrant breathing fire."

Right. Rolling his shoulders didn't really do much to ease the strain. He needed to get it together. Diah wasn't breakable—she'd proved that from the start. Plus, she didn't want Memphis advertising that she was more than an employee to him.

An awkward position to be in, but for Diah, he'd played along.

Though it wasn't easy, Memphis tried to look like no more than a concerned boss. "Fine, so what's the problem?" He hadn't imagined that troubled expression she'd worn, and he couldn't credit the idea that Remmy had caused it.

"I told her she was allowed to have a relationship and didn't have to pretend otherwise. I mean, it's obvious when you two look at each other, and it's been what now? Over a month since you met."

"Six weeks," Memphis murmured, well aware that Diah had a timeline on things.

"And she hasn't exactly been sleeping in her own cabin." Before Memphis could remark on that, he added, "Not that I was keeping track..."

"It'd be hard to miss." Memphis couldn't pull his gaze from her. With Tuff between them, she and the woman had taken a seat on the steps and were chatting like old friends.

To him, Ms. Robertson had been demanding and pushy. To Diah, she was friendliness personified. "Diah looked upset a minute ago."

"Not my doing. We were chatting and then she saw something, or thought of something, that really hit her. For a second there, I thought she'd keel over. She went white and sort of wobbly."

"What the hell?"

Hurrying now, Remmy said, "But you know Diah. She got it together and insisted she was fine."

"Is she?"

"Overall, sure. She doesn't seem to realize it, but she's tough as nails most of the time." Remmy watched the women. "You know, she treats me like a..." He tugged at his ear. "Hell, I don't know. Maybe a cross between a brother and a friend. It's weird."

Only because Remmy wasn't used to anything that meaningful with women. There was Jodi, but that relationship had restrictions, thanks to Hunter's watchfulness. "Weird but nice?"

"Yeah." He worked his jaw. "She has a way of looking at a person, it's almost like she sees inside my head."

Accurate. Curious how Remmy felt about it, he asked, "Does it bother you?"

"She asked me the same thing. It's not what I'm used to, that's all."

Memphis smiled. "She's not what I'm used to, either." She was better.

Remmy nodded at the newcomer. "I don't mind handling this for you, but what's your gut saying? Hire her or not?"

"I'm more interested in what your gut says, since you're the resident expert on shady characters."

Remmy didn't look away from the woman, which meant they were both now staring. And naturally that drew her attention, as well as Diah's.

Standing, Diah gave Remmy a "well?" gesture, which more or less meant, *Get over here.*

The funny part was, Remmy obeyed. He tightened his mouth, squared his shoulders and strode forward as if heading into battle.

Memphis would have laughed if he wasn't concerned for Diah.

He watched as they passed each other, Diah and Tuff on their way to him, Remmy on his way to the other woman. Sparks would fly, Memphis was sure of it. It could be entertaining, but not right now. Not when Diah was a priority.

As soon as she reached him, she went on tiptoe and softly pressed her mouth to his.

Like a statement. Like a declaration.

More than ready to end the pretense, Memphis kissed her back. *Like a claim.*

"No more hiding," she whispered.

Hoping he understood, he gathered her closer. "Hiding?"

"Us. Being together." Her face went warm and she grumbled, "Or whatever you'd call it. Not trying to pressure you or anything."

"We're together," he stated. For her, any relationship was a big step, so it pleased him to be a part of it. "This isn't because of Ms. Robertson, is it?"

Diah smiled. "No."

"And not because of Remmy?"

"I like him, but no." Her fingertips touched over his chest, toying with his shirt. "There are things I need to tell you."

Every fiber of his being sparked to attention. "Excellent. Let's go talk."

Though he was prepared to hear something momentous, she shifted verbal gears on him. "She seems nice."

"Who?"

Nodding at Remmy and the woman, she said, "Lane Robertson."

"Nice?" Wasn't the impression he'd gotten. "Not sure that's how I'd describe her."

Diah leaned into him. "She's really pretty, too, with her fluffy hair and round face."

"A baby face. She claims she's twenty-three but doesn't look it to me." She'd easily pass for seventeen or even younger. "As far as being pretty, I hadn't noticed."

"Bull. Then what did you notice?"

He lifted a shoulder. "She's tall for a girl, with a sturdy build and innocent face—at least until she opens her mouth. Then nothing about her seems innocent."

Diah glanced back at her. "She's only a year younger than me. Her build isn't sturdy, just strong." She studied the woman a moment more. "I think like me, she has to be here."

Oh, how he wanted to dig into that, at least as it pertained to Diah. "You got that impression from something she said?"

"More how she acted. She's desperate for a job here." Her gaze flicked to his face. "There's no way you missed it."

Of course he hadn't, and now he could see that it mattered to Diah. "No, I didn't."

"Will Remmy hire her?"

Making yet another split-second decision, Memphis stated, "He will if that's what you want."

Since Tuff stretched out in the grass, his attention on Remmy and Lane, Diah relaxed her hold on the leash and smiled up at Memphis wonderingly. "You'd do that for me?"

What wouldn't he do for her? It bothered him that he was so committed, yet he sensed that she was still skirting any real trust. "Say the word."

She seemed to give it some thought, her attention shifting from his face to the chatting pair nearby and back again. "Thank you, but you left it up to Remmy so let's see what he decides."

Honestly, he no longer cared what happened between Remmy and the woman. "You have something to tell me?"

"I'm probably overreacting. You know how I am when I get spooked, but it was the weirdest thing—seeing it and then having this awful feeling come over me."

"Tell me." Then they could work it out.

Again, she glanced at Remmy, which also drew

Memphis's gaze. Given that the woman's pointy finger was now aimed at Remmy, things were heating up over there.

Nodding toward them, Diah said, "Let's get that settled, then maybe talk inside."

Damn it, another delay. Struggling for lost patience, Memphis went along. As they approached the others, he heard the woman snap, "You're being unreasonable."

"Is he?" Diah asked, sidling up to them with Tuff, and dragging Memphis along. "How so?"

Lane didn't appear at all comfortable with Diah's question.

Remmy crossed his arms and scowled. "I told her I'd have to do a background check."

"Standard," Memphis agreed.

"Is that the only holdup?" Glancing at each man, Diah asked, "If she passes the background check, you'll hire her?"

Memphis deferred to Remmy.

Put on the spot, Remmy took his time before relenting. "Probably."

"Great." Ready to get things moving, Memphis put his arm around Diah, took the leash for Tuff and said, "Go ahead and do the background check now. She can wait with you while you do."

Arms dropping, Remmy went blank. "Now?"

"We're opening in a week. No time like the present." Plus, that'd keep them both busy long enough for him to talk with Diah. "Dinner in thirty minutes, though, so don't drag your feet."

Enjoying Remmy's discomfort, Lane lifted her chin. "Fine by me."

She probably assumed Remmy couldn't find much

in that short time frame, but Memphis knew better. He'd already helped Remmy set up an advanced search program. He'd also secured Remmy's private internet connection. In half the time allotted, he could uncover anything outstanding of interest.

Later, when he didn't have business with Diah, Memphis would do his own thorough check on the girl.

The second they stepped into his cabin, Tuff made a beeline for the kitchen, meaning he wanted to be fed. At the same time, Diah gave an appreciative sniff of the air. "Something smells good."

"Chili." Unwilling to be put off any longer, he caught her arm and steered her to the kitchen. "Dinner will keep until after our talk."

"I'll make it short, because I'm hungry." Going to the low cabinet where they kept Tuff's supplies, Diah got out the dog's food and poured it into his bowl, then refreshed his water dish, too.

"You're stalling."

Stopping with her back to him, she said in a low, barely audible tone, "That's because you're going to be mad at me."

Memphis wasn't sure if that was true or not, but he said only, "If I am, you can tell me to stuff it."

Incredulous, she jerked around to face him. "I can?"

Taking her shoulders, Memphis said, "In this, with what's between us, I'm not your boss. We're just a couple in an even relationship and you never have to worry about what you say to me. If it bothers me, I'll say so." But he wouldn't stop caring about her. "And even if it does, so what? I've been bothered before and survived it." He'd rather have all her secrets out in the open.

"Are you sure you want to get drawn into my problems?"

He was sure of many things, but obviously she wasn't. "Quit stalling." He punctuated that with a firm kiss. "You're only making this harder. Especially on me."

Her mouth twisted to the side in doubt. "This might affect the campground, too."

"Then I definitely need to know."

"Fine." Groaning, she dropped her head to his chest. "I found things in Glover's belongings, things he didn't want me to see unless…until…he was gone."

At the prospect of her finally telling him everything, Memphis's heart started punching like a jackhammer. "I vote you tell me what those things are."

"At this point, I think I have to." Pressing away from him, she went to the sink and washed her hands, up her forearms, and then splashed her face.

Throwing up his hands, he growled, "Swear to God—"

"I just need a second," she snapped back.

They glared at each other. "I've been patient."

Softer, she said, "I know."

"I've resisted finding the truth for myself—but I *could*, Diah. I'm about to get started right now."

After rolling her eyes, she dried her hands and asked, "Can we sit?"

"We can do whatever you want." Impatient, he followed her example, washing up in the sink with overly brisk energy.

Rushing her wasn't the answer. *Can waiting six weeks be called rushing?* No, he decided. He'd given her more than enough time. Possibly too much, even. She'd gotten comfortable with having everything her way.

It wasn't like him, damn it. He didn't let others dictate his life. Sure, this was the new him, the guy trying to make a difference, but he couldn't do that by sitting in the dark.

Diah was already in her chair, her hands folded primly on the tabletop, when he took his own seat. He didn't say anything else. Why bother? She'd either trust him or she wouldn't. Instead, he just watched her and waited.

With one finger, she pushed her glasses farther up the bridge of her nose.

It was telling that she'd wear them now. Lately, she'd taken them off whenever they were alone.

"So," she said, shifting restlessly. "I know I should have told you already, just as I know I probably wouldn't have if I hadn't seen his name."

Not what he'd expected. "Whose name?"

"Rusty's."

Following along wasn't easy. "Your stepbrother? You saw his name...where?"

"It's carved in one of your picnic tables." In that fixed way of hers, she watched him. "A table by one of the newer cabins."

It took him a second, but given the way she'd explained it, the math clicked into place. Those cabins were only eight years old, but Rusty should have died ten years ago. Had one of them been moved? He thought aloud, "The original tables with the oldest cabins have concrete bases."

She nodded. "This was a steel base table."

Definitely one of the newer ones. He had a hard time bending his brain around it. "You think Rusty was here, at this campground?"

"I know he was. We all were. My stepfather brought us here a couple of times when I was a lot younger."

"On…what? Vacation?" Then with incredulity, *"Here?"* It would be an outrageous distance to travel with a wife and kids just to visit what had been a downtrodden campground—unless her stepfather had done specific business here. Given what he knew, that seemed possible.

Diah nodded. "He was definitely doing some kind of deal. He and Rusty would go out for a big part of the day. I wanted to go, too, but my mother always said I had to stay in the camper where it was safe. I remember because I was bored during those times. When I could get out and look around, it wasn't so bad."

"That would've been more than eight years ago."

She nodded. "It's why I came here, Memphis. This campground was familiar to my family, maybe more so to my stepfather and stepbrother since they did some kind of business here."

"And Glover was involved then, too?"

"He had this specific place circled on a map." She paused, her gaze almost pleading, then she said, "He'd also written on it."

Memphis went stiff. "What did it say?"

"Just Rusty's name, underlined." Before he could react to that awful admission, she said urgently, "I can feel that I'm getting closer. There's a clue here somewhere that could tell me who murdered my family. Who wanted to murder *me*."

That explained why she'd snuck out at night, and why she'd gotten into the floor of the cabin. It also emphasized the risks she'd taken. "You don't even know what you're looking for."

She caught her bottom lip in her teeth, then said, "I was starting to wonder if I was wrong, if maybe this place had nothing to do with the past. But now there's Rusty's name on the table, and Glover's interest in the place."

He pinched the bridge of his nose, knowing she was right. "I don't believe in coincidence."

"I don't, either. *Something* is here. Maybe a sealed box of some sort that has photos, or a recording of something they did."

"Seems like a box would have been easy to spot."

"I know. I've looked everywhere, even in the supply building. When I didn't find anything… I'd sort of given up." She worried her lip again, then admitted, "It had stopped being such a priority for me."

That confession grabbed him. "Why?"

"Being with you, enjoying you so much, I guess stuff about the past lost some of its importance." She removed the glasses to rub her eyes. "I'd decided that until I found the person responsible, until I solved the mystery, I'd never be safe."

In his opinion, she wasn't wrong.

"Now, seeing Rusty's name…" She let that trail off. "I can't let it go."

Drumming his fingertips on the table, he was so mired in dark thoughts that the touch of her small hand hit him like a jolt. He felt it all the way to his heart. Turning his hand over, he clasped her fingers.

"I'm afraid Rusty might still be around." Her eyes turned beseeching. "Memphis, what if he's the one who set the fire?"

That'd mean her stepbrother had wanted her to die.

It'd mean he'd killed not only his stepmother, but his

own father, too. That'd make him an utterly ruthless murderer. A man without a conscience. A man with a lot to lose if Diah exposed him. "If Rusty orchestrated a fire and wanted people to believe he'd died, why carve his name into a table?"

"I never said he was smart, just mean."

Or, Memphis thought, he might have put the name there as a marker. Perhaps the table had something to do with whatever the miserable bastard had hidden. *If* he had hidden anything.

Straightforward plans were so much easier than decade-old twists and turns.

Three bodies had been found in the fire, assumed to be Diah's mother, stepfather and Rusty. So who else had died that day? "This all seems far-fetched. You realize that."

"Yes." Pulling her hands free, she rubbed her arms as if chilled. "Something tells me Rusty is still around, and that he'll show up here."

"Could his name be the evidence you wanted?" Didn't seem like much to go on.

"I don't think so. I figured it'd be something specific about a job, or maybe the person they worked for."

Seemed more plausible than a name that could have been carved by anyone. "He was…what? A gangster? A crook?"

"Glover never spelled out what they each did, but he admitted to being protection for someone, and that he did really bad things. Since Rusty worked with him, he probably did the same, right?"

"Sounds logical to me." Yet, it was also possible that Rusty was worse.

"I've been going on the assumption that their boss—

whoever he might be—was the one who'd planned the fire. That's who I'd hoped to expose."

Memphis could only stare at her. "Jesus, Diah. Do you know how risky that would be?" He definitely should have pushed for answers sooner.

"I need to know. I *have* to know."

Yes, he supposed she did. He'd have felt the same. Even if the threat was over, not knowing would be terrible.

And if it wasn't over?

Her gaze searched his, and she reached for his hands again. "I should have told you sooner." She shook her head. "No, I should never have come here in the first place. When I saw you outside that first day…I didn't care that I'd be using you and your place to get what I wanted. I just wanted it. I wanted to uncover all the secrets so I didn't have to keep moving."

"You wanted to put an end to it all."

Closing her eyes and lowering her face, she nodded. "I'm sorry."

"I'm not."

Her head came up. "I've kept things from you. Even though we've…"

Cocking a brow, he waited.

"Remmy called it *banging*."

Drawing a blank, Memphis asked, "He…what?"

She shrugged. "We talked a little."

Anger vied with humor. Remmy hadn't given him details, damn him. "About us having sex?"

"Basically, he said I shouldn't act like nothing is going on, when obviously it is." She eyed him. "It is, right?"

All kinds of things were going on, mostly him falling in love. "If you have to ask, clearly I've been subpar."

"What?" She leaned forward in a rush. "No way. You're *amazing*. Before you, I didn't know it could be like that. Shoot, I think about it—about you—all the time." She scowled. "Why the hell do you think I jump your bones every night?"

"I thought I was doing the jumping, but whatever." At least physically, she was hooked. "Forget Remmy for the moment, and forget that you kept things from me. That's over, right?"

Warily, she nodded.

"Good. Far as I'm concerned, you're here now, with me, and I'm glad. It doesn't matter how we got to this point, we'll figure out the rest together."

She tried to pull her hands away, but he held on.

"The bodies in the fire would have been identified."

She nodded. "Unless Rusty found a way around that." Thinking it through, she said, "Glover told me that we couldn't trust the cops in that area, because his boss had a few of them on his payroll."

This just kept getting worse and worse. "Start at the beginning, and tell me everything you know."

After a bracing breath, she nodded. "I found a map in Glover's stash. On it, he'd circled this place and written Rusty's name. Maybe he was planning something, but then he got sick…"

"When did he do that, do you know?"

"No idea." Her mouth flattened. "But it's probably why he kept us moving so often. He suspected Rusty, and he knew he'd be the only one able to help me."

The only one who'd *want* to help her. "Christ."

"I don't know for sure why he kept us on the run, but

if he suspected Rusty, or worse, if he *knew* Rusty had survived, he'd likely assume that I was still in danger."

"If Rusty found you, he'd finish what he started."

Her fingers tightened on his. "You have to understand, Memphis. If I'm right, if my own stepbrother set that fire, he'd be desperate to cover his involvement, meaning he'd kill me—and anyone near me."

"Not a fucking chance." Memphis would never let that happen.

"I'm sorry. I want to do things your way, but more than that, I don't want you hurt."

Offense burned through his blood. "I'm not the pathetic dupe you think I am."

"I've never thought you were pathetic," she denied hotly. "Even when you were singing naked outside, I didn't think it."

Memphis huffed. He'd probably never live that down.

"You've always been incredible and patient and kind—"

"Don't saint me," he said dryly.

"—and that's why I should probably go."

She said it, but her eyes…those fascinating eyes… He could see that she didn't want to leave him, and for Memphis that was reason enough for him to take over. "You're not going anywhere, babe. Not now." *Not ever.* "Forget it."

At the unfamiliar tone from him, her eyes widened. "But—"

"You're going to stay put, and we're going to figure this out." Once and for all, and then she'd be safe.

Even better, she'd be his.

"But…how?"

He had a lot to think about, and Remmy should arrive soon to eat. "You know, this elusive evidence of Glover's could be about the fire. It could be proof that Rusty is responsible."

"I know and I've racked my brain, but I can't imagine what that proof would be."

"Me, either, but I know who could find out." Maybe it was time to call in the big guns.

"Who?"

"Do you trust me?"

She did that mesmerizing stare thing, but Memphis didn't blink, didn't falter, and finally, with a tiny smile, she nodded. "I really do."

"Perfect." Overflowing with satisfaction, he said, "Leave it to me."

CHAPTER TWELVE

USING THE EXCLUSIVE program Memphis had installed, Remmy went through a few files that had popped up on his search. Where Memphis had gotten the elite program, Remmy could guess: Madison. She had access to things exclusive to the military.

And now somehow he'd become a part of it.

Memphis trusted him. Diah liked him. Jodi was his friend. Hunter accepted him.

So many upstanding, amazing people, and they'd welcomed him into their sphere.

Sometimes he didn't know himself anymore. One thing was certain, he respected this new stranger version of himself a hell of a lot more than his former self.

The floor squeaked when Lane shifted again.

He kept glancing at her. In the narrow wooden chair opposite him at the tiny two-seater table, she worried. Her mounting tension was a live, electric current filling his small cabin.

With him six feet tall, and her probably five-eight, their knees kept bumping. He pretended not to notice, but she squirmed around uneasily, doing her best to avoid the contact.

Being contrary, Remmy bumped her again.

She glared at him from beneath dark brown brows,

her blue eyes nearly snapping like the center of a hot flame.

What poetic bullshit.

They were just blue eyes, plain old blue, framed with long brown eyelashes under level brows.

Her brown curly hair had a mind of its own. She kept tugging it down and tucking it behind her ears, and then *poof*, it'd fluff up again.

"You going to research or gawk at me?"

"I can do both." He sat back in his seat. "You know, with that particular expression plastered on your face, you look guilty as hell."

Drawing up in indignation, she demanded, "Guilty of *what*?"

"That's what I'm trying to find out."

"Screw this." Noisily scraping back her chair, she shot to her feet and stalked toward the door. There was zero sway in her hips, and her hands were curled tight into fists.

"Giving up?" Remmy asked softly, knowing she wasn't. "You'll leave now?"

Halting, her shoulders bunched, she slowly turned back to glare at him. "No. Not until you hire me."

With her seat moved away from the table, he stretched out his legs and laced his fingers together over his midsection—a man at his leisure, without a care. "You've been arrested."

An infinitesimal tightening of her face gave her away. "Hire me."

Using his foot, Remmy snagged the leg of her chair and drew it closer. "Sit with me."

Her eyes widened at that *with me* part, but she reluctantly dragged herself closer and lowered herself to the chair as if sitting in boiling oil.

"You were eighteen at the time?"

She hitched her chin. "Eighteen and stupid and I did a load of community service, paid my debt as they say, and I haven't been in trouble since."

He disagreed. She was in trouble now. "Before coming here, you worked for Otto Woodall." And that, he knew, meant trouble of the worst kind.

Her gaze darted away in a panic, then finally crawled back. "I'm not working for him anymore."

Or was she? First, Ed and his crew of misfits agreed to a job, and now this girl was here. "What does Otto want?"

A dozen emotions flitted over her face before she deflated. "Look, he's a dick and I despise him, okay? It's not like I wanted to work for him." Bitter with accusation, she glared at him. "You probably have no clue what it's like to be forced into something, but let me tell you, it sucks donkey balls."

Forced? He kept his tone neutral and asked, "That bad, huh?"

Again, she pushed back her chair, this time more quietly and with pride stamped on her expression. "I know, not your problem."

"I didn't say that." For whatever reason, it felt very much like his problem.

"You didn't have to. Been here, done this, have the T-shirt."

"Dramatic much?" Before she reached the door, Remmy stepped in front of her, blocking her escape—and that's what it was, an escape. She wanted the job, but she did not want to discuss Otto, which of course made him more determined to learn the truth. "Are you working for him now?"

Her short, quiet laugh lacked any humor. "Weren't you listening?" Tired and not bothering to hide it, she rubbed her forehead. "Look, I'm trying to put Otto far behind me, but that's hard to do when he manages to shut me down on every job I apply for." She squared off with him. "I've been searching for work for three weeks now. Apparently, everyone has gotten the word that they better not hire me. No offense, but this place was a last shot kind of effort."

Funny, but he believed her and his take on things was starting to shift. "So if I don't hire you, what will you do?"

"If?" She perked up at that. "Meaning…you still might?"

Seeing so much hope in her face affected him profoundly. He was not a guy who softened over big eyes and desperation, not when he'd seen it a hundred times before, in a hundred different places. Even so, he heard himself say, "Considering it."

She breathed faster. "If you don't, I'll start driving and get as far out of town as I can before I run out of money. Honestly, I don't have much to go on, though. Otto held my wages for the past month and when I left… Well, I couldn't get them."

"Why not?"

She winced. "I didn't give notice, all right? I just left but it was the only way! He wouldn't have let me leave otherwise, but every day it got harder and I—" Appalled at herself, she slapped a hand over her mouth.

Could anyone fake an expression like that? Maybe, but he didn't think she was.

Gently, he brought her hand down and, when she didn't object, he kept her wrist captured. She wasn't as fine-boned as Jodi and Diah, but she was a hell of a lot smaller than him and he didn't like knowing someone had scared her. "You're saying a lot, Lane, most of it alarming."

Gaze wary, she took a step back, freeing herself from his hold. "Alarming how?"

"Otto is keeping you from getting a job, he wouldn't have *let* you leave. What exactly does all that mean?"

New emotions filled her eyes, indecision, uncertainty. Calculations.

Quickly, she looked away.

"That won't help," he informed her.

Her gaze swung back to his. "What?"

"Dodging me. Trying to think up a pretty lie. If you actually want this job and the dubious pleasure of working here, you may as well rip off the bandage. Tell me what you're up against and I'll decide if I can help."

"What makes you think I want your help?"

"So if I offer you an extra hundred for your exit from town, you won't take it?"

Her eyes flared at the offer.

Now he wondered, would she take his money and bail, or stick it out?

Picking at a fingernail, she hesitated, then settled on saying, "I'd rather you give me a job so I can make my own money."

"So let's talk about that."

She blinked. "For real?"

"I'm not ruling it out. But if I catch you in a lie, I'll can you real fast."

A fat smile came over her face, making her look

like an excited kid. "I'll be the best worker this place has ever seen."

"Is that an insult to me or Diah?"

"What? No. I meant..." She scowled. "You know what I meant."

Remmy glanced over her. "You don't look twenty-three."

"I know." Copping an attitude, she held out her arms. "That's one of the things Otto liked about me, the perv."

By the second, Remmy's bad feelings expanded. He worried that if he sent her off without the job, she'd never be seen again. "Spill it—and you better be truthful. What exactly did you do for him?"

Her shoulders dropped. "Probably not what you're thinking, though I was never sure if that was completely off the table." She leaned back on the short counter in his minuscule kitchen, her hands braced beside her hips. "Basically, I did whatever I was told. Took out trash, washed and restocked the linens, mopped the halls, worked in the kitchen, cleaned rooms...there are always chores in a hotel." Her gaze fixed on his and her voice lowered. "Sometimes Otto would want to see me."

"For what reason?"

"Mostly to toy with me, I think." Her jaw flexed. "His favorite game was finding fault. He'd get out this stupid book where he supposedly tallied my debt."

"Your debt?"

"Yeah, see, I owed him money."

A bad error but he didn't say so. "Go on."

"He'd muse over it, like it was freaking calculus or something, then he'd say that I hadn't done a good enough job with this or that and he had to have someone else redo it, which actually cost him money, so enough money never came off."

"Meaning you were never going to be free?" He didn't need her to answer that. He knew the game only too well. "I've never met Otto, but I know him by reputation. Why would you borrow money from him in the first place?"

"Borrow it? Get real." The seconds ticked by while she stewed in silence, then she closed her eyes and shook her head. "So in a nutshell, Otto kept me out of jail a second time." Looking at him again, she swore, "On my life, I was falsely accused, but you know how it is. If you've got a record and a history, you always top the list of suspects."

Yeah, he did know it. In his case, the accusations had often been accurate. "What were you accused of?"

"I had a job at a restaurant waiting tables, and a bunch of money went missing from the register. No idea who took it, but I know it wasn't me. I loved that stupid job, even though I barely made enough to get by. Anyway, everyone immediately assumed it was me. The waitresses were cursing me where customers could hear, and the boss was threatening to call the cops..." Distraught and embarrassed, she visibly shored herself up. "It sucked *so hard*, that when this total stranger said he'd hand over the money and I could repay him, I agreed. You don't have to say it, I know it wasn't my brightest move, but I just wanted out of there."

Remmy didn't judge her for that. At her age, in her position, he couldn't say what he might do. "How did you think he'd want repayment?"

"I asked him that right off," she said, pacing away and then back again. "I mean, I sure as hell wasn't going to screw him for it." She snorted as if the very idea was ludicrous. "Not that he's a bad-looking guy, but there's something skeevy about him… When I made it clear that sex wasn't on the table, he laughed like I'd told a joke, and then he explained that I could work for him at his hotel."

Still sounded damned risky to Remmy. "Tell me you didn't get in a car with him."

"No, I had—*have*—an old beater that gets me where I need to go." Again, she glanced away.

Hmm. So there was something about her car that she didn't want him to know. "Where are you parked, anyway?"

"Back at the entrance. I wasn't sure if I'd be allowed to drive in since the place isn't open yet. When I opted to walk, I didn't realize it'd be so far."

For now, he'd let that go. Shortly, he'd be able to see her car through Memphis's various spy cams. Handy things, those. "Sable doesn't need a full-time helper—" his raised voice cut off her immediate protest "—but we could use someone at the gatehouse to check in the guests."

Relieved, she blew out a breath and said, "Awesome. Count me in."

"Can you start tomorrow?"

Eagerness flashed in her eyes again. Ordinary blue eyes, he reminded himself. Actually, everything about her was ordinary—if any woman could be called that. This one…maybe not.

Holding herself tensed, as if to pounce, she nodded hard. "Absolutely."

"Seven AM?" Admittedly, that was earlier than he

and Diah usually got started, but he wasn't above testing Lane a little.

"No problem." She seemed to be holding her breath, her gaze expectant.

Hmm. "Fine. Consider yourself hired."

Her sudden screech and jostling dance startled him enough that he braced for an attack—until he realized the reason behind her ridiculous show. Paying no attention to his growled curse, she grabbed him and bounced around as if she'd just won the damned lottery and expected him to celebrate with her.

"Lane," he tried to say while being wildly jostled. *"Lane."* With one small tug, she landed against his body, which effectively ended her not-so-slick dance moves.

Wide eyes stared up at him, and finally—belatedly, to his mind—a little reserve crept in. "Oh," she whispered, glancing down at where their chests had collided.

Yup, Remmy was pretty damned aware of it, too. Not good. He lifted his hands as if in surrender.

He wasn't made of ice, after all.

Hastily, she pressed away, all flustered and tongue-tied before she needlessly smoothed her clothes as if he'd somehow displaced them.

In his head, maybe, because her hot body had felt incredibly good all smooshed up to his. In reality, all he'd done was get her attention.

Knowing it was past time for him to send her on her way, he turned for the door, opened it and waited for her to get it in gear. When he looked back, she was still rooted to the spot, her absorbed gaze locked on him.

"It's getting late," he said, not at all subtle. "I need to wash up and join the others for dinner."

"Dinner," she repeated, as if she'd never heard of such a thing. Finally, though, it clicked. She blinked fast. "Oh, right." A high, forced laugh. "Gotcha. Didn't mean to overstay. I'll get on my way right now." She bustled past him, over the small wooden deck and down the steps. "Thanks again for the job. You won't regret it."

Remmy stood there watching her.

Damn it, it was dark now. She had her head down, her arms swinging at her sides as she power-walked away with long strides. The urge to follow her, to ensure she got safely to her car, gnawed on his peace of mind.

Instead, he closed and locked his door and jogged to Memphis's cabin. Tuff went nuts at his two-rap knock and a second later, Memphis opened the door.

Pushing his way in, Remmy said, "Pull her up on one of your cameras, will you?"

"Ms. Robertson?"

"Yeah, Lane. She supposedly parked at the entrance, but it's dark now."

Diah said with accusation, "And you let her walk there alone?"

"Let her?" he asked, on his way to the window so he could watch her as long as possible. "That's funny, coming from someone as bullheaded as you."

Squeezing in next to him, Diah said, "She's almost out of sight."

"At least we got those brighter lights up."

"Won't stop a wolf, or a moose, or—"

"Damn it," Remmy said. Her needling spurred his own worry to a sharpened edge.

"Got her." Memphis sat at the table, his phone before him.

Relieved, Remmy got behind his chair and peered over his shoulder, watching as Lane continued on without once glancing around her.

"She seems on a mission." Diah pulled her seat next to Memphis. "It's like she's late for something."

"Or nervous," Memphis said.

"I should have gone with her." It pissed Remmy off to be in this position. He was still sorting out his own life. He couldn't exactly take on someone else's problems.

"Ah." Diah grinned. "She has a pop-up camper."

Memphis rubbed a hand over his face. "So she does."

Breath held, Remmy saw her climb into her car. The lighting wasn't good enough to see much, but there was no missing the small camper in back. Would she drive off? To go where? "She knows Otto."

"Knows him, or *knows* him?"

Briefly, he scowled at Memphis. "Worked for him at his hotel, but she swears that's over. I can find out more tomorrow when I—" His explanations ended with *"Son of a bitch,"* when Lane navigated the car around and drove down the entry toward the camp.

Together, they left their seats and headed to the front door with Tuff leading the way. Diah quickly leashed the dog and Remmy jerked open the door.

Beneath floodlights, Lane maneuvered to one of the hookup sites, expertly backed in her tiny camper and parked.

All without acknowledging them as her spellbound audience.

"Did you tell her she could stay here?" Memphis quietly asked.

"Nope." Then he added, "But I'm glad she is. Will it be a problem?"

Diah answered before Memphis could. "She'll be safer here."

Yes, she would—but safe from what?

Smiling at both men, Diah said, "I'll take a bowl of chili to her. Tomorrow we can all get better acquainted."

"I'll take it." Remmy headed back into the house. "She'll probably need help getting that pop-up open, and until I know more about her, I don't think you should get too close."

THE NEXT MORNING over coffee, Memphis called Madison while Diah listened in. She hadn't met Madison yet, but since Memphis trusted her, she supposed she would as well.

Before coming here, it'd been only her and Tuff. She hadn't trusted another living soul. Then there was Memphis, and he'd won her over so easily. She'd also gained Remmy as a friend. With everything Memphis had told her about his brother and sister-in-law, she automatically trusted them, too.

Her world was expanding rapidly, and she liked it.

The call was answered with, "About damn time! Whew. You know I was on pins and needles, waiting until you needed my help. You do need my help, right? Say yes, Memphis."

Grinning, Memphis replied, "Hello to you, too, Madison. I have you on speaker with Jedidiah Stephens."

"Ooooh, hello there, Diah. It's a pleasure."

Pulling others into her troubles went against the grain. Memphis had insisted, though, assuring her that everything would be fine, and she had to admit, Madison had a very cheery way about her. "Since Memphis didn't answer, I will. Yes, we could use your help."

"Ha! I'm so glad you're agreeable. Thank you. You're taking good care of my number-one guy, right?"

Diah grinned. Madison was more upbeat than Memphis, and that was saying something. "Trying, but he's always so chipper, there's not much I can do for him."

"What? But you're just what he needed. Hasn't he told you that yet?" And then, "Memphis, you disappoint me. Tell her already."

Rolling his eyes, Memphis said, "Your husband is your number-one guy."

"Oh, for sure," she replied in a purr. "And believe me, I tell him *often* that he's just what I need. Hint, hint."

By the second, Diah liked her more. "Memphis is the most patient, understanding and generous person I've ever met."

"Wow, I might have to dust off his halo."

Memphis snorted.

"His wicked sense of humor doesn't bother you?" Madison asked.

"Everything about him bothers every part of me—but always in a really good way."

"Lovely. I have a feeling you two are going to need each other."

Memphis snapped to attention. "What does that mean?"

"Well..." After dragging out the word, she sighed. "You can't be that surprised that I jumped the gun a wee bit. You *know* me, Memphis."

His jaw locked. "I was clear."

Madison rushed on with, "Right. You didn't want me snooping around in her background—and I tried to respect that, I really did, but I had a feeling and so... I did, anyway."

Diah stared at Memphis's set face and his obvious displeasure. He'd told his oh-so-awesome research genius BFF to stay out of her business?

How sweet was that?

Not that he looked sweet at the moment. More like ready to spit nails.

Reaching for his large, capable hand and lacing her fingers with his, Diah mouthed *Thank you*, so Madison wouldn't hear.

So much strength tempered with such a giving heart and endless good humor—how could any woman be immune to that? Especially when that awesome package of great qualities was all wrapped up in sinfully sexy good looks and a superior bod?

Rhetorical question, because obviously she couldn't.

Clearing her throat, Diah asked the obvious. "I take it you learned something?"

"Oh, a great many things." Shaking off the apologetic tone, Madison got right to it. "Your stepbrother was never solidly identified in the fire, a fire I suspect he set, though it was made to look as if your stepfather fell asleep while drinking and smoking." She waited.

Neither Diah nor Memphis said anything.

"Ah, so you already had suspicions as well? Excellent." She rushed on. "Get this. Rusty Wilson had been in a bar that night. According to his friends, he'd had too much to drink and they'd driven him home. That's all true, as far as I can tell from security tapes, and it's close to the only evidence they had to identify him. The usual protocol used wasn't possible."

"Usual protocol being dental records?" Memphis asked, loosening just a little. "Medical records or anything like that?"

"Diah's stepbrother had no major surgeries, breaks or implants to annotate, so the medical records were a bust. Dental records—get this. The dentist retired that month, moved to Florida and then died shortly after when he ran his car off the road. Convenient, right?"

"The dentist might disagree," Memphis said.

"*Poof*, dental records are gone and without the dentist to say where they are, they're impossible to recover."

"So how'd they ID him?"

"His melted cell phone was found near the body. An easy plant, of course. And although the clothes were burned away, there were a few pieces found under the body that matched what Rusty had been wearing earlier in the night."

Picturing the grisly scene, Diah cringed.

In the next second, Memphis had her in his lap, his arms around her, his warm mouth pressed to her temple.

Don't be cowardly. That was her biggest goal, to step up and do what had to be done. To make a difference. After a calming breath, she relaxed against Memphis and forced herself to ask, "So who did the body belong to?"

"The million-dollar question, right? I didn't find any missing people reports that would fit for the general area, in Rusty's size and age, but rest assured I'm on it."

"Diah has info for you, too." When her gaze met his, he asked, "You want to tell her about the name or should I?"

Held so warm and safe by Memphis, she no longer felt ill. "I can." As briefly as possible, she shared what she'd found in Glover's things, and then the name she'd located carved onto the table. "I know it's not much to go on."

"It's a great starting point," Madison said. "I'll back-track through any records at the campground. Too bad the guy who previously owned it wasn't as high-tech as Memphis."

"No video?" Memphis asked.

"Not surprising for the time, but you'd think there'd be something."

"He gave lowlifes free rein, so probably not surprising at all."

"Never fear," Madison said. "I'm all over it and I'm sure there's a business somewhere nearby that'll have a clue."

It boggled Diah's mind that anyone could access data that old, especially from such a remote location. "Knockoff isn't exactly a happening place."

"Oh, I don't know," Madison drawled. "Memphis is there, and Remmy and now you. Bound to be all kinds of fascinating things taking place."

"Ha!" Diah laughed. "Good point."

"I'll check back as soon as I have something to share. In the meantime, I'll be keeping an eye on all of you."

"Madison," Memphis warned…but she'd already disconnected.

Unsure of Memphis's mood, Diah touched his face. "She means well."

He surprised her by grinning. "She does, and she's talented beyond belief. I'm glad she's on board."

It took her a second, and then she said, "You big faker. You weren't at all annoyed with her, were you?"

"Little bit." He leaned in for a quick smooch before explaining, "With Madison, it's better to grab whatever control I can before she starts plowing over me."

"Would she do that?"

"Take over? In a hot minute. It's in her nature. She's from a family of alphas that just naturally think they can do everything better—and usually they're not wrong." Expression tender, he smoothed back her hair and straightened her glasses. "When it comes to your safety I won't cut corners, and that means letting Madison do her thing. But it's also personal, so I want to know what's happening every step of the way."

Tilting in for another taste of him, she wished she had the guts to ask, *How personal?* For her, yeah, things were getting pretty serious. So serious, in fact, that she could no longer imagine a day-to-day existence without him. What would that even look like?

How would she get through it?

For much of her life, she'd been tackling problems: the negligence of her mom, the abuse from Rusty, the brutal deaths of her entire family, being on the run with Glover and then his passing. She'd stupidly thought she'd gone through enough, that she would never again need another person.

Now she knew that wasn't true.

Derailing her thoughts, Memphis deepened the kiss and soon his mouth was open, hot, damp, eating at hers while his hands roamed down her back to her behind. Unable to think at all, she could only feel…until Tuff loudly whined.

Pulling away, Diah looked blankly at her dog. It took her thoughts a second to focus, and then she realized her glasses were askew, too. She righted them, cleared her throat and tried to get herself in order.

"That dog is a cock-blocker." Tuff squirreled closer, knowing Memphis meant him. "Yeah, you." He reached out to pat the dog with affection. "Don't worry, though, you're still my bud."

Leave it to Memphis to lighten the moment. "He's used to me being up and at work by now." That reminded her and she turned to look through the window. "Think Remmy is waiting for me?"

"He's busy with our new hire."

"How do you know?"

"I texted him this morning." Lifting her to her feet, Memphis stood and then put his hands to her shoulders. "Only two more days before we open."

After working so hard to get everything ready, she felt a sense of pride for all they'd accomplished. "The reservations are full." Soon the grounds would be overflowing with campers, fifth wheels, RVs and tents. The dark quiet nights she enjoyed so much would be overtaken with chatter, lights and activity.

"The first few days will be an adjustment." Taking her hand and heading for the front door with Tuff, Memphis said, "Don't go anywhere alone."

How exactly did he think that would work? "People will be everywhere. I doubt I could find time alone even if I wanted to." Which she didn't. Every spare minute she had, she enjoyed spending with Memphis. It was the oddest thing to go from being content in her isolation, set on her course, to leaning—emotionally and physically—on someone else.

"That's the problem. We'll be overrun with strangers and I can't keep track of all of them." They stepped out to his yard where Tuff immediately went the length of his leash to investigate a bush. "Just stay near Remmy or me at all times."

"How am I supposed to do my job?"

Where he'd been playful and sexual just a minute before, Memphis was now intractable. Without any real anger, he stated, "Your job isn't important."

Her jaw dropped. "I've worked hard!" Damn it, the place looked great, and she'd had a hand in making that happen.

"Believe me, I know. Sometimes I think you're trying to work yourself into the ground. Now that we're opening, you can lighten up."

"Not likely." She glanced around, imagining every spot taken. "There will always be issues. Endless issues. I'm your maintenance technician and that means when the problems pop up, I have to take care of them."

His brows scrunched together and those dark blue eyes narrowed. "Not. Without. Me or Remmy."

Such an autocratic tone! Reminding herself that he only wanted to protect her, Diah crossed her arms. "Am I allowed to check on Sable? Lane?" The two women would be stationed a good distance apart, with Lane at the entry gate and Sable at the camp store. Surely, he didn't think one of them would need to escort her back and forth.

It was obvious he wanted to deny her, but after working his jaw, he said, "If you let me know what you're doing, then it should be fine."

Un-freaking-believable. "I have to check in with you?"

His gaze went to Tuff when he said, "Recall that I'm the employer, you're the employ—"

"Asshat!"

His expression hardened but he muttered, "Bad joke."

"*Was* it a joke?"

The question soured his mood even more. "You know damn good and well that you're more than that."

"More, yes." A bed warmer, a dinner mooch—hell, she mooched *every* meal—on top of being a constant distraction, a worry. He was trying to do one thing, and she kept derailing him. Hurt seemed to choke her as she thought of everything he'd given…while she'd merely done her job. "You're right. You are the boss and I shouldn't bitch about doing things your way." Didn't mean she had to like it, though.

"Diah." He bent to look into her eyes. "Why are you deliberately putting the worst spin on this?"

"I'm not, but…" The denial faded. Damn it, hadn't she just told Madison how wonderful he was? She had. And there were definite reasons to be extra cautious.

She wasn't oblivious to the danger, so then why was she fighting with him? Feeling like an ungrateful jerk, she muttered, "Sorry."

"Does that contrite tone mean you'll cooperate?"

"I'm not an idiot, Memphis. I would have been careful anyway, but since it's important to you, yes, I'll check in."

His shoulders loosened. "Thank you." A quick look around ensured they were still alone, but he lowered his voice anyway. "Keep in mind that some of our reservations are from return guests, like Ed. Others are known troublemakers. I don't trust any of them, so I don't want you to, either." He brushed his knuckles over her cheek. "Look at it this way, would you risk Tuff, knowing the caliber of people who'll be here?"

"Of course not. I love Tuff too much to chance his safety."

Wearing a slight smile, he whispered, "Multiply that

by a hundred and maybe you'll get a clue about why I'm being overprotective."

Her heart skipped a beat. Could he be talking about love? *For her?* God, she hoped so, because she knew where Memphis Osborn was concerned, she was a total goner. Falling in love? Ha! She was already there.

She, Jedidiah Stephens, was completely, irrevocably in love with Memphis Osborn. Huh.

Now that she'd admitted it to herself, she almost wanted to laugh. "You don't realize, do you?"

Aggrieved all over again, he huffed. "The danger? Of course I do. Why do you think I'm—"

"No." She pressed her fingertips to his mouth. That sexy, teasing, oh-so-talented mouth. "I meant you don't realize what you mean to me. Not to put you on the spot, but you've become the most important person in my world. I've never had anyone to..." No, she wouldn't say *love*. There was no reason to pressure him like that. It'd be unfair, especially when he was already doing so much for her. *Everything* for her. Truly, it boggled her mind that anyone could be that invested in her.

Lightly catching her wrist, he lowered her hand and asked gruffly, "To...?"

She was known for her unwavering gaze, but the keen way he watched her now was pretty darned intense. "To lean on," she whispered. "To completely trust. To care about and lust after and know, one hundred percent, that you would never hurt me."

"Never," he agreed.

How nice it was to have Memphis on her side. "If it wasn't a threat to me, which makes it a threat to you, the past wouldn't matter anymore." Compared to the present, it faded like a vague shadow. "But there is a threat, so I want you to be careful, too."

Indulgent, he smiled and said, "Okay."

It was obvious that he discounted any such threat to himself. *Men.* Wonderful, strong, sexy men.

Memphis knew his brother was a hero, but he didn't yet realize that he was a hero as well.

Giving him a light shove that didn't move him a single inch, she said, "Butthead," while laughing and leaning into him.

He held Tuff's leash with one hand, and tangled the other in her hair. "Somehow that insult sounded like forgiveness."

Because it was. How could she be mad at him for caring? "Will you try to remember that you're not invincible?"

"Of course."

"You're important to me, Memphis."

"I'm glad."

He was *glad*? Definitely a butthead—but for now he was hers, and she didn't want him distracted with her when he could be catching bad actors in the middle of bad things. "Okay, here's the deal. I won't take any chances, and you'll try to trust me. If anything feels off, or if anyone seems a threat, I swear I'll let you know. Can you do that?"

"It won't be easy."

Those take-charge tendencies of his were trying to take over since talking to Madison. She rested her hand on his chest. "A big boy like you will manage, I'm sure."

"Tease." Half smiling, half frowning, he nodded. "I'll do my best—which won't be perfect." His hand opened to cradle her cheek. “Keep in mind that if anything happened to you it would completely level me.”

Whoa, that sounded serious. Diah would have liked to ask for details, but just then Lane’s camper door opened with a loud squeak. Tuff gave a bark until he saw Lane, then he wagged his tail and headed toward her. She hopped out with enough energy to rattle the entire tiny camper, then took a moment to stroke the dog’s neck.

From right behind her, Remmy emerged. He had to bend down to fit through the shorter doorway.

Huh. Interesting.

The budget camper had collapsible screens for windows, currently zipped closed so Diah couldn’t see through them. The open door gave her a quick glimpse of a compact, badly dated, miniature stove and sink area. The refrigerator was the size of a cooler. Another pop-out section from the rear provided a sleeping space.

Before she and Memphis could make too many assumptions, Remmy said, “She had a blown fuse and wasn’t sure how to change it.”

“Now I know,” Lane said, still with her attention on the dog.

Memphis nodded as if that explained everything.

Frowning, Remmy added, “The camper is old and needs repairs, but it’s solid.”

“It’s perfect.” Walking backward away from them, Lane said, “Thanks for letting me stay here.”

“Did I have a choice?” Memphis asked.

“I told Remmy to just deduct it from my pay.”

Cutting off whatever Memphis would have replied, Diah said, “I look forward to getting to know you better.”

“Great. Same.” She flagged a hand to indicate her

destination. "I'm going to check out the camp store, and then the gatehouse to familiarize myself. After that, if I can pitch in with anything, just let me know."

Together, they all watched her go.

"I like her," Diah announced.

Remmy said, "You don't really know her, but yeah, she's all right." He turned to Memphis. "She'll have to use the public restrooms. There's not enough room in that little camper even to add a portable toilet. She'll be sleeping on a skinny foam matt at the end of the camper, without a single solid wall to protect her."

Diah eyed the canvas sides and sloping canvas roof. "Does she seem concerned?"

Frowning, Remmy shook his head. "She appears to love the setup. Said she slept great last night."

Adventures, Diah knew, came in various packages. For her, being here, falling in love with Memphis, making friends with Remmy, had turned into the best kind of adventure. Maybe for Lane it'd be the same.

"Find out if there's anything she needs. I might have extra stuff in my cabin she could use."

Both men stared at her. Right. It wasn't actually *her* cabin anymore. All she did was store her stuff there. She should offer it up for Memphis to rent, but wouldn't that look pushy, as if she expected to live with him?

Uncomfortable now, she looked up at Memphis and tried for a casual smile. "That is, if you wouldn't mind. I know some stuff has to stay with the cabin—"

He leaned down and took her mouth in a warm, not-so-brief kiss. "It's a great idea." Another kiss, and then he straightened. He, too, affected a casual smile. "Maybe we should consider offering the cabin to Lane."

With a roll of his eyes, Remmy said, "You two crack

me up. All this dancing around when there isn't any music playing."

Diah scowled at him. "We should get to work." She took Tuff's leash from Memphis and turned to go. "I need to grab some stuff from the supply shed first. I'll be ready in five minutes."

"Remember your promise," Memphis called after her.

She blew him a kiss, and when Remmy laughed, she blew him one, too.

Right now it felt like she lived in two worlds—one full of promises and protection, and one shadowy with possible danger.

Juggling them both was going to get dicey, but with any luck she'd get through it all, settle her past, gain her freedom…and maybe get her own personal hero, too.

All in all, worth the risks.

CHAPTER THIRTEEN

Otto relaxed back in his desk chair, his thoughts centered on the two new women at the hotel. They were both young and attractive, happy to have shelter and protection. So often, his offer felt like a lifeline to those without resources. Desperate girls with nowhere to go, no one to turn to. Grooming them was easy.

Except it hadn't been easy with Lane. She fought against him, sharpening his interest in the process.

And then she'd gotten away.

Lately, his every thought circled around to loss. The loss so long ago—one that still haunted him. His more recent loss of Lane.

There'd been no sign of her. His men had scoured the area, warning every business owner to alert him if she showed up. Oh, she'd been spotted. Pretty much everywhere. But no one hired her and she kept slipping away.

Bad planning on his part.

He changed tactics, ordering *everyone* to hire her on the spot if she showed up again, yet it was already too late. He had a gut-clenching dread that he'd never see her again. Somehow she'd gotten out of town. Even her fucking beat-up car was now missing, though the keys he'd taken from her were still in his locked desk drawer, one to an apartment he'd closed out, another to a car that was barely roadworthy. The only other thing on the key ring was a quarter-sized smiley face charm. It mocked him.

Fuck Lane. She'd never been that important, anyway. He'd used her as filler, that's all. She'd taken the place of the one he really wanted.

Thinking it made his jaw tighten. Lane had been unimportant, yes, but he'd fucking *owned* her. How dare she run away?

There was a brief rap on his door.

"Enter."

Ed stepped in, paused and gave him a wary look, like a rat might eye a pissed-off cat.

Time to redirect his thoughts. He needed to concentrate on his hotel, Castle Getaway—*where you're treated like a king.* He was the king, not anyone else, but with all the women working there most men felt special. It was part of the service he offered, a service forever growing in popularity.

"You sent for me?" Ed asked.

"Yes." It was always easiest to do his business away from the hotel, and now that the campgrounds were opening again—something he'd never thought would happen—they'd be perfect for two reasons, only one of them business.

He had to reclaim what was his.

When he'd stashed it, he'd figured it was safe. Hell, everyone had assumed the run-down place would stay closed. When last he'd seen the campground, it was badly overgrown and in disrepair. Using it had seemed like a good idea at the time.

Now people would be tromping everywhere, so…

plans changed. Once he had his shit, he'd destroy it, which is what he should have done in the first place.

Over the past ten years, he'd gained power by taking zero shit from others. The days of him being a punching bag, taking the blame for anything, were long gone. He hired good men as retaliators, and never took unnecessary risks.

Years ago, though? Yeah, on the off chance he might use the evidence someday, he'd been reluctant to let it go. Wasn't his wisest move. Very soon he'd correct that error and then he could put all his concentration on more important things.

Hands linked loosely over his stomach, he asked Ed, "Everything is good to go?"

Ed said, "I have the camper lined up and the reservation made. I got one of the sites farthest from the entry, back in the woods." Pulling a crumpled, folded paper from his pocket, he dropped it on the desk. "I printed the layout of the place when I made the online reservation. The spot I circled is booked for a week. Is that good enough?"

Filled with distaste, Otto eyed the paper. This is what separated goons from organizers. Ed was a straight-up goon. Point at a person you wanted smashed, and Ed would smash them. Direct him to stab someone in the back, and he'd get wood while doing it—the sick prick.

Sadly, though, he had no respect for presentation. Ed certainly couldn't have run a thriving hotel that catered to the whims of special guests.

Brushing aside the layout without looking at it, Otto asked, "How long can you keep your friend's camper?"

"Long as we need it."

Since he'd expected nothing less, he smiled. Those who knew his name, also knew to stay on his good side. "Does the setup still leave room for one car to park beside the camper?"

"Yeah. Plus, the spot I got is remote enough that we could park a second car even."

He only needed one additional car, which would make it easy for him to leave once he'd finished his business.

"I figured I'd make it look real official, you know? Maybe even spend an afternoon fishing in the lake."

Uncaring what he did in his off time, Otto said, "I may go along."

Taken aback, Ed repeated, "Go along?"

"I wouldn't want anyone to know I was in the camper. Do you understand me?"

After some loose-jawed surprise, Ed nodded. "Yeah, sure, Otto. No problem."

If only he could trust Ed to handle this… But no. He wouldn't chance it. His entire life was built off a single brilliant plan. Now he was the king. Successful. He had everything he wanted.

Almost.

He wouldn't chance a fuckup that could ruin him at this point.

Every precaution was needed. "First thing when you get there, check closely for hidden security. Get the names and working hours of other employees. See how involved the owner is in running things." He gave it some thought. "And keep an eye on Remmy. I have a difficult time believing he's working there."

Practically jumping on that, Ed said, "An honest

job?" He snorted. "Not Remmy's speed. I bet he's up to something."

"Likely, but it doesn't matter." Plenty of people would be there to do business. "As long as he doesn't get in our way, leave him be."

"Right, got it. I'll be chill." He hesitated. "I figured I'd take one of the other guys with me. Probably Charlie."

Since it was in his nature to be cruel, a fact he'd long ago accepted, Otto laughed. "Let me guess. You're afraid of Remmy?"

"No!"

Otto chuckled. "Don't worry. If he becomes a problem, we'll kill him, but *away* from the campgrounds." Sitting forward, Otto gave Ed a dead stare. "Fuck this up for me and you won't be given another chance."

Ed scowled. "I've got it covered. No problem."

He'd better, because at the end of the opening week Otto hoped to have the entire thing wrapped up. His property retrieved, evidence destroyed and arrangements made.

After that, he could find a new girl, one without disturbing eyes. One who looked as young and innocent as Lane. When he did, she wouldn't get away as the others had. She'd be his… Forever.

THEIR FIRST FULL week was chaos, all in a very good way. It seemed every spot was taken and they had a growing list of reservations. When Memphis had started this, he'd never once considered that the campground might actually be a financial success. Most of his income was from wise investments in real estate and stock, but now, using his hands and actually living and working at his own campground… Damn, it was rewarding in ways he'd never expected.

As Diah hustled past him with a guest and a toolbox in her hand, he knew that she had a lot to do with his current level of satisfaction. Everything about her suited him in ways he'd never considered.

Before Diah, he'd had a plan laid out and it hadn't included involvement. Then she'd showed up, refused to leave, mesmerized him with her bold stare and confounded him with her fearless determination.

In the end, it was her touching vulnerability that completely stole his heart. It was almost like she intuitively knew when to be disagreeable or sweet to wrench the strongest response from him. Around her, he perpetually wanted to smile.

Looking down at Tuff since the dog was his companion today, Memphis said, "We're lucky guys, aren't we?"

"Fft."

He stroked the dog's neck. Like Memphis, Tuff kept his gaze on Diah as she stopped outside a camper and shared an animated conversation with a woman and man that apparently had something to do with the steps not working on their RV. He had complete faith that Diah would have it figured out in no time.

"You look content."

Turning to find his brother standing there, Memphis grinned. "Hey, when did you get here?"

"Few minutes ago. Remmy let us in. We parked out of the way and since the women are looking around, I figured I'd let you know we're here."

Leery of Hunter's smile, Memphis repeated, "Women?"

"Jodi…and Madison."

"Ah, hell." He quickly searched the immediate surroundings. "Where?"

"Relax. They'll be on their best behavior."

"Yeah, right." Just the fact that he didn't see Madison was alarming. It was never a good thing to have her nosing around. She'd either initiate a problem, or solve one in her own unique, over-the-top way. Truthfully, Jodi wasn't much different.

Overall, they were amazing—and he didn't want them wreaking havoc today.

Hunter knelt down to lavish some attention on Tuff. "When I get home, Turbo will smell the dog on me and have a fit."

"Lots of quacking?" Hunter's dog had the most amusing bark, very different from Tuff's generally quiet way. "You could have brought him with you." Better the dog than Madison. Not that he wouldn't be happy to see her, but right now he was so busy. It'd be better when he had more time to keep an eye on her, and to do a proper introduction to Diah.

"Wasn't enough room in my truck with both women determined to come along. Plus, Turbo was snoring in his dog bed. He'd played in the yard for an hour with Madison before we left. She wore him out."

Both dreading the answer, and somewhat hopeful, he asked, "Has Madison found out anything? Is that why she's here?"

"Could be," Hunter said in an annoyingly cagey way. "When I tried to get concrete answers, she patted me like I was a curious boy and said it was your business and she'd discuss it with you first."

Yeah, sounded like Madison. "Apparently, she wants

to discuss it in person," Memphis muttered, his gaze again drawn to Diah. The steps were now working fine and the couple, whom he knew were buying drugs from another camper, thanked her before going into their RV and closing the door.

He'd already gotten the info for everyone involved and done some background work on them. They weren't big-time drug dealers, only into personal use. As long as they weren't trafficking anything dangerous, selling to kids or driving while incapacitated, he'd leave them to their recreational choices.

Hunter asked, "Do you have time to visit, or do you need to keep vigil on the girl?"

He snorted. "You're the one who told me she's a woman, remember?"

"Yeah, I do." Hunter smiled. "Seems you figured that out for yourself, though."

"I'm in deep," Memphis admitted. Because Hunter was his brother and he not only loved him, he also respected him more than anyone he knew, confiding in him was easy. He'd already told him some of the details around Diah, and he assumed Jodi had filled in the rest, which she'd no doubt gotten from Madison. "I don't suppose there are any secrets left for me to tell you?"

"Not really, no. It's not the same as talking to you face-to-face, though."

Very true. "I've wanted to see you," Memphis admitted. "We've been swamped here with prep, though, and I don't want to leave Diah alone until we have everything sorted out."

"I get it. I felt the same with Jodi, like if I let her out of my sight I'd somehow lose her."

"That's about it." He watched Diah hurry by again, but at nearly every RV, she got stopped for a question. When she disappeared from sight, he thought about going after her.

A second later, his phone dinged. Knowing it'd be Diah, he said to his brother, "Give me just a sec."

"Take your time." Hunter relieved him of the leash and walked a short distance away with Tuff.

The text from Diah said, Problem with a leak in laundry. Done in 30 or less. No I don't need ur help.

The building for the laundry wasn't far away, and others would be in and out of there. Didn't matter. When she was out of his sight, it worried him.

Remember your promise

To which she replied: :)

Huh. Maybe she'd gotten used to him worrying. Just to be sure, he sent: I'm checking on u in 20. He waited, but didn't get a reply, which was probably her way of letting him know to chill. She had promised, and he knew she understood the risks.

But seriously, he made note of the time before heading to Hunter. "You want anything to drink?"

"A cola would be great." His gaze searched Memphis's face. "Why don't we sit out here? I get the feeling you won't relax if we're inside."

"Thanks. Be right back." In the kitchen, he grabbed two cold colas and a glass of water to refresh Tuff's bowl on the deck, but he also grabbed him a treat. He thought it was important for Tuff to know how much he appreciated his good behavior. The dog was watchful but friendly, and best of all, he trusted Memphis to keep Diah safe. That counted for a lot.

Used to be, Tuff wouldn't have left her side. Now Memphis liked to think that Tuff knew he could relax his guard. Such a good boy he was.

Hunter had taken one of the two chairs on the short deck with Tuff resting next to him, his chin on his paws as he watched campers go by. Memphis set the drinks on the table, dumped Tuff's old water and refilled the dish, then offered the dog the treat.

With his tail sweeping back and forth across the deck, Tuff lifted his head enough to accept the bone-shaped goodie, and got down to devouring it.

Knowing he'd stalled long enough, Memphis sat, his drink ignored, elbows on knees as he considered all the issues and how to put them into words.

"Tell me what concerns you most."

Leave it to his brother to cut to the heart of things. "The threat to Diah. That's top of the list. I can't shake the feeling that something terrible is going to happen."

"Don't ignore it," Hunter warned, now more alert. "People are a hell of a lot more intuitive than they want to believe. When those internal alarm bells go off, you don't have to be polite. You don't have to worry about offending someone. You don't even have to be logical. Just protect yourself."

"And protect Diah."

"Anyone you care about," Hunter agreed. "I'm not saying you have to be an obnoxious asshole, and you definitely don't need to borrow trouble. Just stay prepared."

"I don't know how you do it." Memphis sat back with

a humorless laugh. "All this, shit happening left and right with campers, and it doesn't bother me. Madison breathing down my neck, piece of cake. But anything with Diah keeps me awake at night. I stay on edge. It's like..."

"You want to hold on extra tight, do whatever it takes to keep her with you."

Memphis looked away. "To make her want to stay."

Frowning, Hunter slowly sat forward. "She's planning to leave?"

"Fucked if I know." He unleashed the frustration he'd so far managed to keep in check. "I mean, I don't think so. She agreed to see out the season with me."

"The season." Hunter grunted at that open-ended arrangement.

"Hey, try living it."

"Did, with Jodi. Not knowing if or when she'd bail was the worst. Don't put me through that hell again."

"What do I do, then? I've only known her seven weeks."

"Keeping count?"

"Seven freaking weeks." That felt like a lifetime. "Not like I can propose."

"Marriage? Might be better to give it a little more time," Hunter said, as if he knew Memphis would head down that road eventually.

And he would. With Diah. *If* she felt the same.

"You could ask her to move in with you."

"Yeah, she stays here anyway, but she still has her own cabin. It's like she's with me, but with one foot out the door." It made him nuts. She'd only recently admitted they even had a relationship, so how could he push for more of a commitment from her?

Hunter gave that some thought. "She's had an odd life. A lot of moving."

"Always on the run," Memphis said. "Even when Glover did settle with her, he wanted her constantly vigilant." Almost as if he knew someone would still come after her. Why did it feel like danger was breathing down his neck?

"Staying in one place might spook her, especially now that Glover is gone. She might feel unsettled."

Glover had been her protector. Now Memphis wanted her to trust him to keep her safe. More than that, he wanted her to *be* safe. He wanted her to know that whatever had happened in her past, it would stay in her past. She could move forward, with him.

Hunter shrugged. "Sometimes, when worry crowds in, moving is the only thing you can do."

Memphis thought of how Hunter had packed up and moved away from everything familiar. "Was it like that for you?"

A few seconds ticked by before he spoke. "When I left, it was to escape the daily reminders, all the memories around me." He fell silent a moment more. "Pretty sure I ran from myself, too."

They'd never discussed it in depth. Memphis was just glad to have his brother back, to know he was okay. He hadn't wanted to pressure Hunter, but now he said, "It killed me how isolated you were, how you cut us all out."

"I know and I'm sorry." He watched the activity in the campground, then reached down to stroke the dog. "I felt guilty for that, but now I don't regret it."

"Course not." With a half smile, Memphis glanced at him. "Now you have Jodi."

"And Diah has you." Hunter set his gaze on Memphis. "I think she'll see that."

But what if she didn't? "She was hurt so badly as a kid." He explained to Hunter about her being dragged from her bed. "It eats me up whenever I think about it, but she doesn't seem to realize that it traumatized her."

"Or she's hiding it pretty deep."

Tunneling his fingers into his hair, Memphis considered that. Yes, Diah still hid a lot of shit.

He wished she wouldn't hide anything from him.

He let out a tense breath. "She has this fearless attitude about everything, but denies it because things can startle her. Like anyone is immune from that?"

"Startles how?"

"She said she freezes up, and she might a little but she still does what she needs to." He shared the way Remmy had scared her at the cabin, and how she'd jolted into action, locking the doors. "The way Glover took her from her bed, it's no wonder. Can you imagine getting jarred awake with a hand over your mouth, smoke in the air, while someone too big for you to fight dragged you out a window?"

Very quietly, Hunter said, "Can't imagine it and don't want to."

Memphis heard the same sympathy that nearly smothered him sometimes. "She sizes people up easily, knowing almost from the start if they're a threat or not." He shook his head, because that didn't really cover it. "You know that Glover had done some pretty bad things."

"I'm aware. He worked for a real bastard until the night of the fire. The man did not have clean hands."

"No, but he turned it around to protect Diah and just as she can't discount that, neither can I."

Hunter was silent a moment, then asked, "How did Glover know about the fire?"

Good question. "Diah said he never talked about it much with her. All she knows is that he rescued her."

Being the analytical sort, the kind of man who saw things that others didn't, Hunter turned thoughtful.

Memphis kept silent, waiting to see what conclusions Hunter would draw. God knew he hadn't been able to sort it out. He had access to everything a computer could find, research records, video recordings, paper trails, but he couldn't read minds and he couldn't put together the vagaries of tainted souls.

To him, it sounded like Glover had bonded with Diah early on. That much Memphis could understand, because everything about Diah fascinated him, though admittedly in different ways.

Perhaps seeing her as a neglected, sometimes mistreated little girl had struck a chord in Glover's otherwise black heart. Whatever his reasons, Memphis would be eternally grateful that she'd had him.

"It occurs to me," Hunter said, "that we might be looking at this all wrong."

Awareness prickled over Memphis. He tried not to jump the gun, but he knew his brother, and he knew he was putting puzzle pieces together. "Don't hold back. Let me hear it."

"It's an ugly thought, but it's the only thing that makes sense to me."

Memphis waited.

Turning to face him, Hunter said, "Glover was probably involved in the plan for killing her family. How else could he have known every detail, including exactly when the fire would start, how to get in and get her out without being seen, and what to do once he had her? That takes a lot of prearranging."

Hating that thought, Memphis said, "Diah claimed he had everything ready. He grabbed her, got in a truck and they took off."

"If that was spur of the moment, it would have left too much evidence behind—unless he'd already arranged to cover his tracks."

"Diah said he gave up everything for her."

Hunter gave it a quick thought. "Seems like Glover could have been in on the planning, but then had a change of heart. He knew the threat wasn't over, because he knew he'd screwed the ultimate plans."

"To destroy the whole family." Rage squeezed Memphis's windpipe, making his voice harsh as he whispered the ugly part out loud. "And that would have included Diah."

For the entire week, she'd stayed too busy to worry much, yet Diah still heeded Memphis's warnings. She was alert and always careful, but the opening was much as she'd expected—nonstop assistance needed with one thing after another. Far too often, people went out in campers, fifth wheels and RVs without really knowing how to operate them. Time and again she reminded herself that people had different talents. One of hers was understanding how things worked. She looked at control panels and just seemed to know.

Today she'd helped people hook up their water, level their RVs, get their TVs set up, and showed a great many of them how to pitch their tents. No matter what she did or where, it seemed she spotted Memphis or Remmy keeping an eye on her.

Funny, but instead of feeling crowded, she felt… Well, it wasn't bad. Was actually kind of nice. Like being part of a real family. Appreciated. Cared for.

Now, as she left the laundry, she didn't see either of them, but she did spot Ed again.

A few times throughout the week she'd noticed him. He was often wandering around, occasionally heading out to fish at the lake, a few times just walking with the other man he'd brought along. Memphis said his name was Charlie and he'd warned her to steer clear of them both.

No problem. They gave her the creeps.

She'd been the one at the gate, giving Lane time to take her break, when they'd checked in. She'd done her best not to stare in any way. Wasn't easy with the way *they* had stared. Now, with neither Memphis nor Remmy around, she saw Ed again.

Before Ed glanced her way, she headed back toward Memphis, or at least that had been her intent until she and Lane crossed paths.

With a smile of greeting, Lane said, "Remmy's at the gate. It's a quiet time right now so I figured I'd check on Sable, see if she needs anything."

Because she felt it, Diah glanced back and found Ed stopped dead in his tracks, staring at them. His interest felt especially sharp-edged, sending uneasiness to prickle along her neck. In the next second, he lifted his phone and took a picture.

Of *her*?

Rapidly switching direction, she decided to stick close to Lane and headed for the dubious safety of the camp store. "I'll go with you."

At first surprised, Lane said, "Okay, sure. You've been running all day. I imagine you could use a break—"

The thought went unfinished as Diah hooked Lane's arm and hustled them along double-time, doing her utmost to resist another glance at Ed. As soon as they stepped into the store, she closed the door and said, "I need to text Memphis real quick."

Lane tipped her head. "Is something wrong?"

"No, sorry. It's just..." *I'm terrible when I panic.* No, she wouldn't say that to Lane. "I just want to make sure he doesn't need anything."

Without looking convinced, Lane said, "Got it. Take your time." She headed over to Sable.

Stepping away, Diah got out her phone and quickly texted a message to Memphis.

Nothing serious, but could you come to camp store?

He replied, Ur okay?

What if Ed hadn't been taking the photo of her? What if he hadn't taken a photo at all? He might have been reading a text and holding up the phone to avoid the glare of the sun.

Feeling ridiculous, hesitant to alarm him, she returned, Yes.

B there soon. Hunter is here.

His brother had dropped in to visit? Now she felt bad for bothering him. She hesitated only three seconds, waffling on what to say, before she sent a simple, Thx. After all, she was in the store with both Sable and Lane. Other campers weren't that far away. A scream would probably bring people running. Knowing Memphis, he wouldn't keep her waiting.

She was safe.

Just as she tucked her phone back in her pocket, Ed stepped in.

The look of glee on his face sent her heart galloping in fear…except, he didn't even notice her.

All his attention was on Lane.

Worse, Lane stared back at him in shock and horror.

Smile broad and walk cocky, Ed moved toward her. "Ah, Lane, it's good to see you."

Lane scuttled behind the counter with Sable, though that little barrier offered no real protection. "Go away."

Now that Diah realized his attention wasn't for her, her composure returned. "What are you doing, Ed?"

He spared her a glance that turned into a full-body perusal. "I'm flattered you know my name, doll, but this doesn't concern you, so butt out." Turning back to Lane, he said, "We have unfinished business. Isn't that right, honey?"

She shook her head and whispered, "No."

"You slipped away without paying your debt."

"I paid it twice over."

"I'm not the only one who disagrees."

Galvanized by her friend's fear, Diah stormed forward to put herself between him and Lane. "You're upsetting an employee. Now get out."

He laughed at her. "I don't think so." Grabbing her upper arm, he tried to move her away. Determined to shield Lane, Diah resisted.

The door opened and a low, husky voice intruded. "Am I interrupting?"

Diah looked up to see two women. She recognized Jodi, Memphis's sister-in-law, as the one who'd spoken. The other, tall and slim with dark hair, looked like a model, especially while smiling.

"Yeah, you are," Ed said, as he shoved his way past Diah.

Before he could touch Lane, she bounded right back. Arms open like a barricade, she explained, "He's bothering Lane."

Jodi stared at Ed. "I suggest you leave them both alone."

With a laugh, Ed asked, "Or what? You'll hurt me?"

The taller woman said, "Well, if she doesn't, I will." She gave him a delighted smile. "Wouldn't take me more than ten seconds, tops."

"Bullshit," Ed growled, losing a bit of his amusement.

"Or," Jodi said, lifting the side of her shirt enough to show the butt of a gun, "I could finish it in two." Her grin was evil, not delighted. "Bullets travel fast."

No longer amused, Ed latched on to Diah and dragged her in front of him, locking one beefy arm around her. He squeezed her so tightly that her toes left the ground. Both surprised and scared, she went entirely blank.

Ed snarled, "You shouldn't go threatening a man like that."

Jodi's smile dimmed. "I don't threaten, I act, so I'm telling you, your best bet on survival is to let her go. Now."

The model said, "Oh, let me. Please? I need the exercise."

Diah wished she had even an ounce of their courage. Around the constriction of his hold and her fear, she thought to rasp, "I messaged Memphis."

Sighing, the tall one said, "Well, that changes everything, doesn't it?"

And from there, everything seemed to happen at once.

The door opened with Memphis and Hunter still in conversation—until they saw what was happening.

The warmth in Memphis's gaze iced over to something hard and dangerous. Outrage carried him forward like a human wrecking ball. He didn't shout, not Memphis, but his calm order, said so quietly, held more warning than a shout could have. "Get your fucking hands off her."

Too fast for her to guess his intent, Ed shoved Diah back into Lane. As the two of them stumbled, Ed threw a vicious punch at Memphis's face.

Diah flinched as if she'd felt the impact of that massive fist. Lane covered her mouth on a short cry.

Sable grumbled, "Screw this," and quickly sidled out of range.

Barely budging from the blow, Memphis narrowed his eyes, worked his jaw and smiled. "You just made three critical mistakes."

"Three?" Ed put up his fists, ready to deliver more damage. "How you figure that?"

Memphis loosened his stance. "One, you hit me."

Diah noticed that Hunter didn't look alarmed. Jodi and the tall woman lifted their brows.

"Two, you only threw one punch."

"Ha! You wanting more?" Ed withdrew a big blade that he flashed in front of him. "You don't have Remmy here to protect you now."

Diah barely swallowed back a scream. Instinctively, she started looking for a weapon to even the odds. All she found was a large can of baked beans.

"Three," Memphis continued calmly, "you stood there listening while I shook off the daze." And with that, Memphis struck him.

Diah almost dropped the can.

Okay, she'd assumed Memphis could hold his own, but the way he moved…

Ed tried to thrust the knife forward, only Memphis caught his wrist, using his own momentum against him to pull him off balance, and landing a hard knee into Ed's groin.

The knife fell from his hand with a clatter, already forgotten as Memphis followed up with a punch to Ed's face, hard enough to send him stumbling back, his arms pinwheeling in the air and blood spraying out of his nose.

She felt sick, but Memphis didn't slow. He struck again, this time with his left hand going to Ed's middle.

Startled, squeamish, more than a little afraid, Diah made a grab for the knife and got clipped in the side of the head by moving bodies. Her glasses went flying, along with her wits. Falling onto her butt, she saw stars dancing in front of her eyes, but she had the knife gripped firmly in hand and she wasn't about to let it go.

"Diah!" Lane grabbed her, urging her to the side, and good thing given the way Ed's body landed hard on the floor right next to her feet. Memphis crouched over him, striking him twice more.

Without her noticing, Hunter had moved to her side. He got her to her feet and out of range, dusted her off and gently but firmly relieved her of the knife. "You okay?"

Unable to take her eyes off Memphis, she nodded. There was a dull sting on her temple, but it was mostly the harsh pumping of her heart that she felt.

"Good." Hunter tucked Lane behind him, then put his arm loosely over Diah's shoulders, and she wasn't sure if it was to comfort her or keep her in place so she couldn't interfere again.

Seconds later, when Memphis stood, Ed didn't. His big body sprawled awkwardly over the floor, blood on his mouth and coming out his nose, eyes swollen shut, a purpling bruise on his jaw, and loose hands cradling his privates. He appeared more unconscious than otherwise, and as she stared at him in macabre horror, he went limp.

Frantically, her gaze went all over Memphis, but when she started forward, Hunter held her back. Other than the single bruise on his cheek from Ed's first punch, Memphis looked fine. Incandescent with rage, yes, but unharmed. "Memphis—"

Slowly turning to face her, Memphis growled, *"What the hell were you thinking?"*

So much silence descended in the small store, Diah heard herself swallow. Humiliation left her hollow. Never had she heard that enraged tone from Memphis. There was no gentle teasing, no humor or compassion or acceptance.

She opened her mouth, but nothing came out. Given half a chance, she'd happily remove herself from the scene, and yet her feet seemed rooted to the floor.

"Ass," Jodi accused, shouldering past Memphis as if heaving, enraged men were an everyday occurrence.

Memphis's nostrils flared as he sucked in a long breath that didn't seem to do him a bit of good. He flexed his hands, staring at Diah as violence churned just below the surface of his control.

She wasn't sure what to do. Well, she wanted to cry, but she wouldn't. Hell no. Not with all of Memphis's friends and family standing around her. Not with the way he'd just spoken to her.

Undaunted, Jodi said, "FYI, Hunter, if you ever speak to me like that, we'll have a huge problem."

Hunter gave Diah a brief, one-armed hug. "Men say stupid things when they're scared shitless. You'd forgive me, Jodi—once you understood."

"It's true," the tall woman said. "Crosby always turns into a caveman when he thinks I'm in danger. I know it's from love, so I don't worry about it too much."

Love? If that's what love looked like, Diah wanted no part of it. Currently, Memphis didn't appear to possess any soft emotions at all.

He looked like a stranger.

"I'm so sorry," Lane whispered. Given how she held

herself, she was as rattled as Diah was. "So damn sorry. This is all my fault."

Memphis finally looked away from Diah, and it was as if he'd freed her from some invisible bond. Her lungs filled with needed oxygen, her joints all loosened and her muscles turned to noodles.

Wobbly on her feet, she was extra grateful that his brother led her to Sable's chair. "Sit a minute. It'll be all right. You'll see." Near her ear, he whispered, "Go easy on him, okay? You gave him a hell of a fright."

Unsure what that meant, she sank into the chair… *Sable.* She'd forgotten all about her. "Where's Sable?"

Poking her head out from behind shelves, Sable took in the crowd, then scowled at Ed's downed body. "I'm not cleaning that up."

Jodi snickered.

Still struggling, Memphis ran a hand over his face.

A part of Diah wanted to go to him so badly. She wanted her old Memphis back, the funny, easygoing guy.

Maybe to break the tension, Jodi said, "Didn't know you could fight like that, Memphis."

"Seriously?" Hunter quirked a brow. "He's my brother. We tangled all the time."

"Yeah, I guess some of your badassery was bound to rub off on him."

With a shrug in his tone, Hunter said, "We're both physical and athletic, so yeah, we played hard and occasionally we got into it."

With tension still roughening his words, Memphis said, "You always went easy on me."

It relieved Diah to hear him speak, even though he didn't look at her.

"You're my brother," Hunter said. "I recall you pulling back a few times as well. Overall, we taught each other."

How could they all stand around chatting as if nothing had happened while Ed groaned on the floor?

Suddenly, a slim hand appeared in front of her face. "I'm Madison, by the way. Memphis's very dear friend. His *best* friend. It's so nice to finally meet you in person."

Blinking, Diah looked up at her. Way up because Madison was really tall. This was his BFF? The woman she'd spoken to about Glover and Rusty? Memphis should have told her that Madison was downright stunning. Feeling like a vague shadow in comparison, Diah took her hand and said a very weak, "Hi."

Madison's fingers curled warmly around Diah's and she leaned close to whisper, "Deep breaths, okay? The adrenaline will wear off in a few minutes and then you'll feel better. It took me years to learn to push through it. Now it's like nothing. Piece of cake. You'll be fine."

No, pretty sure she wouldn't, not with Memphis furious at her and everyone else trying to pretend nothing much had happened.

As she stepped away, Madison said, "So this is Ed, in the flesh." She toed the downed man. "Doesn't look like much right now, does he?"

Memphis said, "Don't poke at him."

Oh, for Madison he sounded a little more reasonable! Damn it, that hurt her, too.

"He works for Otto." Stoic and very alone, Lane stared at Ed. "He recognized me."

So he hadn't taken the photo of Diah? Spurred by her new friend's guilt, Diah forgot her own upset and hurried to her side. She wasn't sure what Ed had done to Lane, but she figured it had to be bad. "Thank God you weren't alone."

Lane's face was pale. "I have to leave now," she whispered. "If…if you could give me thirty minutes before you let him go—"

"No."

Everyone turned to Memphis. Gradually, he got it together. Madison, damn her, hugged up to his arm and patted his chest as if soothing a rabid beast.

Diah wanted to pat him—but yeah, she wasn't making the first move. They were all too blasé about things and she was most definitely out of her depth.

"This was *my* fault," Memphis said, ignoring how Madison continued to keep his arm. "Remmy told me you had worked for Otto Woodall. We should have warned you that Ed was here."

"You didn't know that I…that they…" Lane shook her head and stiffened her shoulders. "I should have left when I had a chance. I didn't have enough money, though, and I thought—"

Putting her arm around her, Diah led Lane to the chair she'd vacated. "You stayed here because you thought you'd be safe, right?"

Lane said nothing.

Diah wasn't deterred. "You *are* safe here. Memphis won't let anyone hurt you." She glared at Memphis, no longer thinking of his anger or her fear. Lane needed help, and by God she'd get it. "Tell her."

Instead, Memphis folded his arms. "Do you believe it, Diah?"

"I..." The words strangled in her throat. Damn it, this wasn't about *her*. She hugged Lane a little closer. "We're not talking about me."

Lane looked back and forth between them.

Memphis moved closer, his midnight eyes staring into hers. "Do you feel safe here?"

She couldn't look away. Her emotions had just gone on a roller-coaster ride of fear, anger, hurt...and now hope. Regardless, she couldn't lie to him. "I feel completely safe with you." Here, anywhere... All she knew was that she'd found him, and now she didn't want to be apart from him.

Satisfaction softened his mouth until the corners actually lifted in a small smile. His eyes warmed, too.

Well, hello. There's the Memphis I know and love.

He turned to Lane. His tone was gentle when he said, "I need you to stay here with us, okay? No more running."

Fear flared in her eyes. "You're going to contact Otto?"

"Maybe, but I won't let him anywhere near you. You have my word."

Lane chewed her bottom lip. "I believe you mean well, but once Otto knows I'm here, it won't be safe for any of you."

"I understand your worry, I swear I do, but can you try to trust me just a little?"

Ready to lend a hand, Diah said, "Please, Lane? He wouldn't lie to you."

Reluctance showed in her tense posture and in the shallow way she breathed, but Lane nodded.

"Good, thank you." Memphis put a hand on her shoulder. "For now, I want you to stay here with my friends, okay?"

"I volunteer to be her personal bodyguard," Madison announced. "She can't get better than me."

Hunter and Jodi both rolled their eyes.

"What?" Madison asked. "I assumed you two would clean the garbage from the floor."

The garbage being Ed. Most definitely, she was out of her league with these people, yet it was an oddly reassuring thought. They were all so calmly capable. And the lethal way Memphis had fought… She still wasn't sure what to make of that.

With her cell phone already out, Jodi said, "I'll call Remmy. He's going to be pissed that he missed the fireworks."

"Probably." Memphis glanced at Lane again. "He'll want to talk to you."

Lane hesitated, her gaze flickering to Ed as he groaned and rolled to his side, before coming back to Diah and then Memphis. "Thank you."

On impulse, Diah hugged her close. "We're friends now. Always feel free to talk to me. About anything, okay?"

Returning the embrace, Lane smiled tremulously. "I will—if you will."

With a gentle hold, Memphis drew Diah away. "I think for now, you and I need to talk."

"Here?" She didn't relish an audience.

"Outside." His gaze sought Sable's. "You're okay?"

Leaning against the wall, appearing a little rattled, Sable nodded. "You impressed me. Not easy to do."

For only a second, Memphis cracked a smile. "Could you draw up a Temporarily Closed sign to tape to the door? I don't want any customers coming into this mess."

Sable's chin lifted. "Will I still get paid?"

Diah couldn't believe that was her top concern. It pleased her when Memphis said, "Regular day's pay. Now get on that sign."

With a groan, Ed pushed into a sitting position against the counter. Using one sleeve, he swiped away the blood from his nose, then flinched. "You fucked up." Through swollen eyes he glared at Memphis, and then Lane. "You'll pay, girl—"

When Hunter crouched in front of him, he cut off the threat really fast. "Not another word, or you'll have more than a broken nose and bruised balls. Got it?"

"What will your brother do to him?" Lane whispered.

With a shrug, Memphis said, "Hunter will figure it out, and I'll rejoin him soon."

"I don't want to be anywhere near him."

Madison said, "Where are you staying? We'll go there. I won't leave you, I promise."

"She really is all the protection you need," Memphis seconded. "Especially with Ed in here."

There was a little more shuffling—agreements about who would do what, though Diah didn't quite follow—and then Memphis had her hand and was urging her from the building. Madison and Lane followed.

Once outside, Madison said to Memphis, "Take your time and do it right." She winked at Diah. "He's the best. Remember that."

It was something she already knew, yet she stayed silent as Madison and Lane walked off to Lane's camper. When she saw Madison look up at the sky, she realized that storm clouds had rolled in. While they'd been in the store, the weather had drastically changed.

Leaning against the side of the building, she asked, "Where's Tuff?"

"In my cabin. He's relaxed his guard enough that he didn't mind going inside to continue his nap."

"I'm glad. He would have wanted a piece of Ed, too, but he could have gotten hurt in the process." She peeked at Memphis. He still looked pretty darned intense. It almost killed her to think how badly things could have turned out. Only he'd surprised her. "I had no idea you could fight like that."

"I know what you've always thought." He leaned against the building, shoulder to shoulder with her. "None of it has ever been flattering."

CHAPTER FOURTEEN

It infuriated Otto to be stuck inside the borrowed camper, forced to wait. Now that he was here, he wanted to reclaim his property and formulate plans. It had been a slow week of Ed scouting out all the security cameras, too many of them really, but he finally had a plan.

To enact it, he needed Ed to watch his back.

He should have returned by now, but there was no sign of him.

Knowing it'd storm soon, he got antsier by the minute. Striding to a window and parting the blinds, he peeked out.

That's when he spotted Lane.

What. The. Fuck.

Soaking up the sight of her, Otto noted the shell-shocked look on her face. Young, afraid… She appeared much as she had the day he'd acquired her from the restaurant.

Damn it, did her hunted expression have something to do with Ed's delay? If that pig had touched her, Otto would kill him. *She's mine.*

Accompanied by a tall, breathtakingly gorgeous woman, Lane made her way toward a ratty little pop-up camper that looked like it might blow away in the storm.

Was she staying *here*? He almost laughed. No wonder he hadn't been able to find the bitch.

Rubbing a hand over his mouth, he thought of everything he'd planned for Lane, everything he'd thought was forever lost but was now back within reach. He breathed deeper as new plans formed in rapid succession. First, he had to get his evidence, then he'd grab Lane and exit the campground.

He was just about to duck away from the window when movement near the camp store drew his gaze.

His fucking knees almost buckled. *"Jedidiah,"* he whispered aloud, struggling to believe his own eyes. But most definitely, that was her. She'd matured, her body lusher now and Christ, he craved her.

Everything collided, his past, his future, what he wanted—and what he wanted to bury. All in this goddamned dump?

He should burn the entire thing to the ground. Actually…yeah. Not a bad idea.

Once he got the women.

Having watched her too long, Jedidiah glanced up, which forced him to stumble back so quickly he lost his footing and landed half on the couch, half on the floor. The metal blinds on the window clattered and the camper shook. He drew three deep breaths then scrambled forward to slide the lock on the metal door, ensuring no one could come snooping.

He had to make new plans and fast. Plans that included Lane…and his long-lost little sister.

DIAH KNEW SHE was jumpy, but seriously, it had felt like someone watched her. She looked toward Ed's camper, thinking maybe it was Charlie, but then she spotted him chatting to some female campers at one of the smaller cabins. She supposed they'd have to talk to him soon.

As Ed's brother, Charlie was bound to notice when he didn't return.

Putting those worries aside for the moment, she looked up at Memphis. He stared straight ahead, his posture deceptively relaxed though she could still sense the tension in him.

"I didn't know you could handle yourself like that because you've deliberately led me to believe you're all laid-back and good-natured."

"Because I am those things."

Without even meaning to move, she turned so that she stood against Memphis, her hands on his chest where she could still feel his warmth and the steady beat of his heart. "You're also total hero material."

"Knowing how to fight doesn't make you a hero," he countered.

"I agree. Knowing when to fight does, though. The truth is that I've seen you as a hero for a while now."

His gaze dipped down to her. "Why?"

"So, so many reasons. Most recently, it was how you agreed to help Lane."

"Did you give me a choice?"

"Did you need one?"

His brows came together. "No."

"Of course not." She tried a smile that he didn't return. "I really do trust you, you know. Totally, completely, one hundred percent."

His chin hitched a little higher. "Enough to stay?"

"For how long?"

Slowly, his eyes closed. He clasped her arms and started to lever her away.

Diah didn't let him. "Are you asking for forever?" The look he gave her said it all.

He was, and her heart did a few leaps.

Emotions like hope, need…definitely love, caused pure pandemonium to her senses. Determined, she hugged herself tight against him and said more softly, "Are you offering me forever?"

His arms loosened, scaring her half to death because she thought he'd move away.

Instead, he lifted them to wrap her in close and put his forehead to hers. "We don't have much time. I now have a few dozen things that need immediate attention."

She was being selfish. "I know."

"So I have to get right to it."

Embarrassed at her own reaction, she worked up a placid smile and found her pride. "Of course."

"I'm sorry I yelled at you."

She nodded, thought about it and shook her head. "You're forgiven if you'll try not to do it again."

He gave her a slight smile, then frowned as he looked over her face. "I'm so sorry you got hurt."

Damn it, her heart felt trampled. "I'm fine."

"You have a bruise here." He pressed a featherlight kiss to her temple. "And your glasses are gone."

At the moment, she didn't care about her glasses. "Your jaw is bruised and so are your knuckles."

"But we're both fine?"

She nodded.

His gaze moved over her face then settled on her eyes. "Diah, will you please stay with me forever?"

He said it again! More emotions welled up, choking her so that all she could do was nod fast.

"Yes?"

"Yes, I'd like that." Feeling ridiculously shy, she asked, "Are you sure?" She spoke again before he could.

"You have to be sure. You can't say any of this if you don't mean it. You don't get to change your mind." That thought brought up another and she frowned. "You don't get to yell at me, either."

"I'm sure that I want you with me." He drew a strained breath. "I'm equally sure that I never want to see you manhandled again." His hands cupped her face. "You should have gotten away from us to be safe."

"He had a knife."

"And I died twice knowing what he could have done to you with it."

She shoved his shoulder. "Well, I was dying, too, because he planned to use it on you!"

"Shh." He smiled as he shushed her. "Everyone in the camp will hear you."

Knowing she loved him, knowing she never wanted to be away from him, she groaned. "I'll forgive you for shouting at me if you understand that I had to try to help."

"Fearless," he complained with a smile.

Just then they both saw Remmy jogging toward them. Memphis pointed toward Lane's camper. "Madison is with her."

Scowling, he turned and headed to the camper—still hurrying. They watched as he gave a knock, and a second later the door opened and Remmy went inside.

Diah knew her time was up. "Those million things you need to do…"

"For now, will you be okay with Madison and Remmy?"

"I'd rather be with you."

His expression softened, but he started her on the way to Lane's. "I'd like that, too, but I can't be divided right now. Hopefully, I won't be too long and I'll tell you everything once we get it worked out."

She didn't want to stay behind, but she knew he was right. Plus, Lane needed a friend right now. Yes, there was Remmy, but maybe she could help, too. "All right, but I'd rather we all wait at your house. I don't want to leave Tuff alone much longer."

"Good idea." Once they reached Lane's camper, Madison stepped out, attempting to look humble.

Diah could have told her that it wasn't a natural fit for a woman like her.

She grabbed Diah in a hug. "Oh, good, you look happier. You'll stay here with Remmy and Lane, okay? I need to…assist Memphis."

Memphis started to speak, to explain the plan.

"I have things to tell you." Her smile wouldn't fool anyone. "Things for your ears only—at least for now."

Proving something important, something Diah couldn't completely define but still cherished, Memphis said, "You can include Diah on anything."

"Yes, of course." Her smile held. "And I'm sure we will. You first, though. You know how I am. Words pour out and I'm not always as tactful as I should be. Remember, she's had an ordeal." Madison turned to Diah. "You've had an ordeal."

Whatever it was that Madison had to share, Diah figured she could wait. Dramatically, she put the back of her hand to her forehead and said, "Yes, such a trial. I need my rest." She dropped her hand and grinned. "Go on, you two." She pointed at Memphis. "But you will fill me in soon, right?"

"Yes." Looking really pleased, and maybe even proud, he said to Madison, "Her dog is in my cabin.

We'll take them there first, then you and I can join Hunter and Jodi."

Those arrangements were made quickly. Remmy appeared glad to move to the cabin instead of the flimsy camper, especially with the way the wind had picked up. Keeping a hand at Lane's back, Remmy guided them on a silent trek past other campers and RVs. Lightning streaked across the darkening sky, and a cold drizzle began to fall.

At the small deck to the cabin, Diah dug out her keys. Tuff barked in excitement from behind the closed door.

She said to Memphis, "Go on before you get soaked. We'll be fine."

With the rainfall steadily increasing, he leaned in for one more kiss. "Lock the door behind you. Remmy, I trust you not to budge."

"I'm not going anywhere," he stated, taking the keys from Diah and unlocking the door so Lane could go inside. Tuff was right there at the door to greet them.

Madison hooked her arm through Memphis's. "Not that I'm afraid of a little rain, but we have a lot to do so let's go."

He hesitated. Yeah, Diah felt it, too. The sense of danger, which made no sense at all now that Ed was contained. She didn't want to hold him up, didn't want to be a burden, so she said very softly, "Thank you for asking me to stay."

In kind, he answered, "Thank you for agreeing."

Stepping inside, Diah closed and locked the door. From the kitchen she heard the muted voices of Lane and Remmy, but Tuff was right there, ecstatic to see her. She knelt to give him a hug and a promise. "We have a permanent home now, bud, here with Memphis. Isn't that awesome?" Tuff snuffled against her neck, making her smile past the nagging worry. "Only a few more things to work out, then I'll be able to breathe easy, and so will you." *Only a few more things.*

It seemed her entire life had been spent on the edge, never knowing when violence might happen again. She was so close now, not only to peace, but to a life with a man unlike any other. A man she loved.

They'd get through this. She had to believe that.

So then why did it feel like ice trickled down her spine?

OTTO FOUND CHARLIE under the awning of a camper, flirting with a pretty woman who had to be wasted if she found Charlie interesting.

Despite the frigid rain, Otto wore his most pleasant expression when he said, "Charlie, there you are."

In his midforties, Ed was no prize, but at least he was loyal and dedicated to the job. Charlie, fifteen years younger, was a total dunce and easily distracted, evidenced by how he looked at Otto now, saying, "Huh?"

Simply put, Otto wanted to rip out his heart. Here he was, exposing himself to a camper, never mind that the woman barely paid him any attention as she stumbled to a little table to pick up her drink. Tonight, right now in fact, Otto needed Charlie.

With a grand sweep of his hand, Otto said, "We have some business to attend to. Tell your lovely friend good-night."

The *lovely friend* seemed to doze off on her feet, so Charlie merely gave her a look before warily joining Otto. "What's up, boss?"

"This way, please."

Charlie glanced up at the sky. "It's raining."

"Since I'm soaked, you can assume I'm aware of the weather."

"Oh, yeah." Frowning now, Charlie stepped out with him then followed as he led him along to the meager shelter of heavy tree limbs.

The rich scent of wet pine permeated the air and his breath fogged before him. A miserable day, which made it perfect for what he had planned. "Are you aware of your brother's whereabouts?"

Charlie rubbed rainwater off his head. "He was fishing last I knew."

Idiot. "You're familiar with the camp store?"

"Yeah, sure."

"I believe Ed is there now. The store has up a Temporarily Closed sign." Since he'd watched the owner, Memphis, along with the tall woman, head to the store, knock, then be allowed inside, his suspicions had been churning. He just knew Ed was in there, and understanding Ed's caliber, it didn't look good for him. "I want you to check on him. If he's fine, inform him—without anyone hearing—that I need a word with him."

Charlie's eyes had rounded. "And if he ain't fine?"

Good riddance to both of you. Otto fashioned yet another smile. "Then you'll quietly assist him, won't you? That's what brothers do. However, you will not under any circumstances mention my name or acknowledge me in any way. Is that clear?"

"Right. Ed told me we can't ever talk about you to anyone else."

"Ed is correct." While Charlie was off attempting to rescue his brother, Otto would collect his property, then he'd collect some vengeance. "I'll meet you back at the camper in thirty minutes." Unwilling to waste a second more, Otto walked off into the storm, deliberately going one way until he was too far away for Charlie to see him, then veering off to the campsite where he'd hid his evidence.

It was unfortunate that campers appeared to be using the site, but with the storm, he doubted they'd venture out. Even if they did, he could claim to be a part of maintenance or something.

He found the picnic table easily enough. Luckily, it hadn't been moved. Memphis Osborn had kept almost everything the same, other than cleaning it up a little.

Remembering a long ago time, when he'd been a little afraid and a lot desperate, Otto traced his fingertips over the engraving of his name.

A stupid thing to do, but he'd worried that he might forget, that he'd need the evidence and not be able to find it. Now Jedidiah was here. His mouth curved as he thought of how she'd react when she saw him. For years she'd lived in fear of him, always tormenting him with that eerily probing gaze that seemed to see all the shit he tried so hard to hide.

No more hiding now.

He was a *king*. He was invincible.

Soon he'd prove it to her.

It took a little effort, but he upended the table. It fell to the side with a quiet thud, thanks to the drenched earth. He felt along the steel frame until he found the seam where joints connected. There, well hidden, was the flash drive. It should still be okay, given what he'd paid for the special metal casing. Waterproof, shockproof, uncrushable and undetectable by X-ray, he expected to find it intact, but if it was corrupted, oh, well. The job was done for him.

Using a knife, he pried it loose, cutting himself once before finally getting it free. Thunder rumbled, shaking the ground, and the rain came down in a torrent.

Any idiots using tents would be carried off by the storm. As he was thinking it, the lights flickered…and died. It wasn't that late yet, but the storm made it feel like night.

Fate was on his side. Now would be the perfect time to strike. He pocketed the flash drive, wiped his bleeding hand on his pants and pushed through the storm—to where he knew Jedidiah and Lane were waiting.

MADISON STAYED TIGHTLY latched to his arm, making Memphis think her news was pretty damned important.

He wished he'd been wrong.

The second they stepped into the shop, she practically dragged Memphis to the other side of the room. Jodi joined them, and even Hunter stepped closer, though he also kept an eye on Ed.

Voice low, Madison said, "We assumed Otto was at his hotel, but he's not."

Memphis felt his blood freeze. "He's here."

"Yes." Her grip tightened. "But that's not the most important thing." She cleared her throat.

"For God's sake, spit it out."

Because he never snapped, Madison patted him. "I'm sorry I didn't put it together sooner, but Otto is actually Diah's stepbrother, Rusty."

Memphis almost bolted. He needed to be with Diah. *Now.*

Hunter added his hold to Madison's. "What the hell is this?"

"Voice low," Jodi cautioned with a nod at Ed.

Right, like Ed could do anything now?

"The less he knows, the better," Madison explained. "It'll make it easier to trip him up once he's questioned. He believes the man he works for is Otto, but I compared pictures using facial ID technology. It's most definitely him."

"I need to go to Diah." Nothing else mattered to him. Not the campground, not his intent to catch crooks—*nothing.*

A knock on the door stalled things. Jodi started to answer it, but Hunter pulled her around. "This is one of those times where I need you to compromise."

She rolled her eyes, but gave in. "I'll just keep Ed quiet, then." Smiling at the downed man, she strode closer and said, "Make a sound, and I'll take out your kneecap."

The credible threat would have worked if Hunter hadn't allowed in Ed's brother Charlie. At that point, it all went to hell.

Charlie entered with a fake smile that vanished the second he spotted his brother. He tried to flee, but Hunter caught him in a headlock, holding him tight until he passed out.

Ed raged for his brother, until Jodi tapped him none-to-gently on the head with her weapon.

In rapid order, the men were tightly bound together. Madison stood over them. "What does Otto want?"

Charlie, who'd just come around, started to speak but Ed silenced him.

"Nobility for your boss?" Memphis worked his jaw.

"How about I just add a few more bruises to Ed until you change your mind?"

"He doesn't know!" Ed protested.

"Okay, then, I'll pound on good old Charlie and when you think he's had enough, you can share what you know." Memphis didn't wait for agreement before slugging Charlie in the gut.

The man nearly vomited.

"Christ." Ed put his head back, eyes closed. "Otto doesn't confide in me. I work for him, that's all. I was supposed to check out your security, and if it was as weak as we suspected, he'd pick up business here again."

"Where is he now?"

"In the camper. Since I'm tied up here, I'm late to meet with him, and that's probably why he sent Charlie after me."

Charlie nodded, then whispered, "We weren't supposed to mention his name." Thunder boomed, making Charlie jump. "We're good as dead now."

Memphis stood. He was about to defer to Madison when the lights went out. "Damn it." He couldn't dismiss a feeling of dread. Using the flashlight on his cell phone, he located a utility light behind the counter, flicked it on to see the faces of his brother and friends, then said, "I'm going to Diah."

Hunter grabbed his arm. "This could be a trap."

"Against Diah, I know." He pressed away, but Hunter kept up with him.

"Stop and *think*, damn it. You can't just run out there. That'll endanger you both."

Madison said, "Lights are out because of the storm. I just verified it." Without her usual smiles, she said, "Remmy isn't answering my text, though. Could be that the storm is causing a problem, but I doubt it since my reception is fine."

New urgency burned into Memphis. "I *have* to go."

"We're the most qualified," Jodi said fast. "It'd make more sense if you stayed here to watch these buffoons and we—"

"Not happening." Memphis started away.

"Hunter," she insisted, as if expecting him to wield some sway.

Instead of trying to dissuade him, Hunter said, "He has to do this—same as I would for you."

Glad to have his brother's backing, Memphis drew a breath. He couldn't, wouldn't, risk others, so he thought fast, then said, "I have a plan."

"Share quickly," Madison said, "and I can help you perfect it. Foolproof planning, even on the fly, is what I do."

Combined, this group of family and friends had all the ability needed—as long as he got to Diah in time.

AT THE SOUND of breaking glass, Tuff went nuts, snarling and trying to lunge out of the kitchen. "What was that?" Luckily, she'd just leashed him to let him out before the storm worsened. It made it easier for her to keep him by her side.

"The way the wind's howling, it could be anything." Gun in hand, Remmy left his seat at the kitchen table. "Stay put. Neither of you moves, got it?"

It was all Diah could do to hold on to the dog. Her heart beat hard, accompanied by the near-constant drone of thunder. She nodded, but since Remmy wasn't looking at her, was instead staring into the shadowy hallway, she said, "I'll be right here with Lane and Tuff."

She told the dog, "Shh, now. Quiet," and he stopped fighting her, but stayed keenly alert.

Lane asked, "Do you have another gun?"

"No." Remmy started out of the kitchen. "I'll be right back." Steps nearly silent, he left the room.

Diah thought of the rifle under Memphis's bed, and the Glock in his nightstand, but she decided not to mention them in front of Lane. When Remmy returned, she'd find a way to tell him, just in case the weapons were needed.

The seconds seemed to be hours until Remmy called out to say, "Looks like a big branch came through the bedroom window."

Relief had barely begun to settle in when another crash sounded, closer this time but still not in the same room. She shot to her feet and stared, willing Remmy to say something, to explain. There was a boom of thunder…

No, wait… Dear God, *that was gunfire!*

Lane shot out of her seat, her hands over her mouth. Snarling, Tuff strained against Diah's hold. Panic tried to seize her, but she fought it when she heard another thump.

And then Remmy called out, "Run!" right before another, louder thump.

The scream lodged in her throat, but fortunately she seemed to go on autopilot. In seconds, she had Lane's hand as they raced to the front door. It took her too long trying to get the door open and still hold on to Tuff, so Lane took the leash from her.

Diah opened the locks, twisted the doorknob—and the wind ripped it out of her hand, then nearly knocked them down when it blew back again.

Lane stepped out with Tuff. Using her shoulder to

keep the door open, she struggled with the dog. "Hurry. We have to get help."

Just as Diah started to step out, a hand snagged in her hair and she got dragged back inside. There was the flash of Lane's horrified face, the maniacal way Tuff reacted, then the door slammed shut.

Lane would get help, she thought frantically. Until then, Diah knew she had to fight, not freeze up. *She had to.*

When she started to struggle, the fist in her hair yanked her back and into a solid body. Near her ear, a dark voice said, "I've got you now."

Her blood ran cold. She knew that voice.

Trying to twist to see him, Diah whispered, "Rusty?"

"That's right, and you're coming with me." He kept her locked to his body as he hauled her down the hall. "We have unfinished business, little sister. And this time, fucking Glover isn't here to protect you."

No, she didn't have Glover.

Rusty might have killed Remmy.

If she let this happen, she might never see Memphis again.

And in that moment, the oddest thing happened. A lifetime of terror seemed to fade away.

Things Glover had taught her clicked into place. She tried to sound terrorized when she asked, "Where are you taking me?"

"We'll go back out the window, and if you want to live, you won't make a sound." Step by step, he hauled her along toward Memphis's bedroom.

Where there were weapons.

Keep your head, Diah, and fight, was Glover's most basic lesson.

Pay attention to everything, Remmy had told her.

In a split second, she came up with a plan. Not a great plan, but it was better than simply going along out of fear.

Without warning, uncaring that she lost a lot of hair in the process, Diah twisted around to claw at Rusty's face. She didn't have punching power so she'd have to inflict pain other ways.

While Rusty screamed and fought to subdue her, she raked her nails over his face, aiming for his eyes. Viciously cursing, he pressed her back, but she still ripped at his ear and nose, inflicting deep, bloody scratches. She wildly kicked and thrashed, and managed to land a knee close enough to his privates to hurt him, but not disable him.

He gripped her arm with viselike force, wrenching her back so violently, it felt like he tore her shoulder from the socket, but she didn't relent. Instead, she bent her head and sank her teeth into his forearm, biting down as hard as she could.

Howling, he desperately clubbed her in the side of the head, once, twice. She saw stars and when her legs went weak, he slammed her back against the wall.

He held his arm, staring in macabre horror at the blood seeping between his fingers. Rage seemed to well inside him. "Bitch!"

When he swung his fist at her, she tried to duck, and mostly took the hit to her shoulder.

It knocked her against the bedroom doorframe.

Her entire body ached, from her stinging scalp all the way down to her feet, but she kept her head enough to rapidly shift into the bedroom—and slam the door.

When Rusty's body landed against it, she knew the flimsy lock wouldn't hold. She had mere seconds.

Urgently, she turned into the room and nearly tripped over Remmy's downed body. He was sprawled out across the floor on his back, his head and shoulder bleeding.

Horror and heartache washed over her, taking out her knees so that she dropped beside him. "Remmy?" she whispered brokenly, touching her hand to his chest. When she felt the gentle rise and fall of his breathing, hope renewed her.

The door splintered open behind her.

Spurred into action, Diah dove over Remmy's body and crawled frantically under the bed.

Rusty laughed and grabbed her ankle. "You can't hide, you stupid bitch."

She kicked back with her unhindered leg, scrambling fast. *Almost within reach.*

"No, you don't." He twisted her ankle. "I'm going to make you pay. You'll be so fucking sorry when I'm done with you!"

He roughly dragged her out, deliberately causing her as much pain as he could.

Diah didn't fight him now, because she was ready. The second she could, she twisted to her back—and aimed the rifle directly at Rusty's smug face. Even seeing the damage she'd done with her nails, her hands didn't shake. Despite fearing for Remmy's life and her own, her heart didn't stutter.

"You," she said, "should have died a long time ago."

After approaching silently through the hall, Memphis peeked into the room and saw the shock on Rusty's face.

He couldn't see Diah yet and it galvanized him with fear-driven determination. Two more steps, his movements drowned out by the accommodating storm, and finally she came into view.

Slowly, the worst of his terror receded. Proud, strong, fearless Diah.

She was not only alive, she was handling the situation.

Seeing her battered face infuriated him. Rusty would pay for that.

Despite her awkward position on the floor, she didn't waver. The rifle in her hands was held steady. Would she shoot Rusty?

To protect Remmy, to save herself, damn right she would.

He couldn't quite process all the emotions stampeding through him. Fear, yes, because she was caught in an untenable situation no matter how calmly she handled it. Pride also, because she'd gone up against her darkest fear and yet managed to have it in hand.

Love. So much love. It didn't matter if he'd known her a day or a decade, she was the one for him. Once she was safe again, he'd tell her so and then they could face the future together.

Unaware of Memphis behind him, Rusty backed away from Diah. The problem, of course, was that Rusty held his own gun. It was only a matter of who fired first, and no way in hell did Memphis like those odds.

From outside the broken window, Hunter closed in. In another thirty seconds, his brother would have a clear shot of Rusty. Madison was out front, ready to take Rusty down if he somehow got away. His incredible BFF had already called in the big guns. They'd arrived in stealth mode to remove not only Rusty, but Ed and Charlie, too.

It was nice having connections.

Praying Diah wouldn't shoot, Memphis crept closer. If he could just get near enough to get his hands on the bastard…

Diah glanced at him, then away. As if she knew Hunter would be near, she also glanced toward the window.

Rusty tried to take advantage, but Diah just pinned him in her sights. "Go ahead," she whispered. "Dare you."

Rusty went still again. "Your precious Glover was in on it, you know."

"Don't know what you're talking about," Diah said. "Don't care." Her aim never faltered.

"You're doing it again," he accused a little wildly. "Staring at me like the witch you are."

She didn't deny it. "I see right through you, Rusty. Every rotten, cowardly inch."

Shit. It wouldn't help for Diah to provoke him, but it did give Memphis the advantage to slip forward another step.

Rusty sneered, "You didn't see through Glover, did you? Our whole family was supposed to die. Glover agreed to help make it happen."

Instead of being devastated by that news, Diah remarked, "And yet, you're still here."

Her voice was controlled and she exuded confidence, but Memphis knew her better than Rusty did, so he saw the pain in her eyes.

"I have proof," Rusty stated.

"Something you'd hidden here?" She gave the smallest of smiles and said in a patronizing tone, "Glover knew. I knew. I would have found it soon."

"Never," he denied.

The smile widened. "I saw your name on the picnic table."

Rusty stepped back—within Memphis's reach.

Though Diah could clearly see Memphis now, she continued as if he wasn't right there. "I bet you thought you were so clever, didn't you? Poor Rusty. You fail at everything you do."

Just then, Remmy groaned, and that changed everything. Diah's gaze shifted, Rusty lifted his gun—and Memphis grabbed his gun hand, forcing it down hard and fast.

At almost the same time that Hunter vaulted through the open window, Rusty squeezed the trigger, reflexively or on purpose, Memphis didn't know. And it didn't matter.

Diah's brother had just shot himself in the foot.

"THANK GOD FOR Hunter and Jodi." Diah leaned tiredly into Memphis's side. "I'm glad they're handling everything at the campground."

He pressed a kiss to her forehead. "Hunter insisted."

The hospital was crowded with other people, many of them giving her looks because of her bruised face. She didn't care. For the first time that she could remember, she felt utterly, completely free. Stronger, braver, *better*. A woman without dark secrets chasing after her.

Memphis said, "The surprise is that Sable is sticking around, too. Hunter said she's being helpful."

"Proof that you have great instincts when it comes to employees." After all, he'd hired her, and she hoped to spend the rest of her life showing him what a great decision he'd made.

Beside her, Lane sat quietly, her arms around herself, one foot tapping anxiously as they waited. She was so withdrawn that it pained Diah. The cops had spoken with Lane endlessly, as had Madison. She probably needed to sleep and eat, yet she wouldn't leave the hospital. She, too, wanted to be here for Remmy.

At Memphis's insistence, the doctor had already looked over Diah and her paltry injuries. Sure, she hurt, but it was the mere physical pain of a scuffle—bruises and scrapes that would quickly heal.

Those pains were nothing compared to the heart-wrenching agony of neglect, fear and isolation she'd known for much of her life. Now, finally, she'd ended the dark specter of danger that had haunted her for so many years.

Gently, Memphis coasted his fingertips over her cheek. "I want to kill him for this," he whispered, so only she could hear.

Because that was the tenth time he'd said it, Diah smiled at him. "Being locked away will be worse for Rusty. He's not a man cut out for prison life."

"No longer a king," Lane whispered.

Diah gave her a brief hug. Thanks to Madison and her very connected family, Rusty Wilson, aka Otto Woodall, was completely exposed. After getting treated for his injuries at the hospital, he'd been taken into custody. An FBI task force had overtaken his hotel and arrested others who were complicit in the forced work programs, kidnapping and human trafficking that had helped shore up Rusty's warped ego.

Hours ago, Madison had promised her, "Rusty will

not skate by. He will never again be a problem for you." Diah believed her.

Now they waited to visit Remmy. The worst of his injury was the gunshot to his shoulder that had required surgery. All had gone well and Remmy was in recovery.

From what they could surmise, he'd hit his head in a fall after getting shot, and that had knocked him out. Blood loss had complicated things, but Remmy should make a full recovery.

Just then a nurse stepped into the waiting room, searched a moment, spotted them and headed in their direction. She, Memphis and Lane were already on their feet when he reached them.

Finally, Remmy was in a private room and allowed visitors, but they were warned not to overstay because he needed a lot of rest.

Lane led the way, her rapid footfalls very close to a run. Diah and Memphis hurried to keep up with her, and they filed into the room close together.

Eyes barely open, Remmy glanced at each of them, then his gaze lingered on Diah before he asked Memphis, "Everything okay?"

Tears swam in Lane's eyes. Memphis nudged her forward while saying, "Everything but you." Taking a position by the bed, he explained, "Other than Diah getting a few bruises, no one else got hurt. How do you feel?"

"Like I should have my ass kicked for fucking up."

Lane made a strangled sound that prompted Diah to take her hand.

"Madison is doing her thing. Otto and his crew are under wraps and staying that way." In very brief terms, Memphis explained the broadness of the operation and the number of arrests that would be made.

"Good going, Memphis." When Remmy paused to swallow, Memphis lifted the cup of water and straw to his mouth so he could drink. "The campground?"

"Protected," Memphis promised.

"Still in operation?"

Understanding his meaning, Memphis nodded. "Hunter and Jodi are there now. Far as any of the guests know, there were a few injuries from the storm, that's all. No one suspects anything."

"Otto had powerful friends, you know that, right?"

"I assumed." Memphis put a hand to Remmy's uninjured shoulder. "That's in the works, too, okay? All you have to worry about is recovering."

Tiredly, he closed his eyes, but said, "Diah? I'm sorry, hon."

"Hush." She released Lane to squeeze in close to Memphis. "You gave us warning. It's because of you that we're all okay. If you hadn't called out, Lane might not have been able to go for help." Diah's throat thickened. "And Tuff might have been killed." She knew without a doubt that Rusty wouldn't hesitate to shoot a dog, but to her, Tuff was so much more. "Thank you for making it possible for us all to survive. Now, because you were there, my past can't bother me anymore."

He managed the slightest of smiles. "Have to admit, getting shot wasn't part of my agenda. I was still functional, but then I stumbled back… That's all I remember."

Diah stroked her fingers over his hair. "Because you hit your head."

"You've got a massive goose egg," Memphis said.

"Maybe that's why it feels like a boulder on my shoulders."

"You need to rest," she proclaimed, seeing the pain in his expression.

He looked at her again. "So do you."

"I'll take care of her," Memphis promised.

Lane had been quiet so far, but out of the blue, she said, "I'm staying here."

They all stared at her.

Frowning, she searched the room, spotted a padded chair in the corner and pointed at it. "Right there." Then defiantly, she added, "I'm not budging."

Remmy started to speak, but Diah beat him to it. "Thank you, Lane. I'll feel better knowing someone is with him."

Memphis followed up with, "Do you need anything? I'd be happy to drive back if you make me a list."

Lane shook her head. "I'm fine, but thanks."

"You need to eat," Remmy said. "And sleep."

Diah loved this moment, everyone caring and helping each other. She was a part of this, of them, and it touched her. "We'll get you some food before we go, and we'll ask the nurse to bring in another pillow and blanket."

Memphis moved the chair close to the bed, near enough that Lane could hold Remmy's hand, then he gave her a hug. "We'll get by without you—but you're still an employee. Don't even think about quitting on me."

Her lips quirked in a quick, grateful smile. "Never."

Seeing the way Remmy watched Lane, Diah knew he'd be sticking around, too.

It was super late, or maybe super early, by the time they got back to Memphis's cabin. Diah knew she should have been dragging, but she felt energized instead. Anxious to see Tuff, to settle things with Memphis, and more than ready to start her new life.

Madison was inside with Tuff when they arrived, and the dog went nuts at finally getting Diah back. She knelt on the floor and hugged him, petting him and talking to him until he finally calmed. Over and over, she said, "I love you, too, Tuff. So much."

Madison stood there, looking exactly as she had earlier, not a hair out of place. Hands on her hips, she asked, "Do you want to sleep and then talk? Eat first? What works for you?"

"Talk," Diah stated. "Then I'll eat, and if Hunter and Jodi can stick around, maybe we'll catch a few hours of sleep."

Memphis smiled at her. "Hunter's only leaving long enough to get his dog. Everything is covered."

By silent agreement they convened to the kitchen. This time Tuff sat right at Diah's side, his head resting over her knees while she stroked his ears and along his neck.

"The flash drive," Madison said, knowing that'd be the top concern. "It did seem incriminating, or at least it would to anyone without experience."

"The cops didn't take it?" Diah asked.

Madison gave her a long look. "Let's just say I have access."

Memphis grinned. "Friends in high places."

"I'm your BFF. Of course I'll look out for you." She squeaked when Memphis hauled her in close for a tight squeeze.

For once, Madison looked surprised, prompting Diah to grin.

She recovered quickly. "So… There are recorded

conversations between Rusty and Glover about an order given by their boss. Before you ask, yes, I've already uncovered the boss. He died years ago by a rival. Far as I can tell, Rusty wasn't involved in that."

"Good riddance," Memphis said. "One less loose end around to concern us."

Diah knew he was still stressed from the close call. Once Rusty had been subdued, Memphis had held her for the longest time, rocking her, kissing her, devastated over each small scrape or mark that he found on her. It had taken a lot of convincing on her end before he'd accepted that she really was okay.

She understood his reaction, oh, yes, she did. When Rusty's gun had fired… The worst fear imaginable had nearly stopped her heart—until she saw that Memphis wasn't hurt.

"Glover seemed to agree to the plan to remove all of you because your stepfather had outlived his usefulness. The plan was for Rusty to escape all along by using a surrogate body. Then the boss would have elevated Rusty and Glover to higher positions in his organization. An organization, by the way, that wasn't all that complex or advanced. It, too, was destroyed by rivals."

Diah realized that she didn't really care about any of it. Even if Glover had been involved, he'd long since made up for that mistake with the love he'd given to her. He hadn't directly killed her mother, and that mattered for a lot.

"Glover, of course, had no intention of seeing it through. If he'd said that, though, he wouldn't have lived long enough to save you. He was super stealthy about the way he arranged things."

"Not stealthy enough for you," Memphis commented, giving Madison her due.

"Very few are." She smiled. "I was only able to backtrack over Glover's plans for that first year. After that, he—and you, Diah—truly fell off the radar. Glover did his job well."

"He always knew Rusty was alive." Memphis scowled over that. "That in itself was a risk to Diah."

"In some ways. Yet, he usually stayed a step ahead." Apologetic, she explained to Diah, "I don't think he actually wanted anyone to die. My belief, just based off experience, is that Glover thought once he'd stolen you away, the rest of the plan would be scrapped. Unfortunately, Rusty must have suspected something because he stepped up the timeline. The fire wasn't originally planned to happen until two AM. The bar closed at one, he'd need time to get home and get in place, and then he'd instigate the fire."

Such a gruesome plan, and yet it didn't surprise Diah that Rusty would do something so vile.

"Instead, Rusty got things going two hours early. I spotted him on a traffic cam. Glover tailed him, staying far enough away that Rusty wouldn't spot him."

"Maybe," Memphis speculated, "Glover would have found a gentler way to get her out of the house, instead of terrorizing her."

"It doesn't matter." Diah smiled at each of them. "I love Glover for what he did, regardless of how he did it." She looked at Memphis with a heart full of emotion. "And I love you for caring."

His wide-eyed gaze locked on hers.

"Ahem." Tucking her laptop under her arm, Madison stood. "I'll take that as my cue to depart."

"Wait." Diah rose from her chair, too, which had Memphis and Tuff both jumping to their feet. "Are you leaving?"

"Only to your cabin for now." She gave Diah a brief, one-arm embrace. "Hope you don't mind. I'm going to grab a little sleep and then see what I can do to help out around here. Just for a day, maybe two."

Normally, Memphis would have cautioned Madison about getting too involved. Hadn't he told Diah that Madison always took over? This time, though, he merely nodded, his gaze still on Diah. "Thanks."

Banking her smile, Diah wrapped both arms around Madison and hugged her for all she was worth. Not a quick hug. Not simply a reciprocal hug. A long, tight, *thank you so much* hug meant to convey all the things she felt. "I'm so glad Memphis has such an astounding, talented and caring BFF."

Swallowing hard, a tear in her eye, Madison whispered, "Oh, you really are special."

"She is," Memphis agreed softly.

They walked with Madison to the door, and once she headed off for Diah's cabin, they let Tuff visit the yard. For now, the campground seemed peaceful. These were the designated quiet hours, when campers were discouraged from making noise that might disturb others. The storm had blown over and the twilight sky had lightened from black to deep purple as dawn approached. It wouldn't be much longer before guests began to awaken and a new day would be underway.

Keeping her voice to a whisper, Diah said, "I really do love you, you know. Not just because you sing silly songs while showering naked outside."

Holding Tuff's leash, Memphis smiled at her. "You'll never let me live that down."

"Never." She wanted a lifetime to tease him, and to love him. "It's not because you love my dog, either."

"Tuff is my buddy." The dog gazed at him adoringly…while still piddling.

"You've done everything you could to keep me safe, but that's not why I love you."

"Good to know, because as fearless as you are, keeping you safe is a big job."

Diah bit back a laugh. "And it's not just because you're incredibly hot in the sack."

His smile tweaked into a grin. "Keep in mind, I might have an off day here and there. Not from lack of effort, you understand. But I'm not perfect."

"You're perfect for me." Her heart kept tripping her up, making her voice unsteady.

"Diah," he said softly, drawing her in. "I love you, too."

"You keep thinking I'm fearless when I'm not. I'm still afraid of so many things."

"That's understandable."

"But I'm not afraid of loving you. I'm not afraid of a future here." Her voice cracked again. "Mostly I'm afraid of a life without you." She rushed on, wanting him to know he had options. "I could do it, though."

"I know that." Tuff came to sit between them, his furry brows up in curiosity. "It wouldn't be nearly as exciting, though, right? Us, here together, listening to critters around a bonfire."

Her heart swelled. "Sharing morning coffee."

"And meals."

"A bed."

"And the shower."

Oh, how she loved him. "All that. Everything. But only with *you*."

"Will you give up your cabin and live with me?"

"Yes." She curled her hands into his shirt, keeping him close.

"Great. So while you're in an agreeable mood… Will you marry me?"

Her eyes filled with tears. She nodded fast, whispering, "Yes, yes, *yes!*" She put a hand over her mouth. "Sorry. This is the quiet time."

"This is the time," he corrected, "for us to start the rest of our lives."

Diah grinned. "Together." The past might have been difficult, but it had led her to Memphis. Knowing how it turned out, she wouldn't have changed a thing.

* * * * *